WOODSTOCK;

OR,

THE CAVALIER.

PRINTED BY BALLANTYNE AND COMPANY, PAUL'S WORK, EDINBURGH.

INTRODUCTION

TO

WOODSTOCK.

———

THE busy period of the great Civil War was one in which the character and genius of different parties were most brilliantly displayed, and, accordingly, the incidents which took place on either side were of a striking and extraordinary character, and afforded ample foundation for fictitious composition. The author had in some measure attempted such in Peveril of the Peak; but the scene was in a remote part of the kingdom, and mingled with other national differences, which left him still at liberty to glean another harvest out of so ample a store.

In these circumstances, some wonderful adventures which happened at Woodstock in the year 1649, occurred to him as something he had long ago read of, although he was unable to tell where, and of which the hint appeared sufficient, although, doubtless, it might have been much better handled if the author had not, in the lapse of time, lost every thing like an accurate recollection of the real story.

It was not until about this period, namely, 1831, that the author, being called upon to write this Introduction, obtained a general account of what really happened upon the marvellous occasion in question, in a work termed " The Every-day Book," published by Mr Hone, and full of curious antiquarian research, the object being to give a variety of original information concerning manners, illustrated by curious instances, rarely to be found elsewhere. Among other matter, Mr Hone quotes an article from the British Magazine for 1747, in the following words, and which is probably the document which the author of Woodstock had formerly perused, although he was unable to refer to the source of his information. The tract is entitled, " The Genuine History of the Good Devil of Woodstock, famous in the world, in the year 1649, and never accounted for, or at all understood to this time."

The teller of this " Genuine History" proceeds verbatim as follows :

" Some original papers having lately fallen into my hands, under the name of ' Authentic Memoirs of the Memorable Joseph Collins of Oxford, commonly known by the name of Funny Joe, and now intended for the press,' I was extremely delighted to find in them a circumstantial and unquestionable account of the most famous of all invisible agents, so well known in the year 1649, under the name of the Good Devil of Woodstock, and even adored by the people of that place, for the vexation and distress it occasioned some people they were not much pleased with. As this famous story, though related by a thousand people, and attested in all its circumstances, beyond all possibility of doubt, by people of rank, learning, and reputation, of Oxford and the adjacent towns, has never yet been generally accounted for, or at all understood, and is perfectly explained, in a manner that can admit of no doubt, in these papers, I could not refuse my readers the pleasure it gave me in reading."

There is, therefore, no doubt that, in the

year 1649, a number of incidents, supposed to
be supernatural, took place at the King's palace
of Woodstock, which the Commissioners of
Parliament were then and there endeavouring
to dilapidate and destroy. The account of this
by the Commissioners themselves, or under
their authority, was repeatedly published, and
in particular, is inserted as relation sixth of
Satan's Invisible World Discovered, by George
Sinclair, Professor of Philosophy in Glasgow,
an approved collector of such tales.

It was the object of neither of the great political parties of that day to discredit this narrative, which gave great satisfaction both to
the cavaliers and roundheads; the former conceiving that the license given to the demons,
was in consequence of the impious desecration
of the King's furniture and apartments, so that
the citizens of Woodstock almost adored the
supposed spirits, as avengers of the cause of
royalty; while the friends of the Parliament,
on the other hand, imputed to the malice of the
fiend the obstruction of the pious work, as
they judged that which they had in hand.

At the risk of prolonging a curious quotation, I include a page or two from Mr Hone's
Every-day Book.

" The honourable the Commissioners arrived at Woodstock manor-house, October 13th, and took up their residence in the King's own rooms. His Majesty's bedchamber they made their kitchen, the council-hall their pantry, and the presence-chamber was the place where they sat for dispatch of business. His Majesty's dining-room they made their wood-yard, and stowed it with no other wood but that of the famous Royal Oak from the High Park, which, that nothing might be left with the name of the King about it, they had dug up by the roots, and bundled up into fagots for their firing.

" October 16th. This day they first sat for the dispatch of business. In the midst of their first debate there entered a large black dog, (as they thought,) which made a terrible howling, overturned two or three of their chairs, and doing some other damage, went under the bed, and there gnawed the cords. The door this while continued constantly shut, when, after some two or three hours, Giles Sharp, their secretary, looking under the bed, perceived that the creature was vanished, and that a plate of meat that the servants had hid there was untouched, and showing them to their

honours, they were all convinced there could
be no real dog concerned in the case; the said
Giles also deposed on oath, that, to his certain
knowledge, there was not.

"October 17th. As they were this day sitting at dinner in a lower room, they heard
plainly the noise of persons walking over head,
though they well knew the doors were all locked, and there could be none there. Presently
after they heard also all the wood of the King's
Oak brought by parcels from the dining-room,
and thrown with great violence into the presence-chamber, as also the chairs, stools, tables,
and other furniture, forcibly hurled about the
room, their own papers of the minutes of their
transactions torn, and the ink-glass broken.
When all this had some time ceased, the said
Giles proposed to enter first into these rooms,
and, in presence of the Commissioners, of whom
he received the key, he opened the door and
entered the room, their honours following him.
He there found the wood strewed about the
room, the chairs tossed about and broken, the
papers torn, and the ink-glass broken over
them all as they had heard, yet no footsteps
appeared of any person whatever being there,
nor had the doors ever been opened to admit

or let out any persons since their honours were last there. It was therefore voted, *nem. con.*, that the person who did this mischief could have entered no other way than at the key-hole of the said doors.

" In the night following this same day, the said Giles, and two other of the Commissioners' servants, as they were in bed in the same room with their honours, had their bed's feet lifted up so much higher than their heads, that they expected to have their necks broken, and then they were let fall at once with such violence as shook them up from the bed to a good distance; and this was repeated many times, their honours being amazed spectators of it. In the morning the bedsteads were found cracked and broken, and the said Giles and his fellows declared they were sore to the bones with the tossing and jolting of the beds.

" October 19th. As they were all in bed together, the candles were all blown out together with a sulphurous smell, and instantly many trenchers of wood were hurled about the room; and one of them putting his head above the clothes, had not less than six thrown at him, which wounded him very grievously. In the morning the trenchers were all found lying about the room, and were observed to be the same they had eaten on the day before, none being found remaining in the pantry.

" October 20th. This night the candles were put out as before ; the curtains of the bed in which their honours lay, were drawn to and fro many times with great violence : their honours received many cruel blows, and were much bruised beside, with eight great pewter dishes, and three dozen wooden trenchers, which were thrown on the bed, and afterwards heard rolling about the room.

" Many times also this night they heard the forcible falling of many fagots by their bedside, but in the morning no fagots were found there, no dishes or trenchers were there seen either ; and the aforesaid Giles attests, that by their different arranging in the pantry, they had assuredly been taken thence, and after put there again.

" October 21st. The keeper of their ordinary and his bitch lay with them : This night they had no disturbance.

" October 22d. Candles put out as before. They had the said bitch with them again, but were not by that protected ; the bitch set up a very piteous cry ; the clothes of their beds were all pulled off, and the bricks, without any wind, were thrown off the chimney tops into the midst.

"October 24th. The candles put out as before. They thought all the wood of the King's Oak was violently thrown down by their bedsides; they counted sixty-four fagots that fell with great violence, and some hit and shook the bed,—but in the morning none were found there, nor the door of the room opened in which the said fagots were.

" October 25th. The candles put out as before. The curtains of the bed in the drawing-room were many times forcibly drawn; the wood thrown out as before; a terrible crack like thunder was heard; and one of the servants, running to see if his master was not killed, found, at his return, three dozen trenchers laid smoothly upon his bed under the quilt.

" October 26th. The beds were shaken as before; the windows seemed all broken to pieces, and glass fell in vast quantities all about the room. In the morning they found the windows all whole, but the floor strewed with broken glass, which they gathered and laid by.

" October 29th. At midnight candles went

out as before; something walked majestically through the room, and opened and shut the window; great stones were thrown violently into the room, some whereof fell on the beds, others on the floor; and about a quarter after one, a noise was heard as of forty cannon discharged together, and again repeated at about eight minutes' distance. This alarmed and raised all the neighbourhood, who, coming into their honours' room, gathered up the great stones, fourscore in number, many of them like common pebbles and boulters, and laid them by, where they are to be seen to this day, at a corner of the adjoining field. This noise, like the discharge of cannon, was heard throughout the country for sixteen miles round. During these noises, which were heard in both rooms together, both the Commissioners and their servants gave one another over for lost, and cried out for help; and Giles Sharp, snatching up a sword, had wellnigh killed one of their honours, taking him for the spirit as he came in his shirt into the room. While they were together, the noise was continued, and part of the tiling of the house, and all the windows of an upper room, were taken away with it.

"October 30th. Something walked into the chamber, treading like a bear; it walked many times about, then threw the warming-pan violently upon the floor, and so bruised it that it was spoiled. Vast quantities of glass were now thrown about the room, and vast numbers of great stones and horses' bones were thrown in; these were all found in the morning, and the floors, beds, and walls were all much damaged by the violence they were thrown in.

"November 1st. Candles were placed in all parts of the room, and a great fire made. At midnight, the candles all yet burning, a noise like the burst of a cannon was heard in the room, and the burning billets were tossed all over the room and about the beds; and had not their honours called in Giles and his fellows, the house had assuredly been burnt. An hour after the candles went out, as usual, the clack of many cannon was heard, and many pailfuls of green stinking water were thrown on their honours in bed; great stones were also thrown in as before, the bed-curtains and bedsteads torn and broken: the windows were now all really broken, and the whole neighbourhood alarmed with the noises; nay, the very rabbit-stealers that were abroad that

Funny Joe, was himself this very devil;—
that, under the feigned name of Giles Sharp,
he hired himself as a servant to the Commissioners;—that by the help of two friends—an
unknown trapdoor in the ceiling of the bedchamber, and a pound of common gunpowder—he played all these extraordinary tricks
by himself;—that his fellow-servants, whom
he had introduced on purpose to assist him, had
lifted up their own beds; and that the candles
were contrived, by a common trick of gunpowder, to be extinguished at a certain time.

The dog who began the farce was, as Joe
swore, no dog at all, but truly a bitch, who
had shortly before whelped in that room, and
made all this disturbance in seeking for her
puppies; and which, when she had served his
purpose, he (Joe Sharp, or Collins,) let out,
and then looked for. The story of the hoof
and sword he himself bore witness to, and was
never suspected as to the truth of them, though
mere fictions. By the trapdoor his friends let
down stones, fagots, glass, water, &c., which
they either left there, or drew up again, as best
suited his purpose; and by this way let themselves in and out, without opening the doors,
or going through the keyholes; and all the

2

noises described, he declares he made by placing quantities of white gunpowder over pieces of burning charcoal, on plates of tin, which, as they melted, exploded with a violent noise.

I am very happy in having an opportunity of setting history right about these remarkable events, and would not have the reader disbelieve my author's account of them, from his naming either white gunpowder exploding when melted, or his making the earth about the pot take fire of its own accord; since, however improbable these accounts may appear to some readers, and whatever secrets they might be in Joe's time, they are now well known in chemistry. As to the last, there needs only to mix an equal quantity of iron filings, finely powdered, and powder of pure brimstone, and make them into a paste with fair water. This paste, when it hath lain together about twenty-six hours, will of itself take fire, and burn all the sulphur away with a blue flame and a bad smell. For the others, what he calls white gunpowder, is plainly the thundering powder called by our chemists *pulvis fulminans*. It is composed of three parts of saltpetre, two parts of pearl ashes or salt of tartar, and one part of flower of brimstone, mixed together and beat to a fine powder; a small quantity of this held on the point of a knife over a candle, will not go off till it melt, and then it gives a report like that of a pistol; and this he might easily dispose of in larger quantities, so as to make it explode of itself, while he, the said Joe, was with his masters.

Such is the explanation of the ghostly adventures of Woodstock, as transferred by Mr Hone from the pages of the old tract, termed the Authentic Memoirs of the memorable Joseph Collins of Oxford, whose courage and loyalty were the only wizards which conjured up those strange and surprising apparitions and works of spirits, which passed as so unquestionable in the eyes of the Parliamentary Commissioners, of Dr Plot, and other authors of credit. The *pulvis fulminans*, the secret principle he made use of, is now known to every apothecary's apprentice.

If my memory be not treacherous, the actor of these wonders made use of his skill in fireworks upon the following remarkable occasion. The Commissioners had not, in their zeal for the public service, overlooked their own private interests, and a deed was drawn up upon parchment, recording the share and nature of the advantages which they privately agreed to concede to each other; at the same time they were, it seems, loath to intrust to any one of their number the keeping of a document in which all were equally concerned.

They hid the written agreement within a flower-pot, in which a shrub concealed it from the eyes of any chance spectator. But the rumour of the apparitions having gone abroad, curiosity drew many of the neighbours to Woodstock, and some in particular, to whom the knowledge of this agreement would have afforded matter of scandal. As the Commissioners received these guests in the saloon where the flower-pot was placed, a match was suddenly set to some fireworks placed there by Sharp the secretary. The flower-pot burst to pieces with the concussion, or was prepared so as to explode of itself, and the contract of the Commissioners, bearing testimony to their private roguery, was thrown into the midst of the visitors assembled. If I have recollected this incident accurately, for it is more than forty years since I perused the tract, it is probable, that in omitting it from the novel, I may also have passed over, from want of memory, other matters which might have made an essential addition to the story. Nothing, indeed, is more certain, than that incidents which are real, preserve an infinite advantage in works of this nature over such as are fictitious. The tree, however, must remain where it has fallen.

Having occasion to be in London in October 1831, I made some researches in the British Museum, and in that rich collection, with the kind assistance of the Keepers, who manage it with so much credit to themselves and advantage to the public, I recovered two original pamphlets, which contain a full account of the phenomena at Woodstock in 1649.* The first is a satirical poem, published in that year, which plainly shows that the legend was current among the people in the very shape in which it was afterwards made public. I have not found the explanation of Joe Collins, which, as mentioned by Mr Hone, resolves the whole into confederacy. It might, however, be recovered by a stricter search than I had leisure for. In the meantime, it may be observed, that neither the name of Joe Collins, nor Sharp, occurs among the *dramatis*

* See Appendix.

personæ given in these tracts, published when
he might have been endangered by any thing
which directed suspicion towards him, at least
in 1649, and perhaps might have exposed him
to danger even in 1660, from the malice of a
powerful though defeated faction.

1st *August*, 1832.

APPENDIX.

No. I.

———

THE WOODSTOCK SCUFFLE;

OR,

MOST DREADFUL APPARITIONS THAT WERE LATELY
SEENE IN THE MANNOR-HOUSE OF WOODSTOCK, NEERE
OXFORD, TO THE GREAT TERROR AND WONDERFUL
AMAZEMENT OF ALL THERE THAT DID BEHOLD THEM.

[Printed in the year 1649.   4to.]

IT were a wonder if one unites,
And not of wonders and strange sights;
For ev'ry where such things affrights
        Poore people,

That men are ev'n at their wits' end;
God judgments ev'ry where doth send,
And yet we don't our lives amend,
        But tipple,

And sweare, and lie, and cheat, and ——,
Because the world shall drown no more,
As if no judgments were in store
               But water ;

But by the stories which I tell,
You'll heare of terrors come from hell,
And fires, and shapes most terrible
               For matter.

It is not long since that a child
Spake from the ground in a large field,
And made the people almost wild
               That heard it,

Of which there is a printed book,
Wherein each man the truth may look ;
If children speak, the matter's took
               For verdict.

But this is stranger than that voice,
The wonder's greater, and the noyse ;
And things appeare to men, not boyes,
               At *Woodstock ;*

Where *Rosamond* had once a bower,
To keep her from Queen *Elinour,*
And had escap'd her poys'nous power
               By good-luck,

But fate had otherwise decreed,
And *Woodstock* Mannor saw a deed,
Which is in *Hollinshed* or *Speed*
    Chro-nicled ;

But neither *Hollinshed* nor *Stow,*
Nor no historians such things show,
Though in them wonders we well know
    Are pickled ;

For nothing else is history
But pickle of antiquity,
Where things are kept in memory
    From stincking,

Which otherwaies would have lain dead,
As in oblivion buried,
Which now you may call into head
    With thinking.

The dreadful story, which is true,
And now committed unto view,
By better pen, had it its due,
    Should see light ;

But I, contented, doe indite,
Not things of wit, but things of right ;
You can't expect that things that fright
    Should delight.

O hearken, therefore, harke and shake !
My very pen and hand doth quake !
While I the true relation make
                    O' th' wonder,

Which hath long time, and still appeares
Unto the State's Commissioners,
And puts them in their beds to feares
                    From under.

They come, good men, imploi'd by th' State,
To sell the lands of Charles the late,
And there they lay, and long did waite
                    For chapmen.

You may have easy pen'worths, woods,
Lands, ven'son, householdstuf, and goods ;
They little thought of dogs that wou'd
                    There snap-men.

But when they'd sup'd, and fully fed,
They set up remnants and to bed,
Where scarce they had laid down a head
                    To slumber,

But that their beds were heav'd on high ;
They thought some dog under did lie,
And meant i' th' chamber (fie, fie, fie,)
                    To scumber.

Some thought the cunning cur did mean
To eat their mutton (which was lean)
Reserv'd for breakfast, for the men
    Were thrifty;

And up one rises in his shirt,
Intending the slie cur to hurt,
And forty thrusts made at him for't,
    Or fifty.

But empty came his sword again,
He found hee thrust but all in vain;
The mutton safe, hee went amain
    To's fellow.

And now (assured all was well)
The bed again began to swell,
The men were frighted, and did smell
    O' th' yellow.

From heaving, now the cloaths it pluckt;
The men, for feare, together stuck,
And in their sweat each other duck't.
    They wished

A thousand times that it were day
'Tis sure the divell! Let us pray.
They pray'd amain; and, as they say,

   * * *

Approach of day did cleere the doubt,
For all devotions were run out,
They now waxt strong and something stout ;
     One peaked

Under the bed, but nought was there ;
He view'd the chamber ev'ry where,
Nothing apear'd but what, for feare,
     They leaked.

Their stomachs then return'd apace,
They found the mutton in the place,
And fell unto it with a grace.
     They laughed

Each at the other's pannick feare,
And each his bed-fellow did jeere,
And having sent for ale and beere,
     They quaffed.

And then abroad the summons went,
Who'll buy king's-land o' th' Parliament ?
A paper-book contein'd the rent,
     Which lay there ;

That did contein the severall farmes,
Quit-rents, knight services, and armes ;
But that they came not in by swarmes
     To pay there.

Night doth invite to bed again,
The grand Commissioners were lain,
But then the thing did heave amain,
   It busled,

And with great clamor fill'd their eares,
The noyse was doubled, and their feares;
Nothing was standing but their haires,
   They nuzled.

Oft were the blankets pul'd, the sheete
Was closely twin'd betwixt their feete,
It seems the spirit was discreete
   And civill.

Which makes the poore Commissioners
Feare they shall get but small arreares,
And that there's yet for cavaliers
   One divell.

They cast about what best to doe;
Next day they would to wise men goe,
To neighb'ring towns som cours to know;
   For schollars

Come not to Woodstock, as before,
And Allen's dead as a nayle-doore,
And so's old John (eclep'd the poore)
   His follower;

Rake Oxford o're, there's not a man
That rayse or lay a spirit can,
Or use the circle, or the wand,
                    Or conjure;

Or can say (Boh!) unto a divell,
Or to a goose that is uncivill,
Nor where Keimbolton purg'd out evill,
                    'Tis sin sure.

There were two villages hard by,
With teachers of presbytery,
Who knew the house was hidiously
                    Be-pestred;

But 'lasse! their new divinity
Is not so deep, or not so high;
Their witts doe (as their meanes did) lie
                    Sequestred;

But Master Joffman was the wight
Which was to exorcise the spright;
Hee'll preach and pray you day and night
                    At pleasure.

And by that painfull gainfull trade,
He hath himselfe full wealthy made;
Great store of guilt he hath, 'tis said,
                    And treasure.

But no intreaty of his friends
Could get him to the house of fiends,
He came not over for such ends
    From Dutch-land;

But worse divinity hee brought,
And hath us reformation taught,
And, with our money, he hath bought
    Him much land.

Had the old parsons preached still,
The div'l should nev'r have had his wil;
But those that had or art or skill
    Are outed;

And those to whom the pow'r was giv'n
Of driving spirits, are out-driv'n;
Their colledges dispos'd, and livings,
    To grout-heads.

There was a justice who did boast,
Hee had as great a gift almost,
Who did desire him to accost
    This evill;

But hee would not employ his gifts,
But found out many sleights and shifts;
Hee had no prayers, nor no snifts,
    For th' divell.

Some other way they cast about,
These brought him in, they throw not out ;
A woman, great with child, will do't ;
                    They got one.

And she i' th' room that night must lie ;
But when the thing about did flie,
And broke the windows furiously,
                    And hot one

Of the contractors o're the head,
Who lay securely in his bed,
The woman, shee-affrighted, fled
                *   *   *

And now they lay the cause on her,
That e're that night the thing did stir,
Because her selfe and grandfather
                    Were Papists ;

They must be barnes-regenerate,
(A *Hans en Kelder* of the state,
Which was in reformation gatt,)
                    They said, which

Doth make the divell stand in awe,
Pull in his hornes, his hoof, his claw ;
But having none, they did in draw
                *   *   *

But in the night there was such worke,
The spirit swaggered like a Turke ;
The bitch had spi'd where it did lurke,
           And howled

In such a wofull manner, that
Their very hearts went pit a pat
    *   *   *   *   *
          *   *   *

The stately rooms, where kings once lay ;
But the contractors shew'd the way.
But mark what now I tell you, pray,
           'Tis worth it.

That book I told you of before,
Wherein were tenants written store,
A register for many more
           Not forth yet ;

That very book, as it did lie,
Took of a flame, no mortall eye
Seeing one jot of fire thereby,
           Or taper ;

For all the candles about flew,
And those that burned, burned blew,
Never kept soldiers such a doe
           Or vaper.

The book thus burnt and none knew how,
The poore contractors made a vow
To worke no more ; this spoil'd their plow
           In that place.

Some other part o' th' house they'll find
To which the devill hath no mind,
But hee, it seems, is not inclin'd
           With that grace ;

But other prancks it play'd elsewhere.
An oake there was stood many a yeere,
Of goodly growth as any where,
           Was hewn down,

Which into fewell-wood was cut,
And some into a wood-pile put,
But it was hurled all about
           And thrown down.

In sundry formes it doth appeare ;
Now like a grasping claw to teare ;
Now like a dog, anon a beare,
           It tumbles ;

And all the windows battered are,
No man the quarter enter dare ;
All men (except the glasier)
           Doe grumble.

Once in the likenesse of a woman,
Of stature much above the common,
'Twas seene, but spak a word to no man,
   And vanish'd.

'Tis thought the ghost of some good wife
Whose husband was depriv'd of life,
Her children cheated, land in strife
   She banist.

No man can tell the cause of these
So wondrous dreadfull outrages;
Yet if upon your sinne you please
   To discant,

You'le find our actions out doe hell's;
O wring your hands and cease the bells,
Repentance must, or nothing else
   Appease can't.

No. II.

THE

JUST DEVIL OF WOODSTOCK;

OR,

A TRUE NARRATIVE OF THE SEVERAL APPARITIONS, THE FRIGHTS AND PUNISHMENTS, INFLICTED UPON THE RUMPISH COMMISSIONERS SENT THITHER TO SURVEY THE MANNORS AND HOUSES BELONGING TO HIS MAJESTIE.

[London, printed in the year 1660.   4to.]

The names of the persons in the ensuing Narrative mentioned, with others.

Captain Cockaine.	Captain Roe.
Captain Hart.	Mr Crook, the Lawyer.
Captain Crook.	Mr Browne, the Surveyor.
Captain Carelesse.	

Their three Servants.

Their Ordinary-keeper, and others.

The Gate-keeper, with the Wife and Servants. Besides many more, who each night heard the noise; as Sir Gerrard Fleetwood and his lady, with his family, Mr Hyans, with his family, and several others, who lodged in the outer courts; and during the three last nights, the inhabitants of Woodstock town, and other neighbor villages.

And there were many more, both divines and others, who came out of the country, and from Oxford, to see the glass and stones, and other stuffe, the devil had brought, wherewith to beat out the Commissioners; the marks upon some walls remain, and many, this to testifie.

THE PREFACE TO THE ENSUING NARRATIVE.

Since it hath pleased the Almighty God, out of his infinite mercy, so to make us happy, by restoring of our native King to us, and us unto our native liberty through him, that now the good may say, *magna temporum felicitas ubi sentire quæ velis, et dicere licet quæ sentias*, we cannot but esteem ourselves engaged, in the highest of degrees, to render unto him the highest thanks we can express, although, surpris'd with joy, we become as lost in the performance; when gladness and admiration strikes us silent, as we look back upon the precipiece of our late condition, and those miraculous deliverances beyond expression; freed from the slavery, and those desperate perils, we dayly lived in fear of, during the tyrannical times of that detestable usurper, Oliver Cromwell; he who had raked up such judges, as would wrest the most innocent language into high treason, when

he had the cruel conscience to take away our lives,
upon no other ground of justice or reason, (the
stones of London streets would rise to witness it,
if all the citizens were silent.)   And with these
judges had such councillors, as could advise him
unto worse, which will less want of witness.   For
should the many auditors be silent, the press (as
God would have it) hath given it us in print,
where one of them (and his conscience-keeper, too,)
speaks out, What shall we do with these men?
saith he ; *Æger intemperans crudelem facit medi-
cum, et immedicabile vulnus ense recidendum.*   Who
these men are that should be brought to such Scici-
lian vespers, the former page sets forth—those
which conceit *Vtopias,* and have their day-dreams
of the return of, I know not what golden age, with
the old line.   What usage, when such a privy councillor had power, could he expect, who then had
published this narrative?   This much so plainly
shows the devil himself dislikit their doings, (so
much more bad were they than he would have them
be,) severer sure then was the devil to their Commissioners at Woodstock; for he warned them, with
dreadful noises, to drive them from their work.
This councillor, without more ado, would have all
who retain'd conceits of allegiance to their soveraign,
to be absolutely cut off by the usurper's sword.   A
sad sentence for a loyal party, to a lawful king.   But
Heaven is always just; the party is repriv'd, and

do acknowledge the hand of God in it, as is rightly applyed, and as justly sensible of their deliverançe: in that the foundation which the councillor saith was already so well laid, is now turned up, and what he calls day-dreams are come to passe. That old line which (as with him) there seemed *aliquid divini* to the contrary, is now restored. And that rock which, as he saith, the prelates and all their adherents, nay, and their master and supporter, too, with all his posterity, have split themselves upon, is nowhere to be heard. And that posterity are safely arrived in their ports, and masters of that mighty navy, their enemies so much encreased to keep them out with. The eldest sits upon the throne, his place by birthright and descent,

" Pacatumque regit Patriis virtutibus orbem ;"

upon which throne long may he sit, and reign in peace, that by his just government, the enemies of ours, the true Protestant Church, of that glorious martyr, our late sovereign, and of his royal posterity, may be either absolutely converted, or utterly confounded.

If any shall now ask thee why this narrative was not sooner published, as neerer to the times wherein the things were acted, he hath the reason for it in the former lines ; which will the more clearly appear unto his apprehension, if he shall perpend how much cruelty is requisite to the maintenance

of rebellion ; and how great care is necessary in the supporters, to obviate and divert the smallest things that tend to the unblinding of the people ; so that it needs will follow, that they must have accounted this amongst the great obstructions to their sales of his majestie's lands, the devil not joining with them in the security ; and greater to the pulling down the royal pallaces, when their chapmen should conceit the devil would haunt them in their houses, for building with so ill got materials ; as no doubt but that he hath, so numerous and confident are the relations made of the same, though scarce any so totally remarkeable as this, (if it be not that others have been more concealed,) in regard of the strange circumstances as long continuances, but especially the number of the persons together, to whom all things were so visibly both seen and done, so that surely it exceeds any other ; for the devils thus manifesting themselves, it appears evidently that there are such things as devils, to persecute the wicked in this world as in the next.

Now, if to these were added the diverse reall phantasms seen at White-Hall in Cromwell's times, which caused him to keep such mighty guards in and about his bedchamber, and yet so oft to change his lodgings ; if those things done at Saint James', where the devil so joal'd the centinels against the sides of the queen's chappell doors, that some of them fell sick upon it, and others, not taking warning by it, kild one outright, whom they buried in the place, and all other such dreadful things, those that inhabited the royal houses have been affrighted with; and if to these were likewise added, a relation of all those regicides and their abettors the devil hath entred into, as he did the Gadarenes' swine, with so many more of them who hath fallen mad, and dyed in hideous forms of such distractions,—that which hath been of this within these 12 last years in England, (should all of this nature our chronicles do tell, with all the superstitious monks have writ, be put together,) would make the greater volume, and of more strange occurrents.

And now as to the penman of this narrative, know that he was a divine, and at the time of those things acted, which are here related, the minister and schoolmaster of Woodstock; a person learned and discreet, not byassed with factious humours, his name Widows, who each day put in writing what he heard from their mouthes, (and such things as they told to have befallen them the night before,) therein keeping to their own words; and, never thinking that what he had writ should happen to be made publick, gave it no better dress to set it forth. And because to do it now shall not be construed to change the story, the reader hath it here accordingly exposed.

THE JUST DEVIL OF WOODSTOCK.

The 16th day of *October*, in the year of our Lord, 1649, the commissioners for surveying and valuing his majestie's mannor house, parks, woods, deer, demesnes, and all things thereunto belonging, by name Captain Crook, Captain Hart, Captain Cockaine, Captain Carelesse, and Captain Roe, their messenger, with Mr Browne, their secretary, and two or three servants, went from Woodstock town, (where they had lain some nights before,) and took up their lodgings in his majestie's house after this manner :—The bedchamber and with-drawing-room they both lodged in and made their kitchen ; the presence-chamber their room for dis-patch of their business with all comers ; of the council-hall their brew-house, as of the dining-room their wood-house, where they laid in the clefts of that antient standard in the High-Park, for many ages beyond memory known by the name of the King's Oak, which they had chosen out, and caused to be dug up by the roots.

October 17th. About the middle of the night, these new guests were first awaked by a knocking at the presence-chamber door, which they also con-ceived did open, and something to enter, which came through the room, and also walkt about that room with a heavy step during half an hour, then crept under the bed where Captain Hart and Captain Carelesse lay, where it did seem (as it were) to bite and gnaw the mat and bed-coards, as if it would tear and rend the feather beds ; which having done a while, then would heave a while, and rest ; then heave them up again in the bed more high than it did before, sometime on the one side, sometime on the other, as if it had tried which captain was heaviest. Thus having heaved some half an hour, from thence it walkt out and went under the servants' bed, and did the like to them ; hence it walkt into a withdrawing-room, and there did the same to all who lodged there. Thus, having welcomed them for more than two hours' space, it walkt out as it came in, and shut the outer door again, but with a clap of some mightie force. These guests were in a sweat all this while, but out of it falling into a sleep again, it became morning first before they spake their minds ; then would they have it to be a dog, yet they described it more to the likeness of a great bear ; so fell to the examining under the beds, where, finding only the mats scracht, but the bed-coards whole, and the quarter of beef which lay on the floor untoucht, they entertained other thoughts.

October 18*th.* They were all awaked as the night before, and now conceived that they heard all the great clefts of the King's Oak brought into the presence-chamber, and there thumpt down, and after roul about the room ; they could hear their chairs and stools tost from one side of the room unto the other, and then (as it were) altogether josled. Thus having done an hour together, it walkt into the withdrawing-room, where lodged the two captains, the secretary, and two servants: here stopt the thing a while, as if it did take breath, but raised a hideous one, then walkt into the bed-chamber, where lay those as before, and under the bed it went, where it did heave and heave again, that now they in bed were put to catch hold upon the bed-posts, and sometimes one of the other, to prevent their being tumbled out upon the ground; then coming out as from under the bed, and taking hold upon the bed-posts, it would shake the whole bed, almost as if a cradle rocked. Thus having done here for half an hour, it went into the with-drawing-room, where first it came and stood at the bed's feet, and heaving up the bed's feet, flopt down again a while, until at last it heaved the feet so high that those in bed thought to have been set upon their heads; and having thus for two hours entertained them, went out as in the night before, but with a great noise.

October 19th. This night they awaked not until the midst of the night; they perceived the room to shake with something that walkt about the bed-chamber, which having done so a while, it walkt into a withdrawing room, where it took up a brasse warming pan, and returning with it into the bedchamber, therein made so loud a noise, in these captains' own words, it was as loud and scurvie as a ring of five untuned bells rung backward; but the captains, not to seem afraid, next day made mirth of what had passed, and jested at the devil in the pan.

October 20*th*. These captains and their company, still lodging as before, were awakened in this night, with some things flying about the rooms, and out of one room into the other, as thrown with some great force. Captain Hart, being in a slumber, was taken by the shoulder and shaked until he did sit up in his bed, thinking that it had been one of his fellows, when suddenly he was taken on the pate with a trencher, that it made him shrink down into the bed-clothes, and all of them in both rooms kept their heads at least within their sheets, so fiercely did three dozen of trenchers fly about the rooms; yet Captain Hart ventured again to peep out to see what was the matter, and what it was that threw, but then the trenchers came so fast and neer about his ears, that he was fain quickly to couch again. In the morning they found all their trenchers, pots, and spits, upon and about their beds, and all such things as were of common use scattered about the rooms. This night there were also, in several parts of the room and outer rooms, such noises of beating at doors, and on the walls, as if that several smiths had been at work; and yet our captains shrunk not from their work, but went on in that, and lodged as they had done before.

October 21st.   About midnight they heard great knocking at every door; after a while the doors flew open, and into the withdrawing-room entered something as of a mighty proportion, the figure of it they knew not how to describe.   This walkt awhile about the room shaking the floor at every step, then came it up close to the bedside, where lay Captains Crook and Carelesse; and after a little pause, as it were, the bed-curtains, both at sides and feet, were drawn up and down slowly, then faster again for a quarter of an hour, then from end to end as fast as imagination can fancie the running of the rings, then shaked it the beds, as if the joints thereof had crackt; then walkt the thing into the bedchamber, and so plaied with those beds there; then took up eight peuter dishes, and bouled them about the room and over the servants in the truckle-beds; then sometimes were the dishes taken up and thrown crosse the high beds and against the walls, and so much battered; but there were more dishes wherein was meat in the same room, that were not at all removed.   During this, in the presence-chamber there was stranger noise of weightie things thrown down, and, as they supposed, the clefts of the King's Oak did roul about the room, yet at the wonted hour went away, and left them to take rest such as they could.

October 22d. Hath mist of being set down; the officers, imployed in their work farther off, came not that day to Woodstock.

October 23d. Those that lodged in the with-drawing-room, in the midst of the night were awakened with the cracking of fire, as if it had been with thorns and sparks of fire burning, whereupon they supposed that the bedchamber had taken fire, and listning to it farther, they heard their fellows in bed sadly groan, which gave them to suppose they might be suffocated; wherefore they called upon their servants to make all possible haste to help them. When the two servants were come in, they found all asleep, and so brought back word, but that there were no bed-clothes upon them; wherefore they were sent back to cover them, and to stir up and mend the fire. When the servants had covered them and were come to the chimney, in the corners they found their wearing apparrel, boots, and stockings, but they had no sooner toucht the embers, when the firebrands flew about their ears so fast, that away ran they into the other room for the shelter of their cover-lids; then after them walkt something that stampt about the room as if it had been exceeding angry, and likewise threw about the trenchers, platters, and all such things in the room—after two hours went out, yet stampt again over their heads.

October 24th. They lodged all abroad.

October 25th. This afternoon was come unto them Mr Richard Crook the lawyer, brother to Captain Crook, and now deputy-steward of the mannor unto Captain Parsons and Major Butler, who had put out Mr Hyans, his majestie's officer. To entertain this new guest, the Commissioners caused a very great fire to be made, of neer the chimney-full of wood of the King's oak, and he was lodged in the withdrawing-room with his brother, and his servant in the same room. About the midst of the night a wonderful knocking was heard, and into the room something did rush, which coming to the chimney-side, dasht out the fire as with the stamp of some prodigious foot, then threw down such weighty stuffe, what ere it was, (they took it to be the residue of the clefts and roots of the King's Oak,) close by the bed-side, that the house and bed shook with it. Captain Cockaine and his fellow arose, and took their swords to go unto the Crooks. The noise ceased at their rising, so that they came to the door and called. The two brothers, though fully awaked, and heard them call, were so amazed, that they made no answer until Captain Cockaine had recovered the boldness to call very loud, and came unto the bedside; then faintly first, after some more assurance, they came to understand one another, and comforted the lawyer. Whilst this was thus, no noise was heard, which made them think the time was past of that night's trouble, so that, after some little conference, they applied themselves to take some rest. When Captain Cockaine was come to his own bed, which he had left open, he found it closely covered, which he much wondered at; but turning the clothes down, and opening it to get in, he found the lower sheet strewed over with trenchers. Their whole three dozens of trenchers were orderly disposed between the sheets, which he and his fellow endeavouring to cast out, such noise arose about the room, that they were glad to get into bed with some of the trenchers. The noise lasted a full half hour after this. This entertainment so ill did like the lawyer, and being not so well studied in the point as to resolve this the devil's law case, that he next day resolved to be gone; but having not dispatcht all that he came for, profit and perswasions prevailed with him to stay the other hearing, so that he lodged as he did the night before.

October 26th. This night each room was better furnished with fire and candle than before; yet about twelve at night came something in that dasht all out, then did walk about the room, making a noise, not to be set forth by the comparison with any other thing; sometimes came it to the bedsides and drew the curtains to and fro, then twerle them, then walk about again, and return to the bed-posts, shake them with all the bed, so that they in bed were put to hold one upon the other, then walk

about the room again, and come to the servants'
bed, and gnaw and scratch the wainscot head, and
shake altogether in that room; at the time of this
being in doing, they in the bedchamber heard such
strange dropping down from the roof of the room,
that they supposed 'twas like the fall of money by
the sound. Captain Cockaine, not frightened with
so small a noise, (and lying near the chimney,) stept
out, and made shift to light a candle, by the light
of which he perceived the room strewed over with
broken glass, green, and some of it as it were pieces
of broken bottles; he had not long been considering
what it was, when suddenly his candle was hit out,
and glass flew about the room, that he made haste
to the protection of the coverlets; the noise of thundering rose more hideous then at any time before;
yet, at a certain time, all vanisht into calmness.
The morning after was the glass about the room,
which the maid that was to make clean the rooms
swept up into a corner, and many came to see it.
But Mr Richard Crook would stay no longer, yet
as he stopt, going through Woodstock town, he
was there heard to say, that he would not lodge
amongst them another night for a fee of L.500.

October 27th. The Commissioners had not yet
done their work, wherefore they must stay; and
being all men of the sword, they must not seem
afraid to encounter with any thing, though it be the
devil; therefore, with pistols charged, and drawn

swords laied by their bedsides, they applied themselves to take some rest, when something in the midst of night, so opened and shut the window casements with such claps, that it awakened all that slept; some of them peeping out to look what was the matter with the windows, stones flew about the rooms as if hurled with many hands; some hit the walls, and some the beds' heads close above the pillows, the dints of which were then, and yet (it is conceived) are to be seen, thus sometime throwing stones, and sometime making thundering noise; for two hours space it ceast, and all was quiet till the morn. After their rising, and the maid come in to make the fire, they looked about the rooms; they found fourscore stones brought in that night, and going to lay them together in the corner where the glass (before mentioned) had been swept up, they found that every piece of glass had been carried away that night. Many people came next day to see the stones, and all observed that they were not of such kind of stones as are naturall in the countrey thereabout; with these were noise like claps of thunder, or report of cannon planted against the rooms, heard by all that lodged in the outer courts, to their astonishment, and at Woodstock town, taken to be thunder.

October 28*th*. This night, both strange and differing noise from the former first awakened Captain Hart, who lodged in the bedchamber, who, hearing

Roe and Brown to groan, called out to Cockaine and Crook to come and help them, for Hart could not now stir himself; Cockaine would faine have answered, but he could not, or look about; something, he thought, stopt both his breath and held down his eye-lids. Amazed thus, he struggles and kickt about, till he had awaked Captain Crook, who, half asleep, grew very angry at his kicks, and multiplied words, it grew to an appointment in the field; but this fully recovered Cockaine to remember that Captain Hart had called for help, wherefore to them he ran in the other room, whom he found sadly groaning, where, scraping in the chimney, he both found a candle and fire to light it; but had not gone two steps, when something blew the candle out, and threw him in the chair by the bedside, when presently cried out Captain Carelesse, with a most pittiful voice, "Come hither, O come hither, brother Cockaine, the thing's gone of me." Cockaine, scarce yet himself, helpt to set him up in his bed, and after Captain Hart, and having scarce done that to them, and also to the other two, they heard Captain Crook crying out, as if something had been killing him. Cockaine snatcht up the sword that lay by their bed, and ran into the room to save Crook, but was in much more likelyhood to kill him, for at his coming, the thing that pressed Crook went of him, at which Crook started out of his bed, whom Cockaine thought a spirit, made at him, at which Crook cried out, " Lord help, Lord save me ;" Cockaine let fall his hand, and Crook, embracing Cockaine, desired his reconcilement, giving him many thanks for his deliverance. Then rose they all and came together, discoursed sometimes godly and sometimes praied, for all this while was there such stamping over the roof of the house, as if 1000 horse had there been trotting ; this night all the stones brought in the night before, and laid up in the withdrawing-room, were all carried again away by that which brought them in, which at the wonted time left of, and, as it were, went out, and so away.

October 29*th.* Their businesse having now received so much forwardnesse as to be neer dispatcht, they encouraged one the other, and resolved to try further; therefore, they provided more lights and fires, and further, for their assistance, prevailed with their ordinary keeper to lodge amongst them, and bring his mastive bitch ; and it was so this night with them, that they had no disturbance at all.

October 30*th.* So well they had past the night before, that this night they went to bed, confident and carelesse ; untill about twelve of the clock, something knockt at the door as with a smith's great hammer, but with such force as if it had cleft the door ; then ent'red something like a bear, but seem'd to swell more big, and walkt about the room, and out of one room into the other, treading so heavily, as the floare had not been strong enough to bear it. When it came into the bedchamber, it dasht against the beds' heads some kind of glass vessell, that broke in sundry pieces, and sometimes would take up those pieces, and hurle them about the room, and into the other room; and when it did not hurle the glasse at their heads, it did strike upon the tables, as if many smiths, with their greatest hammers, had been laying on as upon an anvil; sometimes it thumpt against the walls as if it would beat a hole through; then upon their heads, such stamping, as if the roof of the house were beating down upon their heads; and having done thus, during the space (as was conjectured) of two hours, it ceased and vanished, but with a more fierce shutting of the doors than at any time before. In the morning they found the pieces of glass about the room, and observed, that it was much differing from that glasse brought in three nights before, this being of a much thicker substance, which severall persons which came in carried away some pieces of. The Commissioners were in debate of lodging there no more; but all their businesse was not done, and some of them were so conceited as to believe, and to attribute the rest they enjoyed, the night before this last, unto the mastive bitch; wherefore, they resolved to get more company, and the mastive bitch, and try another night.

October 31st. This night, the fires and lights prepared, the ordinary keeper and his bitch, with another man perswaded by him, they all took their beds and fell asleep. But about twelve at night, such rapping was on all sides of them, that it wakened all of them; as the doors did seem to open, the mastive bitch fell fearfully a yelling, and presently ran fiercely into the bed to them in the truckle-bed; as the thing came by the table, it struck so fierce a blow on that, as that it made the frame to crack, then took the warming-pan from off the table, and stroke it against the walls with so much force as that it was beat flat together, lid and bottom. Now were they hit as they lay covered over head and ears within the bed-clothes. Captain Carelesse was taken a sound blow on the head with the shoulder-blade bone of a dead horse, (before they had been but thrown at, when they peept up, and mist;) Browne had a shrewed blow on the leg with the backbone, and another on the head, and every one of them felt severall blows of bones and stones through the bed-clothes, for now these things were thrown as from an angry hand that meant further mischief; the stones flew in at window as shot out of a gun, nor was the bursts lesse (as from without) than of a cannon, and all the windows broken down. Now as the hurling of the things did cease, and the thing walkt up and down, Captain Cockaine and Hart cried out, In the name of the Father, Son, and Holy Ghost, what are you? What would you have ? What have we done that you disturb us thus ? No voice replied, (as the Captains said, yet some of their servants have said otherwise,) and the noise ceast. Hereupon Captain Hart and Cockaine rose, who lay in the bedchamber, renewed the fire and lights, and one great candle, in a candlestick, they placed in the door, that might be seen by them in both the rooms. No sooner were they got to bed, but the noise arose on all sides more loud and hideous than at any time before, insomuch as (to use the Captain's own words) it returned and brought seven devils worse than itself; and presently they saw the candle and candlestick in the passage of the door, dasht up to the roof of the room, by a kick of the hinder parts of a horse, and after with the hoof trode out the snuff, and so dasht out the fire in the chimnies. As this was done, there fell, as from the sieling, upon them in the truckle-beds, such quantities of water, as if it had been poured out of buckets, which stunk worse than any earthly stink could make ; and as this was in doing, something crept under the high beds, tost them up to the roof of the house, with the Commissioners in them, until the testers of the beds were beaten down upon, and the bedsted-frames broke under them ; and here some pause being made, they all, as if with one consent, started up, and ran down the stairs until they came into the Councel Hall, where two sate up a-brewing, but now were fallen asleep ; those they scared much with wakening of them, having been much perplext before with the strange noise, which commonly was taken by them abroad for thunder, sometimes for rumbling wind. Here the Captains and their company got fire and candle, and every one carrying something of either, they returned into the Presence-Chamber, where some applied themselves to make the fire, whilst others fell to prayers, and having got some clothes about them, they spent the residue of the night in singing psalms and prayers ; during which, no noise was in that room, but most hideously round about, as at some distance.

It should have been told before, how that when Captain Hart first rose this night, (who lay in the bedchamber next the fire,) he found their book of valuations crosse the embers smoaking, which he snacht up and cast upon the table there, which the night before was left upon the table in the presence amongst their other papers : this book was in the morning found a handful burnt, and had burnt the table where it lay; Browne the clerk said, he would not for a 100 and a 100*l.* that it had been burnt a handful further.

This night it happened that there were six cony-stealers, who were come with their nets and ferrets to the cony-burrows by Rosamond's Well; but with the noise this night from the Mannor-house, they were so terrified, that like men dis-

tracted away they ran, and left their haies all ready
pitched, ready up, and the ferrets in the cony-burrows.

Now the Commissioners, more sensible of their
danger, considered more seriously of their safety,
and agreed to go and confer with Mr Hoffman, the
minister of Wotton, (a man not of the meanest note
for life or learning, by some esteemed more high,)
to desire his advice, together with his company and
prayers. Mr Hoffman held it too high a point to
resolve on suddenly and by himself, wherefore desired time to consider upon it, which being agreed
unto, he forthwith rode to Mr Jenkinson and Mr
Wheat, the two next Justices of Peace, to try
what warrant they could give him for it. They
both (as 'tis said from themselves) encouraged him
to be assisting to the Commissioners, according to
his calling.

But certain it is, that when they came to fetch
him to go with them, Mr Hoffman answered, that
he would not lodge there one night for 500*l.*, and
being asked to pray with them, he held up his hands
and said, that he would not meddle upon any terms.

Mr Hoffman refusing to undertake the quarrel,
the Commissioners held it not safe to lodge where
they had been thus entertained any longer, but
caused all things to be removed into the chambers
over the gatehouse, where they staid but one night,
and what rest they enjoyed there, we have but an

uncertain relation of, for they went away early the
next morning ; but if it may be held fit to set down
what hath been delivered by the report of others,
they were also the same night much affrighted with
dreadful apparitions, but observing that these passages spread much in discourse, to be also in particulars taken notice of, and that the nature of it
made not for their cause, they agreed to the concealing of things for the future ; yet this is well-
known and certain, that the gate-keeper's wife was
in so strange an agony in her bed, and in her bedchamber such noise, (whilst her husband was above
with the Commissioners,) that two maids in the
next room to her, durst not venture to assist her,
but affrighted ran out to call company, and their
master, and found the woman (at their coming in)
gasping for breath : and the next day said, that
she saw and suffered that, which for all the world
she would not be hired to again.

From Woodstock the Commissioners removed
unto Euelme, and some of them returned to Woodstock the Sunday se'nnight after, (the book of Valuations wanting something that was for haste left
imperfect,) but lodged not in any of those rooms
where they had lain before, and yet were not unvi-
sited (as they confess themselves) by the devil,
whom they called their nightly guest ; Captain
Crook came not untill Tuesday night, and how he
sped that night the gate-keeper's wife can tell if

she dareth, but what she hath whispered to her gossips, shall not be made a part of this our narrative, nor many more particulars which have fallen from the Commissioners themselves and their servants to other persons; they are all or most of them alive, and may add to it when they please, and surely have not a better way to be revenged of him who troubled them, than according to the proverb, tell truth and shame the devil.

There remains this observation to be added, that on a Wednesday morning all these officers went away; and that since then diverse persons of severall qualities, have lodged often and sometimes long in the same rooms, both in the presence, withdrawing-room, and bedchamber belonging unto his sacred Majesty; yet none have had the least disturbance, or heard the smallest noise, for which the cause was not as ordinary as apparent, except the Commissioners and their company, who came in order to the alienating and pulling down the house, which is wellnigh performed.

A SHORT SURVEY OF WOODSTOCK, NOT TAKEN BY ANY OF THE BEFORE-MENTIONED COMMISSIONERS

The noble seat, called Woodstock, is one of the ancient honours belonging to the crown. Severall

* This Survey of Woodstock is appended to the preceding pamphlet.

mannors owe suite and service to the place; but the custom of the countrey giving it but the title of a mannor, we shall erre with them to be the better understood.

The mannor-house hath been a large fabrick, and accounted amongst his majestie's standing houses, because there was alwaies kept a standing furniture. This great house was built by King Henry the First, but ampleyfied with the gate-house and outsides of the outer-court, by King Henry the Seventh, the stables by King James.

About a bow-shoot from the gate south-west, remain foundation signs of that structure, erected by King Henry the Second, for the security of Lady Rosamond, daughter of Walter Lord Clifford, which some poets have compared to the Dedalian labyrinth, but the form and circuit both of the place and ruins shew it to have been a house and of one pile, perhaps of strength, according to the fashion of those times, and probably was fitted with secret places of recess, and avenues to hide or convey away such persons as were not willing to be found if narrowly sought after. About the midst of the place ariseth a spring, called at present Rosamond's Well; it is but shallow, and shews to have been paved and walled about, likely contrived for the use of them within the house, when it should be of danger to go out.

A quarter of a mile distant from the King's house,

is seated Woodstock town, new and old. This new Woodstock did arise by some buildings which Henry the Second gave leave to be erected, (as received by tradition,) at the suite of the Lady Rosamond, for the use of out-servants upon the wastes of the mannor of Bladon, where is the mother church; this is a hamlet belonging to it, though encreased to a market town by the advantage of the Court residing sometime near, which of late years they have been sensible of the want of; this town was made a corporation in the 11th year of Henry the Sixth, by charter, with power to send two burgesses to parliament or not, as they will themselves.

Old Woodstock is seated on the west side of the brook, named Glyme, which also runneth through the park; the town consists not of above four or five houses, but it is to be conceived that it hath been much larger, (but very anciently so,) for in some old law historians there is mention of the assize at Woodstock, for a law made in a Micelge-mote (the name of parliaments before the coming of the Norman) in the days of King Ethelred.

And in like manner, that thereabout was a king's house, if not in the same place where Henry the First built the late standing pile before his; for in such days those great councils were commonly held in the King's palaces. Some of those lands have belonged to the orders of the Knights Templers there being records which call them, *Terras quas Rex excambiavit cum Templariis.*

But now this late large mannor-house is in a manner almost turned into heaps of rubbish; some seven or eight rooms left for the accommodation of a tenant that should rent the King's meadows, (of those who had no power to let them,) with several high uncovered walls standing, the prodigious spectacles of malice unto monarchy, which ruines still bear semblance of their state, and yet aspire, in spight of envy or of weather, to shew, What kings do build, subjects may sometimes shake, but utterly can never overthrow.

That part of the park called the High-park, hath been lately subdivided by Sir Arthur Haselrig, to make pastures for his breed of colts, and other parts plowed up. Of the whole saith Roffus Warwicensis, in MS. Hen. I. p. 122, *Fecit iste Rex Parcum de Woodstock, cum Palatio infra prædictum Parcum, qui Parcus erat primus Parcus Angliæ, et continet in circuitu septem Miliaria; constructus erat Anno 14 hujus Regis, aut parum post.* Without the Park the King's demesne woods were, it cannot well be said now are, the timber being all sold off, and underwoods so cropt and spoiled by that beast the Lord Munson, and other greedy cattle, that they are hardly recoverable. Beyond which lieth Stonefield, and other mannors that hold of Woodstock, with other woods, that have been aliened by former kings, but with reservation of liberty for his majestie's deer, and other beasts of forrest, to harbour in at pleasure, as in due place is to be shewed.

END OF APPENDIX.

WOODSTOCK;

OR,

THE CAVALIER.

PREFACE.

———

It is not my purpose to inform my readers how the manuscripts of that eminent antiquary, the Rev. J. A. Rochecliffe, D.D., came into my possession. There are many ways in which such things happen, and it is enough to say they were rescued from an unworthy fate, and that they were honestly come by As for the authenticity of the anecdotes which I have gleaned from the writings of this excellent person, and put together with my own unrivalled facility, the name of Doctor Rochecliffe will warrant accuracy, wherever that name happens to be known.

With his history the reading part of the world are well acquainted; and we might refer the tyro to honest Anthony a Wood, who looked up to him as one of the pillars of High

Church, and bestows on him an exemplary character in the *Athenæ Oxonienses*, although the Doctor was educated at Cambridge, England's other eye.

It is well known that Doctor Rochecliffe early obtained preferment in the Church, on account of the spirited share which he took in the controversy with the Puritans; and that his work, entitled *Malleus Hæresis*, was considered as a knock-down blow by all except those who received it. It was that work which made him, at the early age of thirty, Rector of Woodstock, and which afterwards secured him a place in the Catalogue of the celebrated Century White;—and, worse than being shown up by that fanatic, among the catalogues of scandalous and malignant priests admitted into benefices by the prelates, his opinions occasioned the loss of his living of Woodstock by the ascendency of Presbytery. He was chaplain, during most part of the Civil War, to Sir Henry Lee's regiment, levied for the service of King Charles; and it was said he engaged more than once personally in the field. At least it is certain that Doctor Rochecliffe was repeatedly in great danger, as will appear from more passages than one in the following history, which speaks of his own exploits, like Cæsar, in the third person. I suspect, however, some Presbyterian commentator has been guilty of interpolating two or three passages. The manuscript was long in possession of the Everards, a distinguished family of that persuasion.*

During the Usurpation, Doctor Rochecliffe was constantly engaged in one or other of the premature attempts at a restoration of monarchy; and was accounted, for his audacity, presence of mind, and depth of judgment, one of the greatest undertakers for the King in that busy time; with this trifling drawback, that the plots in which he busied himself were almost constantly detected. Nay, it was suspected that Cromwell himself sometimes contrived to suggest to him the intrigues in which he engaged, by which means the wily Protector made experiments on the fidelity of doubtful friends, and became well acquainted with the plots of declared enemies, which he thought it more easy to disconcert and disappoint than to punish severely.

* It is hardly necessary to say, unless to some readers of very literal capacity, that Doctor Rochecliffe and his manuscripts are alike apocryphal.

Upon the Restoration, Doctor Rochecliffe regained his living of Woodstock, with other church preferment, and gave up polemics and political intrigues for philosophy. He was one of the constituent members of the Royal Society, and was the person through whom Charles required of that learned body solution of their curious problem, "Why, if a vessel is filled brimful of water, and a large live fish plunged into the water, nevertheless it shall not overflow the pitcher?" Doctor Rochecliffe's exposition of this phenomenon was the most ingenious and instructive of four that were given in; and it is certain the Doctor must have gained the honour of the day, but for the obstinacy of a plain, dull, country gentleman, who insisted that the experiment should be, in the first place, publicly tried. When this was done, the event showed it would have been rather rash to have adopted the facts exclusively on the royal authority; as the fish, however curiously inserted into his native element, splashed the water over the hall, and destroyed the credit of four ingenious essayists, besides a large Turkey carpet.

Doctor Rochecliffe, it would seem, died about 1685, leaving many papers behind him

of various kinds, and, above all, many valuable
anecdotes of secret history, from which the
following Memoirs have been extracted, on
which we intend to say only a few words by
way of illustration.

The existence of Rosamond's Labyrinth,
mentioned in these pages, is attested by Drayton in the reign of Queen Elizabeth.

" Rosamond's Labyrinth, whose ruins, together with her Well, being paved with square
stones in the bottom, and also her Tower, from
which the Labyrinth did run, are yet remaining, being vaults arched and walled with stone
and brick, almost inextricably wound within
one another, by which, if at any time her
lodging were laid about by the Queen, she
might easily avoid peril imminent, and, if need
be, by secret issues take the air abroad, many
furlongs about Woodstock in Oxfordshire."*

It is highly probable, that a singular piece
of phantasmagoria, which was certainly played off upon the Commissioners of the Long
Parliament, who were sent down to dispark
and destroy Woodstock, after the death of
Charles I., was conducted by means of the

* Drayton's England's Heroical Epistles, Note A, on the
Epistle, Rosamond to King Henry.

secret passages and recesses in the ancient Labyrinth of Rosamond, round which successive Monarchs had erected a Hunting-seat or Lodge.

There is a curious account of the disturbance given to those Honourable Commissioners, inserted by Doctor Plot, in his Natural History of Oxfordshire. But as I have not the book at hand, I can only allude to the work of the celebrated Glanville upon Witches, who has extracted it as an highly accredited narrative of supernatural dealings. The beds of the Commissioners, and their servants, were hoisted up till they were almost inverted, and then let down again so suddenly, as to menace them with broken bones. Unusual and horrible noises disturbed those sacrilegious intromitters with royal property. The devil, on one occasion, brought them a warming-pan; on another, pelted them with stones and horses' bones. Tubs of water were emptied on them in their sleep; and so many other pranks of the same nature played at their expense, that they broke up housekeeping, and left their intended spoliation only half completed. The good sense of Doctor Plot suspected, that these eats were wrought by conspiracy and confederation, which Glanville of course endeavours to refute with all his might; for it could scarce be expected, that he who believed in so convenient a solution as that of supernatural agency, would consent to relinquish the service of a key, which will answer any lock, however intricate.

Nevertheless, it was afterwards discovered, that Doctor Plot was perfectly right; and that the only demon who wrought all these marvels, was a disguised royalist—a fellow called Trusty Joe, or some such name, formerly in the service of the Keeper of the Park, but who engaged in that of the Commissioners, on purpose to subject them to his persecution. I think I have seen some account of the real state of the transaction, and of the machinery by which the wizard worked his wonders; but whether in a book, or a pamphlet, I am uncertain. I remember one passage particularly, to this purpose. The Commissioners having agreed to retain some articles out of the public account, in order to be divided among themselves, had entered into an indenture for ascertaining their share in the peculation, which they hid in a bow-pot for security. Now, when an assembly of divines, aided by the most strict religious characters in the neighbourhood of Woodstock, were assembled to conjure down the supposed demon, Trusty Joe had contrived a firework, which he let off in the midst of the exorcism, and which destroyed the bow-pot; and, to the shame and confusion of the Commissioners, threw their secret indenture into the midst of the assembled ghost-seers, who became thus acquainted with their secret schemes of peculation.

It is, however, to little purpose for me to strain my memory about ancient and imperfect recollections concerning the particulars of these fantastic disturbances at Woodstock, since Doctor Rochecliffe's papers give such a much more accurate narrative than could be obtained from any account in existence before their publication. Indeed, I might have gone much more fully into this part of my subject, for the materials are ample;—but, to tell the reader a secret, some friendly critics were of opinion they made the story hang on hand; and thus I was prevailed on to be more concise on the subject than I might otherwise have been.

The impatient reader, perhaps, is by this time accusing me of keeping the sun from him with a candle. Were the sunshine as bright, however, as it is likely to prove; and the

flambeau, or link, a dozen of times as smoky,
my friend must remain in the inferior atmosphere a minute longer, while I disclaim the
idea of poaching on another's manor. Hawks,
we say in Scotland, ought not to pick out
hawks' eyes, or tire upon each other's quarry;
and, therefore, if I had known that, in its
date and its characters, this tale was likely to
interfere with that recently published by a
distinguished contemporary, I should unquestionably have left Doctor Rochecliffe's manuscript in peace for the present season. But
before I was aware of this circumstance, this
little book was half through the press; and I
had only the alternative of avoiding any in-
tentional imitation, by delaying a perusal of
the contemporary work in question. Some
accidental collision there must be, when works
of a similar character are finished on the same
general system of historical manners, and the
same historical personages are introduced. Of
course, if such have occurred, I shall be probably the sufferer. But my intentions have
been at least innocent, since I look on it as
one of the advantages attending the conclusion of WOODSTOCK, that the finishing of my

own task will permit me to have the pleasure of reading BRAMBLETYE-HOUSE, from which I have hitherto conscientiously abstained.

WOODSTOCK;

OR,

THE CAVALIER.

WOODSTOCK.

CHAPTER I.

Some were for gospel ministers,
And some for red-coat seculars,
As men most fit t' hold forth the word,
And wield the one and th' other sword.
                         BUTLER's *Hudibras*.

THERE is a handsome parish church in the town
of Woodstock,—I am told so, at least, for I never
saw it, having scarce time, when at the place, to
view the magnificence of Blenheim, its painted
halls, and tapestried bowers, and then return in
due season to dine in hall with my learned friend,
the provost of ——; being one of those occasions
on which a man wrongs himself extremely, if he
lets his curiosity interfere with his punctuality. I
had the church accurately described to me, with a
view to this work; but, as I have some reason to
doubt whether my informant had ever seen the
inside of it himself, I shall be content to say that
it is now a handsome edifice, most part of which was
rebuilt forty or fifty years since, although it still
contains some arches of the old chantry, founded,

it is said, by King John. It is to this more ancient part of the building that my story refers.

On a morning in the end of September, or beginning of October, in the year 1652, being a day appointed for a solemn thanksgiving for the decisive victory at Worcester, a respectable audience was assembled in the old chantry, or chapel of King John. The condition of the church and character of the audience both bore witness to the rage of civil war, and the peculiar spirit of the times. The sacred edifice showed many marks of dilapidation. The windows, once filled with stained glass, had been dashed to pieces with pikes and muskets, as matters of and pertaining to idolatry. The carving on the reading-desk was damaged, and two fair screens of beautiful sculptured oak had been destroyed, for the same pithy and conclusive reason. The high altar had been removed, and the gilded railing, which was once around it, was broken down and carried off. The effigies of several tombs were mutilated, and now lay scattered about the church,

> Torn from their destined niche,—unworthy meed
> Of knightly counsel or heroic deed !

The autumn wind piped through empty aisles, in which the remains of stakes and trevisses of rough-hewn timber, as well as a quantity of scattered hay and trampled straw, seemed to intimate that the hallowed precincts had been, upon some late emergency, made the quarters of a troop of horse.

The audience, like the building, was abated in

splendour. None of the ancient and habitual worshippers during peaceful times, were now to be seen in their carved galleries, with hands shadowing their brows, while composing their minds to pray where their fathers had prayed, and after the same mode of worship. The eye of the yeoman and peasant sought in vain the tall form of old Sir Henry Lee of Ditchley, as, wrapped in his laced cloak, and with beard and whiskers duly composed, he moved slowly through the aisles, followed by the faithful mastiff, or bloodhound, which in old time had saved his master by his fidelity, and which regularly followed him to church. Bevis, indeed, fell under the proverb which avers, " He is a good dog which goes to church;" for, bating an occasional temptation to warble along with the accord, he behaved himself as decorously as any of the congregation, and returned as much edified, perhaps, as most of them. The damsels of Woodstock looked as vainly for the laced cloaks, jingling spurs, slashed boots, and tall plumes, of the young cavaliers of this and other high-born houses, moving through the streets and the churchyard with the careless ease, which indicates perhaps rather an overweening degree of self-confidence, yet shows graceful when mingled with good-humour and courtesy. The good old dames, too, in their white hoods and black velvet gowns—their daughters, "the cynosure of neighbouring eyes,"—where were they all now, who, when they entered the church, used to divide men's thoughts between them and

Heaven? "But, ah! Alice Lee—so sweet, so gentle, so condescending in thy loveliness—[thus proceeds a contemporary annalist, whose manuscript we have deciphered]—why is my story to turn upon thy fallen fortunes? and why not rather to the period when, in the very dismounting from your palfrey, you attracted as many eyes as if an angel had descended,—as many blessings as if the benignant being had come fraught with good tidings? No creature wert thou of an idle romancer's imagination—no being fantastically bedizened with inconsistent perfections;—thy merits made me love thee well—and for thy faults—so well did they show amid thy good qualities, that I think they made me love thee better."

With the house of Lee had disappeared from the chantry of King John others of gentle blood and honoured lineage, — Freemantles, Winklecombes, Drycotts, &c.; for the air that blew over the towers of Oxford was unfavourable to the growth of Puritanism, which was more general in the neighbouring counties. There were among the congregation, however, one or two that, by their habits and demeanour, seemed country gentlemen of consideration, and there were also present some of the notables of the town of Woodstock, cutlers or glovers chiefly, whose skill in steel or leather had raised them to a comfortable livelihood. These dignitaries wore long black cloaks, plaited close at the neck, and, like peaceful citizens, carried their Bibles and memorandum-books at their girdles, instead of knife or sword.* This respectable, but least numerous part of the audience, were such decent persons as had adopted the Presbyterian form of faith, renouncing the liturgy and hierarchy of the Church of England, and living under the tuition of the Rev. Nehemiah Holdenough, much famed for the length and strength of his powers of predication. With these grave seniors sat their goodly dames in ruff and gorget, like the portraits which in catalogues of paintings are designed " wife of a burgomaster ;" and their pretty daughters, whose study, like that of Chaucer's physician, was not always in the Bible, but who were, on the contrary, when a glance could escape the vigilance of their honoured mothers, inattentive themselves, and the cause of inattention in others.

But, besides these dignified persons, there were in the church a numerous collection of the lower orders, some brought thither by curiosity, but many of them unwashed artificers, bewildered in the theological discussions of the time, and of as many various sects as there are colours in the rainbow. The presumption of these learned Thebans being in exact proportion to their ignorance, the last was total, and the first boundless. Their behaviour in the church was any thing but reverential or edifying. Most of them affected a cynical contempt for all that was only held sacred by human sanction—the church was to these men but a steeple-house, the clergyman, an ordinary person ; her ordinances,

* This custom among the Puritans is mentioned often in old plays, and among others in the Widow of Watling Street.

dry bran and sapless pottage,* unfitted for the spiritualized palates of the saints, and the prayer. an address to Heaven, to which each acceded or not, as in his too critical judgment he conceived fit.

The elder amongst them sat or lay on the benches, with their high steeple-crowned hats pulled over their severe and knitted brows, waiting for the Presbyterian parson, as mastiffs sit in dumb expectation of the bull that is to be brought to the stake. The younger mixed, some of them, a bolder license of manners with their heresies; they gazed round on the women, yawned, coughed, and whispered, eat apples, and cracked nuts, as if in the gallery of a theatre ere the piece commences.

Besides all these, the congregation contained a few soldiers, some in corslets and steel caps, some in buff, and others in red coats. These men of war had their bandoleers, with ammunition, slung round them, and rested on their pikes and muskets. They, too, had their peculiar doctrines on the most difficult points of religion, and united the extravagances of enthusiasm with the most determined courage and resolution in the field. The burghers of Woodstock looked on these military saints with no small degree of awe; for though not often sullied with deeds of plunder or cruelty, they had the power of both absolutely in their hands, and the peaceful citizens had no alternative, save submission to whatever the ill-regulated and enthusiastic imaginations of their martial guides might suggest.

* See a curious vindication of this indecent simile here for the Common Prayer, in Note, end of Chapter.

After some time spent in waiting for him, Mr Holdenough began to walk up the aisles of the chapel, not with the slow and dignified carriage with which the old Rector was of yore wont to maintain the dignity of the surplice, but with a hasty step, like one who arrives too late at an appointment, and bustles forward to make the best use of his time. He was a tall thin man, with an adust complexion, and the vivacity of his eye indicated some irascibi· lity of temperament. His dress was brown, not black, and over his other vestments he wore, in honour of Calvin, a Geneva cloak of a blue colour, which fell backwards from his shoulders as he post- ed on to the pulpit. His grizzled hair was cut as short as shears could perform the feat, and covered with a black silk scullcap, which stuck so close to his head, that the two ears expanded from under it as if they had been intended as handles by which to lift the whole person. Moreover, the worthy divine wore spectacles, and a long grizzled peaked beard, and he carried in his hand a small pocket- bible with silver clasps. Upon arriving at the pul- pit, he paused a moment to take breath, then began to ascend the steps by two at a time.

But his course was arrested by a strong hand, which seized his cloak. It was that of one who had detached himself from the group of soldiery. He was a stout man of middle stature, with a quick eye, and a countenance, which, though plain, had yet an expression that fixed the attention. His dress, though not strictly military, partook of that character. He wore large hose made of calves-leather, and a tuck, as it was then called, or rapier, of tremendous length, balanced on the other side by a dagger. The belt was morocco, garnished with pistols.

The minister, thus intercepted in his duty, faced round upon the party who had seized him, and demanded, in no gentle tone, the meaning of the interruption.

" Friend," quoth the intruder, " is it thy purpose to hold forth to these good people?"

" Ay, marry is it," said the clergyman, " and such is my bounden duty. Woe to me if I preach not the gospel—Prithee, friend, let me not in my labour"——

" Nay," said the man of warlike mien, " I am myself minded to hold forth; therefore, do thou desist, or if thou wilt do by mine advice, remain and fructify with those poor goslings, to whom I am presently about to shake forth the crumbs of comfortable doctrine."

" Give place, thou man of Satan," said the priest, waxing wroth, " respect mine order—my cloth."

" I see no more to respect in the cut of thy cloak, or in the cloth of which it is fashioned," said the other, " than thou didst in the Bishop's rochets— they were black and white, thou art blue and brown. Sleeping dogs every one of you, lying down, loving to slumber—shepherds that starve the flock, but will not watch it, each looking to his own gain— hum."

Scenes of this indecent kind were so common at the time, that no one thought of interfering; the congregation looked on in silence, the better class scandalized, and the lower orders, some laughing, and others backing the soldier or minister as their fancy dictated. Meantime the struggle waxed fiercer; Mr Holdenough clamoured for assistance.

"Master Mayor of Woodstock," he exclaimed, " wilt thou be among those wicked magistrates who bear the sword in vain?—Citizens, will you not help your pastor?—Worthy Aldermen, will you see me strangled on the pulpit stairs by this man of buff and Belial?—But lo, I will overcome him, and cast his cords from me."

As Holdenough spoke, he struggled to ascend the pulpit stairs, holding hard on the banisters. His tormentor held fast by the skirts of the cloak, which went nigh to the choking of the wearer, until, as he spoke the words last mentioned, in a half-strangled voice, Mr Holdenough dexterously slipped the string which tied it round his neck, so that the garment suddenly gave way; the soldier fell backwards down the steps, and the liberated divine skipped into the pulpit, and began to give forth a psalm of triumph over his prostrate adversary. But a great hubbub in the church marred his exultation, and although he and his faithful clerk continued to sing the hymn of victory, their notes were only heard by fits, like the whistle of a curlew during a gale of wind.

The cause of the tumult was as follows:—The Mayor was a zealous Presbyterian, and witnessed the intrusion of the soldier with great indignation from the very beginning, though he hesitated to interfere with an armed man while on his legs and capable of resistance. But no sooner did he behold the champion of independency sprawling on his back, with the divine's Geneva cloak fluttering in his hands, than the magistrate rushed forward, exclaiming that such insolence was not to be endured, and ordered his constables to seize the prostrate champion, proclaiming, in the magnanimity of wrath, " I will commit every red-coat of them all—I will commit him were he Noll Cromwell himself!"

The worthy Mayor's indignation had overmastered his reason when he made this mistimed vaunt; for three soldiers, who had hitherto stood motionless like statues, made each a stride in advance, which placed them betwixt the municipal officers and the soldier, who was in the act of rising; then making at once the movement of resting arms according to the manual as then practised, their musket-buts rang on the church pavement, within an inch of the gouty toes of Master Mayor. The energetic magistrate, whose efforts in favour of order were thus checked, cast one glance on his supporters, but that was enough to show him that force was not on his side. All had shrunk back on hearing that ominous clatter of stone and iron. He was obliged to descend to expostulation.

" What do you mean, my masters?" he said; " is it like a decent and God-fearing soldiery, who have wrought such things for the land as have never before been heard of, to brawl and riot in the church, or to aid, abet, and comfort a profane fellow, who hath, upon a solemn thanksgiving, excluded the minister from his own pulpit?"

" We have nought to do with thy church, as thou call'st it," said he who, by a small feather in front of his morion, appeared to be the corporal of the party ;—" we see not why men of gifts should not be heard within these citadels of superstition, as well as the voice of the men of crape of old, and the men of cloak now. Wherefore, we will pluck yon Jack Presbyter out of his wooden sentinel-box, and our own watchman shall relieve the guard, and mount thereon, and cry aloud and spare not."

" Nay, gentlemen," said the Mayor, "if such be your purpose, we have not the means to withstand you, being, as you see, peaceful and quiet men— But let me first speak with this worthy minister, Nehemiah Holdenough, to persuade him to yield up his place for the time without farther scandal."

The peace-making Mayor then interrupted the quavering of Holdenough and the clerk, and prayed both to retire, else there would, he said, be certainly strife.

" Strife!" replied the Presbyterian divine, with scorn ; " no fear of strife, among men that dare not testify against this open profanation of the church, and daring display of heresy. Would your neighbours of Banbury have brooked such an insult?"

" Come, come, Master Holdenough," said the Mayor, "put us not to mutiny and cry Clubs. I tell you once more, we are not men of war or blood."

" Not more than may be drawn by the point of a needle," said the preacher, scornfully.—" Ye

tailors of Woodstock !—for what is a glover but a
tailor working on kid-skin?—I forsake you, in scorn
of your faint hearts and feeble hands, and will seek
me elsewhere a flock which will not fly from their
shepherd at the braying of the first wild ass which
cometh from out the great desert."

So saying, the aggrieved divine departed from
his pulpit, and shaking the dust from his shoes, left
the church as hastily as he had entered it, though
with a different reason for his speed. The citizens
saw his retreat with sorrow, and not without a
compunctious feeling, as if conscious that they were
not playing the most courageous part in the world.
The Mayor himself and several others left the
church, to follow and appease him.

The Independent orator, late prostrate, was now
triumphant, and inducting himself into the pulpit
without farther ceremony, he pulled a Bible from
his pocket, and selected his text from the forty-fifth
psalm,—" Gird thy sword upon thy thigh, O most
mighty, with thy glory and thy majesty : and in
thy majesty ride prosperously."—Upon this theme
he commenced one of those wild declamations common at the period, in which men were accustomed
to wrest and pervert the language of Scripture, by
adapting it to modern events.*   The language
which, in its literal sense, was applied to King
David, and typically referred to the coming of the
Messiah, was, in the opinion of the military orator,

* Note, p. 22. Vindication of the Book of Common Prayer,
against the contumelious slanders of the Fanatic Party terming it Porridge.

most properly to be interpreted of Oliver Cromwell, the victorious general of the infant Commonwealth, which was never destined to come of age.
" Gird on thy sword !" exclaimed the preacher
emphatically ; " and was not that a pretty bit of
steel as ever dangled from a corslet, or rung against
a steel saddle ? Ay, ye prick up your ears now, ye
cutlers of Woodstock, as if ye should know something of a good fox broadsword—Did you forge it,
I trow ?—was the steel quenched with water from
Rosamond's well, or the blade blessed by the old
cuckoldy priest of Godstow ? You would have us
think, I warrant me, that you wrought it and welded it, grinded and polished it, and all the while it
never came on a Woodstock stithy ! You were all
too busy making whittles for the lazy crape-men of
Oxford, bouncing priests, whose eyes were so closed
up with fat, that they could not see Destruction till
she had them by the throat. But I can tell you
where the sword was forged, and tempered, and
welded, and grinded, and polished. When you
were, as I said before, making whittles for false
priests, and daggers for dissolute G—d d—n-me
cavaliers, to cut the people of England's throats with
—it was forged at Long Marston Moor, where
blows went faster than ever rung hammer on anvil
—and it was tempered at Naseby, in the best blood
of the cavaliers—and it was welded in Ireland
against the walls of Drogheda—and it was grinded
on Scottish lives at Dunbar—and now of late it was
polished in Worcester, till it shines as bright as the

sun in the middle heaven, and there is no light in England that shall come nigh unto it."

Here the military part of the congregation raised a hum of approbation, which being a sound like the " hear, hear," of the British House of Commons, was calculated to heighten the enthusiasm of the orator, by intimating the sympathy of the audience. " And then," resumed the preacher, rising in energy as he found that his audience partook in these feelings, " what sayeth the text?—Ride on prosperously—do not stop—do not call a halt—do not quit the saddle—pursue the scattered fliers—sound the trumpet—not a levant or a flourish, but a point of war—sound, boot and saddle—to horse and away —a charge!—follow after the young Man!—what part have we in him?—Slay, take, destroy, divide the spoil! Blessed art thou, Oliver, on account of thine honour—thy cause is clear, thy call is undoubted—never has defeat come near thy leading staff, nor disaster attended thy banner. Ride on, flower of England's soldiers! ride on, chosen leader of God's champions! gird up the loins of thy resolution, and be steadfast to the mark of thy high calling!"

Another deep and stern hum, echoed by the ancient embow'd arches of the old chantry, gave him an opportunity of an instant's repose; when the people of Woodstock heard him, and not without anxiety, turn the stream of his oratory into another channel.

" But wherefore, ye people of Woodstock, do I say these things to you, who claim no portion in

our David, no interest in England's son of Jesse?
—You, who were fighting as well as your might
could (and it was not very formidable) for the late
Man, under that old blood-thirsty papist Sir Jacob
Aston—are you not now plotting, or ready to plot,
for the restoring, as ye call it, of the young Man, the
unclean son of the slaughtered tyrant—the fugitive
after whom the true hearts of England are now
following, that they may take and slay him?—
' Why should your rider turn his bridle our way?'
say you in your hearts; ' we will none of him; if
we may help ourselves, we will rather turn us to
wallow in the mire of monarchy, with the sow that
was washed but newly.' Come, men of Woodstock,
I will ask, and do you answer me. Hunger ye
still after the flesh-pots of the monks of Godstow?
and ye will say, Nay;—but wherefore, except that
the pots are cracked and broken, and the fire is
extinguished wherewith thy oven used to boil?
And again, I ask, drink ye still of the well of the
fornications of the fair Rosamond?—ye will say,
Nay;—but wherefore?"—

Here the orator, ere he could answer the question in his own way, was surprised by the following
reply, very pithily pronounced by one of the congregation :—" Because you, and the like of you,
have left us no brandy to mix with it."

All eyes turned to the audacious speaker, who
stood beside one of the thick sturdy Saxon pillars,
which he himself somewhat resembled, being short
of stature, but very strongly made, a squat broad
Little John sort of figure, leaning on a quarterstaff,

and wearing a jerkin, which, though now sorely
stained and discoloured, had once been of the Lincoln green, and showed remnants of having been
laced. There was an air of careless good-humoured audacity about the fellow; and, though under
military restraint, there were some of the citizens
who could not help crying out,—" Well said, Joceline Joliffe!"

" Jolly Joceline, call ye him?" proceeded the
preacher, without showing either confusion or displeasure at the interruption,—" I will make him
Joceline of the jail, if he interrupts me again. One
of your park-keepers, I warrant, that can never
forget they have borne C. R. upon their badges
and bugle-horns, even as a dog bears his owner's
name on his collar—a pretty emblem for Christian
men! But the brute beast hath the better of him,
—the brute weareth his own coat, and the caitiff
thrall wears his master's. I have seen such a wag
make a rope's end wag ere now.—Where was I?
—Oh, rebuking you for your backslidings, men of
Woodstock.—Yes, then ye will say ye have renounced Popery, and ye have renounced Prelacy,
and then ye wipe your mouth like Pharisees as ye
are; and who but you for purity of religion! But
I tell you, ye are but like Jehu the son of Nimshi,
who broke down the house of Baal, yet departed
not from the sons of Jeroboam. Even so ye eat not
fish on Friday with the blinded Papists, nor minced-
pies on the twenty-fifth day of December, like the
slothful Prelatists; but ye will gorge on sack-posset
each night in the year with your blind Presbyterian

guide, and ye will speak evil of dignities, and revile
the Commonwealth; and ye will glorify yourselves
in your park of Woodstock, and say, ' Was it not
walled in first of any other in England, and that
by Henry, son of William called the Conqueror?'
And ye have a princely Lodge therein, and call the
same a Royal Lodge; and ye have an oak which ye
call the King's Oak; and ye steal and eat the venison of the park; and ye say, ' This is the king's
venison, we will wash it down with a cup to the
king's health—better we eat it than those roundheaded commonwealth knaves.'   But listen unto
me, and take warning.   For these things come we
to controversy with you.   And our name shall be
a cannon-shot, before which your Lodge, in the
pleasantness whereof ye take pastime, shall be blown
into ruins; and we will be as a wedge to split
asunder the King's oak into billets to heat a brown
baker's oven; and we will dispark your park, and
slay your deer, and eat them ourselves, neither shall
you have any portion thereof, whether in neck or
haunch.   Ye shall not haft a tenpenny knife with
the horns thereof, neither shall ye cut a pair of
breeches out of the hide, for all ye be cutlers and
glovers; and ye shall have no comfort or support
neither from the sequestrated traitor Henry Lee,
who called himself ranger of Woodstock, nor from
any on his behalf; for they are coming hither who
shall be called Maher-shalal-hash-baz, because he
maketh haste to the spoil."

Here ended this wild effusion, the latter part of
which fell heavy on the souls of the poor citizens

of Woodstock, as tending to confirm a report of an unpleasing nature which had been lately circulated. The communication with London was indeed slow, and the news which it transmitted were uncertain: no less uncertain were the times themselves, and the rumours which were circulated, exaggerated by the hopes and fears of so many various factions. But the general stream of report, so far as Woodstock was concerned, had of late run uniformly in one direction. Day after day they had been informed, that the fatal fiat of Parliament had gone out, for selling the park of Woodstock, destroying its lodge, disparking its forest, and erasing, as far as they could be erased, all traces of its ancient fame. Many of the citizens were likely to be sufferers on this occasion, as several of them enjoyed, either by sufferance or right, various convenient privileges, of pasturage, cutting firewood, and the like, in the royal chase; and all the inhabitants of the little borough were hurt to think, that the scenery of the place was to be destroyed, its edifices ruined, and its honours rent away. This is a patriotic sensation often found in such places, which ancient distinctions and long-cherished recollections of former days, render so different from towns of recent date. The natives of Woodstock felt it in the fullest force. They had trembled at the anticipated calamity; but now, when it was announced by the appearance of those dark, stern, and at the same time omnipotent soldiers—now that they heard it proclaimed by the mouth of one of their military preachers—they considered their fate as inevitable.

The causes of disagreement among themselves were for the time forgotten, as the congregation, dismissed without psalmody or benediction, went slowly and mournfully homeward, each to his own place of abode.

NOTE TO CHAPTER I.

Note, p. 14.—Vindication of the Book of Common Prayer, against the contumelious slanders of the Fanatic Party terming it Porridge.

The author of this singular and rare tract indulges in the allegorical style, till he fairly hunts down the allegory.

" But as for what you call porridge, who hatched the name I know not, neither is it worth the enquiring after, for I hold porridge good food. It is better to a sick man than meat, for a sick man will sooner eat pottage than meat. Pottage will digest with him when meat will not; pottage will nourish the blood, fill the veins, run into every part of a man, make him warmer; so will these prayers do, set our soul and body in a heat, warm our devotion, work fervency in us, lift up our soul to God. For there be herbs of God's own planting in our pottage as you call it—the Ten Commandments, dainty herbs to season any pottage in the world; there is the Lord's Prayer, and that is a most sweet pot-herb cannot be denied; then there is also David's herbs, his prayers and psalms, helps to make our pottage relish well; the psalm of the blessed Virgin, a good pot-herb. Though they be, as some term them, *cock-crowed* pottage, yet they are as sweet, as good, as dainty, and as fresh, as they were at the first. The sun hath not made them sour with its heat, neither hath the cold water taken away their vigour and strength. Compare them with the Scriptures, and see if they be not as well seasoned and crumbed. If you find any thing in them that is either too salt, too fresh, or too bitter, that herb shall be taken out and better put in, if it can be got, or none. And as in kitchen pottage there are many good herbs, so there is likewise in this church pottage, as you call it. For first, there is in kitchen pottage good water to make them; so, on the contrary, in the other pottage there is the water of life. 2. There is salt to season them;

so in the other is a prayer of grace to season their hearts.
3. There is oatmeal to nourish the body, in the other is the bread
of life. 4. There is thyme in them to relish them, and it is
very wholesome—in the other is the wholesome exhortation
not to harden our heart while it is called to-day. This relish-
eth well. 5. There is a small onion to give a taste—in the
other is a good herb, called Lord have mercy on us. These,
and many other holy herbs are contained in it, all boiling in
the heart of man, will make as good pottage as the world can
afford, especially if you use these herbs for digestion,—the
herb repentance, the herb grace, the herb faith, the herb love,
the herb hope, the herb good works, the herb feeling, the herb
zeal, the herb fervency, the herb ardency, the herb constancy,
with many more of this nature, most excellent for digestion."
Ohe! jam satis. In this manner the learned divine hunts his
metaphor at a very cold scent, through a pamphlet of six mortal quarto pages.

CHAPTER II.

Come forth, old man—Thy daughter's side
Is now the fitting place for thee;
When Time hath quell'd the oak's bold pride,
The youthful tendril yet may hide
The ruins of the parent tree.

WHEN the sermon was ended, the military orator
wiped his brow; for, notwithstanding the coolness
of the weather, he was heated with the vehemence
of his speech and action. He then descended from
the pulpit, and spoke a word or two to the corporal
who commanded the party of soldiers, who, replying by a sober nod of intelligence, drew his men
together, and marched them in order to their quarters in the town.

The preacher himself, as if nothing extraordinary had happened, left the church and sauntered
through the streets of Woodstock, with the air of a
stranger who was viewing the town, without seeming to observe that he was himself in his turn
anxiously surveyed by the citizens, whose furtive
yet frequent glances seemed to regard him as something alike suspected and dreadful, yet on no account to be provoked. He heeded them not, but
stalked on in the manner affected by the distinguished fanatics of the day; a stiff solemn pace, a
severe and at the same time a contemplative look,

like that of a man discomposed at the interruptions which earthly objects forced upon him, obliging him by their intrusion to withdraw his thoughts for an instant from celestial things. Innocent pleasures of what kind soever they held in suspicion and contempt, and innocent mirth they abominated. It was, however, a cast of mind that formed men for great and manly actions, as it adopted principle, and that of an unselfish character, for the ruling motive, instead of the gratification of passion. Some of these men were indeed hypocrites, using the cloak of religion only as a covering for their ambition; but many really possessed the devotional character, and the severe republican virtue, which others only affected. By far the greater number hovered between these extremes, felt to a certain extent the power of religion, and complied with the times in affecting a great deal.

The individual, whose pretensions to sanctity, written as they were upon his brow and gait, have given rise to the above digression, reached at length the extremity of the principal street, which terminates upon the park of Woodstock. A battlemented portal of Gothic appearance defended the entrance to the avenue. It was of mixed architecture, but on the whole, though composed of the styles of the different ages when it had received additions, had a striking and imposing effect. An immense gate composed of rails of hammered iron, with many a flourish and scroll, displaying as its uppermost ornament the ill-fated cipher of C. R., was now decayed, being partly wasted with rust, partly by violence.

The stranger paused, as if uncertain whether he should demand or assay entrance. He looked through the grating down an avenue skirted by majestic oaks, which led onward with a gentle curve, as if into the depths of some ample and ancient forest. The wicket of the large iron gate being left unwittingly open, the soldier was tempted to enter, yet with some hesitation, as he that intrudes upon ground which he conjectures may be prohibited—indeed his manner showed more reverence for the scene than could have been expected from his condition and character. He slackened his stately and consequential pace, and at length stood still, and looked around him.

Not far from the gate, he saw rising from the trees one or two ancient and venerable turrets, bearing each its own vane of rare device glittering in the autumn sun. These indicated the ancient hunting seat, or Lodge, as it was called, which had, since the time of Henry II., been occasionally the residence of the English monarchs, when it pleased them to visit the woods of Oxford, which then so abounded with game, that, according to old Fuller, huntsmen and falconers were nowhere better pleased. The situation which the Lodge occupied was a piece of flat ground, now planted with sycamores, not far from the entrance to that magnificent spot, where the spectator first stops to gaze upon Blenheim, to think of Marlborough's victories, and to applaud or criticise the cumbrous magnificence of Vanburgh's style.

There, too, paused our military preacher, but with other thoughts, and for other purpose, than to admire the scene around him. It was not long afterwards when he beheld two persons, a male and a female, approaching slowly, and so deeply engaged in their own conversation that they did not raise their eyes to observe that there stood a stranger in the path before them. The soldier took advantage of their state of abstraction, and, desirous at once to watch their motions and avoid their observation, he glided beneath one of the huge trees which skirted the path, and whose boughs, sweeping the ground on every side, ensured him against discovery, unless in case of an actual search.

In the meantime, the gentleman and lady continued to advance, directing their course to a rustic seat, which still enjoyed the sunbeams, and was placed adjacent to the tree where the stranger was concealed.

The man was elderly, yet seemed bent more by sorrow and infirmity, than by the weight of years. He wore a mourning cloak, over a dress of the same melancholy colour, cut in that picturesque form which Vandyck has rendered immortal. But although the dress was handsome, it was put on and worn with a carelessness which showed the mind of the wearer ill at ease. His aged, yet still handsome countenance, had the same air of consequence which distinguished his dress and his gait. A striking part of his appearance was a long white beard,

which descended far over the breast of his slashed
doublet, and looked singular from its contrast in
colour with his habit.

The young lady, by whom this venerable gentleman seemed to be in some degree supported as
they walked arm in arm, was a slight and sylph-
like form, with a person so delicately made, and so
beautiful in countenance, that it seemed the earth
on which she walked was too grossly massive a
support for a creature so aerial. But mortal beauty must share human sorrows. The eyes of the
beautiful being showed tokens of tears; her colour
was heightened as she listened to her aged companion; and it was plain, from his melancholy yet
displeased look, that the conversation was as dis-
tressing to himself as to her. When they sat
down on the bench we have mentioned, the gentleman's discourse could be distinctly overheard by
the eavesdropping soldier, but the answers of the
young lady reached his ear rather less distinctly.

" It is not to be endured !" said the old man,
passionately ; " it would stir up a paralytic wretch
to start up a soldier. My people have been thin-
ned, I grant you, or have fallen off from me in
these times—I owe them no grudge for it, poor
knaves ; what should they do waiting on me, when
the pantry has no bread and the buttery no ale ?
But we have still about us some rugged foresters
of the old Woodstock breed—old as myself most
of them—what of that ? old wood seldom warps in
the wetting ;—I will hold out the old house, and it

will not be the first time that I have held it against
ten times the strength that we hear of now."

" Alas ! my dear father !"—said the young lady,
in a tone which seemed to intimate his proposal of
defence to be altogether desperate.

" And why, alas ?" said the gentleman, angrily ;
" is it because I shut my door against a score or
two of these blood-thirsty hypocrites ?"

" But their masters can as easily send a regiment or an army, if they will," replied the lady ;
" and what good would your present defence do,
excepting to exasperate them to your utter destruction ?"

" Be it so, Alice," replied her father ; " I have
lived my time, and beyond it. I have outlived the
kindest and most princelike of masters. What
do I do on the earth since the dismal thirtieth of
January ? The parricide of that day was a signal
to all true servants of Charles Stewart to avenge
his death, or die as soon after as they could find a
worthy opportunity !"

" Do not speak thus, sir," said Alice Lee ; " it
does not become your gravity and your worth to
throw away that life which may yet be of service
to your king and country,—it will not and cannot
always be thus. England will not long endure the
rulers which these bad times have assigned her.
In the meanwhile—[here a few words escaped the
listener's ears]—and beware of that impatience,
which makes bad worse."

" Worse ?" exclaimed the impatient old man,
" *What* can be worse ? Is it not at the worst al-

ready ?   Will not these people expel us from the
only shelter we have left—dilapidate what remains
of royal property under my charge—make the palace
of princes into a den of thieves, and then wipe their
mouths and thank God, as if they had done an alms-
deed ?"

"Still," said his daughter, " there is hope behind, and I trust the King is ere this out of their
reach—We have reason to think well of my brother Albert's safety."

"Ay, Albert! there again," said the old man,
in a tone of reproach ; "had it not been for thy
entreaties I had gone to Worcester myself ; but
I must needs lie here like a worthless hound when
the hunt is up, when who knows what service I
might have shown ?   An old man's head is sometimes useful when his arm is but little worth.   But
you and Albert were so desirous that he should go
alone—and now, who can say what has become of
him ?"

"Nay, nay, father," said Alice, "we have good
hope that Albert escaped from that fatal day ; young
Abney saw him a mile from the field."

"Young Abney lied, I believe," said the father,
in the same humour of contradiction—" Young
Abney's tongue seems quicker than his hands, but
far slower than his horse's heels when he leaves the
roundheads behind him.   I would rather Albert's
dead body were laid between Charles and Cromwell, than hear he fled as early as young Abney."

"My dearest father," said the young lady, weep-
ing as she spoke, "what can I say to comfort you ?"

" Comfort me, say'st thou, girl ? I am sick of comfort—an honourable death, with the ruins of Woodstock for my monument, were the only comfort to old Henry Lee. Yes, by the memory of my fathers ! I will make good the Lodge against these rebellious robbers."

" Yet be ruled, dearest father," said the maiden, " and submit to that which we cannot gainsay. My uncle Everard"——

Here the old man caught at her unfinished words. " Thy uncle Everard, wench !—Well, get on.— What of thy precious and loving uncle Everard?"

" Nothing, sir," she said, " if the subject displeases you."

" Displeases me ?" he replied, " why should it displease me ? or if it did, why shouldst thou, or any one, affect to care about it ? What is it that hath happened of late years—what is it can be thought to happen that astrologer can guess at, which can give pleasure to us ?"

" Fate," she replied, " may have in store the joyful restoration of our banished Prince."

" Too late for my time, Alice," said the knight ; " if there be such a white page in the heavenly book, it will not be turned until long after my day.—But I see thou wouldst escape me.—In a word, what of thy uncle Everard ?"

" Nay, sir," said Alice, " God knows I would rather be silent for ever, than speak what might, as you would take it, add to your present distemperature."

" Distemperature !" said her father ; " Oh, thou

art a sweet-lipped physician, and wouldst, I warrant me, drop nought but sweet balm, and honey, and oil, on my distemperature—if that is the phrase for an old man's ailment, when he is wellnigh heart-broken.—Once more, what of thy uncle Everard?"

His last words were uttered in a high and peevish tone of voice; and Alice Lee answered her father in a trembling and submissive tone.

"I only meant to say, sir, that I am well assured that my uncle Everard, when we quit this place"——

"That is to say, when we are kicked out of it by crop-eared canting villains like himself.—But on with thy bountiful uncle—what will he do? will he give us the remains of his worshipful and economical house-keeping, the fragments of a thrice-sacked capon twice a-week, and a plentiful fast on the other five days?—Will he give us beds beside his half-starved nags, and put them under a short allowance of straw, that his sister's husband—that I should have called my deceased angel by such a name!—and 'his sister's daughter, may not sleep on the stones? Or will he send us a noble each, with a warning to make it last, for he had never known the ready-penny so hard to come by? Or what else will your uncle Everard do for us? Get us a furlough to beg? Why, I can do that without him."

"You misconstrue him much," answered Alice, with more spirit than she had hitherto displayed; "and would you but question your own heart, you would acknowledge—I speak with reverence—that your tongue utters what your better judgment would disown. My uncle Everard is neither a miser nor a hypocrite,—neither so fond of the goods of this world that he would not supply our distresses amply, nor so wedded to fanatical opinions as to exclude charity for other sects beside his own."

"Ay, ay, the Church of England is a *sect* with him, I doubt not, and perhaps with thee too, Alice," said the knight. "What is a Muggletonian, or a Ranter, or a Brownist, but a sectary? and thy phrase places them all, with Jack Presbyter himself, on the same footing with our learned prelates and religious clergy! Such is the cant of the day thou livest in, and why shouldst thou not talk like one of the wise virgins and psalm-singing sisters, since, though thou hast a profane old cavalier for a father, thou art own niece to pious uncle Everard?"

"If you speak thus, my dear father," said Alice, "what can I answer you? Hear me but one patient word, and I shall have discharged my uncle Everard's commission."

"Oh, it is a commission then? Surely, I suspected so much from the beginning—nay, have some sharp guess touching the ambassador also.—Come, madam the mediator, do your errand, and you shall have no reason to complain of my patience."

"Then, sir," replied his daughter, "my uncle Everard desires you would be courteous to the commissioners, who come here to sequestrate the parks and the property; or, at least, heedfully to abstain from giving them obstacle or opposition: it can, he says, do no good, even on your own principles, and it will give a pretext for proceeding against you as one in the worst degree of malignity, which he thinks may otherwise be prevented. Nay, he has good hope, that if you follow his counsel, the committee may, through the interest he possesses, be inclined to remove the sequestration of your estate on a moderate fine. Thus says my uncle; and having communicated his advice, I have no occasion to urge your patience with farther argument."

"It is well thou dost not, Alice," answered Sir Henry Lee, in a tone of suppressed anger; "for, by the blessed Rood, thou hast wellnigh led me into the heresy of thinking thee no daughter of mine.—Ah! my beloved companion, who art now far from the sorrows and cares of this weary world, couldst thou have thought that the daughter thou didst clasp to thy bosom, would, like the wicked wife of Job, become a temptress to her father in the hour of affliction, and recommend to him to make his conscience truckle to his interest, and to beg back at the bloody hands of his master's, and perhaps his son's murderers, a wretched remnant of the royal property he has been robbed of!—Why, wench, if I must beg, think'st thou I will sue to those who have made me a mendicant? No. I will never show my grey beard, worn in sorrow for my sovereign's death, to move the compassion of some proud sequestrator, who perhaps was one of the parricides. No. If Henry Lee must sue for food, it shall be of some sound loyalist like himself, who, having but half a loaf remaining, will not nevertheless refuse to share it with him. For his daughter, she may wander her own way, which leads her to a refuge with her wealthy roundhead kinsfolk; but let her no more call him father, whose honest indigence she has refused to share!"

" You do me injustice, sir," answered the young lady, with a voice animated yet faltering, " cruel injustice. God knows, your way is my way, though it lead to ruin and beggary; and while you tread it, my arm shall support you while you will accept an aid so feeble."

" Thou word'st me, girl," answered the old cavalier, " thou word'st me, as Will Shakspeare says —thou speakest of lending me thy arm; but thy secret thought is thyself to hang upon Markham Everard's."

" My father, my father," answered Alice, in a tone of deep grief, " what can thus have altered your clear judgment and kindly heart ?—Accursed be these civil commotions ! not only do they destroy men's bodies, but they pervert their souls; and the brave, the noble, the generous, become suspicious, harsh, and mean ! Why upbraid me with Markham Everard ? Have I seen or spoke to him since you forbid him my company, with terms less kind —I will speak it truly—than was due even to the relationship betwixt you ? Why think I would sacrifice to that young man my duty to you? Know, that were I capable of such criminal weakness, Markham Everard were the first to despise me for it."

She put her handkerchief to her eyes, but she

could not hide her sobs, nor conceal the distress they intimated.   The old man was moved.

"I cannot tell," he said, "what to think of it. Thou seem'st sincere, and wert ever a good and kindly daughter—how thou hast let that rebel youth creep into thy heart I wot not; perhaps it is a punishment on me, who thought the loyalty of my house was like undefiled ermine.   Yet here is a damned spot, and on the fairest gem of all—my own dear Alice.   But do not weep—we have enough to vex us.   Where is it that Shakspeare hath it :—

> ——' Gentle daughter,
> Give even way unto my rough affairs;
> Put you not on the temper of the times,
> Nor be, like them, to Percy troublesome.'"

"I am glad," answered the young lady, "to hear you quote your favourite again, sir. Our little jars are ever wellnigh ended when Shakspeare comes in play."

"His book was the closet-companion of my blessed master," said Sir Henry Lee ; "after the Bible, (with reverence for naming them together!) he felt more comfort in it than in any other ; and as I have shared his disease, why, it is natural I should take his medicine.   Albeit, I pretend not to my master's art in explaining the dark passages; for I am but a rude man, and rustically brought up to arms and hunting."

"You have seen Shakspeare yourself, sir ?" said the young lady.

"Silly wench," replied the knight, "he died when I was a mere child—thou hast heard me say so twenty times; but thou wouldst lead the old man away from the tender subject. Well, though I am not blind, I can shut my eyes and follow. Ben Jonson I knew, and could tell thee many a tale of our meetings at the Mermaid, where, if there was much wine, there was much wit also. We did not sit blowing tobacco in each other's faces, and turning up the whites of our eyes as we turned up the bottom of the wine-pot. Old Ben adopted me as one of his sons in the muses. I have shown you, have I not, the verses, ' To my much beloved son, the worshipful Sir Henry Lee of Ditchley, Knight and Baronet ?' "

" I do not remember them at present, sir," replied Alice.

" I fear ye lie, wench," said her father; " but no matter—thou canst not get any more fooling out of me just now. The Evil Spirit hath left Saul for the present. We are now to think what is to be done about leaving Woodstock—or defending it ?"

" My dearest father," said Alice, " can you still nourish a moment's hope of making good the place ?"

" I know not, wench," replied Sir Henry; " I would fain have a parting blow with them, 'tis certain—and who knows where a blessing may alight ? But then, my poor knaves that must take part with me in so hopeless a quarrel—that thought hampers me, I confess."

" Oh, let it do so, sir," replied Alice; " there

are soldiers in the town, and there are three regiments at Oxford!"

"Ah, poor Oxford!" exclaimed Sir Henry, whose vacillating state of mind was turned by a word to any new subject that was suggested,—"Seat of learning and loyalty! these rude soldiers are unfit inmates for thy learned halls and poetical bowers; but thy pure and brilliant lamp shall defy the foul breath of a thousand churls, were they to blow at it like Boreas. The burning bush shall not be consumed, even by the heat of this persecution."

"True, sir," said Alice, "and it may not be useless to recollect, that any stirring of the royalists at this unpropitious moment will make them deal yet more harshly with the University, which they consider as being at the bottom of every thing which moves for the King in these parts."

"It is true, wench," replied the knight; "and small cause would make the villains sequestrate the poor remains which the civil wars have left to the colleges. That, and the risk of my poor fellows —Well; thou hast disarmed me, girl. I will be as patient and calm as a martyr."

"Pray God you keep your word, sir!" replied his daughter; "but you are ever so much moved at the sight of any of these men, that"——

"Would you make a child of me, Alice?" said Sir Henry. "Why, know you not that I can look upon a viper, or a toad, or a bunch of engendering adders, without any worse feeling than a little disgust? and though a roundhead, and especially a red-coat, are in my opinion more poisonous than vipers, more loathsome than toads, more hateful than knotted adders, yet can I overcome my nature so far, that should one of them appear at this moment, thyself should see how civilly I would entreat him."

As he spoke, the military preacher abandoned his leafy screen, and, stalking forward, stood unexpectedly before the old cavalier, who stared at him, as if he had thought his expressions had actually raised the devil.

" Who art thou?" at length said Sir Henry, in a raised and angry voice, while his daughter clung to his arm in terror, little confident that her father's pacific resolutions would abide the shock of this unwelcome apparition.

" I am one," replied the soldier, " who neither fear nor shame to call myself a poor day-labourer in the great work of England—umph!—Ay, a simple and sincere upholder of the good old cause."

" And what the devil do you seek here?" said the old knight, fiercely.

" The welcome due to the steward of the Lords Commissioners," answered the soldier.

" Welcome art thou as salt would be to sore eyes," said the cavalier; " but who be your Commissioners, man?"

The soldier with little courtesy held out a scroll, which Sir Henry took from him betwixt his finger and thumb, as if it were a letter from a pest-house; and held it at as much distance from his eyes, as his purpose of reading it would permit. He then read aloud, and as he named the parties one by one, he added a short commentary on each name, addressed, indeed, to Alice, but in such a tone that showed he cared not for its being heard by the soldier.

" *Desborough*—the ploughman Desborough—as grovelling a clown as is in England—a fellow that would be best at home, like an ancient Scythian, under the tilt of a waggon—d—n him. *Harrison*, a bloody-minded, ranting enthusiast, who read the Bible to such purpose, that he never lacked a text to justify a murder—d—n him too. *Bletson*—a true-blue Commonwealth's man, one of Harrison's Rota Club, with his noddle full of newfangled notions about government, the clearest object of which is to establish the tail upon the head; a fellow who leaves you the statutes and law of old England, to prate of Rome and Greece—sees the Areopagus in Westminster-Hall, and takes old Noll for a Roman Consul—Adad, he is like to prove a dictator amongst them instead. Never mind—d—n Bletson too."

" Friend," said the soldier, " I would willingly be civil, but it consists not with my duty to hear these godly men, in whose service I am, spoken of after this irreverent and unbecoming fashion. And albeit I know that you malignants think you have a right to make free with that damnation, which you seem to use as your own portion, yet it is superfluous to invoke it against others, who have better hopes in their thoughts, and better words in their mouths."

" Thou art but a canting varlet," replied the

knight; " and yet thou art right in some sense—for it is superfluous to curse men who already are damned as black as the smoke of hell itself."

" I prithee forbear," continued the soldier, "for manners' sake, if not for conscience—grisly oaths suit ill with grey beards."

" Nay, that is truth, if the devil spoke it," said the knight; " and I thank Heaven I can follow good counsel, though old Nick gives it. And so, friend, touching these same Commissioners, bear them this message; that Sir Henry Lee is keeper of Woodstock Park, with right of waif and stray, vert and venison, as complete as any of them have to their estate—that is, if they possess any estate but what they have gained by plundering honest men. Nevertheless, he will give place to those who have made their might their right, and will not expose the lives of good and true men, where the odds are so much against them. And he protests that he makes this surrender, neither as acknowledging of these so termed Commissioners, nor as for his own individual part fearing their force, but purely to avoid the loss of English blood, of which so much hath been spilt in these late times."

" It is well spoken," said the steward of the Commissioners; " and therefore, I pray you, let us walk together into the house, that thou mayst deliver up unto me the vessels, and gold and silver ornaments, belonging unto the Egyptian Pharaoh who committed them to thy keeping."

" What vessels?" exclaimed the fiery old knight; " and belonging to whom? Unbaptized dog, speak

civil of the Martyr in my presence, or I will do a
deed misbecoming of me on that caitiff corpse of
thine!"—And shaking his daughter from his right
arm, the old man laid his hand on his rapier.

His antagonist, on the contrary, kept his temper
completely, and waving his hand to add impression
to his speech, he said, with a calmness which aggravated Sir Henry's wrath, " Nay, good friend, I
prithee be still, and brawl not—it becomes not grey
hairs and feeble arms to rail and rant like drunk-
ards. Put me not to use the carnal weapon in
mine own defence, but listen to the voice of reason.
Seest thou not that the Lord hath decided this
great controversy in favour of us and ours, against
thee and thine? Wherefore render up thy stew-
ardship peacefully, and deliver up to me the chat-
tels of the Man, Charles Stewart."

" Patience is a good nag, but she will bolt," said
the knight, unable longer to rein in his wrath. He
plucked his sheathed rapier from his side, struck
the soldier a severe blow with it, and instantly
drawing it, and throwing the scabbard over the
trees, placed himself in a posture of defence, with
his sword's point within half a yard of the steward's
body. The latter stepped back with activity, threw
his long cloak from his shoulders, and drawing his
long tuck, stood upon his guard. The swords
clashed smartly together, while Alice, in her terror, screamed wildly for assistance. But the combat was of short duration. The old cavalier had
attacked a man as cunning of fence as he himself,
or a little more so, and possessing all the strength

and activity of which time had deprived Sir Henry,
and the calmness which the other had lost in his
passion. They had scarce exchanged three passes
ere the sword of the knight flew up in the air, as
if it had gone in search of the scabbard ; and, burning with shame and anger, Sir Henry stood disarmed, at the mercy of his antagonist. The republican showed no purpose of abusing his victory ;
nor did he, either during the combat, or after the
victory was won, in any respect alter the sour and
grave composure which reigned upon his countenance—a combat of life and death seemed to him a
thing as familiar, and as little to be feared, as an
ordinary bout with foils.

   " Thou art delivered into my hands," he said,
" and by the law of arms I might smite thee under
the fifth rib, even as Asahel was struck dead by
Abner, the son of Ner, as he followed the chase on
the hill of Ammah, that lieth before Giah, in the
way of the wilderness of Gibeon ; but far be it
from me to spill thy remaining drops of blood. True
it is, thou art the captive of my sword and of my
spear ; nevertheless, seeing that there may be a
turning from thine evil ways, and a returning to
those which are good, if the Lord enlarge thy date
for repentance and amendment, wherefore should
it be shortened by a poor sinful mortal, who is,
speaking truly, but thy fellow worm ?"

   Sir Henry Lee remained still confused, and unable to answer, when there arrived a fourth person, whom the cries of Alice had summoned to the
spot. This was Joceline Joliffe, one of the under-

keepers of the walk, who, seeing how matters stood, brandished his quarterstaff, a weapon from which he never parted, and having made it describe the figure of eight in a flourish through the air, would have brought it down with a vengeance upon the head of the steward, had not Sir Henry interposed.

"We must trail bats now, Joceline—our time of shouldering them is past. It skills not striving against the stream—the devil rules the roast, and makes our slaves our tutors."

At this moment another auxiliary rushed out of the thicket to the knight's assistance. It was a large wolf-dog, in strength a mastiff, in form and almost in fleetness a greyhound. Bevis was the noblest of the kind which ever pulled down a stag, tawny-coloured like a lion, with a black muzzle and black feet, just edged with a line of white round the toes. He was as tractable as he was strong and bold. Just as he was about to rush upon the soldier, the words, "Peace, Bevis!" from Sir Henry, converted the lion into a lamb, and, instead of pulling the soldier down, he walked round and round, and snuffed, as if using all his sagacity to discover who the stranger could be, towards whom, though of so questionable an appearance, he was enjoined forbearance. Apparently he was satisfied, for he laid aside his doubtful and threatening demonstrations, lowered his ears, smoothed down his bristles, and wagged his tail.

Sir Henry, who had great respect for the sagacity of his favourite, said in a low voice to Alice, "Bevis is of thy opinion, and counsels submission.

There is the finger of Heaven in this to punish the pride, ever the fault of our house.—Friend," he continued, addressing the soldier, " thou hast given the finishing touch to a lesson, which ten years of constant misfortune have been unable fully to teach me. Thou hast distinctly shown me the folly of thinking that a good cause can strengthen a weak arm. God forgive me for the thought, but I could almost turn infidel, and believe that Heaven's blessing goes ever with the longest sword ; but it will not be always thus. God knows his time.—Reach me my Toledo, Joceline, yonder it lies ; and the scabbard, see where it hangs on the tree.—Do not pull at my cloak, Alice, and look so miserably frightened ; I shall be in no hurry to betake me to bright steel again, I promise thee.—For thee, good fellow, I thank thee, and will make way for thy masters without farther dispute or ceremony. Joceline Joliffe is nearer thy degree than I am, and will make surrender to thee of the Lodge and household stuff.—Withhold nothing, Joliffe—let them have all. For me, I will never cross the threshold again —but where to rest for a night ? I would trouble no one in Woodstock—hum—ay—it shall be so. Alice and I, Joceline, will go down to thy hut by Rosamond's Well ; we will borrow the shelter of thy roof for one night at least ; thou wilt give us welcome, wilt thou not ?—How now—a clouded brow ?"

Joceline certainly looked embarrassed, directed first a glance to Alice, then looked to heaven, then to earth, and last to the four quarters of the horizon, and then murmured out, " Certainly—without question—might he but run down to put the house in order."

" Order enough—order enough—for those that may soon be glad of clean straw in a barn," said the knight ; " but if thou hast an ill-will to harbour any obnoxious or malignant persons, as the phrase goes, never shame to speak it out, man. 'Tis true, I took thee up when thou wert but a ragged Robin,* made a keeper of thee, and so forth. What of that ? Sailors think no longer of the wind than when it forwards them on the voyage—thy betters turn with the tide, why should not such a poor knave as thou ?"

" God pardon your honour for your harsh judgment !" said Joliffe. " The hut is yours, such as it is, and should be were it a king's palace, as I wish it were, even for your honour's sake, and Mistress Alice's—only I could wish your honour would condescend to let me step down before, in case any neighbour be there—or—or—just to put matters something into order for Mistress Alice and your honour—just to make things something seemly and shapely."

" Not a whit necessary," said the knight, while Alice had much trouble in concealing her agitation. " If thy matters are unseemly, they are fitter for a defeated knight—if they are unshapely, why, the liker to the rest of a world, which is all unsha-

* The keeper's followers in the New Forest are called in popular language ragged Robins.

ped.   Go thou with that man.—What is thy name, friend ?"

" Joseph Tomkins is my name in the flesh," said the Steward. " Men call me honest Joe, and Trusty Tomkins."

" If thou hast deserved such names, considering what trade thou hast driven, thou art a jewel indeed," said the knight ; " yet if thou hast not, never blush for the matter, Joseph, for if thou art not in truth honest, thou hast all the better chance to keep the fame of it—the title and the thing itself have long walked separate ways. Farewell to thee,—and farewell to fair Woodstock !"

So saying, the old knight turned round, and, pulling his daughter's arm through his own, they walked onward into the forest, in the same manner in which they were introduced to the reader.

CHAPTER III.

Now, ye wild blades, that make loose inns your stage,
To vapour forth the acts of this sad age,
Stout Edgehill fight, the Newberries and the West,
And northern clashes, where you still fought best;
Your strange escapes, your dangers void of fear,
When bullets flew between the head and ear,
Whether you fought by Damme or the Spirit,
Of you I speak.
                                   Legend of Captain Jones.

JOSEPH TOMKINS and Joliffe the keeper remained for some time in silence, as they stood together looking along the path in which the figures of the Knight of Ditchley and pretty Mistress Alice had disappeared behind the trees. They then gazed on each other in doubt, as men who scarce knew whether they stood on hostile or on friendly terms together, and were at a loss how to open a conversation. They heard the knight's whistle summon Bevis; but though the good hound turned his head and pricked his ears at the sound, yet he did not obey the call, but continued to snuff around Joseph Tomkins's cloak.

"Thou art a rare one, I fear me," said the keeper, looking to his new acquaintance. "I have heard of men who have charms to steal both dogs and deer."

1

" Trouble not thyself about my qualities, friend," said Joseph Tomkins, " but bethink thee of doing thy master's bidding."

Joceline did not immediately answer, but at length, as if in sign of truce, stuck the end of his quarterstaff upright in the ground, and leant upon it as he said gruffly,—" So, my tough old knight and you were at drawn bilbo, by way of afternoon service, sir preacher—Well for you I came not up till the blades were done jingling, or I had rung even-song upon your pate."

The Independent smiled grimly as he replied, " Nay, friend, it is well for thyself, for never should sexton have been better paid for the knell he tolled. Nevertheless, why should there be war betwixt us, or my hand be against thine ? Thou art but a poor knave, doing thy master's order, nor have I any desire that my own blood or thine should be shed touching this matter. Thou art, I understand, to give me peaceful possession of the Palace of Woodstock, so called—though there is now no palace in England, no, nor shall be in the days that come after, until we shall enter the palace of the New Jerusalem, and the reign of the Saints shall commence on earth."

" Pretty well begun already, friend Tomkins," said the keeper ; " you are little short of being kings already upon the matter as it now stands ; and for your Jerusalem I wot not, but Woodstock is a pretty nest-egg to begin with.—Well, will you shog—will you on—will you take sasine and livery? —you heard my orders."

"Umph—I know not," said Tomkins. "I must beware of ambuscades, and I am alone here. Moreover, it is the High Thanksgiving appointed by Parliament, and owned to by the army—also the old man and the young woman may want to recover some of their clothes and personal property, and I would not that they were baulked on my account. Wherefore, if thou wilt deliver me possession tomorrow morning, it shall be done in personal presence of my own followers, and of the Presbyterian man the Mayor, so that the transfer may be made before witnesses; whereas, were there none with us but thou to deliver, and I to take possession, the men of Belial might say, Go to, Trusty Tomkins hath been an Edomite—Honest Joe hath been as an Ishmaelite, rising up early and dividing the spoil with them that served the Man—yea, they that wore beards and green jerkins, as in remembrance of the Man and of his government."

Joceline fixed his keen dark eyes upon the soldier as he spoke, as if in design to discover whether there was fair play in his mind or not. He then applied his five fingers to scratch a large shock head of hair, as if that operation was necessary to enable him to come to a conclusion. "This is all fair sounding, brother," said he; "but I tell you plainly, there are some silver mugs, and platters, and flagons, and so forth, in yonder house, which have survived the general sweep that sent all our plate to the smelting-pot, to put our knight's troop on horseback. Now, if thou takest not these off my hand, I may come to trouble, since it may be thought I have minished their numbers.—Whereas, I being as honest a fellow"——

"As ever stole venison," said Tomkins—"nay, I do owe thee an interruption."

"Go to, then," replied the keeper; "if a stag may have come to mischance in my walk, it was no way in the course of dishonesty, but merely to keep my old dame's pan from rusting; but for silver porringers, tankards, and such like, I would as soon have drunk the melted silver, as stolen the vessel made out of it. So that I would not wish blame or suspicion fell on me in this matter. And therefore, if you will have the things rendered even now,—why so—and if not, hold me blameless."

"Ay, truly?" said Tomkins; "and who is to hold me blameless, if they should see cause to think any thing minished? Not the right worshipful Commissioners, to whom the property of the estate is as their own; therefore, as thou say'st, we must walk warily in the matter. To lock up the house and leave it, were but the work of simple ones. What say'st thou to spend the night there, and then nothing can be touched without the knowledge of us both?"

"Why, concerning that," answered the keeper, "I should be at my hut to make matters somewhat conformable for the old knight and Mistress Alice, for my old dame Joan is something dunny, and will scarce know how to manage—and yet, to speak the truth, by the mass I would rather not see Sir Henry to-night, since what has happened to-day hath roused his spleen, and it is a peradventure he may have met something at the hut which will scarce tend to cool it."

"It is a pity," said Tomkins, "that, being a gentleman of such grave and goodly presence, he should be such a malignant cavalier, and that he should, like the rest of that generation of vipers, have clothed himself with curses as with a garment."

"Which is as much as to say, the tough old knight hath a habit of swearing," said the keeper, grinning at a pun, which has been repeated since his time ; "but who can help it? it comes of use and wont.   Were you now, in your bodily self, to light suddenly on a Maypole, with all the blithe morris-dancers prancing around it to the merry pipe and tabor, with bells jingling, ribands fluttering, lads frisking and laughing, lasses leaping till you might see where the scarlet garter fastened the light-blue hose, I think some feeling, resembling either natural sociality, or old use and wont, would get the better, friend, even of thy gravity, and thou wouldst fling thy cuckoldy steeple-hat one way, and that blood-thirsty long sword another, and trip, like the noodles of Hogs-Norton, when the pigs play on the organ."

The Independent turned fiercely round on the keeper, and replied, "How now, Mr Green Jerkin? what language is this to one whose hand is at the plough?   I advise thee to put curb on thy tongue, lest thy ribs pay the forfeit."

"Nay, do not take the high tone with me, brother," answered Joceline; "remember thou hast not the old knight of sixty-five to deal with, but a fellow as bitter and prompt as thyself—it may be a little more so—younger, at all events—and prithee, why shouldst thou take such umbrage at a Maypole? I would thou hadst known one Phil Hazeldine of these parts—He was the best morris-dancer betwixt Oxford and Burford."

"The more shame to him," answered the Independent; "and I trust he has seen the error of his ways, and made himself (as, if a man of action, he easily might) fit for better company than wood-hunters, deer-stealers, Maid Marions, swash-bucklers, deboshed revellers, bloody brawlers, maskers and mummers, lewd men and light women, fools and fiddlers, and carnal self-pleasers of every description."

"Well," replied the keeper, "you are out of breath in time; for here we stand before the famous Maypole of Woodstock."

They paused in an open space of meadow-land, beautifully skirted by large oaks and sycamores, one of which, as king of the forest, stood a little detached from the rest, as if scorning the vicinity of any rival. It was scathed and gnarled in the branches, but the immense trunk still showed to what gigantic size the monarch of the forest can attain in the groves of merry England.

"That is called the King's oak," said Joceline; "the oldest men of Woodstock know not how old it is; they say Henry used to sit under it with fair Rosamond, and see the lasses dance, and the lads of the village run races, and wrestle for belts or bonnets."

" I nothing doubt it, friend," said Tomkins ; " a tyrant and a harlot were fitting patron and patroness for such vanities."

" Thou mayst say thy say, friend," replied the keeper, "so thou lettest me say mine. There stands the Maypole, as thou seest, half a flight-shot from the King's Oak, in the midst of the meadow. The King gave ten shillings from the customs of Woodstock to make a new one yearly, besides a tree fitted for the purpose out of the forest. Now it is warped, and withered, and twisted, like a wasted brier-rod. The green, too, used to be close-shaved, and rolled till it was smooth as a velvet mantle— now it is rough and overgrown."

" Well, well, friend Joceline," said the Independent, " but where was the edification of all this? —what use of doctrine could be derived from a pipe and tabor ? or was there ever aught like wisdom in a bagpipe ?"

" You may ask better scholars that," said Joceline ; " but methinks men cannot be always grave, and with the hat over their brow. A young maiden will laugh as a tender flower will blow—ay, and a lad will like her the better for it ; just as the same blithe Spring that makes the young birds whistle, bids the blithe fawns skip. There have come worse days since the jolly old times have gone by :—I tell thee, that in the holydays which you, Mr Longsword, have put down, I have seen this greensward alive with merry maidens and manly fellows. The good old rector himself thought it was no sin to come for awhile and look on, and his goodly cassock and scarf kept us all in good order, and taught us to limit our mirth within the bounds of discretion. We might, it may be, crack a broad jest, or pledge a friendly cup a turn too often, but it was in mirth and good neighbourhood—Ay, and if there was a bout at single-stick, or a bellyful of boxing, it was all for love and kindness; and better a few dry blows in drink, than the bloody doings we have had in sober earnest, since the presbyter's cap got above the bishop's mitre, and we exchanged our goodly rectors and learned doctors, whose sermons were all bolstered up with as much Greek and Latin as might have confounded the devil himself, for weavers and cobblers, and such other pulpit volunteers, as—as we heard this morning—It will out."

" Well, friend," said the Independent, with patience scarcely to have been expected, " I quarrel not with thee for nauseating my doctrine. If thine ear is so much tickled with tabor tunes and morris tripping, truly it is not likely thou shouldst find pleasant savour in more wholesome and sober food. —But let us to the Lodge, that we may go about our business there before the sun sets."

" Troth, and that may be advisable for more reasons than one," said the keeper; " for there have been tales about the Lodge which have made men afeard to harbour there after nightfall."

" Were not yon old knight, and yonder damsel his daughter, wont to dwell there?" said the Independent. " My information said so."

" Ay, truly did they," said Joceline ; "and while
they kept a jolly household, all went well enough ;
for nothing banishes fear like good ale.   But after
the best of our men went to the wars, and were
slain at Naseby fight, they who were left found
the Lodge more lonesome, and the old knight has
been much deserted of his servants :—marry, it
might be, that he has lacked silver of late to pay
groom and lackey."

" A potential reason for the diminution of a
household," said the soldier.

" Right, sir, even so," replied the keeper. "They
spoke of steps in the great gallery, heard by dead
of the night, and voices that whispered at noon in
the matted chambers ; and the servants pretended
that these things scared them away ; but in my poor
judgment, when Martinmas and Whitsuntide came
round without a penny-fee, the old blue-bottles of
serving-men began to think of creeping elsewhere
before the frost chilled them—No devil so frightful
as that which dances in the pocket where there is
no cross to keep him out."

" You were reduced, then, to a petty household ?" said the Independent.

" Ay, marry, were we," said Joceline ; "but we
kept some half-score together, what with blue-
bottles in the Lodge, what with green caterpillars
of the chase, like him who is yours to command ;
we stuck together till we found a call to take a
morning's ride somewhere or other."

" To the town of Worcester," said the soldier,

"where you were crushed like vermin and palmer worms, as you are ?"

"You may say your pleasure," replied the keeper ; "I'll never contradict a man who has got my head under his belt. Our backs are at the wall, or you would not be here."

"Nay, friend," said the Independent, "thou riskest nothing by thy freedom and trust in me. I can be *bon camarado* to a good soldier, although I have striven with him even to the going down of the sun.—But here we are in front of the Lodge."

They stood accordingly in front of the old Gothic building, irregularly constructed, and at different times, as the humour of the English monarchs led them to taste the pleasures of Woodstock Chase, and to make such improvements for their own accommodation as the increasing luxury of each age required. The oldest part of the structure had been named by tradition Fair Rosamond's Tower ; it was a small turret of great height, with narrow windows, and walls of massive thickness. The tower had no opening to the ground, or means of descending, a great part of the lower portion being solid mason-work. It was traditionally said to have been accessible only by a sort of small drawbridge, which might be dropped at pleasure from a little portal near the summit of the turret, to the battlements of another tower of the same construction, but twenty feet lower, and containing only a winding staircase, called in Woodstock Love's Ladder ; because it is said, that by ascending this staircase to the top of the tower, and then making use of the drawbridge,

Henry obtained access to the chamber of his paramour.

This tradition had been keenly impugned by Dr Rochecliffe, the former rector of Woodstock, who insisted, that what was called Rosamond's Tower, was merely an interior keep, or citadel, to which the lord or warden of the castle might retreat, when other points of safety failed him ; and either protract his defence, or, at the worst, stipulate for reasonable terms of surrender. The people of Woodstock, jealous of their ancient traditions, did not relish this new mode of explaining them away ; and it is even said, that the Mayor, whom we have already introduced, became Presbyterian, in revenge of the doubts cast by the rector upon this important subject, rather choosing to give up the Liturgy than his fixed belief in Rosamond's Tower, and Love's Ladder.

The rest of the Lodge was of considerable extent, and of different ages ; comprehending a nest of little courts, surrounded by buildings which corresponded with each other, sometimes within-doors, sometimes by crossing the courts, and frequently in both ways. The different heights of the buildings announced that they could only be connected by the usual variety of staircases, which exercised the limbs of our ancestors in the sixteenth and earlier centuries, and seem sometimes to have been contrived for no other purpose.

The varied and multiplied fronts of this irregular building were, as Dr Rochecliffe was wont to say, an absolute banquet to the architectural antiquary, as they certainly contained specimens of every style which existed, from the pure Norman of Henry of Anjou, down to the composite, half Gothic half classical architecture of Elizabeth and her successor. Accordingly, the rector was himself as much enamoured of Woodstock as ever was Henry of Fair Rosamond ; and as his intimacy with Sir Henry Lee permitted him entrance at all times to the Royal Lodge, he used to spend whole days in wandering about the antique apartments, examining, measuring, studying, and finding out excellent reasons for architectural peculiarities, which probably only owed their existence to the freakish fancy of a Gothic artist. But the old antiquarian had been expelled from his living by the intolerance and troubles of the times, and his successor, Nehemiah Holdenough, would have considered an elaborate investigation of the profane sculpture and architecture of blinded and blood-thirsty Papists, together with the history of the dissolute amours of old Norman monarchs, as little better than a bowing down before the calves of Bethel, and a drinking of the cup of abominations.—We return to the course of our story.

" There is," said the Independent Tomkins, after he had carefully perused the front of the building, " many a rare monument of olden wickedness about this miscalled Royal Lodge ; verily, I shall rejoice much to see the same destroyed, yea, burned to ashes, and the ashes thrown into the brook Kedron, or any other brook, that the land may be cleansed from the memory thereof, neither remember the iniquity with which their fathers have sinned."

The keeper heard him with secret indignation, and began to consider with himself, whether, as they stood but one to one, and without chance of speedy interference, he was not called upon, by his official duty, to castigate the rebel who used language so defamatory. But he fortunately recollected, that the strife must be a doubtful one—that the advantage of arms was against him—and that, in especial, even if he should succeed in the combat, it would be at the risk of severe retaliation. It must be owned, too, that there was something about the Independent so dark and mysterious, so grim and grave, that the more open spirit of the keeper felt oppressed, and, if not overawed, at least kept in doubt concerning him ; and he thought it wisest, as well as safest, for his master and himself, to avoid all subjects of dispute, and know better with whom he was dealing, before he made either friend or enemy of him.

The great gate of the Lodge was strongly bolted, but the wicket opened on Joceline's raising the latch. There was a short passage of ten feet, which had been formerly closed by a portcullis at the inner end, while three loopholes opened on either side, through which any daring intruder might be annoyed, who, having surprised the first gate, must be thus exposed to a severe fire before he could force the second. But the machinery of the portcullis was damaged, and it now remained a fixture, brandishing its jaw, well furnished with iron fangs, but incapable of dropping it across the path of invasion.

The way, therefore, lay open to the great hall or

outer vestibule of the Lodge. One end of this long and dusky apartment was entirely occupied by a gallery, which had in ancient times served to accommodate the musicians and minstrels. There was a clumsy staircase at either side of it, composed of entire logs of a foot square ; and in each angle of the ascent was placed, by way of sentinel, the figure of a Norman foot-soldier. having an open casque on his head, which displayed features as stern as the painter's genius could devise. Their arms were buff-jackets, or shirts of mail, round bucklers, with spikes in the centre, and buskins which adorned and defended the feet and ankles, but left the knees bare. These wooden warders held great swords, or maces, in their hands, like military guards on duty. Many an empty hook and brace, along the walls of the gloomy apartment, marked the spots from which arms, long preserved as trophies, had been, in the pressure of the war, once more taken down to do service in the field, like veterans whom extremity of danger recalls to battle. On other rusty fastenings were still displayed the hunting trophies of the monarchs to whom the Lodge belonged, and of the silvan knights to whose care it had been from time to time confided.

At the nether end of the hall, a huge, heavy, stone-wrought chimney-piece projected itself ten feet from the wall, adorned with many a cipher, and many a scutcheon of the Royal House of England. In its present state, it yawned like the arched mouth of a funeral vault, or perhaps might be compared to the crater of an extinguished volcano. But the

sable complexion of the massive stone-work, and al
around it, showed that the time had been when i
sent its huge fires blazing up the huge chimney
besides puffing many a volume of smoke over the
heads of the jovial guests, whose royalty or nobility
did not render them sensitive enough to quarre
with such slight inconvenience. On these occasions
it was the tradition of the house, that two cart-loads
of wood was the regular allowance for the fire between noon and curfew, and the andirons, or dogs,
as they were termed, constructed for retaining the
blazing firewood on the hearth, were wrought in
the shape of lions of such gigantic size, as might
well warrant the legend. There were long seats of
stone within the chimney, where, in despite of the
tremendous heat, monarchs were sometimes said to
have taken their station, and amused themselves
with broiling the *umbles*, or *dowsets*, of the deer,
upon the glowing embers, with their own royal
hands, when happy the courtier who was invited to
taste the royal cookery. Tradition was here also
ready with her record, to show what merry gibes,
such as might be exchanged between prince and
peer, had flown about at the jolly banquet which
followed the Michaelmas hunt. She could tell, too,
exactly, where King Stephen sat when he darned
his own princely hose, and knew most of the old
tricks he had put upon little Winkin, the tailor of
Woodstock.

Most of this rude revelry belonged to the Plan-
tagenet times. When the house of Tudor acceded
to the throne, they were more chary of their royal

presence, and feasted in halls and chambers far within, abandoning the outmost hall to the yeomen of the guard, who mounted their watch there, and passed away the night with wassail and mirth, exchanged sometimes for frightful tales of apparitions and sorceries, which made some of those grow pale, in whose ears the trumpet of a French foeman would have sounded as jollily as a summons to the woodland chase.

Joceline pointed out the peculiarities of the place to his gloomy companion more briefly than we have detailed them to the reader. The Independent seemed to listen with some interest at first, but, flinging it suddenly aside, he said, in a solemn tone, " Perish, Babylon, as thy master Nebuchadnezzar hath perished ! He is a wanderer, and thou shalt be a waste place—yea, and a wilderness— yea, a desert of salt, in which there shall be thirst and famine."

" There is like to be enough of both to-night," said Joceline, " unless the good knight's larder be somewhat fuller than it is wont."

" We must care for the creature comforts," said the Independent, " but in due season, when our duties are done.—Whither lead these entrances ?"

" That to the right," replied the keeper, " leads to what are called the state-apartments, not used since the year sixteen hundred and thirty-nine, when his blessed Majesty"——

" How, sir !" interrupted the Independent, in a voice of thunder, " dost thou speak of Charles

Stewart as blessing, or blessed?—beware the proclamation to that effect."

" I meant no harm," answered the keeper, suppressing his disposition to make a harsher reply. " My business is with bolts and bucks, not with titles and state affairs. But yet, whatever may have happed since, that poor King was followed with blessings enough from Woodstock; for he left a glove full of broad pieces for the poor of the place"——

" Peace, friend," said the Independent; " I will think thee else one of those besotted and blinded Papists, who hold, that bestowing of alms is an atonement and washing away of the wrongs and oppressions which have been wrought by the almsgiver. Thou sayest, then, these were the apartments of Charles Stewart?"

" And of his father, James, before him, and Elizabeth, before *him*, and bluff King Henry, who builded that wing, before them all."

" And there, I suppose, the knight and his daughter dwelt?"

" No," replied Joceline; " Sir Henry Lee had too much reverence for—for things which are now thought worth no reverence at all—Besides, the state-rooms are unaired, and in indifferent order, since of late years. The Knight Ranger's apartment lies by that passage to the left."

" And whither goes yonder stair, which seems both to lead upwards and downwards?"

" Upwards," replied the keeper, " it leads to many apartments, used for various purposes, of sleeping, and other accommodation. Downwards, to the kitchen, offices and vaults of the castle, which, at this time of the evening, you cannot see without lights."

" We will to the apartments of your knight, then," said the Independent. " Is there fitting accommodation there ?"

" Such as has served a person of condition, whose lodging is now worse appointed," answered the honest keeper, his bile rising so fast that he added, in a muttering and inaudible tone, " so it may well serve a crop-eared knave like thee."

He acted as the usher, however, and led on towards the ranger's apartments.

This suite opened by a short passage from the hall, secured at time of need by two oaken doors, which could be fastened by large bars of the same, that were drawn out of the wall, and entered into square holes, contrived for their reception on the other side of the portal. At the end of this passage, a small anteroom received them, into which opened the sitting apartment of the good knight—which, in the style of the times, might have been termed a fair summer parlour—lighted by two oriel windows, so placed as to command each of them a separate avenue, leading distant and deep into the forest. The principal ornament of the apartment, besides two or three family portraits of less interest, was a tall full-length picture, that hung above the chimney-piece, which, like that in the hall, was of heavy stone-work, ornamented with carved scutcheons, emblazoned with various devices. The portrait was that of a man about fifty years of age, in complete plate armour, and painted in the harsh and dry manner of Holbein—probably, indeed, the work of that artist, as the dates corresponded. The formal and marked angles, points, and projections of the armour, were a good subject for the harsh pencil of that early school. The face of the knight was, from the fading of the colours, pale and dim, like that of some being from the other world, yet the lines expressed forcibly pride and exultation.

He pointed with his leading-staff, or truncheon, to the background, where, in such perspective as the artist possessed, were depicted the remains of a burning church, or monastery, and four or five soldiers, in red cassocks, bearing away in triumph what seemed a brazen font or laver. Above their heads might be traced in scroll, " *Lee Victor sic voluit.*" Right opposite to the picture, hung, in a niche in the wall, a complete set of tilting armour, the black and gold colours, and ornaments of which, exactly corresponded with those exhibited in the portrait.

The picture was one of those which, from something marked in the features and expression, attract the observation even of those who are ignorant of art. The Independent looked at it until a smile passed transiently over his clouded brow. Whether he smiled to see the grim old cavalier employed in desecrating a religious house—(an occupation much conforming to the practice of his own sect)—whether he smiled in contempt of the old painter's harsh and dry mode of working—or whether the sight of this remarkable portrait revived some other ideas, the under-keeper could not decide.

The smile passed away in an instant, as the soldier looked to the oriel windows. The recesses within them were raised a step or two from the wall. In one was placed a walnut-tree reading-desk, and a huge stuffed arm-chair, covered with Spanish leather. A little cabinet stood beside, with some of its shuttles and drawers open, displaying hawks-bells, dog-whistles, instruments for trimming falcon's feathers, bridle-bits of various constructions, and other trifles connected with silvan sport.

The other little recess was differently furnished. There lay some articles of needle-work on a small table, besides a lute, with a book having some airs written down in it, and a frame for working embroidery. Some tapestry was displayed around the recess, with more attention to ornament than was visible in the rest of the apartment; the arrangement of a few bow-pots, with such flowers as the fading season afforded, showed also the superintendence of female taste.

Tomkins cast an eye of careless regard upon these subjects of female occupation, then stepped into the farther window, and began to turn the leaves of a folio, which lay open on the reading-desk, apparently with some interest. Joceline, who had determined to watch his motions without interfering with them, was standing at some distance in dejected silence, when a door behind the tapestry suddenly opened, and a pretty village maid tripped out with a napkin in her hand, as if she had been about some household duty.

"How now, Sir Impudence ?" she said to Joceline, in a smart tone ; "what do you here prowling about the apartments when the master is not at home ?"

But instead of the answer which perhaps she expected, Joceline Joliffe cast a mournful glance towards the soldier in the oriel window, as if to make what he said fully intelligible, and replied with a dejected appearance and voice, "Alack, my pretty Phœbe, there come those here that have more right or might than any of us, and will use little ceremony in coming when they will, and staying while they please."

He darted another glance at Tomkins, who still seemed busy with the book before him, then sidled close to the astonished girl, who had continued looking alternately at the keeper and at the stranger, as if she had been unable to understand the words of the first, or to comprehend the meaning of the second being present.

"Go," whispered Joliffe, approaching his mouth so near her cheek, that his breath waved the curls of her hair ; "go, my dearest Phœbe, trip it as fast as a fawn down to my lodge—I will soon be there, and"——

"Your lodge, indeed !" said Phœbe ; "you are very bold, for a poor killbuck that never frightened any thing before save a dun deer—*Your* lodge, indeed !—I am like to go there, I think."

"Hush, hush ! Phœbe—here is no time for jesting. Down to my hut, I say, like a deer, for the knight and Mrs Alice are both there, and I fear will not return hither again.—All's naught, girl—and our evil days are come at last with a vengeance—we are fairly at bay and fairly hunted down."

"Can this be, Joceline?" said the poor girl, turning to the keeper with an expression of fright in her countenance, which she had hitherto averted in rural coquetry.

"As sure, my dearest Phœbe, as"——

The rest of the asseveration was lost in Phœbe's ear, so closely did the keeper's lips approach it; and if they approached so very near as to touch her cheek, grief, like impatience, hath its privileges, and poor Phœbe had enough of serious alarm to prevent her from demurring upon such a trifle.

But no trifle was the approach of Joceline's lips to Phœbe's pretty though sunburnt cheek, in the estimation of the Independent, who, a little before the object of Joceline's vigilance, had been more lately in his turn the observer of the keeper's demeanour, so soon as the interview betwixt Phœbe and him had become so interesting. And when he remarked the closeness of Joceline's argument, he raised his voice to a pitch of harshness that would have rivalled that of an ungreased and rusty saw, and which at once made Joceline and Phœbe spring six feet apart, each in contrary directions, and if Cupid was of the party, must have sent him out at the window like a wild-duck flying from a culverin. Instantly throwing himself into the attitude of a preacher and a reprover of vice, "How now!" he

exclaimed, " shameless and impudent as you are !
—What—chambering and wantoning in our very
presence !—How—would you play your pranks before the steward of the Commissioners of the High
Court of Parliament, as ye would in a booth at the
fulsome fair, or amidst the trappings and tracings
of a profane dancing-school, where the scoundrel
minstrels make their ungodly weapons to squeak,
'Kiss and be kind, the fiddler's blind ?'—But here,"
he said, dealing a perilous thump upon the volume
—" Here is the King and high priest of those vices
and follies !—Here is he, whom men of folly profanely call nature's miracle !—Here is he, whom
princes chose for their cabinet-keeper, and whom
maids of honour take for their bedfellow !—Here is
the prime teacher of fine words, foppery and folly—
Here !"—(dealing another thump upon the volume
—and oh ! revered of the Roxburghe, it was the
first folio—beloved of the Bannatyne, it was Hem-
mings and Condel—it was the *editio princeps*)—
" On thee," he continued—" on thee, William
Shakspeare, I charge whate'er of such lawless idle-
ness and immodest folly hath defiled the land since
thy day !"

" By the mass, a heavy accusation," said Joceline, the bold recklessness of whose temper could
not be long overawed ; " Odds pitlikins, is our master's old favourite, Will of Stratford, to answer
for every buss that has been snatched since James's
time ?—a perilous reckoning truly—but I wonder
who is sponsible for what lads and lasses did before
his day ?"

" Scoff not," said the soldier, " lest I, being called thereto by the voice within me, do deal with thee as a scorner. Verily I say, that since the devil fell from Heaven, he never lacked agents on earth ; yet nowhere hath he met with a wizard having such infinite power over men's souls as this pestilent fellow Shakspeare. Seeks a wife a foul example for adultery, here she shall find it—Would a man know how to train his fellow to be a murderer, here shall he find tutoring—Would a lady marry a heathen negro, she shall have chronicled example for it—Would any one scorn at his Maker, he shall be furnished with a jest in this book—Would he defy his brother in the flesh, he shall be accommodated with a challenge—Would you be drunk, Shakspeare will cheer you with a cup—Would you plunge in sensual pleasures, he will soothe you to indulgence, as with the lascivious sounds of a lute. This, I say, this book is the wellhead and source of all those evils which have overrun the land like a torrent, making men scoffers, doubters, deniers, murderers, makebates, and lovers of the wine-pot, haunting unclean places, and sitting long at the evening-wine. Away with him, away with him, men of England! to Tophet with his wicked book, and to the vale of Hinnom with his accursed bones ! Verily but that our march was hasty when we passed Stratford, in the year 1643, with Sir William Waller ; but that our march was hasty"——

" Because Prince Rupert was after you with his cavaliers," muttered the incorrigible Joceline.

" I say," continued the zealous trooper, raising his voice and extending his arm—" but that our march was by command hasty, and that we turned not aside in our riding, closing our ranks each one upon the other as becomes men of war, I had torn on that day the bones of that preceptor of vice and debauchery from the grave, and given them to the next dunghill. I would have made his memory scoff and a hissing !"

" That is the bitterest thing he has said yet," observed the keeper. " Poor Will would have liked the hissing worse than all the rest."

Will the gentleman say any more ?" enquired Phœbe in a whisper. " Lack-a-day, he talks brave words, if one knew but what they meant. But it is a mercy our good knight did not see him ruffle the book at that rate—Mercy on us, there would certainly have been bloodshed.—But oh the father —see how he is twisting his face about !—Is he ill of the colic, think'st thou, Joceline ? Or, may I offer him a glass of strong waters ?"

" Hark thee hither, wench !" said the keeper, " he is but loading his blunderbuss for another volley; and while he turns up his eyes, and twists about his face, and clenches his fist, and shuffles and tramples with his feet in that fashion, he is bound to take no notice of any thing. I would be sworn to cut his purse, if he had one, from his side, without his feeling it."

" La ! Joceline," said Phœbe, " and if he abides here in this turn of times, I dare say the gentleman will be easily served."

" Care not thou about that," said Joliffe; " but tell me softly and hastily, what is in the pantry?"

" Small housekeeping enough," said Phœbe; " a cold capon and some comfits, and the great standing venison pasty, with plenty of spice—a manchet or two besides, and that is all."

" Well, it will serve for a pinch—wrap thy cloak round thy comely body—get a basket and a brace of trenchers and towels, they are heinously impoverished down yonder—carry down the capon and the manchets—the pasty must abide with this same soldier and me, and the pie-crust will serve us for bread."

" Rarely," said Phœbe; " I made the paste myself—it is as thick as the walls of Fair Rosamond's Tower."

" Which two pairs of jaws would be long in gnawing through, work hard as they might," said the keeper. " But what liquor is there?"

" Only a bottle of Alicant, and one of sack, with the stone jug of strong waters," answered Phœbe.

" Put the wine-flasks into thy basket," said Joceline, " the knight must not lack his evening draught—and down with thee to the hut like a lapwing. There is enough for supper, and to-morrow is a new day.—Ha! by heaven I thought yonder man's eye watched us—No—he only rolled it round him in a brown study—Deep enough doubtless, as they all are.—But d—n him, he must be bottomless if I cannot sound him before the night's out.—Hie thee away, Phœbe."

But Phœbe was a rural coquette, and, aware

that Joceline's situation gave him no advantage of
avenging the challenge in a fitting way, she whispered in his ear, " Do you think our knight's friend,
Shakspeare, really found out all these naughty
devices the gentleman spoke of?"

Off she darted while she spoke, while Joliffe
menaced future vengeance with his finger, as he
muttered, " Go thy way, Phœbe Mayflower, the
lightest-footed and lightest-hearted wench that ever
tripped the sod in Woodstock-park!—After her,
Bevis, and bring her safe to our master at the hut."

The large greyhound arose like a human servitor
who had received an order, and followed Phœbe
through the hall, first licking her hand to make her
sensible of his presence, and then putting himself
to a slow trot, so as best to accommodate himself
to the light pace of her whom he convoyed, whom
Joceline had not extolled for her activity without
due reason. While Phœbe and her guardian thread
the forest glades, we return to the Lodge.

The Independent now seemed to start as if from
a reverie. " Is the young woman gone?" said he.

" Ay, marry is she," said the keeper ; " and if
your worship hath farther commands, you must rest
contented with male attendance."

" Commands—umph—I think the damsel might
have tarried for another exhortation," said the soldier—" truly, I profess my mind was much inclined
toward her for her edification."

" Oh, sir," replied Joliffe, " she will be at church
next Sunday, and if your military reverence is
pleased again to hold forth amongst us, she will

have use of the doctrine with the rest. But young maidens of these parts hear no private homilies.— And what is now your pleasure? Will you look at the other rooms, and at the few plate articles which have been left?"

" Umph—no," said the Independent—" it wears late, and gets dark—thou hast the means of giving us beds, friend?"

" Better you never slept in," replied the keeper.

" And wood for a fire, and a light, and some small pittance of creature-comforts for refreshment of the outward man?" continued the soldier.

" Without doubt," replied the keeper, displaying a prudent anxiety to gratify this important personage.

In a few minutes a great standing candlestick was placed on an oaken table. The mighty venison pasty, adorned with parsley, was placed on the board on a clean napkin ; the stone-bottle of strong waters, with a blackjack full of ale, formed comfortable appendages ; and to this meal sat down in social manner the soldier, occupying a great elbow-chair, and the keeper, at his invitation, using the more lowly accommodation of a stool, at the opposite side of the table. Thus agreeably employed, our history leaves them for the present.

CHAPTER IV.

——————————— Yon path of greensward
Winds round by sparry grot and gay pavilion ;
There is no flint to gall thy tender foot,
There's ready shelter from each breeze, or shower.
But duty guides not that way—see her stand,
With wand entwined with amaranth, near yon cliffs.
Oft where she leads thy blood must mark thy footsteps,
Oft where she leads thy head must bear the storm,
And thy shrunk form endure heat, cold, and hunger ;
But she will guide thee up to noble heights,
Which he who gains seems native of the sky,
While earthly things lie stretch'd beneath his feet,
Diminish'd, shrunk, and valueless——

Anonymous.

THE reader cannot have forgotten that after his scuffle with the commonwealth soldier, Sir Henry Lee, with his daughter Alice, had departed to take refuge in the hut of the stout keeper Joceline Joliffe. They walked slow, as before, for the old knight was at once oppressed by perceiving these last vestiges of royalty fall into the hands of republicans, and by the recollection of his recent defeat. At times he paused, and, with his arms folded on his bosom, recalled all the circumstances attending his expulsion from a house so long his home. It seemed to him that, like the champions of romance of whom he had sometimes read, he himself was retiring from the post which it was his duty to guard, defeated by a Paynim knight, for whom the adventure had been reserved by fate. Alice had her own painful subjects of recollection, nor had the tenor of her last conversation with her father been so pleasant as to make her anxious to renew it until his temper should be more composed; for with an excellent disposition, and much love to his daughter, age and misfortunes, which of late came thicker and thicker, had given to the good knight's passions a wayward irritability unknown to his better days. His daughter, and one or two attached servants, who still followed his decayed fortunes, soothed his frailty as much as possible, and pitied him even while they suffered under its effects.

It was a long time ere he spoke, and then he referred to an incident already noticed. " It is strange," he said, " that Bevis should have followed Joceline and that fellow rather than me."

" Assure yourself, sir," replied Alice, " that his sagacity saw in this man a stranger, whom he thought himself obliged to watch circumspectly, and therefore he remained with Joceline."

" Not so, Alice," answered Sir Henry; " he leaves me because my fortunes have fled from me. There is a feeling in nature, affecting even the instinct, as it is called, of dumb animals, which teaches them to fly from misfortune. The very deer there will butt a sick or wounded buck from the herd; hurt a dog, and the whole kennel will fall on him and worry him; fishes devour their own kind when they are wounded with a spear; cut a crow's wing, or break its leg, the others will buffet it to death."

"That may be true of the more irrational kinds of animals among each other," said Alice, "for their whole life is wellnigh a warfare; but the dog leaves his own race to attach himself to ours; forsakes, for his master, the company, food, and pleasure of his own kind; and surely the fidelity of such a devoted and voluntary servant as Bevis hath been in particular, ought not to be lightly suspected."

"I am not angry with the dog, Alice; I am only sorry," replied her father. "I have read, in faithful chronicles, that when Richard II. and Henry of Bolingbroke were at Berkeley Castle, a dog of the same kind deserted the King, whom he had always attended upon, and attached himself to Henry, whom he then saw for the first time. Richard foretold, from the desertion of his favourite, his approaching deposition.* The dog was afterwards kept at Woodstock, and Bevis is said to be of his breed, which was heedfully kept up. What I might foretell of mischief from his desertion, I cannot guess, but my mind assures me it bodes no good."

There was a distant rustling among the withered leaves, a bouncing or galloping sound on the path, and the favourite dog instantly joined his master.

"Come into court, old knave," said Alice, cheerfully, "and defend thy character, which is wellnigh endangered by this absence." But the dog only paid her courtesy by gambolling around them, and instantly plunged back again, as fast as he could scamper.

* The story occurs, I think, in Froissart's Chronicles.

" How now, knave?" said the knight; " thou
art too well trained, surely, to take up the chase
without orders ?" A minute more showed them
Phœbe Mayflower approaching, her light pace so
little impeded by the burden which she bore, that
she joined her master and young mistress just as
they arrived at the keeper's hut, which was the
boundary of their journey. Bevis, who had shot
a-head to pay his compliments to Sir Henry his
master, had returned again to his immediate duty,
the escorting Phœbe and her cargo of provisions.
The whole party stood presently assembled before
the door of the keeper's hut.

In better times, a substantial stone habitation, fit
for the yeoman-keeper of a royal walk, had adorned this place. A fair spring gushed out near the
spot, and once traversed yards and courts, attached to well-built and convenient kennels and mews.
But in some of the skirmishes which were common
during the civil wars, this little silvan dwelling had
been attacked and defended, stormed and burnt.
A neighbouring squire, of the Parliament side of
the question, took advantage of Sir Henry Lee's
absence, who was then in Charles's camp, and of
the decay of the royal cause, and had, without scruple, carried off the hewn stones, and such building
materials as the fire left unconsumed, and repaired
his own manor-house with them. The yeoman-
keeper, therefore, our friend Joceline, had constructed, for his own accommodation, and that of
the old woman he called his dame, a wattled hut,
such as his own labour, with that of a neighbour or

two, had erected in the course of a few days. The walls were plastered with clay, white-washed, and covered with vines and other creeping plants ; the roof was neatly thatched, and the whole, though merely a hut, had, by the neat-handed Joliffe, been so arranged as not to disgrace the condition of the dweller.

The knight advanced to the entrance ; but the ingenuity of the architect, for want of a better lock to the door, which itself was but of wattles curiously twisted, had contrived a mode of securing the latch on the inside with a pin, which prevented it from rising ; and in this manner it was at present fastened. Conceiving that this was some precaution of Joliffe's old housekeeper, of whose deafness they were all aware, Sir Henry raised his voice to demand admittance, but in vain. Irritated at this delay, he pressed the door at once with foot and hand, in a way which the frail barrier was unable to resist ; it gave way accordingly, and the knight thus forcibly entered the kitchen, or outward apartment, of his servant. In the midst of the floor, and with a posture which indicated embarrassment, stood a youthful stranger, in a riding-suit.

" This may be my last act of authority here," said the knight, seizing the stranger by the collar, " but I am still Ranger of Woodstock for this night at least—Who, or what art thou ?"

The stranger dropped the riding-mantle in which his face was muffled, and at the same time fell on one knee.

" Your poor kinsman, Markham Everard," he

1

said, "who came hither for your sake, although he fears you will scarce make him welcome for his own."

Sir Henry started back, but recovered himself in an instant, as one who recollected that he had a part of dignity to perform. He stood erect, therefore, and replied, with considerable assumption of stately ceremony:

"Fair kinsman, it pleases me that you are come to Woodstock upon the very first night that, for many years which have past, is likely to promise you a worthy or a welcome reception."

"Now God grant it be so, that I rightly hear and duly understand you!" said the young man; while Alice, though she was silent, kept her looks fixed on her father's face, as if desirous to know whether his meaning was kind towards his nephew, which her knowledge of his character inclined her greatly to doubt.

The knight meanwhile darted a sardonic look, first on his nephew, then on his daughter, and proceeded—"I need not, I presume, inform Mr Markham Everard, that it cannot be our purpose to entertain him, or even to offer him a seat in this poor hut."

"I will attend you most willingly to the Lodge," said the young gentleman. "I had, indeed, judged you were already there for the evening, and feared to intrude upon you. But if you would permit me, my dearest uncle, to escort my kinswoman and you back to the Lodge, believe me, amongst all which you have so often done of good and kind, you never conferred benefit that will be so dearly prized."

" You mistake me greatly, Mr Markham Everard," replied the knight. " It is not our purpose to return to the Lodge to-night, nor, by Our Lady, to-morrow neither. I meant but to intimate to you in all courtesy, that at Woodstock Lodge you will find those for whom you are fitting society, and who, doubtless, will afford you a willing welcome ; which I, sir, in this my present retreat, do not presume to offer to a person of your consequence."

" For Heaven's sake," said the young man, turning to Alice, " tell me how I am to understand language so mysterious !"

Alice, to prevent his increasing the restrained anger of her father, compelled herself to answer, though it was with difficulty, " We are expelled from the Lodge by soldiers."

" Expelled—by soldiers !" exclaimed Everard, in surprise—" there is no legal warrant for this."

" None at all," answered the knight, in the same tone of cutting irony which he had all along used, " and yet as lawful a warrant, as for aught that has been wrought in England this twelvemonth and more. You are, I think, or were, an Inns-of-Court-man—marry, sir, your enjoyment of your profession is like that lease which a prodigal wishes to have of a wealthy widow. You have already survived the law which you studied, and its expiry doubtless has not been without a legacy—some decent pickings, some merciful increases, as the phrase goes. You have deserved it two ways—you wore buff and bandoleer, as well as wielded pen and ink—I have not heard if you held forth too."

" Think of me and speak of me as harshly as you will, sir," said Everard, submissively. " I have but, in this evil time, guided myself by my conscience, and my father's commands."

" O, an you talk of conscience," said the old knight, " I must have mine eye upon you, as Hamlet says. Never yet did Puritan cheat so grossly as when he was appealing to his conscience; and as for thy *father*"——

He was about to proceed in a tone of the same invective, when the young man interrupted him, by saying, in a firm tone, " Sir Henry Lee, you have ever been thought noble—Say of me what you will, but speak not of my father what the ear of a son should not endure, and which yet his arm cannot resent. To do me such wrong is to insult an unarmed man, or to beat a captive."

Sir Henry paused, as if struck by the remark. " Thou hast spoken truth in that, Mark, wert thou the blackest Puritan whom hell ever vomited, to distract an unhappy country."

" Be that as you will to think it," replied Everard: " but let me not leave you to the shelter of this wretched hovel. The night is drawing to storm —let me but conduct you to the Lodge, and expel those intruders, who can, as yet at least, have no warrant for what they do. I will not linger a moment behind them, save just to deliver my father's message.—Grant me but this much, for the love you once bore me !"

" Yes, Mark," answered his uncle, firmly, but sorrowfully, " thou speakest truth—I did love thee once. The bright-haired boy whom I taught to ride, to shoot, to hunt—whose hours of happiness were spent with me, wherever those of graver labours were employed—I did love that boy—ay, and I am weak enough to love even the memory of what he was.—But he is gone, Mark—he is gone; and in his room I only behold an avowed and determined rebel to his religion and to his king—a rebel more detestable on account of his success, the more infamous through the plundered wealth with which he hopes to gild his villainy.— But I am poor, thou think'st, and should hold my peace, lest men say, ' Speak, sirrah, when you should.'—Know, however, that, indigent and plundered as I am, I feel myself dishonoured in holding even but this much talk with the tool of usurping rebels.—Go to the Lodge, if thou wilt—yonder lies the way—but think not that, to regain my dwelling there, or all the wealth I ever possessed in my wealthiest days, I would willingly accompany thee three steps on the greensward. If I must be thy companion, it shall be only when thy red-coats have tied my hands behind me, and bound my legs beneath my horse's belly. Thou mayst be my fellow traveller then, I grant thee, if thou wilt, but not sooner."

Alice, who suffered cruelly during this dialogue, and was well aware that further argument would only kindle the knight's resentment still more highly, ventured at last, in her anxiety, to make a sign to her cousin to break off the interview, and to retire, since her father commanded his absence in a manner so peremptory. Unhappily she was observed by Sir Henry, who, concluding that what he saw was evidence of a private understanding betwixt the cousins, his wrath acquired new fuel, and it required the utmost exertion of self-command, and recollection of all that was due to his own dignity, to enable him to veil his real fury under the same ironical manner which he had adopted at the beginning of this angry interview.

"If thou art afraid," he said, "to trace our forest glades by night, respected stranger, to whom I am perhaps bound to do honour as my successor in the charge of these walks, here seems to be a modest damsel, who will be most willing to wait on thee, and be thy bow-bearer.—Only, for her mother's sake, let there pass some slight form of marriage between you—Ye need no license or priest in these happy days, but may be buckled like beggars in a ditch, with a hedge for a church-roof, and a tinker for a priest. I crave pardon of you for making such an officious and simple request—perhaps you are a Ranter—or one of the family of Love, or hold marriage rites as unnecessary, as Knipperdoling, or Jack of Leyden?"

"For mercy's sake, forbear such dreadful jesting, my father! and do you, Markham, begone, in God's name, and leave us to our fate—Your presence makes my father rave."

"Jesting!" said Sir Henry, "I was never more serious—Raving!—I was never more composed—

I could never brook that falsehood should approach me—I would no more bear by my side a dishonoured daughter than a dishonoured sword; and this unhappy day hath shown that both can fail."

"Sir Henry," said young Everard, "load not your soul with a heavy crime, which be assured you do, in treating your daughter thus unjustly. It is long now since you denied her to me, when we were poor and you were powerful. I acquiesced in your prohibition of all suit and intercourse. God knoweth what I suffered—but I acquiesced. Neither is it to renew my suit that I now come hither, and have, I do acknowledge, sought speech of her—not for her own sake only, but for yours also. Destruction hovers over you, ready to close her pinions to stoop, and her talons to clutch—Yes, sir, look contemptuous as you will, such is the case! and it is to protect both you and her that I am here."

"You refuse then my free gift," said Sir Henry Lee; "or perhaps you think it loaded with too hard conditions?"

"Shame, shame on you, Sir Henry!" said Everard, waxing warm in his turn; "have your political prejudices so utterly warped every feeling of a father, that you can speak with bitter mockery and scorn of what concerns your own daughter's honour?—Hold up your head, fair Alice, and tell your father he has forgotten nature in his fantastic spirit of loyalty.—Know, Sir Henry, that though I would prefer your daughter's hand to every blessing which Heaven could bestow on me, I would not accept it—my conscience would not permit me to do so—when I knew it must withdraw her from her duty to you."

"Your conscience is over scrupulous, young man;—carry it to some dissenting rabbi, and he who takes all that comes to net, will teach thee it is sinning against our mercies to refuse any good thing that is freely offered to us."

"When it is freely offered, and kindly offered —not when the offer is made in irony and insult. —Fare thee well, Alice—if aught could make me desire to profit by thy father's wild wish to cast thee from him in a moment of unworthy suspicion, it would be that while indulging in such sentiments, Sir Henry Lee is tyrannically oppressing the creature, who of all others is most dependent on his kindness—who of all others will most feel his severity, and whom, of all others, he is most bound to cherish and support."

"Do not fear for me, Mr Everard," exclaimed Alice, aroused from her timidity by a dread of the consequences not unlikely to ensue, where civil war set relations, as well as fellow-citizens, in opposition to each other.—"Oh, begone, I conjure you, begone! Nothing stands betwixt me and my father's kindness, but these unhappy family divisions —but your ill-timed presence here—For Heaven's sake, leave us!"

"Soh, mistress!" answered the hot old cavalier, "you play lady paramount already; and who but you!—you would dictate to our train, I warrant, like Goneril and Regan! But I tell thee, no man shall leave my house—and, humble as it is, *this* is now my house—while he has aught to say to me that is to be spoken, as this young man now speaks, with a bent brow and a lofty tone.—Speak out, sir, and say your worst!"

"Fear not my temper, Mrs Alice," said Everard, with equal firmness and placidity of manner; "and you, Sir Henry, do not think that if I speak firmly, I mean therefore to speak in anger, or officiously. You have taxed me with much, and, were I guided by the wild spirit of romantic chivalry, much which, even from so near a relative, I ought not, as being by birth, and in the world's estimation, a gentleman, to pass over without reply. Is it your pleasure to give me patient hearing?"

"If you stand on your defence," answered the stout old knight, "God forbid that you should not challenge a patient hearing—ay, though your pleading were two parts disloyalty and one blasphemy —Only, be brief—this has already lasted but too long."

"I will, Sir Henry," replied the young man; "yet it is hard to crowd into a few sentences, the defence of a life which, though short, has been a busy one—too busy, your indignant gesture would assert. But I deny it; I have drawn my sword neither hastily, nor without due consideration, for a people whose rights have been trampled on, and whose consciences have been oppressed—Frown not, sir—such is not your view of the contest, but such is mine. For my religious principles, at which you have scoffed, believe me, that though they depend not on set forms, they are no less sincere than

your own, and thus far purer—excuse the word—
that they are unmingled with the bloodthirsty dictates of a barbarous age, which you and others have
called the code of chivalrous honour. Not my own
natural disposition, but the better doctrine which
my creed has taught, enables me to bear your harsh
revilings without answering in a similar tone of
wrath and reproach. You may carry insult to extremity against me at your pleasure—not on account of our relationship alone, but because I am
bound in charity to endure it. This, Sir Henry,
is much from one of our house. But, with forbearance far more than this requires, I can refuse
at your hands the gift, which, most of all things
under Heaven, I should desire to obtain, because
duty calls upon her to sustain and comfort you, and
because it were sin to permit you, in your blind-
ness, to spurn your comforter from your side.—
Farewell, sir—not in anger, but in pity—We may
meet in a better time, when your heart and your
principles shall master the unhappy prejudices by
which they are now overclouded.—Farewell—farewell, Alice!"

The last words were repeated twice, and in a
tone of feeling and passionate grief, which differed
utterly from the steady and almost severe tone
in which he had addressed Sir Henry Lee. He
turned and left the hut so soon as he had uttered
these last words; and, as if ashamed of the tender-
ness which had mingled with his accents, the young
commonwealth's-man turned and walked sternly
and resolvedly forth into the moonlight, which now

was spreading its broad light and autumnal shadows over the woodland.

So soon as he departed, Alice, who had been during the whole scene in the utmost terror that her father might have been hurried, by his natural heat of temper, from violence of language into violence of action, sunk down upon a settle twisted out of willow-boughs, like most of Joceline's few movables, and endeavoured to conceal the tears which accompanied the thanks she rendered in broken accents to Heaven, that, notwithstanding the near alliance and relationship of the parties, some fatal deed had not closed an interview so perilous and so angry. Phœbe Mayflower blubbered heartily for company, though she understood but little of what had passed ; just, indeed, enough to enable her afterwards to report to some half-dozen particular friends, that her old master, Sir Henry, had been perilous angry, and almost fought with young Master Everard, because he had wellnigh carried away her young mistress.—" And what could he have done better ?" said Phœbe, " seeing the old man had nothing left either for Mrs Alice or himself ; and as for Mr Mark Everard, and our young lady, oh ! they had spoken such loving things to each other, as are not to be found in the history of Argalus and Parthenia, who, as the story-book tells, were the truest pair of lovers in all Arcadia, and Oxfordshire to boot."

Old Goody Jellycot had popped her scarlet hood into the kitchen more than once while the scene was proceeding ; but, as the worthy dame was parcel blind, and more than parcel deaf, knowledge was excluded by two principal entrances ; and though she comprehended, by a sort of general instinct, that the gentlefolk were at high words, yet why they chose Joceline's hut for the scene of their dispute, was as great a mystery as the subject of the quarrel.

But what was the state of the old cavalier's mood, thus contradicted, as his most darling principles had been, by the last words of his departing nephew ? The truth is, that he was less thoroughly moved than his daughter expected ; and in all probability his nephew's bold defence of his religious and political opinions rather pacified than aggravated his displeasure. Although sufficiently impatient of contradiction, still evasion and subterfuge were more alien to the blunt old Ranger's nature than manly vindication and direct opposition ; and he was wont to say, that he ever loved the buck best who stood boldest at bay. He graced his nephew's departure, however, with a quotation from Shakspeare, whom, as many others do, he was wont to quote from a sort of habit and respect, as a favourite of his unfortunate master, without having either much real taste for his works, or great skill in applying the passages which he retained on his memory.

" Mark," he said, " mark this, Alice—the devil can quote Scripture for his purpose. Why, this young fanatic cousin of thine, with no more beard than I have seen on a clown playing Maid Marion on May-day, when the village barber had shaved him in too great a hurry, shall match any bearded

Presbyterian or Independent of them all, in laying
down his doctrines and his uses, and bethumping
us with his texts and his homilies. I would worthy
and learned Doctor Rochecliffe had been here, with
his battery ready mounted from the Vulgate, and
the Septuagint, and what not—he would have battered the presbyterian spirit out of him with a
wanion. However, I am glad the young man is
no sneaker; for, were a man of the devil's opinion
in religion, and of Old Noll's in politics, he were
better open on it full cry, than deceive you by hunting counter, or running a false scent. Come—
wipe thine eyes—the fray is over, and not like to
be stirred again soon, I trust."

Encouraged by these words, Alice rose, and,
bewildered as she was, endeavoured to superintend
the arrangements for their meal and their repose
in their new habitation. But her tears fell so fast,
they marred her counterfeited diligence; and it
was well for her that Phœbe, though too ignorant
and too simple to comprehend the extent of her distress, could afford her material assistance, in lack
of mere sympathy.

With great readiness and address, the damsel
set about every thing that was requisite for preparing the supper and the beds; now screaming into
Dame Jellycot's ear, now whispering into her mistress's, and artfully managing, as if she was merely
the agent, under Alice's orders. When the cold
viands were set forth, Sir Henry Lee kindly pressed
his daughter to take refreshment, as if to make up,
indirectly, for his previous harshness towards her;

while he himself, like an experienced campaigner, showed, that neither the mortifications nor brawls of the day, nor the thoughts of what was to come to-morrow, could diminish his appetite for supper, which was his favourite meal. He ate up two-thirds of the capon, and, devoting the first bumper to the happy restoration of Charles, second of the name, he finished a quart of wine ; for he belonged to a school accustomed to feed the flame of their loyalty with copious brimmers. He even sang a verse of " The King shall enjoy his own again," in which Phœbe, half-sobbing, and Dame Jellycot, screaming against time and tune, were contented to lend their aid, to cover Mistress Alice's silence.

At length the jovial knight betook himself to his rest on the keeper's straw pallet, in a recess adjoining to the kitchen, and, unaffected by his change of dwelling, slept fast and deep. Alice had less quiet rest in old Goody Jellycot's wicker couch, in the inner apartment ; while the dame and Phœbe slept on a mattrass, stuffed with dry leaves, in the same chamber, soundly as those whose daily toil gains their daily bread, and whom morning calls up only to renew the toils of yesterday.

CHAPTER V.

My tongue pads slowly under this new language,
And starts and stumbles at these uncouth phrases.
They may be great in worth and weight, but hang
Upon the native glibness of my speech,
Like Saul's plate-armour on the shepherd boy,
Encumbering and not arming him.

                                        J. B.

As Markham Everard pursued his way towards
the Lodge, through one of the long sweeping glades
which traversed the forest, varying in breadth, till
the trees were now so close that the boughs made
darkness over his head, then receding farther to
let in glimpses of the moon, and anon opening yet
wider into little meadows or savannahs, on which
the moonbeams lay in silvery silence ; as he thus
proceeded on his lonely course, the various effects
produced by that delicious light on the oaks, whose
dark leaves, gnarled branches, and massive trunks
it gilded, more or less partially, might have drawn
the attention of a poet or a painter.

But if Everard thought of any thing saving the
painful scene in which he had just played his part,
and of which the result seemed the destruction of
all his hopes, it was of the necessary guard to be
observed in his night-walk.   The times were dan-

gerous and unsettled ; the roads full of disbanded
soldiers, and especially of royalists, who made their
political opinions a pretext for disturbing the country with marauding parties and robberies. Deer-
stealers also, who are ever a desperate banditti,
had of late infested Woodstock Chase. In short,
the dangers of the place and period were such, that
Markham Everard wore his loaded pistols at his
belt, and carried his drawn sword under his arm,
that he might be prepared for whatever peril should
cross his path.

He heard the bells of Woodstock Church ring
curfew, just as he was crossing one of the little
meadows we have described, and they ceased as he
entered an overshadowed and twilight part of the
path beyond. It was there that he heard some one
whistling ; and, as the sound became clearer, it was
plain the person was advancing towards him. This
could hardly be a friend ; for the party to which
he belonged rejected, generally speaking, all music,
unless psalmody. " If a man is merry, let him sing
psalms," was a text which they were pleased to in-
terpret as literally and to as little purpose as they
did some others ; yet it was too continued a sound
to be a signal amongst night-walkers, and too light
and cheerful to argue any purpose of concealment on
the part of the traveller, who presently exchanged
his whistling for singing, and trolled forth the following stanza to a jolly tune, with which the old
cavaliers were wont to wake the night owl :

> Hey for cavaliers ! Ho for cavaliers !
> Pray for cavaliers !

Rub a dub—rub a dub!
Have at old Beelzebub—
Oliver smokes for fear.

"I should know that voice," said Everard, un-cocking the pistol which he had drawn from his belt, but continuing to hold it in his hand. Then came another fragment:

Hash them—slash them—
All to pieces dash them.

"So ho!" cried Markham, "who goes there, and for whom?"

"For Church and King," answered a voice, which presently added, "No, d—n me—I mean *against* Church and King, and for the people that are uppermost—I forget which they are."

"Roger Wildrake, as I guess?" said Everard.

"The same—Gentleman; of Squattlesea-mere, in the moist county of Lincoln."

"Wildrake!" said Markham—"Wildgoose you should be called. You have been moistening your own throat to some purpose, and using it to gabble tunes very suitable to the times, to be sure!"

"Faith, the tune's a pretty tune enough, Mark, only out of fashion a little—the more's the pity."

"What could I expect," said Everard, "but to meet some ranting, drunken cavalier, as desperate and dangerous as night and sack usually make them? What if I had rewarded your melody by a ball in the gullet?"

"Why, there would have been a piper paid—that's all," said Wildrake.—"But wherefore come you this way now?—I was about to seek you at the hut."

" I have been obliged to leave it—I will tell you the cause hereafter," replied Markham.

" What! the old play-hunting cavalier was cross, or Chloe was unkind?"

" Jest not, Wildrake—it is all over with me," said Everard.

" The devil it is," exclaimed Wildrake, " and you take it thus quietly!—Zounds! let us back together—I'll plead your cause for you—I know how to tickle up an old knight and a pretty maiden—Let me alone for putting you *rectus in curia*, you canting rogue.—D—n me, Sir Henry Lee, says I, your nephew is a piece of a Puritan—it won't deny—but I'll uphold him a gentleman and a pretty fellow, for all that.—Madam, says I, you may think your cousin looks like a psalm-singing weaver, in that bare felt, and with that rascally brown cloak; that band, which looks like a baby's clout, and those loose boots, which have a whole calf-skin in each of them,—but let him wear on the one side of his head a castor, with a plume befitting his quality; give him a good Toledo by his side, with a broidered belt and an inlaid hilt, instead of the ton of iron contained in that basket-hilted black Andrew Ferrara; put a few smart words in his mouth—and, blood and wounds! madam, says I"——

" Prithee, truce with this nonsense, Wildrake," said Everard, " and tell me if you are sober enough to hear a few words of sober reason?"

" Pshaw! man, I did but crack a brace of quarts

with yonder puritanic, roundheaded soldiers, up yonder at the town; and rat me but I passed myself for the best man of the party; twanged my nose, and turned up my eyes, as I took my can—Pah! the very wine tasted of hypocrisy. I think the rogue corporal smoked something at last—as for the common fellows, never stir, but *they* asked me to say grace over another quart!"

" This is just what I wished to speak with you about, Wildrake," said Markham—" You hold me, I am sure, for your friend?"

" True as steel.—Chums at College and at Lincoln's-Inn—we have been Nisus and Euryalus, Theseus and Pirithous, Orestes and Pylades; and, to sum up the whole with a puritanic touch, David and Jonathan, all in one breath. Not even politics, the wedge that rends families and friendships asunder, as iron rives oak, have been able to split us."

" True," answered Markham; " and when you followed the King to Nottingham; and I enrolled under Essex, we swore, at our parting, that whichever side was victorious, he of us who adhered to it, should protect his less fortunate comrade."

" Surely, man, surely; and have you not protected me accordingly? Did you not save me from hanging? and am I not indebted to you for the bread I eat?"

" I have but done that, which, had the times been otherwise, you, my dear Wildrake, would, I am sure, have done for me. But, as I said, that is just what I wished to speak to you about. Why render the task of protecting you more difficult than it must necessarily be at any rate? Why thrust thyself into the company of soldiers, or such like, where thou art sure to be warmed into betraying thyself? Why come hollowing and whooping out cavalier ditties, like a drunken trooper of Prince Rupert, or one of Wilmot's swaggering body-guards?"

"Because I may have been both one and t'other in my day, for aught that you know," replied Wildrake. "But, oddsfish! is it necessary I should always be reminding you, that our obligation of mutual protection, our league of offensive and defensive, as I may call it, was to be carried into effect without reference to the politics or religion of the party protected, or the least obligation on him to conform to those of his friend?"

"True," said Everard; "but with this most necessary qualification, that the party should submit to such outward conformity to the times as should make it more easy and safe for his friend to be of service to him. Now, you are perpetually breaking forth, to the hazard of your own safety and my credit."

"I tell you, Mark, and I would tell your namesake the apostle, that you are hard on me. You have practised sobriety and hypocrisy from your hanging sleeves till your Geneva cassock—from the cradle to this day,—and it is a thing of nature to you; and you are surprised that a rough, rattling, honest fellow, accustomed to speak truth all his life, and especially when he found it at the bottom of a flask, cannot be so perfect a prig as thyself!—

Zooks! there is no equality betwixt us—A trained diver might as well, because he can retain his breath for ten minutes without inconvenience, upbraid a poor devil for being like to burst in twenty seconds, at the bottom of ten fathoms' water—And, after all, considering the guise is so new to me, I think I bear myself indifferently well—try me!"

" Are there any more news from Worcester fight?" asked Everard, in a tone so serious that it imposed on his companion, who replied in his genuine character—

" Worse!—d—n me, worse an hundred times than reported—totally broken. Noll hath certainly sold himself to the devil, and his lease will have an end one day—that is all our present comfort."

" What! and would this be your answer to the first red-coat who asked the question?" said Everard. " Methinks you would find a speedy passport to the next corps de garde."

" Nay, nay," answered Wildrake, " I thought you asked me in your own person.—Lack-a-day! a great mercy—a glorifying mercy—a crowning mercy—a vouchsafing—an uplifting—I profess the malignants are scattered from Dan to Beersheba—smitten, hip and thigh, even until the going down of the sun!"

" Hear you aught of Colonel Thornhaugh's wounds?"

" He is dead," answered Wildrake, " that's one comfort—the roundheaded rascal!—Nay, hold! it was but a trip of the tongue—I meant, the sweet godly youth."

"And hear you aught of the young man, King of Scotland, as they call him?" said Everard.

"Nothing, but that he is hunted like a partridge on the mountains. May God deliver him, and confound his enemies!—Zoons, Mark Everard, I can fool it no longer. Do you not remember, that at the Lincoln's-Inn gambols—though you did not mingle much in them, I think—I used always to play as well as any of them, when it came to the action, but they could never get me to rehearse conformably. It's the same at this day. I hear your voice, and I answer to it in the true tone of my heart; but when I am in the company of your snuffling friends, you have seen me act my part indifferent well."

"But indifferent, indeed," replied Everard; "however, there is little call on you to do aught, save to be modest and silent. Speak little, and lay aside, if you can, your big oaths and swaggering looks—set your hat even on your brows."

"Ay, that is the curse! I have been always noted for the jaunty manner in which I wear my castor—Hard when a man's merits become his enemies!"

"You must remember you are my clerk."

"Secretary," answered Wildrake; "let it be secretary, if you love me."

"It must be clerk, and nothing else—plain clerk —and remember to be civil and obedient," replied Everard.

"But you should not lay on your commands with so much ostentatious superiority, Master Markham

Everard. Remember I am your senior of three years standing. Confound me, if I know how to take it !"

Was ever such a fantastic wronghead !—For my sake, if not for thine own, bend thy freakish folly to listen to reason. Think that I have incurred both risk and shame on thy account."

" Nay, thou art a right good fellow, Mark," replied the cavalier, " and for thy sake I will do much —but remember to cough, and cry hem ! when thou seest me like to break bounds—And now tell me whither we are bound for the night ?"

 " To Woodstock Lodge, to look after my uncle's property," answered Markham Everard : " I am informed that soldiers have taken possession—Yet how could that be, if thou foundest the party drinking in Woodstock ?"

" There was a kind of commissary or steward, or some such rogue, had gone down to the Lodge," replied Wildrake ; " I had a peep at him."

" Indeed !" replied Everard.

" Ay, verily," said Wildrake, " to speak your own language. Why, as I passed through the park in quest of you, scarce half an hour since, I saw a light in the Lodge—Step this way, you will see it yourself."

" In the north-west angle ?" returned Everard —" It is from a window in what they call Victor Lee's apartment."

" Well," resumed Wildrake, " I had been long one of Lundsford's lads, and well used to patrolling duty—So, rat me, says I, if I leave a light in my rear, without knowing what it means. Besides, Mark, thou hadst said so much to me of thy pretty cousin, I thought I might as well have a peep, if I could."

" Thoughtless, incorrigible man ! to what dangers do you expose yourself and your friends, in mere wantonness !—But go on."

" By this fair moonshine, I believe thou art jealous, Mark Everard !" replied his gay companion ; " there is no occasion ; for, in any case, I, who was to see the lady, was steeled by honour against the charms of my friend's Chloe—Then the lady was not to see me, so could make no comparisons to thy disadvantage, thou knowest—Lastly, as it fell out, neither of us saw the other at all."

" Of that I am well aware. Mrs Alice left the Lodge long before sunset, and never returned. What *didst* thou see to introduce with such preface ?"

" Nay, no great matter," replied Wildrake ; " only getting upon a sort of buttress, (for I can climb like any cat that ever mewed in any gutter,) and holding on by the vines and creepers which grew around, I obtained a station where I could see into the inside of that same parlour thou spokest of just now."

" And what saw'st thou there ?" once more demanded Everard.

" Nay, no great matter, as I said before," replied the cavalier ; " for in these times it is no new thing to see churls carousing in royal or noble chambers. I saw two rascallions engaged in emptying a solemn stoup of strong waters, and dispatching a huge venison pasty, which greasy mess, for their convenience, they had placed on a lady's work-table— One of them was trying an air on a lute."

"The profane villains!" exclaimed Everard, "it was Alice's."

"Well said, comrade—I am glad your phlegm can be moved. I did but throw in these incidents of the lute and the table, to try if it were possible to get a spark of human spirit out of you, be-sanctified as you are."

"What like were the men?" said young Everard.

"The one a slouch-hatted, long-cloaked, sour-faced fanatic, like the rest of you, whom I took to be the steward or commissary I heard spoken of in the town; the other was a short sturdy fellow, with a wood-knife at his girdle, and a long quarterstaff lying beside him—a black-haired knave, with white teeth and a merry countenance—one of the under-rangers or bow-bearers of these walks, I fancy."

"They must have been Desborough's favourite, trusty Tomkins," said Everard, "and Joceline Joliffe, the keeper. Tomkins is Desborough's right hand—an Independent, and hath pourings forth, as he calls them. Some think that his gifts have the better of his grace. I have heard of his abusing opportunities."

"They were improving them when I saw them," replied Wildrake, "and made the bottle smoke for it—when, as the devil would have it, a stone, which had been dislodged from the crumbling buttress, gave way under my weight. A clumsy fellow like thee would have been so long thinking what was to be done, that he must needs have followed it before he could make up his mind; but I, Mark, I hopped like a squirrel to an ivy twig, and stood fast—was wellnigh shot, though, for the noise alarmed them both. They looked to the oriel, and saw me on the outside; the fanatic fellow took out a pistol—as they have always such texts in readiness hanging beside the little clasped Bible, thou know'st—the keeper seized his hunting-pole —I treated them both to a roar and a grin—thou must know I can grimace like a baboon—I learned the trick from a French player, who could twist his jaws into a pair of nut-crackers—and therewithal I dropped myself sweetly on the grass, and ran off so trippingly, keeping the dark side of the wall as long as I could, that I am wellnigh persuaded they thought I was their kinsman, the devil, come among them uncalled. They were abominably startled."

"Thou art most fearfully rash, Wildrake," said his companion; "we are now bound for the house —what if they should remember thee?"

"Why, it is no treason, is it? No one has paid for peeping since Tom of Coventry's days; and if he came in for a reckoning, belike it was for a better treat than mine. But trust me, they will no more know me, than a man who had only seen your friend Noll at a conventicle of saints, would know the same Oliver on horseback, and charging with his lobster-tailed squadron; or the same Noll cracking a jest and a bottle with wicked Waller the poet."

"Hush! not a word of Oliver, as thou dost value thyself and me. It is ill jesting with the rock you may split on.—But here is the gate—we will disturb these honest gentlemen's recreations."

As he spoke, he applied the large and ponderous knocker to the hall-door.

"Rat-tat-tat-too!" said Wildrake; "there is a fine alarm to you cuckolds and roundheads!" He then half-mimicked, half-sung the march so called :—

"Cuckolds, come dig, cuckolds, come dig;
Round about cuckolds, come dance to my jig!"

"By Heaven! this passes midsummer frenzy," said Everard, turning angrily on him.

"Not a bit, not a bit," replied Wildrake; "it is but a slight expectoration, just like what one makes before beginning a long speech. I will be grave for an hour together, now I have got that point of war out of my head."

As he spoke, steps were heard in the hall, and the wicket of the great door was partly opened, but secured with a chain in case of accidents. The visage of Tomkins, and that of Joceline beneath it, appeared at the chink, illuminated by the lamp which the latter held in his hand, and Tomkins demanded the meaning of this alarm.

"I demand instant admittance!" said Everard. "Joliffe, you know me well?"

"I do, sir," replied Joceline, "and could admit

you with all my heart; but, alas! sir, you see I am
not key-keeper. Here is the gentleman whose warrant I must walk by—The Lord help me, seeing
times are such as they be!"

"And when that gentleman, who I think may
be Master Desborough's valet"——

"His honour's unworthy secretary, an it please
you," interposed Tomkins; while Wildrake whispered in Everard's ear, "I will be no longer secretary. Mark, thou wert quite right—the clerk
must be the more gentlemanly calling."

"And if you are Master Desborough's secretary, I presume you know me and my condition well
enough," said Everard, addressing the Independent,
"not to hesitate to admit me and my attendant to
a night's quarters in the Lodge?"

"Surely not, surely not," said the Independent
—"that is, if your worship thinks you would be
better accommodated here than up at the house of
entertainment in the town, which men unprofitably
call Saint George's Inn. There is but confined
accommodation here, your honour—and we have
been frayed out of our lives already by the visitation
of Satan—albeit his fiery dart is now quenched."

"This may be all well in its place, Sir Secretary," said Everard; "and you may find a corner for
it when you are next tempted to play the preacher.
But I will take it for no apology for keeping me
here in the cold harvest wind; and if not presently
received, and suitably too, I will report you to
your master for insolence in your office."

The secretary of Desborough did not dare offer farther opposition ; for it is well known that Desborough himself only held his consequence as a kinsman of Cromwell ; and the Lord General, who was wellnigh paramount already, was known to be strongly favourable both to the elder and younger Everard. It is true, they were Presbyterians and he an Independent ; and that, though sharing those sentiments of correct morality and more devoted religious feeling, by which, with few exceptions, the Parliamentarian party were distinguished, the Everards were not disposed to carry these attributes to the extreme of enthusiasm, practised by so many others at the time. Yet it was well known that whatever might be Cromwell's own religious creed, he was not uniformly bounded by it in the choice of his favourites, but extended his countenance to those who could serve him, even although, according to the phrase of the time, they came out of the darkness of Egypt. The character of the elder Everard stood very high for wisdom and sagacity ; besides, being of a good family and competent fortune, his adherence would lend a dignity to any side he might espouse. Then his son had been a distinguished and successful soldier, remarkable for the discipline he maintained among his men, the bravery which he showed in the time of action, and the humanity with which he was always ready to qualify the consequences of victory. Such men were not to be neglected, when many signs combined to show that the parties in the state, who

had successfully accomplished the deposition and
death of the king, were speedily to quarrel among
themselves about the division of the spoils. The
two Everards were therefore much courted by
Cromwell, and their influence with him was supposed
to be so great, that trusty Master Secretary Tomkins
cared not to expose himself to risk, by contending
with Colonel Everard for such a trifle as a night's
lodging, or a greater thing.

Joceline was active on his side—more lights
were obtained—more wood thrown on the fire—
and the two newly-arrived strangers were introduced into Victor Lee's parlour, as it was called,
from the picture over the chimney-piece, which we
have already described. It was several minutes ere
Colonel Everard could recover his general stoicism
of deportment, so strongly was he impressed by
finding himself in the apartment, under whose roof
he had passed so many of the happiest hours of his
life. There was the cabinet, which he had seen
opened with such feelings of delight when Sir
Henry Lee deigned to give him instructions in
fishing, and to exhibit hooks and lines, together
with all the materials for making the artificial fly,
then little known. There hung the ancient family
picture, which, from some odd mysterious expressions of his uncle relating to it, had become to his
boyhood, nay, his early youth, a subject of curiosity
and of fear. He remembered how, when left alone
in the apartment, the searching eye of the old
warrior seemed always bent upon his, in whatever

part of the room he placed himself, and how his childish imagination was perturbed at a phenomenon, for which he could not account.

With these came a thousand dearer and warmer recollections of his early attachment to his pretty cousin Alice, when he assisted her at her lessons, brought water for her flowers, or accompanied her while she sung ; and he remembered that while her father looked at them with a good-humoured and careless smile, he had once heard him mutter, " And if it should turn out so—why it might be best for both," and the theories of happiness he had reared on these words. All these visions had been dispelled by the trumpet of war, which called Sir Henry Lee and himself to opposite sides ; and the transactions of this very day had shown, that even Everard's success as a soldier and a statesman seemed absolutely to prohibit the chance of their being revived.

He was waked out of this unpleasing reverie by the approach of Joceline, who, being possibly a seasoned toper, had made the additional arrangements with more expedition and accuracy, than could have been expected from a person engaged as he had been since nightfall.

He now wished to know the Colonel's directions for the night.

" Would he eat any thing ?"

" No."

" Did his honour choose to accept Sir Henry Lee's bed, which was ready prepared ?"

" Yes."

" That of Mistress Alice Lee should be prepared for the Secretary."

" On pain of thine ears—No," replied Everard.

" Where then was the worthy Secretary to be quartered ?"

" In the dog-kennel, if you list," replied Colonel Everard ; " but," added he, stepping to the sleeping apartment of Alice, which opened from the parlour, locking it, and taking out the key, " no one shall profane this chamber."

" Had his honour any other commands for the night ?"

" None, save to clear the apartment of yonder man.—My clerk will remain with me—I have orders which must be written out.—Yet stay—Thou gavest my letter this morning to Mistress Alice ?"

" I did."

" Tell me, good Joceline, what she said when she received it ?"

" She seemed much concerned, sir ; and indeed I think that she wept a little—but indeed she seemed very much distressed."

" And what message did she send to me ?"

" None, may it please your honour—She began to say, ' Tell my cousin Everard that I will communicate my uncle's kind purpose to my father, if I can get fitting opportunity—but that I greatly fear'—and there checked herself, as it were, and said, ' I will write to my cousin ; and as it may be late ere I have an opportunity of speaking with my

father, do thou come for my answer after service.'
—So I went to church myself, to while away the
time; but when I returned to the Chase, I found
this man had summoned my master to surrender,
and, right or wrong, I must put him in possession of
the Lodge.   I would fain have given your honour
a hint that the old knight and my young mistress
were like to take you on the form, but I could not
mend the matter."

" Thou hast done well, good fellow, and I will
remember thee.—And now, my masters," he said,
advancing to the brace of clerks or secretaries, who
had in the meanwhile sat quietly down beside the
stone bottle, and made up acquaintance over a glass
of its contents—" Let me remind you, that the
night wears late."

" There is something cries tinkle, tinkle, in the
bottle yet," said Wildrake, in reply.

" Hem! hem! hem!" coughed the Colonel of
the Parliament service; and if his lips did not curse
his companion's imprudence, I will not answer for
what arose in his heart.—" Well!" he said, observing that Wildrake had filled his own glass and
Tomkins's, " take that parting glass and begone."

" Would you not be pleased to hear first," said
Wildrake, "how this honest gentleman saw the
devil to-night look through a pane of yonder window, and how he thinks he had a mighty strong
resemblance to your worship's humble slave and
varlet scribbler? Would you but hear this, sir, and
just sip a glass of this very recommendable strong
waters?"

"I will drink none, sir," said Colonel Everard sternly; "and I have to tell *you*, that you have drunken a glass too much already.—Mr Tomkins, sir, I wish you good-night."

"A word in season at parting," said Tomkins, standing up behind the long leathern back of a chair, hemming and snuffling as if preparing for an exhortation.

"Excuse me, sir," replied Markham Everard; "you are not now sufficiently yourself to guide the devotion of others."

"Woe be to them that reject!" said the Secretary of the Commissioners, stalking out of the room—the rest was lost in shutting the door, or suppressed for fear of offence.

"And now, fool Wildrake, begone to thy bed—yonder it lies," pointing to the knight's apartment.

"What, thou hast secured the lady's for thyself? I saw thee put the key in thy pocket."

"I would not—indeed I could not sleep in that apartment—I can sleep nowhere—but I will watch in this arm-chair. I have made him place wood for repairing the fire.—Good now, go to bed thyself, and sleep off thy liquor."

"Liquor!—I laugh thee to scorn, Mark—thou art a milksop, and the son of a milksop, and know'st not what a good fellow can do in the way of crushing an honest cup."

"The whole vices of his faction are in this poor fellow individually," said the Colonel to himself, eyeing his protegé askance, as the other retreated into the bedroom, with no very steady pace—"He is reckless, intemperate, dissolute ; and if I cannot get him safely shipped for France, he will certainly be both his own ruin and mine.—Yet, withal, he is kind, brave, and generous, and would have kept the faith with me which he now expects from me ; and in what consists the merit of our truth, if we observe not our plighted word when we have promised to our hurt ?   I will take the liberty, however, to secure myself against farther interruption on his part."

So saying, he locked the door of communication betwixt the sleeping-room, to which the cavalier had retreated, and the parlour ;—and then, after pacing the floor thoughtfully, returned to his seat, trimmed the lamp, and drew out a number of letters.—" I will read these over once more," he said, " that, if possible, the thought of public affairs may expel this keen sense of personal sorrow. Gracious Providence, where is this to end ! We have sacrificed the peace of our families, the warmest wishes of our young hearts, to right the country in which we were born, and to free her from oppression ; yet it appears, that every step we have made towards liberty, has but brought us in view of new and more terrific perils, as he who travels in a mountainous region, is, by every step which elevates him higher, placed in a situation of more imminent hazard."

He read long and attentively, various tedious and embarrassed letters, in which the writers, placing before him the glory of God, and the freedom and liberties of England, as their supreme ends, could not, by all the ambagitory expressions they made use of, prevent the shrewd eye of Markham Everard from seeing, that self-interest and views of ambition were the principal moving-springs at the bottom of their plots.

CHAPTER VI.

Sleep steals on us even like his brother Death—
We know not when it comes—we know it must come—
We may affect to scorn and to contemn it,
For 'tis the highest pride of human misery
To say it knows not of an opiate.
Yet the reft parent, the despairing lover,
Even the poor wretch who waits for execution,
Feels this oblivion, against which he thought
His woes had arm'd his senses, steal upon him,
And through the fenceless citadel —the body—
Surprise that haughty garrison—the mind.

HERBERT.

COLONEL EVERARD experienced the truth contained in the verses of the quaint old bard whom we have quoted above. Amid private grief, and anxiety for a country long a prey to civil war, and not likely to fall soon under any fixed or well-established form of government, Everard and his father had, like many others, turned their eyes to General Cromwell, as the person whose valour had made him the darling of the army, whose strong sagacity had hitherto predominated over the high talents by which he had been assailed in Parliament, as well as over his enemies in the field, and who was alone in the situation to *settle the nation*, as the phrase then went ; or, in other words, to dictate the mode of government. The father and son were both reputed to stand high in the General's favour. But Markham Everard was conscious of some particulars, which induced him to doubt whether Cromwell actually, and at heart, bore either to his father or to himself that good-will which was generally believed. He knew him for a profound politician, who could veil for any length of time his real sentiments of men and things, until they could be displayed without prejudice to his interest. And he moreover knew that the General was not likely to forget the opposition which the Presbyterian party had offered to what Oliver called the Great Matter —the trial, namely, and execution of the King. In this opposition, his father and he had anxiously concurred, nor had the arguments, nor even the half-expressed threats of Cromwell, induced them to flinch from that course, far less to permit their names to be introduced into the commission nominated to sit in judgment on that memorable occasion.

This hesitation had occasioned some temporary coldness between the General and the Everards, father and son. But as the latter remained in the army, and bore arms under Cromwell both in Scotland, and finally at Worcester, his services very frequently called forth the approbation of his commander. After the fight of Worcester, in particular, he was among the number of those officers on whom Oliver, rather considering the actual and practical extent of his own power, than the name under which he exercised it, was with difficulty withheld from imposing the dignity of Knights-Bannerets at his own will and pleasure. It therefore seemed, that all recollection of former disagreement was obliterated, and that the Everards had regained their former stronghold in the General's affections. There were, indeed, several who doubted this, and who endeavoured to bring over this distinguished young officer to some other of the parties which divided the infant Commonwealth. But to these proposals he turned a deaf ear. Enough of blood, he said, had been spilled—it was time that the nation should have repose under a firmly-established government, of strength sufficient to protect property, and of lenity enough to encourage the return of tranquillity. This, he thought, could only be accomplished by means of Cromwell, and the greater part of England was of the same opinion. It is true, that, in thus submitting to the domination of a successful soldier, those who did so, forgot the principles upon which they had drawn the sword against the late King. But in revolutions, stern and high principles are often obliged to give way to the current of existing circumstances; and in many a case, where wars have been waged for points of metaphysical right, they have been at last gladly terminated, upon the mere hope of obtaining general tranquillity, as, after many a long siege, a garrison is often glad to submit on mere security for life and limb.

Colonel Everard, therefore, felt that the support which he afforded Cromwell, was only under the idea, that, amid a choice of evils, the least was likely to ensue from a man of the General's wisdom and valour being placed at the head of the state; and be was sensible, that Oliver himself was likely to consider his attachment as lukewarm and imperfect, and measure his gratitude for it upon the same limited scale.

In the meanwhile, however, circumstances compelled him to make trial of the General's friendship. The sequestration of Woodstock, and the warrant to the Commissioners to dispose of it as national property, had been long granted, but the interest of the elder Everard had for weeks and months deferred its execution. The hour was now approaching when the blow could be no longer parried, especially as Sir Henry Lee, on his side, resisted every proposal of submitting himself to the existing government, and was therefore, now that his hour of grace was passed, enrolled in the list of stubborn and irreclaimable malignants, with whom the Council of State was determined no longer to keep terms. The only mode of protecting the old knight and his daughter, was to interest, if possible, the General himself in the matter; and revolving all the circumstances connected with their intercourse, Colonel Everard felt that a request, which would so immediately interfere with the interests of Desborough, the brother-in-law of Cromwell, and one of the present Commissioners, was putting to a very severe trial the friendship of the latter. Yet no alternative remained.

With this view, and agreeably to a request from Cromwell, who at parting had been very urgent to have his written opinion upon public affairs, Colonel Everard passed the earlier part of the night in arranging his ideas upon the state of the Commonwealth, in a plan which he thought likely to be acceptable to Cromwell, as it exhorted him, under the aid of Providence, to become the saviour of the state, by convoking a free Parliament, and by their aid placing himself at the head of some form of liberal and established government, which might supersede the state of anarchy, in which the nation was otherwise likely to be merged. Taking a general view of the totally broken condition of the Royalists, and of the various factions which now convulsed the state, he showed how this might be done without bloodshed or violence. From this topic he descended to the propriety of keeping up the becoming state of the Executive Government, in whose hands soever it should be lodged, and thus showed Cromwell, as the future Stadtholder, or Consul, or Lieutenant-General of Great Britain and Ireland, a prospect of demesne and residences becoming his dignity. Then he naturally passed to the disparking and destroying of the royal residences of England, made a woful picture of the demolition which impended over Woodstock, and interceded for the preservation of that beautiful seat, as a matter of personal favour, in which he found himself deeply interested.

Colonel Everard, when he had finished his letter, did not find himself greatly risen in his own opinion. In the course of his political conduct, he had till this hour avoided mixing up personal motives with his public grounds of action, and yet he now felt himself making such a composition.

But he comforted himself, or at least silenced this unpleasing recollection, with the consideration, that the weal of Britain, studied under the aspect of the times, absolutely required that Cromwell should be at the head of the government; and that the interest of Sir Henry Lee, or rather his safety and his existence, no less emphatically demanded the preservation of Woodstock, and his residence there. Was it a fault of his, that the same road should lead to both these ends, or that his private interest, and that of the country, should happen to mix in the same letter? He hardened himself, therefore, to the act, made up and addressed his packet to the Lord General, and then sealed it with his seal of arms. This done, he lay back in his chair; and, in spite of his expectations to the contrary, fell asleep in the course of his reflections, anxious and harassing as they were, and did not awaken until the cold grey light of dawn was peeping through the eastern oriel.

He started at first, rousing himself with the sensation of one who awakes in a place unknown to him; but the localities instantly forced themselves on his recollection. The lamp burning dimly in the socket, the wood fire almost extinguished in its own white embers, the gloomy picture over the chimney-piece, the sealed packet on the table—all reminded him of the events of yesterday, and his deliberations of the succeeding night.

"There is no help for it," he said; "it must be Cromwell or anarchy. And probably the sense that his title, as head of the Executive Government, is derived merely from popular consent, may check the too natural proneness of power to render itself arbitrary. If he govern by Parliaments, and with regard to the privileges of the subject, wherefore not Oliver as well as Charles? But I must take measures for having this conveyed safely to the hands of this future sovereign prince. It will be well to take the first word of influence with him, since there must be many who will not hesitate to recommend counsels more violent and precipitate."

He determined to intrust the important packet to the charge of Wildrake, whose rashness was never so distinguished, as when by any chance he was left idle and unemployed; besides, even if his faith had not been otherwise unimpeachable, the obligations which he owed to his friend Everard must have rendered it such.

These conclusions passed through Colonel Everard's mind, as, collecting the remains of wood in the chimney, he gathered them into a hearty blaze, to remove the uncomfortable feeling of chillness which pervaded his limbs; and by the time he was a little more warm, again sunk into a slumber, which was only dispelled by the beams of morning peeping into his apartment.

He arose, roused himself, walked up and down the room, and looked from the large oriel window on the nearest objects, which were the untrimmed hedges and neglected walks of a certain wilderness, as it is called in ancient treatises on gardening, which, kept of yore well ordered, and in all the pride of the topiary art, presented a succession of yew-trees cut into fantastic forms, of close alleys, and of open walks, filling about two or three acres of ground on that side of the Lodge, and forming a boundary between its immediate precincts and the open Park. Its enclosure was now broken down in many places, and the hinds with their fawns fed free and unstartled up to the very windows of the silvan palace.

This had been a favourite scene of Markham's sports when a boy. He could still distinguish, though now grown out of shape, the verdant battlements of a Gothic castle, all created by the gardener's shears, at which he was accustomed to shoot his arrows; or, stalking before it like the knight-errants of whom he read, was wont to blow his horn, and bid defiance to the supposed giant or Paynim knight, by whom it was garrisoned. He remembered how he used to train his cousin, though several years younger than himself, to bear a part in those revels of his boyish fancy, and to play the character of an elfin page, or a fairy, or an enchanted princess. He remembered, too, many particulars of their later acquaintance, from which he had been almost necessarily led to the conclusion, that from an early period their parents had entertained some idea, that there might be a well-fitted match betwixt his fair cousin and himself. A thousand visions, formed in so bright a prospect, had vanished along with it, but now returned like shadows, to remind him of all he had lost—and for what?—" For the sake of England," his proud

consciousness replied,—" Of England, in danger
of becoming the prey at once of bigotry and tyranny." And he strengthened himself with the
recollection, " If I have sacrificed my private happiness, it is that my country may enjoy liberty of
conscience, and personal freedom; which, under a
weak prince and usurping statesman, she was but
too likely to have lost."

But the busy fiend in his breast would not be
repulsed by the bold answer. "Has thy resistance,"
it demanded, "availed thy country, Markham Everard? Lies not England, after so much bloodshed,
and so much misery, as low beneath the sword of a
fortunate soldier, as formerly under the sceptre of
an encroaching prince? Are Parliament, or what
remains of them, fitted to contend with a leader,
master of his soldiers' hearts, as bold and subtle as
he is impenetrable in his designs? This General,
who holds the army, and by that the fate of the
nation in his hand, will he lay down his power because philosophy would pronounce it his duty to
become a subject?"

He dared not answer that his knowledge of Cromwell authorized him to expect any such act of self-
denial. Yet still he considered that in times of such
infinite difficulty, that must be the best government,
however little desirable in itself, which should most
speedily restore peace to the land, and stop the
wounds which the contending parties were daily
inflicting on each other. He imagined that Cromwell was the only authority under which a steady
government could be formed, and therefore had

attached himself to his fortune, though not without considerable and recurring doubts, how far serving the views of this impenetrable and mysterious General was consistent with the principles under which he had assumed arms.

While these things passed in his mind, Everard looked upon the packet which lay on the table addressed to the Lord General, and which he had made up before sleep. He hesitated several times, when he remembered its purport, and in what degree he must stand committed with that personage, and bound to support his plans of aggrandizement, when once that communication was in Oliver Cromwell's possession.

" Yet it must be so," he said at last, with a deep sigh. " Among the contending parties, he is the strongest—the wisest and most moderate—and ambitious though he be, perhaps not the most dangerous. Some one must be trusted with power to preserve and enforce general order, and who can possess or wield such power like him that is head of the victorious armies of England? Come what will in future, peace and the restoration of law ought to be our first and most pressing object. This remnant of a parliament cannot keep their ground against the army, by mere appeal to the sanction of opinion. If they design to reduce the soldiery, it must be by actual warfare, and the land has been too long steeped in blood. But Cromwell may, and I trust will, make a moderate accommodation with them, on grounds by which peace may be preserved; and it is this to which we must look and trust for a settlement of the kingdom, alas! and for the chance of protecting my obstinate kinsman from the consequences of his honest though absurd pertinacity."

Silencing some internal feelings of doubt and reluctance by such reasoning as this, Markham Everard continued in his resolution to unite himself with Cromwell in the struggle which was evidently approaching betwixt the civil and military authorities; not as the course which, if at perfect liberty, he would have preferred adopting, but as the best choice between two dangerous extremities to which the times had reduced him. He could not help trembling, however, when he recollected that his father, though hitherto the admirer of Cromwell, as the implement by whom so many marvels had been wrought in England, might not be disposed to unite with his interest against that of the Long Parliament, of which he had been, till partly laid aside by continued indisposition, an active and leading member. This doubt also he was obliged to swallow, or strangle, as he might; but consoled himself with the ready argument, that it was impossible his father could see matters in another light than that in which they occurred to himself.

CHAPTER VII.

DETERMINED at length to dispatch his packet to the General without delay, Colonel Everard approached the door of the apartment, in which, as was evident from the heavy breathing within, the prisoner Wildrake enjoyed a deep slumber, under the influence of liquor at once and of fatigue. In turning the key, the bolt, which was rather rusty, made a resistance so noisy, as partly to attract the sleeper's attention, though not to awake him. Everard stood by his bedside, as he heard him mutter, " Is it morning already, jailer?—Why, you dog, an you had but a cast of humanity in you, you would qualify your vile news with a cup of sack;—hanging is sorry work, my masters—and sorrow's dry."

" Up, Wildrake—up, thou ill-omened dreamer!" said his friend, shaking him by the collar.

" Hands off!" answered the sleeper.—" I can climb a ladder without help, I trow."—He then sat up in the bed, and opening his eyes, stared around him, and exclaimed, " Zounds! Mark, is it only thou? I thought it was all over with me—fetters were struck from my legs—rope drawn round my gullet—irons knocked off my hands—all ready for a dance in the open element upon slight footing."

"Truce with thy folly, Wildrake! Sure the devil of drink, to whom thou hast, I think, sold thyself"——

"For a hogshead of sack," interrupted Wildrake; "the bargain was made in a cellar in the Vintry."

"I am as mad as thou art, to trust any thing to thee," said Markham; "I scarce believe thou hast thy senses yet."

"What should ail me?" said Wildrake—"I trust I have not tasted liquor in my sleep, saving that I dreamed of drinking small-beer with Old Noll, of his own brewing. But do not look so glum, man—I am the same Roger Wildrake that I ever was; as wild as a mallard, but as true as a game-cock. I am thine own chum, man—bound to thee by thy kind deeds—*devinctus beneficio*—there is Latin for it; and where is the thing thou wilt charge me with, that I will not, or dare not execute, were it to pick the devil's teeth with my rapier, after he had breakfasted upon roundheads?"

"You will drive me mad," said Everard.—— "When I am about to intrust all I have most valuable on earth to your management, your conduct and language are those of a mere Bedlamite. Last night I made allowance for thy drunken fury; but who can endure thy morning madness?—it is unsafe for thyself and me, Wildrake—it is unkind —I might say ungrateful."

"Nay, do not say *that*, my friend," said the cavalier, with some show of feeling; "and do not judge of me with a severity that cannot apply to such as I am. We who have lost our all in these sad jars, who are compelled to shift for our living, not from day to day, but from meal to meal—we whose only hiding-place is the jail, whose prospect of final repose is the gallows,—what canst thou expect from us, but to bear such a lot with a light heart, since we should break down under it with a heavy one?"

This was spoken in a tone of feeling which found a responding string in Everard's bosom. He took his friend's hand, and pressed it kindly.

" Nay, if I seemed harsh to thee, Wildrake, I profess it was for thine own sake more than mine. I know thou hast at the bottom of thy levity, as deep a principle of honour and feeling as ever governed a human heart. But thou art thoughtless—thou art rash—and I protest to thee, that wert thou to betray thyself in this matter in which I trust thee, the evil consequences to myself would not afflict me more than the thought of putting thee into such danger."

" Nay, if you take it on that tone, Mark," said the cavalier, making an effort to laugh, evidently that he might conceal a tendency to a different emotion, " thou wilt make children of us both—babes and sucklings, by the hilt of this bilbo.—Come, trust me ; I can be cautious when time requires it—no man ever saw me drink when an alert was expected—and not one poor pint of wine will I taste until I have managed this matter for thee. Well, I am thy secretary—clerk—I had forgot—and carry thy dispatches to Cromwell, taking good

heed not to be surprised or choused out of my lump
of loyalty, [striking his finger on the packet,] and
I am to deliver it to the most loyal hands to which
it is most humbly addressed—Adzooks, Mark, think
of it a moment longer—Surely thou wilt not carry
thy perverseness so far, as to strike in with this
bloody-minded rebel?—Bid me give him three
inches of my dudgeon-dagger, and I will do it much
more willingly than present him with thy packet."

" Go to," replied Everard, " this is beyond our
bargain. If you will help me, it is well; if not, let
me lose no time in debating with thee, since I think
every moment an age till the packet is in the
General's possession. It is the only way left me to
obtain some protection, and a place of refuge, for
my uncle and his daughter."

" That being the case," said the cavalier, " I
will not spare the spur. My nag up yonder at the
town will be ready for the road in a trice, and thou
mayst reckon on my being with Old Noll—thy
General, I mean—in as short time as man and horse
may consume betwixt Woodstock and Windsor,
where I think I shall for the present find thy friend
keeping possession where he has slain."

" Hush, not a word of that. Since we parted
last night, I have shaped thee a path which will
suit thee better than to assume the decency of language, and of outward manner, of which thou hast
so little. I have acquainted the General that thou
hast been by bad example and bad education"——

" Which is to be interpreted by contraries, I
hope," said Wildrake; " for sure I have been as

well born and bred up as any lad of Leicestershire might desire."

"Now, I prithee hush—thou hast, I say, by bad example, become at one time a malignant, and mixed in the party of the late King. But seeing what things were wrought in the nation by the General, thou hast come to a clearness touching his calling to be a great implement in the settlement of these distracted kingdoms. This account of thee will not only lead him to pass over some of thy eccentricities, should they break out in spite of thee, but will also give thee an interest with him as being more especially attached to his own person."

"Doubtless," said Wildrake, "as every fisher loves best the trouts that are of his own tickling."

"It is likely, I think, he will send thee hither with letters to me," said the Colonel, "enabling me to put a stop to the proceedings of these sequestrators, and to give poor old Sir Henry Lee permission to linger out his days among the oaks he loves to look upon. I have made this my request to General Cromwell, and I think my father's friendship and my own may stretch so far on his regard without risk of cracking, especially standing matters as they now do—thou dost understand?"

"Entirely well," said the cavalier; "stretch, quotha!—I would rather stretch a rope than hold commerce with the old King-killing ruffian. But I have said I will be guided by thee, Markham, and rat me but I will."

"Be cautious then," said Everard, "mark well what he does and says—more especially what he does; for Oliver is one of those whose mind is better known by his actions than by his words—and stay—I warrant thee thou wert setting off without a cross in thy purse?"

" Too true, Mark," said Wildrake, " the last noble melted last night among yonder blackguard troopers of yours."

" Well, Roger," replied the Colonel, " that is easily mended." So saying, he slipped his purse into his friend's hand. " But art thou not an inconsiderate weather-brained fellow, to set forth, as thou wert about to do, without any thing to bear thy charges—what couldst thou have done?"

" Faith, I never thought of that—I must have cried *Stand*, I suppose, to the first pursy townsman, or greasy grazier, that I met o' the heath—it is many a good fellow's shift in these bad times."

" Go to," said Everard; " be cautious—use none of your loose acquaintance—rule your tongue—beware of the wine-pot—for there is little danger if thou couldst only but keep thyself sober—Be moderate in speech, and forbear oaths or vaunting."

" In short, metamorphose myself into such a prig as thou art, Mark?—Well," said Wildrake, " so far as outside will go, I think I can make a *Hope-on-high Bomby** as well as thou canst. Ah! those were merry days when we saw Mills present Bomby at the Fortune playhouse, Mark, ere I had lost my laced cloak and the jewel in my ear, or

* A puritanic character in one of Beaumont and Fletcher's plays.

thou hadst gotten the wrinkle on thy brow, and the puritanic twist of thy mustache!"

"They were like most worldly pleasures, Wild-rake," replied Everard, "sweet in the mouth and bitter in digestion.—But away with thee; and when thou bring'st back my answer, thou wilt find me either here or at Saint George's Inn, at the little borough.—Good luck to thee—Be but cautious how thou bearest thyself."

The Colonel remained in deep meditation.—"I think," he said, "I have not pledged myself too far to the General. A breach between him and the Parliament seems inevitable, and would throw England back into civil war, of which all men are wearied. He may dislike my messenger—yet that I do not greatly fear. He knows I would choose such as I can myself depend on, and hath dealt enough with the stricter sort to be aware that there are among them, as well as elsewhere, men who can hide two faces under one hood."

CHAPTER VIII.

For there in lofty air was seen to stand
The stern Protector of the conquer'd land;
Drawn in that look with which he wept and swore,
Turn'd out the members, and made fast the door,
Ridding the house of every knave and drone,
Forced—though it grieved his soul—to rule alone.
                    The Frank Courtship.—CRABBE.

LEAVING Colonel Everard to his meditations, we follow the jolly cavalier, his companion, who, before mounting at the George, did not fail to treat himself to his morning draught of eggs and muscadine, to enable him to face the harvest wind.

Although he had suffered himself to be sunk in the extravagant license which was practised by the cavaliers, as if to oppose their conduct in every point to the preciseness of their enemies, yet Wildrake, well-born and well-educated, and endowed with good natural parts, and a heart which even debauchery, and the wild life of a roaring cavalier, had not been able entirely to corrupt, moved on his present embassy with a strange mixture of feelings, such as perhaps he had never in his life before experienced.

His feelings as a loyalist led him to detest Cromwell, whom in other circumstances he would scarce have wished to see, except in a field of battle, where he could have had the pleasure to exchange pistol-shots with him. But with this hatred there was mixed a certain degree of fear. Always victorious wherever he fought, the remarkable person whom Wildrake was now approaching had acquired that influence over the minds of his enemies, which constant success is so apt to inspire—they dreaded while they hated him—and joined to these feelings, was a restless meddling curiosity, which made a particular feature in Wildrake's character, who, having long had little business of his own, and caring nothing about that which he had, was easily attracted by the desire of seeing whatever was curious or interesting around him.

"I should like to see the old rascal after all," he said, "were it but to say that I *had* seen him."

He reached Windsor in the afternoon, and felt on his arrival the strongest inclination to take up his residence at some of his old haunts, when he had occasionally frequented that fair town in gayer days. But resisting all temptations of this kind, he went courageously to the principal inn, from which its ancient emblem, the Garter, had long disappeared. The master, too, whom Wildrake, experienced in his knowledge of landlords and hostelries, had remembered a dashing Mine Host of Queen Bess's school, had now sobered down to the temper of the times, shook his head when he spoke of the Parliament, wielded his spigot with the gravity of a priest conducting a sacrifice, wished England a happy issue out of all her afflictions, and greatly lauded his Excellency the Lord General.

Wildrake also remarked, that his wine was better than it was wont to be, the Puritans having an excellent gift at detecting every fallacy in that matter; and that his measures were less and his charges larger—circumstances which he was induced to attend to, by mine host talking a good deal about his conscience.

He was told by this important personage, that the Lord General received frankly all sorts of persons; and that he might obtain access to him next morning, at eight o'clock, for the trouble of presenting himself at the Castle-gate, and announcing himself as the bearer of dispatches to his Excellency.

To the Castle the disguised cavalier repaired at the hour appointed. Admittance was freely permitted to him by the red-coated soldier, who, with austere looks, and his musket on his shoulder, mounted guard at the external gate of that noble building. Wildrake crossed through the under ward, or court, gazing as he passed upon the beautiful Chapel, which had but lately received, in darkness and silence, the unhonoured remains of the slaughtered King of England. Rough as Wildrake was, the recollection of this circumstance affected him so strongly, that he had nearly turned back in a sort of horror, rather than face the dark and daring man, to whom, amongst all the actors in that melancholy affair, its tragic conclusion was chiefly to be imputed. But he felt the necessity of subduing all sentiments of this nature, and compelled himself to proceed in a negotiation intrusted to his conduct

by one to whom he was so much obliged as Colonel
Everard. At the ascent, which passed by the Round
Tower, he looked to the ensign-staff, from which
the banner of England was wont to float. It was
gone, with all its rich emblazonry, its gorgeous
quarterings, and splendid embroidery; and in its
room waved that of the Commonwealth, the cross
of Saint George, in its colours of blue and red, not
yet intersected by the diagonal cross of Scotland,
which was soon after assumed, as if in evidence of
England's conquest over her ancient enemy. This
change of ensigns increased the train of his gloomy
reflections, in which, although contrary to his wont,
he became so deeply wrapped, that the first thing
which recalled him to himself, was the challenge
from the sentinel, accompanied with a stroke of the
but of his musket on the pavement, with an emphasis which made Wildrake start.

"Whither away, and who are you?"

"The bearer of a packet," answered Wildrake,
"to the worshipful the Lord General."

"Stand till I call the officer of the guard."

The corporal made his appearance, distinguished
above those of his command by a double quantity
of band round his neck, a double height of steeple-
crowned hat, a larger allowance of cloak, and a
treble proportion of sour gravity of aspect. It
might be read on his countenance, that he was one
of those resolute enthusiasts to whom Oliver owed
his conquests, whose religious zeal made them even
more than a match for the high-spirited and high-
born cavaliers, that exhausted their valour in vain

defence of their sovereign's person and crown. He looked with grave solemnity at Wildrake, as if he was making in his own mind an inventory of his features and dress; and having fully perused them, he required "to know his business."

"My business," said Wildrake, as firmly as he could—for the close investigation of this man had given him some unpleasant nervous sensations— "my business is with your General."

"With his Excellency the Lord General, thou wouldst say?" replied the corporal. "Thy speech, my friend, savours too little of the reverence due to his Excellency."

"D—n his Excellency!" was at the lips of the cavalier; but prudence kept guard, and permitted not the offensive words to escape the barrier. He only bowed, and was silent.

"Follow me," said the starched figure whom he addressed; and Wildrake followed him accordingly, into the guard-house, which exhibited an interior characteristic of the times, and very different from what such military stations present at the present day.

By the fire sat two or three musketeers, listening to one who was expounding some religious mystery to them. He began half beneath his breath, but in tones of great volubility, which tones, as he approached the conclusion, became sharp and eager, as challenging either instant answer or silent acquiescence. The audience seemed to listen to the speaker with immovable features, only answering him with clouds of tobacco-smoke, which they rolled

from under their thick mustaches.   On a bench lay
a soldier on his face ; whether asleep, or in a fit of
contemplation, it was impossible to decide.   In the
midst of the floor stood an officer, as he seemed by
his embroidered shoulder-belt and scarf round his
waist, otherwise very plainly attired, who was engaged in drilling a stout bumpkin, lately enlisted,
to the manual, as it was then used.   The motions
and words of command were twenty at the very
least ; and until they were regularly brought to an
end, the corporal did not permit Wildrake either
to sit down, or move forward beyond the threshold
of the guard-house.   So he had to listen in succession to—Poise your musket—Rest your musket
—Cock your musket—Handle your primers—and
many other forgotten words of discipline, until at
length the words, " Order your musket," ended the
drill for the time.

    " Thy name, friend ?" said the officer to the
recruit, when the lesson was over.

    " Ephraim," answered the fellow, with an affect-
ed twang through the nose.

    " And what besides Ephraim ?"

    " Ephraim Cobb, from the godly city of Glocos-
ter, where I have dwelt for seven years, serving
apprentice to a praiseworthy cordwainer."

    " It is a goodly craft," answered the officer ; " but
casting in thy lot with ours, doubt not that thou
shalt be set beyond thine awl, and thy last to boot."

    A grim smile of the speaker accompanied this
poor attempt at a pun ; and then turning round to
the corporal, who stood two paces off, with the face

of one who seemed desirous of speaking, said,
" How now, corporal, what tidings ?"

" Here is one with a packet, an please your Excellency," said the corporal—" Surely my spirit
doth not rejoice in him, seeing I esteem him as a
wolf in sheep's clothing."

By these words, Wildrake learned that he was
in the actual presence of the remarkable person to
whom he was commissioned ; and he paused to consider in what manner he ought to address him.

The figure of Oliver Cromwell was, as is generally known, in no way prepossessing. He was
of middle stature, strong, and coarsely made, with
harsh and severe features, indicative, however, of
much natural sagacity and depth of thought. His
eyes were grey and piercing ; his nose too large in
proportion to his other features, and of a reddish
hue.

His manner of speaking, when he had the purpose to make himself distinctly understood, was
energetic and forcible, though neither graceful nor
eloquent. No man could on such occasions put his
meaning into fewer and more decisive words. But
when, as it often happened, he had a mind to play
the orator, for the benefit of people's ears, without
enlightening their understanding, Cromwell was
wont to invest his meaning, or that which seemed
to be his meaning, in such a mist of words, sur-
rounding it with so many exclusions and exceptions,
and fortifying it with such a labyrinth of paren-
theses, that though one of the most shrewd men
in England, he was, perhaps, the most unintelligible

speaker that ever perplexed an audience. It has been long since said by the historian, that a collection of the Protector's speeches would make, with a few exceptions, the most nonsensical book in the world; but he ought to have added, that nothing could be more nervous, concise, and intelligible, than what he really intended should be understood.

It was also remarked of Cromwell, that though born of a good family, both by father and mother, and although he had the usual opportunities of education and breeding connected with such an advantage, the fanatic democratic ruler could never acquire, or else disdained to practise, the courtesies usually exercised among the higher classes in their intercourse with each other. His demeanour was so blunt as sometimes might be termed clownish, yet there was in his language and manner a force and energy corresponding to his character, which impressed awe, if it did not impose respect; and there were even times when that dark and subtle spirit expanded itself, so as almost to conciliate affection. The turn for humour, which displayed itself by fits, was broad, and of a low, and sometimes practical character. Something there was in his disposition congenial to that of his countrymen; a contempt of folly, a hatred of affectation, and a dislike of ceremony, which, joined to the strong intrinsic qualities of sense and courage, made him in many respects not an unfit representative of the democracy of England.

His religion must always be a subject of much doubt, and probably of doubt which he himself could hardly have cleared up. Unquestionably there was a time in his life when he was sincerely enthusiastic, and when his natural temper, slightly subject to hypochondria, was strongly agitated by the same fanaticism which influenced so many persons of the time. On the other hand, there were periods during his political career, when we certainly do him no injustice in charging him with a hypocritical affectation. We shall probably judge him, and others of the same age, most truly, if we suppose that their religious professions were partly influential in their own breast, partly assumed in compliance with their own interest. And so ingenious is the human heart in deceiving itself as well as others, that it is probable neither Cromwell himself, nor those making similar pretensions to distinguished piety, could exactly have fixed the point at which their enthusiasm terminated and their hypocrisy commenced ; or rather, it was a point not fixed in itself, but fluctuating with the state of health, of good or bad fortune, of high or low spirits, affecting the individual at the period.

Such was the celebrated person, who, turning round on Wildrake, and scanning his countenance closely, seemed so little satisfied with what he beheld, that he instinctively hitched forward his belt, so as to bring the handle of his tuck-sword within his reach. But yet, folding his arms in his cloak, as if upon second thoughts laying aside suspicion, or thinking precaution beneath him, he asked the cavalier what he was, and whence he came ?

*

" A poor gentleman, sir,—that is, my lord,"—answered Wildrake ; " last from Woodstock."

" And what may your tidings be, sir *gentleman?*" said Cromwell, with an emphasis. " Truly I have seen those most willing to take upon them that title, bear themselves somewhat short of wise men, and good men, and true men, with all their gentility : Yet gentleman was a good title in old England, when men remembered what it was construed to mean."

" You say truly, sir," replied Wildrake, suppressing, with difficulty, some of his usual wild expletives ; " formerly gentlemen were found in gentlemen's places, but now the world is so changed, that you shall find the broidered belt has changed place with the under spur-leather."

" Say'st thou me?" said the General ; " I profess thou art a bold companion, that can bandy words so wantonly ;—thou ring'st somewhat too loud to be good metal, methinks : And once again what are thy tidings with me ?"

" This packet," said Wildrake, " commended to your hands by Colonel Markham Everard."

" Alas, I must have mistaken thee," answered Cromwell, mollified at the mention of a man's name whom he had great desire to make his own ; " forgive us, good friend, for such, we doubt not, thou art. Sit thee down, and commune with thyself as thou mayst, until we have examined the contents of thy packet. Let him be looked to, and have what he lacks." So saying, the General left the guard-house, where Wildrake took his seat in the corner, and awaited with patience the issue of his mission.

The soldiers now thought themselves obliged to treat him with more consideration, and offered him a pipe of Trinidado, and a black jack filled with October. But the look of Cromwell, and the dangerous situation in which he might be placed by the least chance of detection, induced Wildrake to decline these hospitable offers, and stretching back in his chair, and affecting slumber, he escaped notice or conversation, until a sort of aide-de-camp, or military officer in attendance, came to summon him to Cromwell's presence.

By this person he was guided to a postern-gate, through which he entered the body of the Castle, and penetrating through many private passages and staircases, he at length was introduced into a small cabinet or parlour, in which was much rich furniture, some bearing the royal cipher displayed, but all confused and disarranged, together with several paintings in massive frames, having their faces turned towards the wall, as if they had been taken down for the purpose of being removed.

In this scene of disorder, the victorious General of the Commonwealth was seated in a large easy-chair, covered with damask, and deeply embroidered, the splendour of which made a strong contrast with the plain, and even homely character of his apparel; although in look and action he seemed like one who felt that the seat which might have in former days held a prince, was not too much distinguished for his own fortunes and ambition. Wild-

1

rake stood before him, nor did he ask him to sit down.

"Pearson," said Cromwell, addressing himself to the officer in attendance, "wait in the gallery, but be within call." Pearson bowed, and was retiring. "Who are in the gallery besides?"

"Worthy Mr Gordon, the chaplain, was holding forth but now to Colonel Overton, and four captains of your Excellency's regiment."

"We would have it so," said the General; "we would not there were any corner in our dwelling where the hungry soul might not meet with manna. Was the good man carried onward in his discourse?"

"Mightily borne through," said Pearson; "and he was touching the rightful claims which the army, and especially your Excellency, hath acquired, by becoming the instruments in the great work;—not instruments to be broken asunder and cast away when the day of their service is over, but to be preserved and held precious, and prized for their honourable and faithful labours, for which they have fought and marched, and fasted and prayed, and suffered cold and sorrow; while others, who would now gladly see them disbanded, and broken, and cashiered, eat of the fat and drink of the strong."

"Ah, good man!" said Cromwell, "and did he touch upon this so feelingly? I could say something—but not now. Begone, Pearson, to the gallery. Let not our friends lay aside their swords, but watch as well as pray."

Pearson retired; and the General, holding the

VOL. XXXIX. K

letter of Everard in his hand, looked again for a long while fixedly at Wildrake, as if considering in what strain he should address him.

When he did speak, it was, at first, in one of those ambiguous discourses which we have already described, and by which it was very difficult for any one to understand his meaning, if, indeed, he knew it himself. We shall be as concise in our statement, as our desire to give the very words of a man so extraordinary will permit.

" This letter," he said, " you have brought us from your master, or patron, Markham Everard ; truly an excellent and honourable gentleman as ever bore a sword upon his thigh, and one who hath ever distinguished himself in the great work of delivering these three poor and unhappy nations. Answer me not : I know what thou wouldst say.— And this letter he hath sent to me by thee, his clerk, or secretary, in whom he hath confidence, and in whom he prays me to have trust, that there may be a careful messenger between us. And lastly, he hath sent thee to me—Do not answer—I know what thou wouldst say,—to me, who, albeit I am of that small consideration, that it would be too much honour for me even to bear a halberd in this great and victorious army of England, am nevertheless exalted to the rank of holding the guidance and the leading-staff thereof.—Nay, do not answer, my friend—I know what thou wouldst say. Now, when communing thus together, our discourse taketh, in respect to what I have said, a threefold argument, or division : First, as it concerneth thy

master; secondly, as it concerneth us and our office; thirdly and lastly, as it toucheth thyself.——
Now, as concerning this good and worthy gentleman, Colonel Markham Everard, truly he hath played the man from the beginning of these unhappy buffetings, not turning to the right or to the left, but holding ever in his eye the mark at which he aimed. Ay, truly, a faithful, honourable gentleman, and one who may well call me friend; and truly I am pleased to think that he doth so. Nevertheless, in this vale of tears, we must be governed less by our private respects and partialities, than by those higher principles and points of duty, whereupon the good Colonel Markham Everard hath ever framed his purposes, as, truly, I have endeavoured to form mine, that we may all act as becometh good Englishmen and worthy patriots. Then, as for Woodstock, it is a great thing which the good Colonel asks, that it should be taken from the spoil of the godly, and left in keeping of the men of Moab, and especially of the malignant, Henry Lee, whose hand hath been ever against us when he might find room to raise it; I say, he hath asked a great thing, both in respect of himself and me. For we of this poor but godly army of England, are holden, by those of the Parliament, as men who should render in spoil for them, but be no sharer of it ourselves; even as the buck, which the hounds pull to earth, furnisheth no part of their own food, but they are lashed off from the carcass with whips, like those which require punishment for their forwardness, not reward for their services.

Yet I speak not this so much in respect of this grant of Woodstock, in regard that, perhaps, their Lordships of the Council, and also the Committee-men of this Parliament, may graciously think they have given me a portion in the matter, in relation that my kinsman Desborough hath an interest allowed him therein ; which interest, as he hath well deserved it for his true and faithful service to these unhappy and devoted countries, so it would ill become me to diminish the same to his prejudice, unless it were upon great and public respects. Thus thou seest how it stands with me, my honest friend, and in what mind I stand touching thy master's request to me ; which yet I do not say that I can altogether, or unconditionally, grant or refuse, but only tell my simple thoughts with regard thereto. Thou understandest me, I doubt not?"

Now, Roger Wildrake, with all the attention he had been able to pay to the Lord General's speech, had got so much confused among the various clauses of the harangue, that his brain was bewildered, like that of a country clown when he chances to get himself involved among a crowd of carriages, and cannot stir a step to get out of the way of one of them, without being in danger of being ridden over by the others.

The General saw his look of perplexity, and began a new oration, to the same purpose as before ; —spoke of his love for his kind friend the Colonel,—his regard for his pious and godly kinsman, Master Desborough,—the great importance of the Palace and Park of Woodstock,—the determination of the Parliament that it should be confiscated, and the produce brought into the coffers of the state,—his own deep veneration for the authority of Parliament, and his no less deep sense of the injustice done to the army,—how it was his wish and will that all matters should be settled in an amicable and friendly manner, without self-seeking, debate, or strife, betwixt those who had been the hands acting, and such as had been the heads governing, in that great national cause,—how he was willing, truly willing, to contribute to this work, by laying down, not his commission only, but his life also, if it were requested of him, or could be granted with safety to the poor soldiers, to whom, silly poor men, he was bound to be as a father, seeing that they had followed him with the duty and affection of children.

And here he arrived at another dead pause, leaving Wildrake as uncertain as before, whether it was or was not his purpose to grant Colonel Everard the powers he had asked for the protection of Woodstock against the Parliamentary Commissioners. Internally he began to entertain hopes that the justice of Heaven, or the effects of remorse, had confounded the regicide's understanding. But no—he could see nothing but sagacity in that steady stern eye, which, while the tongue poured forth its periphrastic language in such profusion, seemed to watch with severe accuracy the effect which his oratory produced on the listener.

" Egad," thought the cavalier to himself, becoming a little familiar with the situation in which he was placed, and rather impatient of a conversation which led to no visible conclusion or termination, " if Noll were the devil himself, as he is the devil's darling, I will not be thus nose-led by him. I'll e'en brusque it a little, if he goes on at this rate, and try if I can bring him to a more intelligible mode of speaking."

Entertaining this bold purpose, but half afraid to execute it, Wildrake lay by for an opportunity of making the attempt, while Cromwell was apparently unable to express his own meaning. He was already beginning a third panegyric upon Colonel Everard, with sundry varied expressions of his own wish to oblige him, when Wildrake took the opportunity to strike in, on the General's making one of his oratorical pauses.

" So please you," he said, bluntly, " your worship has already spoken on two topics of your discourse, your own worthiness, and that of my master, Colonel Everard. But, to enable me to do mine errand, it would be necessary to bestow a few words on the third head."

" The third !" said Cromwell.

" Ay," said Wildrake, " which, in your honour's subdivision of your discourse, touched on my unworthy self. What am I to do—what portion am I to have in this matter ?"

Oliver started at once from the tone of voice he had hitherto used, and which somewhat resembled the purring of a domestic cat, into the growl of the tiger when about to spring. " *Thy* portion, jail-bird !" he exclaimed, " the gallows—thou shalt hang

as high as Haman, if thou betray counsel!—But,"
he added, softening his voice, " keep it like a true
man, and my favour will be the making of thee.
Come hither—thou art bold, I see, though somewhat saucy. Thou hast been a malignant—so writes
my worthy friend Colonel Everard; but thou hast
now given up that falling cause. I tell thee, friend,
not all that the Parliament or the army could do
would have pulled down the Stewarts out of their
high places, saving that Heaven had a controversy
with them.   Well, it is a sweet and comely thing
to buckle on one's armour in behalf of Heaven's
cause; otherwise truly, for mine own part, these
men might have remained upon the throne even
unto this day.   Neither do I blame any for aiding
them, until these successive great judgments have
overwhelmed them and their house.   I am not a
bloody man, having in me the feeling of human
frailty; but, friend, whosoever putteth his hand to
the plough, in the great actings which are now on
foot in these nations, had best beware that he do
not look back; for, rely upon my simple word, that
if you fail me, I will not spare on you one foot's
length of the gallows of Haman. Let me therefore
know, at a word, if the leaven of thy malignancy
is altogether drubbed out of thee ?"

" Your honourable lordship," said the cavalier,
shrugging up his shoulders, " has done that for
most of us, so far as cudgelling to some tune can
perform it."

" Sayst thou?" said the General, with a grim
smile on his lip, which seemed to intimate that he

was not quite inaccessible to flattery; " yea, truly, thou dost not lie in that—we have been an instrument. Neither are we, as I have already hinted, so severely bent against those who have striven against us as malignants, as others may be. The parliament-men best know their own interest and their own pleasure; but, to my poor thinking, it is full time to close these jars, and to allow men of all kinds the means of doing service to their country; and we think it will be thy fault if thou art not employed to good purpose for the state and thyself, on condition thou puttest away the old man entirely from thee, and givest thy earnest attention to what I have to tell thee."

" Your lordship need not doubt my attention," said the cavalier.

And the republican General, after another pause, as one who gave his confidence not without hesitation, proceeded to explain his views with a distinctness which he seldom used, yet not without his being a little biassed now and then, by his long habits of circumlocution, which indeed he never laid entirely aside, save in the field of battle.

" Thou seest," he said, " my friend, how things stand with me. The Parliament, I care not who knows it, love me not—still less do the Council of State, by whom they manage the executive government of the kingdom. I cannot tell why they nourish suspicion against me, unless it is because I will not deliver this poor innocent army, which has followed me in so many military actions, to be now pulled asunder, broken piecemeal and reduced, so that they who have protected the state at the expense of their blood, will not have, perchance, the means of feeding themselves by their labour; which, methinks, were hard measure, since it is taking from Esau his birthright, even without giving him a poor mess of pottage."

" Esau is likely to help himself, I think," replied Wildrake.

" Truly, thou sayst wisely," replied the General; " it is ill starving an armed man, if there is food to be had for taking—nevertheless, far be it from me to encourage rebellion, or want of due subordination to these our rulers. I would only petition in a due and becoming, a sweet and harmonious manner, that they would listen to our conditions, and consider our necessities. But, sir, looking on me, and estimating me so little as they do, you must think that it would be a provocation in me towards the Council of State, as well as the Parliament, if, simply to gratify your worthy master, I were to act contrary to their purposes, or deny currency to the commission under their authority, which is as yet the highest in the State—and long may it be so for me—to carry on the sequestration which they intend. And would it not also be said, that I was lending myself to the malignant interest, affording this den of the bloodthirsty and lascivious tyrants of yore, to be in this our day a place of refuge to that old and inveterate Amalekite, Sir Henry Lee, to keep possession of the place in which he hath so long glorified himself? Truly it would be a perilous matter."

" Am I then to report," said Wildrake, " an it please you, that you cannot stead Colonel Everard in this matter?"

" Unconditionally, ay—but, taken conditionally, the answer may be otherwise,"—answered Cromwell. " I see thou art not able to fathom my purpose, and therefore I will partly unfold it to thee. —But take notice, that, should thy tongue betray my council, save in so far as carrying it to thy master, by all the blood which has been shed in these wild times, thou shalt die a thousand deaths in one!"

" Do not fear me, sir," said Wildrake, whose natural boldness and carelessness of character was for the present time borne down and quelled, like that of falcons in the presence of the eagle.

" Hear me, then," said Cromwell, " and let no syllable escape thee. Knowest thou not the young Lee whom they call Albert, a malignant like his father, and one who went up with the young man to that last ruffle which we had with him at Worcester—May we be grateful for the victory !"

" I know there is such a young gentleman as Albert Lee," said Wildrake.

" And knowest thou not—I speak not by way of prying into the good Colonel's secrets, but only as it behoves me to know something of the matter, that I may best judge how I am to serve him— Knowest thou not that thy master, Markham Everard, is a suitor after the sister of this same malignant, a daughter of the old Keeper, called Sir Henry Lee ?"

" All this I have heard," said Wildrake, " nor can I deny that I believe in it."

" Well then, go to.—When the young man Charles Stewart fled from the field of Worcester, and was by sharp chase and pursuit compelled to separate himself from his followers, I know by sure intelligence that this Albert Lee was one of the last who remained with him, if not indeed the very last."

" It was devilish like him," said the cavalier, without sufficiently weighing his expressions, considering in what presence they were to be uttered —" And I'll uphold him with my rapier, to be a true chip of the old block !"

" Ha, swearest thou ?" said the General. " Is this thy reformation ?"

" I never swear, so please you," replied Wildrake, recollecting himself, " except there is some mention of malignants and cavaliers in my hearing ; and then the old habit returns, and I swear like one of Goring's troopers."

" Out upon thee," said the General ; " what can it avail thee to practise a profanity so horrible to the ears of others, and which brings no emolument to him who uses it ?"

" There are, doubtless, more profitable sins in the world than the barren and unprofitable vice of swearing," was the answer which rose to the lips of the cavalier ; but that was exchanged for a profession of regret for having given offence. The truth was, the discourse began to take a turn which rendered it more interesting than ever to Wildrake, who therefore determined not to lose the opportunity for obtaining possession of the secret that seemed to be suspended on Cromwell's lips ; and that could only be through means of keeping guard upon his own.

" What sort of a house is Woodstock ?" said the General, abruptly.

" An old mansion," said Wildrake, in reply ; " and, so far as I could judge by a single night's lodgings, having abundance of backstairs, also subterranean passages, and all the communications under ground, which are common in old raven-nests of the sort."

" And places for concealing priests, unquestionably," said Cromwell " It is seldom that such ancient houses lack secret stalls wherein to mew up these calves of Bethel."

" Your Honour's Excellency," said Wildrake, " may swear to that."

" I swear not at all," replied the General drily.— " But what think'st thou, good fellow ?—I will ask thee a blunt question—Where will those two Worcester fugitives that thou wottest of be more likely to take shelter—and that they must be sheltered somewhere, I well know—than in this same old palace, with all the corners and concealments whereof young Albert hath been acquainted ever since his earliest infancy ?"

" Truly," said Wildrake, making an effort to answer the question with seeming indifference, while the possibility of such an event, and its consequences, flashed fearfully upon his mind,—" Truly, I should be of your honour's opinion, but that I think the company, who, by the commission of Parliament, have occupied Woodstock, are likely to fright them thence, as a cat scares doves from a pigeon-house. The neighbourhood, with reverence, of Generals Desborough and Harrison, will suit ill with fugitives from Worcester field."

"I thought as much, and so, indeed, would I have it," answered the General. "Long may it be ere our names shall be aught but a terror to our enemies! But in this matter, if thou art an active plotter for thy master's interest, thou mightst, I should think, work out something favourable to his present object."

"My brain is too poor to reach the depth of your honourable purpose," said Wildrake.

"Listen then, and let it be to profit," answered Cromwell. "Assuredly the conquest at Worcester was a great and crowning mercy; yet might we seem to be but small in our thankfulness for the same, did we not do what in us lies towards the ultimate improvement and final conclusion of the great work which has been thus prosperous in our hands, professing, in pure humility and singleness of heart, that we do not, in any way, deserve our instrumentality to be remembered, nay, would rather pray and entreat, that our name and fortunes were forgotten, than that the great work were in itself incomplete. Nevertheless, truly, placed as we now are, it concerns us more nearly than others,— that is, if so poor creatures should at all speak of themselves as concerned, whether more or less, with these changes which have been wrought around, not, I say, by ourselves, or our own power, but by the destiny to which we were called, fulfilling the same with all meekness and humility,—I say it concerns us nearly that all things should be done in conformity with the great work which hath been wrought, and is yet working, in these lands. Such is my plain and simple meaning. Nevertheless, it is much to be desired that this young man, this King of Scots, as he called himself—this Charles Stewart—should not escape forth from the nation, where his arrival has wrought so much disturbance and bloodshed."

" I have no doubt," said the cavalier, looking down, " that your lordship's wisdom hath directed all things as they may best lead towards such a consummation ; and I pray your pains may be paid as they deserve."

" I thank thee, friend," said Cromwell, with much humility ; " doubtless we shall meet our reward, being in the hands of a good paymaster, who never passeth Saturday night. But understand me, friend—I desire no more than my own share in the good work. I would heartily do what poor kindness I can to your worthy master, and even to you in your degree—for such as I do not converse with ordinary men, that our presence may be forgotten like an every-day's occurrence. We speak to men like thee for their reward or their punishment ; and I trust it will be the former which thou in thine office wilt merit at my hand."

"Your honour," said Wildrake, "speaks like one accustomed to command."

"True ; men's minds are linked to those of my degree by fear and reverence," said the General; —"but enough of that, desiring, as I do, no other dependency on my special person than is alike to us all upon that which is above us. But I would desire to cast this golden ball into your master's lap. He hath served against this Charles Stewart and his father. But he is a kinsman near to the old knight, Lee, and stands well affected towards his daughter. *Thou* also wilt keep a watch, my friend—that ruffling look of thine will procure thee the confidence of every malignant, and the prey cannot approach this cover, as though to shelter, like a cony in the rocks, but thou wilt be sensible of his presence."

"I make a shift to comprehend your Excellency," said the cavalier ; "and I thank you heartily for the good opinion you have put upon me, and which, I pray I may have some handsome opportunity of deserving, that I may show my gratitude by the event. But still, with reverence, your Excellency's scheme seems unlikely, while Woodstock remains in possession of the sequestrators. Both the old knight and his son, and far more such a fugitive as your honour hinted at, will take special care not to approach it till they are removed."

"It is for that I have been dealing with thee thus long," said the General.—"I told thee that I was something unwilling, upon slight occasion, to dispossess the sequestrators by my own proper warrant, although having, perhaps, sufficient authority in the state both to do so, and to despise the murmurs of those who blame me. In brief, I would be loath to tamper with my privileges, and make experiments between their strength, and the powers of the commission granted by others, without pressing need, or at least great prospect of advantage. So, if thy Colonel will undertake, for his love of the Republic, to find the means of preventing its worst and nearest danger, which must needs occur from the escape of this young man, and will do his endeavour to stay him, in case his flight should lead him to Woodstock, which I hold very likely, I will give thee an order to these sequestrators, to evacuate the palace instantly; and to the next troop of my regiment, which lies at Oxford, to turn them out by the shoulders, if they make any scruples— Ay, even, for example's sake, if they drag Desborough out foremost, though he be wedded to my sister."

"So please you, sir," said Wildrake, "and with your most powerful warrant, I trust I might expel the commissioners, even without the aid of your most warlike and devout troopers."

"That is what I am least anxious about," replied the General; "I should like to see the best of them sit after I had nodded to them to begone —always excepting the worshipful House, in whose name our commissions run; but who, as some think, will be done with politics ere it be time to renew them. Therefore, what chiefly concerns me to know, is, whether thy master will embrace a traffic which

hath such a fair promise of profit with it. I am well
convinced that, with a scout like thee, who hast been
in the cavalier's quarters, and canst, I should guess,
resume thy drinking, ruffianly, health-quaffing manners whenever thou hast a mind, he must discover
where this Stewart hath ensconced himself. Either
the young Lee will visit the old one in person, or
he will write to him, or hold communication with
him by letter. At all events, Markham Everard
and thou must have an eye in every hair of your
head." While he spoke, a flush passed over his
brow, he rose from his chair, and paced the apartment in agitation. " Woe to you, if you suffer the
young adventurer to escape me !—you had better
be in the deepest dungeon in Europe, than breathe
the air of England, should you but dream of playing me false. I have spoken freely to thee, fellow
—more freely than is my wont—the time required
it. But, to share my confidence is like keeping a
watch over a powder-magazine, the least and most
insignificant spark blows thee to ashes ! Tell your
master what I have said—but not how I said it—
Fie, that I should have been betrayed into this distemperature of passion !—begone, sirrah. Pearson
shall bring thee sealed orders—Yet, stay—thou
hast something to ask."

" I would know," said Wildrake, to whom the
visible anxiety of the General gave some confidence,
" what is the figure of this young gallant, in case I
should find him ?"

" A tall, rawboned, swarthy lad, they say he
has shot up into. Here is his picture by a good

hand, some time since." He turned round one of the portraits which stood with its face against the wall; but it proved not to be that of Charles the Second, but of his unhappy father.

The first motion of Cromwell indicated a purpose of hastily replacing the picture, and it seemed as if an effort was necessary to repress his disinclination to look upon it. But he did repress it, and, placing the picture against the wall, withdrew slowly and sternly, as if, in defiance of his own feelings, he was determined to gain a place from which to see it to advantage. It was well for Wildrake that his dangerous companion had not turned an eye on him, for *his* blood also kindled when he saw the portrait of his master in the hands of the chief author of his death. Being a fierce and desperate man, he commanded his passion with great difficulty; and if, on its first violence, he had been provided with a suitable weapon, it is possible Cromwell would never have mounted higher in his bold ascent towards supreme power.

But this natural and sudden flash of indignation, which rushed through the veins of an ordinary man like Wildrake, was presently subdued, when confronted with the strong yet stifled emotion displayed by so powerful a character as Cromwell. As the cavalier looked on his dark and bold countenance, agitated by inward and indescribable feelings, he found his own violence of spirit die away and lose itself in fear and wonder. So true it is, that as greater lights swallow up and extinguish the display of those which are less, so men of great, ca-

pacious, and overruling minds, bear aside and sub-
-due, in their climax of passion, the more feeble wills
and passions of others; as, when a river joins a
brook, the fiercer torrent shoulders aside the small-
er stream.

Wildrake stood a silent, inactive, and almost a
terrified spectator, while Cromwell, assuming a firm
sternness of eye and manner, as one who compels
himself to look on what some strong internal feeling renders painful and disgustful to him, proceeded, in brief and interrupted expressions, but yet
with a firm voice, to comment on the portrait of
the late King. His words seemed less addressed
to Wildrake, than to be the spontaneous unburden-
ing of his own bosom, swelling under recollection
of the past and anticipation of the future.

" That Flemish painter," he said—" that Anto-
nio Vandyke—what a power he has! Steel may
mutilate, warriors may waste and destroy—still the
King stands uninjured by time; and our grand-
children, while they read his history, may look on
his image, and compare the melancholy features
with the woful tale.—It was a stern necessity—it
was an awful deed! The calm pride of that eye
might have ruled worlds of crouching Frenchmen,
or supple Italians, or formal Spaniards; but its
glances only roused the native courage of the stern
Englishman.—Lay not on poor sinful man, whose
breath is in his nostrils, the blame that he falls,
when Heaven never gave him strength of nerves to
stand! The weak rider is thrown by his unruly
horse, and trampled to death—the strongest man,

the best cavalier, springs to the empty saddle, and uses bit and spur till the fiery steed knows its master. Who blames him, who, mounted aloft, rides triumphantly amongst the people, for having succeeded, where the unskilful and feeble fell and died? Verily he hath his reward: Then, what is that piece of painted canvass to me more than others? No; let him show to others the reproaches of that cold, calm face, that proud yet complaining eye: Those who have acted on higher respects have no cause to start at painted shadows. Not wealth nor power brought me from my obscurity. The oppressed consciences, the injured liberties of England, were the banner that I followed."

He raised his voice so high, as if pleading in his own defence before some tribunal, that Pearson, the officer in attendance, looked into the apartment; and observing his master, with his eyes kindling, his arm extended, his foot advanced, and his voice raised, like a general in the act of commanding the advance of his army, he instantly withdrew.

" It was other than selfish regards that drew me forth to action," continued Cromwell, " and I dare the world—ay, living or dead I challenge—to assert that I armed for a private cause, or as a means of enlarging my fortunes. Neither was there a trooper in the regiment who came there with less of personal evil will to yonder unhappy"——

At this moment the door of the apartment opened, and a gentlewoman entered, who, from her resemblance to the General, although her features were soft and feminine, might be immediately recognised as his daughter. She walked up to Cromwell, gently but firmly passed her arm through his, and said to him in a persuasive tone, " Father, this is not well—you have promised me this should not happen."

The General hung down his head, like one who was either ashamed of the passion to which he had given way, or of the influence which was exercised over him. He yielded, however, to the affectionate impulse, and left the apartment, without again turning his head towards the portrait which had so much affected him, or looking towards Wildrake, who remained fixed in astonishment.

CHAPTER IX.

Doctor.—Go to, go to—You have known what you should not.
Macbeth.

WILDRAKE was left in the cabinet, as we have said, astonished and alone. It was often noised about, that Cromwell, the deep and sagacious states-man, the calm and intrepid commander, he who had overcome such difficulties, and ascended to such heights, that he seemed already to bestride the land which he had conquered, had, like many other men of great genius, a constitutional taint of melancholy, which sometimes displayed itself both in words and actions, and had been first observed in that sudden and striking change, when, abandoning entirely the dissolute freaks of his youth, he embraced a very strict course of religious observances, which, upon some occasions, he seemed to consider as bringing him into more near and close contact with the spiritual world. This extraordinary man is said sometimes, during that period of his life, to have given way to spiritual delusions, or, as he himself concei-ved them, prophetic inspirations of approaching grandeur, and of strange, deep, and mysterious agencies, in which he was in future to be engaged, in the same manner as his younger years had been marked by fits of exuberant and excessive frolic and debaucheries. Something of this kind seemed to explain the ebullition of passion which he had now manifested.

With wonder at what he had witnessed, Wild-rake felt some anxiety on his own account. Though not the most reflecting of mortals, he had sense enough to know, that it is dangerous to be a witness of the infirmities of men high in power; and he was left so long by himself, as induced him to entertain some secret doubts, whether the General might not be tempted to take means of confining or removing a witness, who had seen him lowered, as it seemed, by the suggestions of his own conscience, beneath that lofty flight, which, in general, he affected to sustain above the rest of the sublunary world.

In this, however, he wronged Cromwell, who was free either from an extreme degree of jealous suspicion, or from any thing which approached towards blood-thirstiness. Pearson appeared, after a lapse of about an hour, and, intimating to Wildrake that he was to follow, conducted him into a distant apartment, in which he found the General seated on a low couch. His daughter was in the apartment, but remained at some distance, apparently busied with some female needle-work, and scarce turned her head as Pearson and Wildrake entered.

At a sign from the Lord General, Wildrake approached him as before. " Comrade," he said, "your old friends the cavaliers look on me as their enemy, and conduct themselves towards me as if they desired to make me such. I profess they are labour-

ing to their own prejudice; for I regard, and have
ever regarded them, as honest and honourable fools,
who were silly enough to run their necks into nooses,
and their heads against stone-walls, that a man
called Stewart, and no other, should be king over
them.   Fools! are there no words made of letters
that would sound as well as Charles Stewart, with
that magic title beside them?   Why, the word
King is like a lighted lamp, that throws the same
bright gilding upon any combination of the alpha-
bet, and yet you must shed your blood for a name!
But thou, for thy part, shalt have no wrong from
me.   Here is an order, well warranted, to clear
the Lodge at Woodstock, and abandon it to thy
master's keeping, or those whom he shall appoint.
He will have his uncle and pretty cousin with him,
doubtless.   Fare thee well—think on what I told
thee.   They say beauty is a loadstone to yonder
long lad, thou dost wot of; but I reckon he has
other stars at present to direct his course than
bright eyes and fair hair.   Be it as it may, thou
knowest my purpose—peer out, peer out; keep a
constant and careful look-out on every ragged patch
that wanders by hedge-row or lane—these are days
when a beggar's cloak may cover a king's ransom.
There are some broad Portugal pieces for thee—
something strange to thy pouch, I ween.—Once
more, think on what thou hast heard, and," he added, in a lower and more impressive tone of voice,
" forget what thou hast seen.   My service to thy
master;—and, yet once again, *remember*—and *for-*

get."—Wildrake made his obeisance, and, returning to his inn, left Windsor with all possible speed.

It was afternoon in the same day when the cavalier rejoined his roundhead friend, who was anxiously expecting him at the inn in Woodstock appointed for their rendezvous.

" Where hast thou been?—what hast thou seen? —what strange uncertainty is in thy looks?—and why dost thou not answer me?"

" Because," said Wildrake, laying aside his riding cloak and rapier, " you ask so many questions at once. A man has but one tongue to answer with, and mine is wellnigh glued to the roof of my mouth."

" Will drink unloosen it?" said the Colonel; " though I dare say thou hast tried that spell at every alehouse on the road. Call for what thou wouldst have, man, only be quick."

" Colonel Everard," answered Wildrake, " I have not tasted so much as a cup of cold water this day."

" Then thou art out of humour for that reason," said the Colonel; " salve thy sore with brandy, if thou wilt, but leave being so fantastic and unlike to thyself as thou showest in this silent mood."

" Colonel Everard," replied the cavalier, very gravely, " I am an altered man."

" I think thou dost alter," said Everard, " every day in the year, and every hour of the day. Come, good now, tell me, hast thou seen the General, and got his warrant for clearing out the sequestrators from Woodstock?"

"I have seen the devil," said Wildrake, "and have, as thou sayst, got a warrant from him."

"Give it me," said Everard, hastily catching at the packet.

"Forgive me, Mark," said Wildrake; "if thou knewest the purpose with which this deed is granted —if thou knewest—what it is not my purpose to tell thee—what manner of hopes are founded on thy accepting it, I have that opinion of thee, Mark Everard, that thou would'st as soon take a redhot horseshoe from the anvil with thy bare hand, as receive into it this slip of paper."

"Come, come," said Everard, "this comes of some of your exalted ideas of loyalty, which, excellent within certain bounds, drive us mad when encouraged up to some heights. Do not think, since I must needs speak plainly with thee, that I see without sorrow the downfall of our ancient monarchy, and the substitution of another form of government in its stead; but ought my regret for the past to prevent my acquiescing and aiding in such measures as are likely to settle the future? The royal cause is ruined, hadst thou and every cavalier in England sworn the contrary; ruined, not to rise again,—for many a day at least. The Parliament, so often draughted and drained of those who were courageous enough to maintain their own freedom of opinion, is now reduced to a handful of statesmen, who have lost the respect of the people, from the length of time during which they have held the supreme management of affairs. They cannot stand long unless they were to reduce

the army ; and the army, late servants, are now
masters, and will refuse to be reduced. They know
their strength, and that they may be an army
subsisting on pay and free quarters throughout
England as long as they will. I tell thee, Wildrake,
unless we look to the only man who can rule and
manage them, we may expect military law throughout the land ; and I, for mine own part, look for
any preservation of our privileges that may be
vouchsafed to us, only through the wisdom and
forbearance of Cromwell. Now you have my secret.
You are aware that I am not doing the best I would,
but the best I can. I wish—not so ardently as
thou, perhaps—yet I *do* wish that the King could
have been restored on good terms of composition,
safe for us and for himself. And now, good Wildrake, rebel as thou thinkest me, make me no worse
a rebel than an unwilling one. God knows, I never
laid aside love and reverence to the King, even in
drawing my sword against his ill advisers."

" Ah, plague on you," said Wildrake, " that is
the very cant of it—that's what you all say. All
of you fought against the King in pure love and
loyalty, and not otherwise. However, I see your
drift, and I own that I like it better than I expected.
The army is your bear now, and old Noll is your
bearward ; and you are like a country constable,
who makes interest with the bearward that he may
prevent him from letting bruin loose. Well, there
may come a day when the sun will shine on our
side of the fence, and thereon shall you, and all the

good fair-weather folks who love the stronger party, come and make common cause with us."

Without much attending to what his friend said, Colonel Everard carefully studied the warrant of Cromwell. "It is bolder and more peremptory than I expected," he said. "The General must feel himself strong, when he opposes his own authority so directly to that of the Council of State and the Parliament."

"You will not hesitate to act upon it?" said Wildrake.

"That I certainly will not," answered Everard; "but I must wait till I have the assistance of the Mayor, who, I think, will gladly see these fellows ejected from the Lodge. I must not go altogether upon military authority, if possible." Then, stepping to the door of the apartment, he dispatched a servant of the house in quest of the Chief Magistrate, desiring he should be made acquainted that Colonel Everard desired to see him with as little loss of time as possible.

"You are sure he will come, like a dog at a whistle," said Wildrake. "The word captain, or colonel, makes the fat citizen trot in these days, when one sword is worth fifty corporation charters. But there are dragoons yonder, as well as the grim-faced knave whom I frightened the other evening when I showed my face in at the window. Think'st thou the knaves will show no rough play?"

"The General's warrant will weigh more with them than a dozen acts of Parliament," said Everard.—" But it is time thou eatest, if thou hast in truth ridden from Windsor hither without baiting."

" I care not about it," said Wildrake : " I tell thee, your General gave me a breakfast, which, I think, will serve me one while, if I am ever able to digest it. By the mass, it lay so heavy on my conscience, that I carried it to church to see if I could digest it there with my other sins. But not a whit."

" To church !—To the door of the church, thou meanest," said Everard. " I know thy way—thou art ever wont to pull thy hat off reverently at the threshold, but for crossing it, that day seldom comes."

" Well," replied Wildrake, " and if I do pull off my castor and kneel, is it not seemly to show the same respects in a church which we offer in a palace ? It is a dainty matter, is it not, to see your Anabaptists, and Brownists, and the rest of you, gather to a sermon with as little ceremony as hogs to a trough ? But here comes food, and now for a grace, if I can remember one."

Everard was too much interested about the fate of his uncle and his fair cousin, and the prospect of restoring them to their quiet home, under the protection of that formidable truncheon which was already regarded as the leading-staff of England, to remark, that certainly a great alteration had taken place in the manners and outward behaviour at least of his companion. His demeanour frequently evinced a sort of struggle betwixt old habits of indulgence, and some newly formed resolutions of abstinence ; and it was almost ludicrous to see how often

the hand of the neophyte directed itself naturally
to a large black leathern jack, which contained two
double flagons of strong ale, and how often, diverted
from its purpose by the better reflections of the
reformed toper, it seized, instead, upon a large ewer
of salubrious and pure water.

It was not difficult to see that the task of sobriety
was not yet become easy, and that, if it had the
recommendation of the intellectual portion of the
party who had resolved upon it, the outward man
yielded a reluctant and restive compliance. But
honest Wildrake had been dreadfully frightened at
the course proposed to him by Cromwell, and, with
a feeling not peculiar to the Catholic religion, had
formed a solemn resolution within his own mind,
that, if he came off safe and with honour from this
dangerous interview, he would show his sense of
Heaven's favour, by renouncing some of the sins
which most easily beset him, and especially that of
intemperance, to which, like many of his wild com-
peers, he was too much addicted.

This resolution, or vow, was partly prudential
as well as religious ; for it occurred to him as very
possible, that some matters of a difficult and delicate nature might be thrown into his hands at the
present emergency, during the conduct of which it
would be fitting for him to act by some better oracle
than that of the Bottle, celebrated by Rabelais. In
full compliance with this prudent determination, he
touched neither the ale nor the brandy which were
placed before him, and declined peremptorily the
sack with which his friend would have garnished

the board. Nevertheless, just as the boy removed
the trenchers and napkins, together with the large
black-jack which we have already mentioned, and
was one or two steps on his way to the door, the
sinewy arm of the cavalier, which seemed to elon-
gate itself on purpose, (as it extended far beyond
the folds of the threadbare jacket,) arrested the
progress of the retiring Ganymede, and seizing on
the black-jack, conveyed it to the lips, which were
gently breathing forth the aspiration, " D—n—I
mean, Heaven forgive me—we are poor creatures
of clay—one modest sip must be permitted to our
frailty."

So murmuring, he glued the huge flagon to his
lips, and as the head was slowly and gradually inclined backwards in proportion as the right hand
elevated the bottom of the pitcher, Everard had
great doubts whether the drinker and the cup were
likely to part until the whole contents of the latter
had been transferred to the person of the former.
Roger Wildrake stinted, however, when, by a moderate computation, he had swallowed at one draught
about a quart and a half.

He then replaced it on the salver, fetched a long
breath to refresh his lungs, bade the boy get him
gone with the rest of the liquors, in a tone which
inferred some dread of his constancy, and then,
turning to his friend Everard, he expatiated in
praise of moderation, observing that the mouthful
which he had just taken had been of more service
to him than if he had remained quaffing healths at
table for four hours together.

His friend made no reply, but could not help being privately of opinion that Wildrake's temperance had done as much execution on the tankard in his single draught, as some more moderate topers might have effected if they had sat sipping for an evening. But the subject was changed by the entrance of the landlord, who came to announce to his honour Colonel Everard, that the worshipful Mayor of Woodstock, with the Rev. Master Holdenough, were come to wait upon him.

CHAPTER X.

——— Here we have one head
Upon two bodies—your two-headed bullock
Is but an ass to such a prodigy.
These two have but one meaning, thought, and counsel;
And, when the single noddle has spoke out,
The four legs scrape assent to 't.

Old Play.

In the goodly form of the honest Mayor, there
was a bustling mixture of importance and embarrassment, like the deportment of a man who was
conscious that he had an important part to act, if
he could but exactly discover what that part was.
But both were mingled with much pleasure at seeing Everard, and he frequently repeated his wel-
comes and all-hails before he could be brought to
attend to what that gentleman said in reply.

" Good, worthy Colonel, you are indeed a desirable sight to Woodstock at all times, being, as
I may say, almost our townsman, as you have dwelt
so much and so long at the palace. Truly, the
matter begins almost to pass my wit, though I have
transacted the affairs of this borough for many a
long day ; and you are come to my assistance like,
like"———

" *Tanquam Deus ex machina,* as the Ethnic poet
hath it," said Master Holdenough, " although I do

not often quote from such books.—Indeed, Master Markham Everard—or worthy Colonel, as I ought rather to say—you are simply the most welcome man who has come to Woodstock since the days of old King Harry."

" I had some business with you, my good friend," said the Colonel, addressing the Mayor; " I shall be glad if it should so happen at the same time, that I may find occasion to pleasure you or your worthy pastor."

" No question you can do so, good sir," interposed Master Holdenough ; " you have the heart, sir, and you have the hand; and we are much in want of good counsel, and that from a man of action. I am aware, worthy Colonel, that you and your worthy father have ever borne yourselves in these turmoils like men of a truly Christian and moderate spirit, striving to pour oil into the wounds of the land, which some would rub with vitriol and pepper ; and we know you are faithful children of that church which we have reformed from its papistical and prelatical tenets."

" My good and reverend friend," said Everard, " I respect the piety and learning of many of your teachers; but I am also for liberty of conscience to all men. I neither side with sectaries, nor do I desire to see them the object of suppression by violence."

" Sir, sir," said the Presbyterian, hastily, " all this hath a fair sound ; but I would you should think what a fine country and church we are like to have of it, amidst the errors, blasphemies, and schisms, which are daily introduced into the church and kingdom of England, so that worthy Master Edwards, in his Gangrena, declareth, that our native country is about to become the very sink and cess-pool of all schisms, heresies, blasphemies, and confusions, as the army of Hannibal was said to be the refuse of all nations—*Colluvies omnium gentium.*—Believe me, worthy Colonel, that they of the Honourable House view all this over lightly, and with the winking connivance of old Eli. These instructors, the schismatics, shoulder the orthodox ministers out of their pulpits, thrust themselves into families, and break up the peace thereof, stealing away men's hearts from the established faith."

"My good Master Holdenough," replied the Colonel, interrupting the zealous preacher, "there is ground of sorrow for all these unhappy discords; and I hold with you, that the fiery spirits of the present time have raised men's minds at once above sober-minded and sincere religion, and above decorum and common sense. But there is no help save patience. Enthusiasm is a stream that may foam off in its own time, whereas it is sure to bear down every barrier which is directly opposed to it.— But what are these schismatical proceedings to our present purpose?"

" Why, partly this, sir," said Holdenough, "although perhaps you may make less of it than I should have thought before we met.—I was myself —I, Nehemiah Holdenough, [he added consequentially,] was forcibly expelled from my own pulpit, even as a man should have been thrust out of his own house, by an alien, and an intruder, a wolf, who was not at the trouble even to put on sheep's clothing, but came in his native wolfish attire of buff and bandoleer, and held forth in my stead to the people, who are to me as a flock to the lawful shepherd.   It is too true. sir—Master Mayor saw it, and strove to take such order to prevent it as man might,—though," turning to the Mayor, "I think still you might have striven a little more."

"Good now, good Master Holdenough, do not let us go back on that question," said the Mayor. "Guy of Warwick, or Bevis of Hampton, might do something with this generation; but truly, they are too many and too strong for the Mayor of Woodstock."

"I think Master Mayor speaks very good sense," said the Colonel; "if the Independents are not allowed to preach, I fear me they will not fight;— and then if you were to have another rising of cavaliers?"

"There are worse folks may rise than cavaliers," said Holdenough.

"How, sir?" replied Colonel Everard.   "Let me remind you, Master Holdenough, that is no safe language in the present state of the nation."

"I say," said the Presbyterian, "there are worse folk may rise than cavaliers; and I will prove what I say.   The devil is worse than the worst cavalier that ever drank a health, or swore an oath—and the devil has arisen at Woodstock Lodge!"

"Ay, truly hath he," said the Mayor, "bodily

and visibly, in figure and form—An awful time we live in !"

" Gentlemen, I really know not how I am to understand you," said Everard.

" Why, it was even about the devil we came to speak with you," said the Mayor; " but the worthy minister is always so hot upon the sectaries"——

" Which are the devil's brats, and nearly akin to him," said Master Holdenough. " But true it is, that the growth of these sects has brought up the Evil One even upon the face of the earth, to look after his own interest, where he finds it most thriving."

" Master Holdenough," said the Colonel, " if you speak figuratively, I have already told you that I have neither the means nor the skill sufficient to temper these religious heats. But if you design to say that there has been an actual apparition of the devil, I presume to think that you, with your doctrine and your learning, would be a fitter match for him than a soldier like me."

" True, sir; and I have that confidence in the commission which I hold, that I would take the field against the foul fiend without a moment's delay," said Holdenough ; " but the place in which he hath of late appeared, being Woodstock, is filled with those dangerous and impious persons, of whom I have been but now complaining ; and though, confident in my own resources, I dare venture in disputation with their Great Master himself, yet without your protection, most worthy Colonel, I see not that I may with prudence trust myself with the tossing and goring ox Desborough, or the bloody and devouring bear Harrison, or the cold and poisonous snake Bletson—all of whom are now at the Lodge, doing license and taking spoil as they think meet ; and, as all men say, the devil has come to make a fourth with them."

"In good truth, worthy and noble sir," said the Mayor, " it is even as Master Holdenough says— our privileges are declared void, our cattle seized in the very pastures. They talk of cutting down and disparking the fair Chase, which has been so long the pleasure of so many kings, and making Woodstock of as little note as any paltry village. I assure you we heard of your arrival with joy, and wondered at your keeping yourself so close in your lodgings. We know no one save your father or you, that are like to stand the poor burgesses' friend in this extremity, since almost all the gentry around are malignants, and under sequestration. We trust, therefore, you will make strong intercession in our behalf."

" Certainly, Master Mayor," said the Colonel, who saw himself with pleasure anticipated ; " it was my very purpose to have interfered in this matter ; and I did but keep myself alone until I should be furnished with some authority from the Lord General."

" Powers from the Lord General !" said the Mayor, thrusting the clergyman with his elbow— " Dost thou hear that ?—What cock will fight that cock ? We shall carry it now over their necks, and Woodstock shall be brave Woodstock still !"

" Keep thine elbow from my side, friend," said
Holdenough, annoyed by the action which the Mayor
had suited to his words ; " and may the Lord send
that Cromwell prove not as sharp to the people of
England as thy bones against my person ! Yet I
approve that we should use his authority to stop the
course of these men's proceedings."

" Let us set out, then," said Colonel Everard ;
" and I trust we shall find the gentlemen reasonable and obedient."

The functionaries, laic and clerical, assented with
much joy ; and the Colonel required and received
Wildrake's assistance in putting on his cloak and
rapier, as if he had been the dependent whose part
he acted. The cavalier contrived, however, while
doing him these menial offices, to give his friend a
shrewd pinch, in order to maintain the footing of
secret equality betwixt them.

The Colonel was saluted, as they passed through
the streets, by many of the anxious inhabitants, who
seemed to consider his intervention as affording the
only chance of saving their fine Park, and the rights
of the corporation, as well as of individuals, from
ruin and confiscation.

As they entered the Park, the Colonel asked his
companions, " What is this you say of apparitions
being seen amongst them ?"

" Why, Colonel," said the clergyman, " you
know yourself that Woodstock was always haunted ?"

" I have lived therein many a day," said the Colonel ; " and I know that I never saw the least sign

of it, although idle people spoke of the house as they do of all old mansions, and gave the apartments ghosts and spectres to fill up the places of as many of the deceased great, as had ever dwelt there."

" Nay, but, good Colonel," said the clergyman, " I trust you have not reached the prevailing sin of the times, and become indifferent to the testimony in favour of apparitions, which appears so conclusive to all but atheists, and advocates for witches ?"

" I would not absolutely disbelieve what is so generally affirmed," said the Colonel ; " but my reason leads me to doubt most of the stories which I have heard of this sort, and my own experience never went to confirm any of them."

" Ay, but trust me," said Holdenough, " there was always a demon of one or the other species about this Woodstock. Not a man or woman in the town but has heard stories of apparitions in the forest, or about the old castle. Sometimes it is a pack of hounds, that sweep along, and the whoops and hollows of the huntsmen, and the winding of horns and the galloping of horse, which is heard as if first more distant, and then close around you— and then anon it is a solitary huntsman, who asks if you can tell him which way the stag is gone. He is always dressed in green ; but the fashion of his clothes is some five hundred years old. This is what we call Demon Meridianum—the noonday spectre."

" My worthy and reverend sir," said the Colonel,

" I have lived at Woodstock many seasons, and have traversed the Chase at all hours. Trust me, what you hear from the villagers, is the growth of their idle folly and superstition."

" Colonel," replied Holdenough, " a negative proves nothing. What signifies, craving your pardon, that you have not seen any thing, be it earthly, or be it of the other world, to detract from the evidence of a score of people who have ?—And, besides, there is the Demon Nocturnum—the being that walketh by night—He has been among these Independents and schismatics last night.—Ay, Colonel, you may stare ; but it is even so—they may try whether he will mend their gifts, as they profanely call them, of exposition and prayer. No, sir, I trow, to master the foul fiend there goeth some competent knowledge of theology, and an acquaintance of the humane letters, ay, and a regular clerical education, and clerical calling."

" I do not in the least doubt," said the Colonel, " the efficacy of your qualifications to lay the devil ; but still I think some odd mistake has occasioned this confusion amongst them, if there has any such in reality existed. Desborough is a blockhead, to be sure ; and Harrison is fanatic enough to believe any thing. But there is Bletson, on the other hand, who believes nothing.—What do you know of this matter, good Master Mayor?"

" In sooth, and it was Master Bletson who gave the first alarm," replied the magistrate, " or, at least, the first distinct one. You see, sir, I was in bed with my wife, and no one else ; and I was as fast asleep as a man can desire to be at two hours after midnight, when, behold you, they came knocking at my bedroom door, to tell me there was an alarm in Woodstock, and that the bell of the Lodge was ringing at that dead hour of the night, as hard as ever it rung when it called the court to dinner."

" Well, but the cause of this alarm?" said the Colonel.

" You shall hear, worthy Colonel, you shall hear," answered the Mayor, waving his hand with dignity; for he was one of those persons who will not be hurried out of their own pace. " So Mrs Mayor would have persuaded me, in her love and affection, poor wretch, that to rise at such an hour out of my own warm bed, was like to bring on my old complaint the lumbago, and that I should send the people to Alderman Dutton.—Alderman Devil, Mrs Mayor, said I ;—I beg your reverence's pardon for using such a phrase—Do you think I am going to lie a-bed when the town is on fire, and the cavaliers up, and the devil to pay ?—I beg pardon again, parson.—But here we are before the gate of the Palace; will it not please you to enter ?"

" I would first hear the end of your story," said the Colonel; " that is, Master Mayor, if it happens to have an end."

" Every thing hath an end," said the Mayor, " and that which we call a pudding hath two.— Your worship will forgive me for being facetious. Where was I ?—O, I jumped out of bed, and put on my red plush breeches, with the blue nether stocks, for I always make a point of being dressed suitably to my dignity, night and day, summer or winter, Colonel Everard; and I took the Constable along with me, in case the alarm should be raised by night-walkers or thieves, and called up worthy Master Holdenough out of his bed, in case it should turn out to be the devil. And so I thought I was provided for the worst—and so away we came; and, by and by, the soldiers who came to the town with Master Tomkins, who had been called to arms, came marching down to Woodstock as fast as their feet would carry them; so I gave our people the sign to let them pass us, and outmarch us, as it were, and this for a twofold reason."

"I will be satisfied," interrupted the Colonel, "with one good reason. You desired the red-coats should have the *first* of the fray?"

"True, sir, very true;—and also that they should have the *last* of it, in respect that fighting is their especial business. However, we came on at a slow pace, as men who are determined to do their duty without fear or favour, when suddenly we saw something white haste away up the avenue towards the town, when six of our constables and assistants fled at once, as conceiving it to be an apparition called the White Woman of Woodstock."

"Look you there, Colonel," said Master Holdenough, "I told you there were demons of more kinds than one, which haunt the ancient scenes of royal debauchery and cruelty."

"I hope you stood your own ground, Master Mayor?" said the Colonel.

" I—yes—most assuredly—that is, I did not, strictly speaking, keep my ground ; but the town-clerk and I retreated—retreated, Colonel, and without confusion or dishonour, and took post behind worthy Master Holdenough, who, with the spirit of a lion, threw himself in the way of the supposed spectre, and attacked it with such a siserary of Latin as might have scared the devil himself, and thereby plainly discovered that it was no devil at all, nor white woman, neither woman of any colour, but worshipful Master Bletson, a member of the House of Commons, and one of the commissioners sent hither upon this unhappy sequestration of the Wood, Chase, and Lodge of Woodstock."

" And this was all you saw of the demon ?" said the Colonel.

" Truly, yes," answered the Mayor ; " and I had no wish to see more. However, we conveyed Master Bletson, as in duty bound, back to the Lodge, and he was ever maundering by the way how that he met a party of scarlet devils incarnate marching down to the Lodge ; but, to my poor thinking, it must have been the Independent dragoons who had just passed us."

" And more incarnate devils I would never wish to see," said Wildrake, who could remain silent no longer. His voice, so suddenly heard, showed how much the Mayor's nerves were still alarmed, for he started and jumped aside with an alacrity of which no one would at first sight suppose a man of his portly dignity to have been capable. Everard imposed silence on his intrusive attendant ; and, desirous to hear the conclusion of this strange story, requested the Mayor to tell him how the matter ended, and whether they stopped the supposed spectre.

" Truly, worthy sir," said the Mayor, " Master Holdenough was quite venturous upon confronting, as it were, the devil, and compelling him to appear under the real form of Master Joshua Bletson, member of Parliament for the borough of Little-faith."

" In sooth, Master Mayor," said the divine, " I were strangely ignorant of my own commission and its immunities, if I were to value opposing myself to Satan, or any Independent in his likeness, all of whom, in the name of Him I serve, I do defy, spit at, and trample under my feet ; and because Master Mayor is something tedious, I will briefly inform your honour that we saw little of the Enemy that night, save what Master Bletson said in the first feeling of his terrors, and save what we might collect from the disordered appearance of the Honourable Colonel Desborough and Major-General Harrison."

" And what plight were they in, I pray you ?" demanded the Colonel.

" Why, worthy sir, every one might see with half an eye that they had been engaged in a fight wherein they had not been honoured with perfect victory ; seeing that General Harrison was stalking up and down the parlour, with his drawn sword in his hand, talking to himself, his doublet unbuttoned, his points untrussed, his garters loose, and like to throw him down as he now and then trode on them, and gaping and grinning like a mad player. And yonder sat Desborough with a dry pottle of sack before him, which he had just emptied, and which, though the element in which he trusted, had not restored him sense enough to speak, or courage enough to look over his shoulder. He had a Bible in his hand, forsooth, as if it would of itself make battle against the Evil One; but I peered over his shoulder, and, alas! the good gentleman held the bottom of the page uppermost. It was as if one of your musketeers, noble and valiant sir, were to present the but of his piece at the enemy instead of the muzzle—ha, ha, ha! it was a sight to judge of schismatics by; both in point of head, and in point of heart, in point of skill, and in point of courage.—Oh! Colonel, then was the time to see the true character of an authorized pastor of souls over those unhappy men, who leap into the fold without due and legal authority, and will, forsooth, preach, teach, and exhort, and blasphemously term the doctrine of the church saltless porridge and dry chips!"

" I have no doubt you were ready to meet the danger, reverend sir; but I would fain know of what nature it was, and from whence it was to be apprehended?"

" Was it for me to make such enquiry?" said the clergyman, triumphantly. " Is it for a brave soldier to number his enemies, or enquire from what quarter they are to come?—No, sir, I was there with match lighted, bullet in my mouth, and my harquebuss shouldered, to encounter as many devils as hell could pour in, were they countless as motes in the sunbeam, and although they came from all points of the compass. The Papists talk of the temptation of St Anthony—pshaw! let them double all the myriads which the brain of a crazy Dutch painter hath invented, and you will find a poor Presbyterian divine—I will answer for one at least, —who, not in his own strength, but his Master's, will receive the assault in such sort, that far from returning against him as against yonder poor hound, day after day, and night after night. he will at once pack them off as with a vengeance to the uttermost parts of Assyria!"

" Still," said the Colonel, " I pray to know whether you saw any thing upon which to exercise your pious learning ?"

" Saw ?" answered the divine ; " no, truly, I saw nothing, nor did I look for any thing. Thieves will not attack well-armed travellers, nor will devils or evil spirits come against one who bears in his bosom the word of truth, in the very language in which it was first dictated. No, sir, they shun a divine who can understand the holy text, as a crow is said to keep wide of a gun loaded with hailshot."

They had walked a little way back upon their road, to give time for this conversation ; and the Colonel, perceiving it was about to lead to no satisfactory explanation of the real cause of alarm on the preceding night, turned round, and observing it was time they should go to the Lodge, began to move in that direction with his three companions.

It had now become dark, and the towers of Woodstock arose high above the umbrageous shroud which the forest spread around the ancient and venerable mansion. From one of the highest turrets, which could still be distinguished as it rose against the clear blue sky, there gleamed a light like that of a candle within the building. The Mayor stopt short, and catching fast hold of the divine, and then of Colonel Everard, exclaimed, in a trembling and hasty, but suppressed tone,

" Do you see yonder light ?"

" Ay, marry do I," said Colonel Everard; " and what does that matter ?—a light in a garret-room of such an old mansion as Woodstock is no subject for wonder, I trow."

" But a light from Rosamond's Tower is surely so ?" said the Mayor.

" True," said the Colonel, something surprised, when, after a careful examination, he satisfied him-self that the worthy magistrate's conjecture was right. " That is indeed Rosamond's Tower; and as the drawbridge by which it was accessible has been destroyed for centuries, it is hard to say what chance could have lighted a lamp in such an inac-cessible place."

" That light burns with no earthly fuel," said the Mayor; "neither from whale nor olive oil, nor bees-wax, nor mutton-suet either. I dealt in these commodities, Colonel, before I went into my pre-sent line; and I can assure you I could distinguish

1

the sort of light they give, one from another, at a greater distance than yonder turret—Look you, that is no earthly flame.—See you not something blue and reddish upon the edges ?—that bodes full well where it comes from.—Colonel, in my opinion we had better go back to sup at the town, and leave the Devil and the red-coats to settle their matters together for to-night ; and then when we come back the next morning, we will have a pull with the party that chances to keep a-field."

" You will do as you please, Master Mayor," said Everard, " but my duty requires me that I should see the Commissioners to-night."

" And mine requires me to see the foul Fiend," said Master Holdenough, " if he dare make himself visible to me. I wonder not that, knowing who is approaching, he betakes himself to the very citadel, the inner and the last defences of this ancient and haunted mansion. He is dainty, I warrant you, and must dwell where is a relish of luxury and murder about the walls of his chamber. In yonder turret sinned Rosamond, and in yonder turret she suffered ; and there she sits, or, more likely, the Enemy in her shape, as I have heard true men of Woodstock tell.—I wait on you, good Colonel— Master Mayor will do as he pleases. The strong man hath fortified himself in his dwelling-house, but, lo, there cometh another stronger than he."

" For me," said the Mayor, " who am as un-learned as I am unwarlike, I will not engage either with the powers of the Earth, or the Prince of the Powers of the Air, and I would we were again at

Woodstock ;—and hark ye, good fellow," slapping Wildrake on the shoulder, " I will bestow on thee a shilling wet and a shilling dry if thou wilt go back with me."

" Gadzookers, Master Mayor," said Wildrake, neither flattered by the magistrate's familiarity of address, nor captivated by his munificence—" I wonder who the devil made you and me fellows ? and, besides, do you think I would go back to Woodstock with your worshipful cod's-head, when, by good management, I may get a peep of fair Rosamond, and see whether she was that choice and incomparable piece of ware, which the world has been told of by rhymers and ballad-makers ?"

" Speak less lightly and wantonly, friend," said the divine ; " we are to resist the Devil that he may flee from us, and not to tamper with him, or enter into his counsels, or traffic with the merchandise of his great Vanity Fair."

" Mind what the good man says, Wildrake," said the Colonel ; " and take heed another time how thou dost suffer thy wit to outrun discretion."

" I am beholden to the reverend gentleman for his advice," answered Wildrake, upon whose tongue it was difficult to impose any curb whatever, even when his own safety rendered it most desirable. " But, gadzookers, let him have had what experience he will in fighting with the Devil, he never saw one so black as I had a tussle with—not a hundred years ago."

" How, friend," said the clergyman, who understood every thing literally when apparitions were

mentioned, " have you had so late a visitation of
Satan ? Believe me, then, that I wonder why thou
darest to entertain his name so often and so lightly, as I see thou dost use it in thy ordinary discourse. But when and where didst thou see the
Evil One ?"

Everard hastily interposed, lest by something
yet more strongly alluding to Cromwell, his imprudent squire should, in mere wantonness, betray
his interview with the General. " The young
man raves," he said, " of a dream which he had the
other night, when he and I slept together in Victor
Lee's chamber, belonging to the ranger's apartments
at the Lodge."

" Thanks for help at a pinch, good patron," said
Wildrake, whispering into Everard's ear, who in
vain endeavoured to shake him off,—" a fib never
failed a fanatic."

" You, also, spoke something too lightly of these
matters, considering the work which we have in
hand, worthy Colonel," said the Presbyterian divine. " Believe me, the young man, thy servant,
was more likely to see visions than to dream merely
idle dreams in that apartment ; for I have always
heard, that, next to Rosamond's Tower, in which,
as I said, she played the wanton, and was afterwards poisoned by Queen Eleanor, Victor Lee's
chamber was the place in the Lodge of Woodstock
more peculiarly the haunt of evil spirits.—I pray
you, young man, tell me this dream or vision of
yours."

" With all my heart, sir," said Wildrake—then

addressing his patron, who began to interfere, he said, " Tush, sir, you have had the discourse for an hour, and why should not I hold forth in my turn ? By this darkness, if you keep me silent any longer I will turn Independent preacher, and stand up in your despite for the freedom of private judgment. —And so, reverend sir, I was dreaming of a carnal divertisement called a bull-baiting ; and methought they were venturing dogs at head, as merrily as e'er I saw them at Tutbury Bull-running ; and methought I heard some one say, there was the Devil come to have a sight of the bull-ring. Well, I thought that, gadswoons, I would have a peep at his Infernal Majesty. So I looked, and there was a butcher in greasy woollen, with his steel by his side ; but he was none of the Devil. And there was a drunken cavalier, with his mouth full of oaths, and his stomach full of emptiness, and a gold-laced waistcoat in a very dilapidated condition, and a ragged hat, with a piece of a feather in it ; and he was none of the Devil neither. And there was a miller, his hands dusty with meal, and every atom of it stolen : and there was a vintner, his green apron stained with wine, and every drop of it sophisticated ; but neither was the old gentleman I looked for to be detected among these artisans of iniquity. At length, sir, I saw a grave person with cropped hair, a pair of longish and projecting ears, a band as broad as a slobbering bib under his chin, a brown coat surmounted by a Geneva cloak, and I had old Nicholas at once in his genuine paraphernalia, by —— !"

"Shame, shame!" said Colonel Everard. "What! behave thus to an old gentleman and a divine!"—

"Nay, let him proceed," said the minister, with perfect equanimity, "if thy friend, or secretary, is gibing, I must have less patience than becomes my profession, if I could not bear an idle jest, and forgive him who makes it. Or if, on the other hand, the Enemy has really presented himself to the young man in such a guise as he intimates, wherefore should we be surprised that he, who can take upon him the form of an angel of light, should be able to assume that of a frail and peccable mortal, whose spiritual calling and profession ought, indeed, to induce him to make his life an example to others, but whose conduct, nevertheless, such is the imperfection of our unassisted nature, sometimes rather presents us with a warning of what we should shun?"

"Now, by the mass, honest dominie—I mean reverend sir—I crave you a thousand pardons," said Wildrake, penetrated by the quietness and patience of the presbyter's rebuke. "By St George, if quiet patience will do it, thou art fit to play a game at foils with the Devil himself, and I would be contented to hold stakes."

As he concluded an apology, which was certainly not uncalled for, and seemed to be received in perfectly good part, they approached so close to the exterior door of the Lodge, that they were challenged with the emphatic *Stand*, by a sentinel who mounted guard there. Colonel Everard replied, *A friend;* and the sentinel repeating his command,

" Stand, friend," proceeded to call the corporal of the guard. The corporal came forth, and at the same time turned out his guard. Colonel Everard gave his name and designation, as well as those of his companions, on which the corporal said, " he doubted not there would be orders for his instant admission , but, in the first place, Master Tomkins must be consulted, that he might learn their honours' mind."

" How, sir !" said the Colonel, " do you, knowing who I am, presume to keep me on the outside of your post ?"

" Not if your honour pleases to enter," said the corporal, " and undertakes to be my warranty ; but such are the orders of my post."

" Nay, then, do your duty," said the Colonel ; " but are the cavaliers up, or what is the matter, that you keep so close and strict a watch ?"

The fellow gave no distinct answer, but muttered between his mustaches something about the Enemy, and the roaring Lion who goeth about seeking whom he may devour. Presently afterwards Tomkins appeared, followed by two servants, bearing lights in great standing brass candlesticks. They marched before Colonel Everard and his party, keeping as close to each other as two cloves of the same orange, and starting from time to time ; and shouldering as they passed through sundry intricate passages, they led up a large and ample wooden staircase, the banisters, rail, and lining of which were executed in black oak, and finally into a long saloon, or parlour, where there was a prodigious fire, and about twelve candles of the largest size distributed in sconces against the wall. There were seated the Commissioners, who now held in their power the ancient mansion and royal domain of Woodstock.

CHAPTER XI.

The bloody bear, an independent beast,
Unlick'd to forms, in groans his hate express'd—
. . . .
Next him the buffoon ape, as atheists use,
Mimick'd all sects, and had his own to choose.
Hind and Panther.

THE strong light in the parlour which we have
described, served to enable Everard easily to re-
cognise his acquaintances, Desborough, Harrison,
and Bletson, who had assembled round an oak table
of large dimensions, placed near the blazing chimney, on which were arranged wine, and ale, and
materials for smoking, then the general indulgence
of the time. There was a species of movable cupboard set betwixt the table and the door, calculated
originally for a display of plate upon grand occasions, but at present only used as a screen ; which
purpose it served so effectually, that, ere he had
coasted around it, Everard heard the following
fragment of what Desborough was saying, in his
strong coarse voice :—" Sent him to share with us,
I'se warrant ye—It was always his Excellency my
brother-in-law's way—if he made a treat for five
friends, he would invite more than the table could
hold—I have known him ask three men to eat two
eggs."

" Hush, hush," said Bletson; and the servants
making their appearance from behind the tall cupboard, announced Colonel Everard. It may not be
uninteresting to the reader to have a description of
the party into which he now entered.

Desborough was a stout, bull-necked man, of
middle-size, with heavy vulgar features, grizzled
bushy eyebrows, and wall-eyes. The flourish of
his powerful relative's fortunes had burst forth in
the finery of his dress, which was much more ornamented than was usual among the roundheads.
There was embroidery on his cloak, and lace upon
his band; his hat displayed a feather with a golden
clasp, and all his habiliments were those of a cavalier, or follower of the court, rather than the plain
dress of a parliamentarian officer. But, Heaven
knows, there was little of courtlike grace or dignity in the person or demeanour of the individual,
who became his fine suit as the hog on the sign-
post does his gilded armour. It was not that he
was positively deformed, or mishaped, for, taken
in detail, the figure was well enough. But his
limbs seemed to act upon different and contradic-
tory principles. They were not, as the play says,
in a concatenation accordingly;—the right hand
moved as if it were upon bad terms with the left,
and the legs showed an inclination to foot it in
different and opposite directions. In short, to use
an extravagant comparison, the members of Colonel
Desborough seemed rather to resemble the dispu-
tatious representatives of a federative congress, than
the well-ordered union of the orders of the state,

in a firm and well-compacted monarchy, where each holds his own place, and all obey the dictates of a common head.

General Harrison, the second of the Commissioners, was a tall, thin, middle-aged man, who had risen into his high situation in the army, and his intimacy with Cromwell, by his dauntless courage in the field, and the popularity he had acquired by his exalted enthusiasm amongst the military saints, sectaries, and Independents, who composed the strength of the existing army. Harrison was of mean extraction, and bred up to his father's employment of a butcher. Nevertheless, his appearance, though coarse, was not vulgar, like that of Desborough, who had so much the advantage of him in birth and education. He had a masculine height and strength of figure, was well made, and in his manner announced a rough military character, which might be feared, but could not easily become the object of contempt or ridicule. His aquiline nose and dark black eyes set off to some advantage a countenance otherwise irregular, and the wild enthusiasm that sometimes sparkled in them as he dilated on his opinions to others, and often seemed to slumber under his long dark eyelashes as he mused upon them himself, gave something strikingly wild, and even noble, to his aspect. He was one of the chief leaders of those who were called Fifth-monarchy men, who, going even beyond the general fanaticism of the age, presumptuously interpreted the Book of the Revelations after their own fancies, considered that the second Advent of the Messiah, and the Millennium, or reign of the Saints upon earth, was close at hand, and that they themselves, illuminated, as they believed, with the power of foreseeing these approaching events, were the chosen instruments for the establishment of the New Reign, or Fifth Monarchy, as it was called, and were fated also to win its honours, whether celestial or terrestrial.

When this spirit of enthusiasm, which operated like a partial insanity, was not immediately affecting Harrison's mind, he was a shrewd worldly man, and a good soldier; one who missed no opportunity of mending his fortune, and who, in expecting the exaltation of the Fifth Monarchy, was, in the meanwhile, a ready instrument for the establishment of the Lord General's supremacy. Whether it was owing to his early occupation, and habits of indifference to pain or bloodshed acquired in the shambles, to natural disposition and want of feeling, or, finally, to the awakened character of his enthusiasm, which made him look upon those who opposed him, as opposing the Divine will, and therefore meriting no favour or mercy, is not easy to say; but all agreed, that after a victory, or the successful storm of a town, Harrison was one of the most cruel and pitiless men in Cromwell's army; always urging some misapplied text to authorize the continued execution of the fugitives, and sometimes even putting to death those who had surrendered themselves prisoners. It was said, that at times the recollection of some of those cruelties troubled his conscience, and disturbed the dreams of beatification in which his imagination indulged.

When Everard entered the apartment, this true representative of the fanatical soldiers of the day, who filled those ranks and regiments which Cromwell had politically kept on foot, while he procured the reduction of those in which the Presbyterian interest predominated, was seated a little apart from the others, his legs crossed, and stretched out at length towards the fire, his head resting on his elbow, and turned upwards, as if studying, with the most profound gravity, the half-seen carving of the Gothic roof.

Bletson remains to be mentioned, who, in person and figure, was diametrically different from the other two. There was neither foppery nor slovenliness in his exterior, nor had he any marks of military service or rank about his person. A small walking rapier seemed merely worn as a badge of his rank as a gentleman, without his hand having the least purpose of becoming acquainted with the hilt, or his eye with the blade. His countenance was thin and acute, marked with lines which thought rather than age had traced upon it; and a habitual sneer on his countenance, even when he least wished to express contempt on his features, seemed to assure the individual addressed, that in Bletson he conversed with a person of intellect far superior to his own. This was a triumph of intellect only, however; for on all occasions of difference respecting speculative opinions, and indeed on all controversies whatsoever, Bletson avoided the ultimate *ratio* of blows and knocks.

Yet this peaceful gentleman had found himself obliged to serve personally in the Parliamentary army at the commencement of the Civil War, till happening unluckily to come in contact with the fiery Prince Rupert, his retreat was judged so precipitate, that it required all the shelter his friends could afford, to keep him free of an impeachment or a court-martial. But as Bletson spoke well, and with great effect in the House of Commons, which was his natural sphere, and was on that account high in the estimation of his party, his behaviour at Edgehill was passed over, and he continued to take an active share in all the political events of that bustling period, though he faced not again the actual front of war.

Bletson's theoretical politics had long inclined him to espouse the opinions of Harrington and others, who adopted the visionary idea of establishing a pure democratical republic in so extensive a country as Britain. This was a rash theory, where there is such an infinite difference betwixt ranks, habits, education, and morals—where there is such an immense disproportion betwixt the wealth of individuals—and where a large portion of the inhabitants consists of the inferior classes of the large towns and manufacturing districts—men unfitted to bear that share in the direction of a state, which must be exercised by the members of a republic in the proper sense of the word. Accordingly, as soon as the experiment was made, it became obvious that no such form of government could be adopted with the smallest chance of stability ; and the question came only to be, whether the remnant, or, as it was vulgarly called, the Rump of the Long Parliament, now reduced by the seclusion of so many of the members to a few scores of persons, should continue, in spite of their unpopularity, to rule the affairs of Britain ? Whether they should cast all loose by dissolving themselves, and issuing writs to convoke a new Parliament, the composition of which no one could answer for, any more than for the measures they might take when assembled ? Or, lastly, Whether Cromwell, as actually happened, was not to throw the sword into the balance, and boldly possess himself of that power which the remnant of the Parliament were unable to hold, and yet afraid to resign ?

Such being the state of parties, the Council of State, in distributing the good things in their gift, endeavoured to soothe and gratify the army, as a beggar flings crusts to a growling mastiff.   In this view Desborough had been created a Commissioner in the Woodstock matter to gratify Cromwell, Harrison to soothe the fierce Fifth-monarchy men, and Bletson as a sincere republican, and one of their own leaven.

But if they supposed Bletson had the least intention of becoming a martyr to his republicanism, or submitting to any serious loss on account of it, they much mistook the man. He entertained their principles sincerely, and not the less that they were found impracticable ; for the miscarriage of his experiment no more converts the political speculator, than the explosion of a retort undeceives an alchymist. But Bletson was quite prepared to submit to Cromwell, or any one else who might be possessed of the actual authority. He was a ready subject in practice to the powers existing, and made little difference betwixt various kinds of government, holding in theory all to be nearly equal in imperfection, so soon as they diverged from the model of Harrington's Oceana. Cromwell had already been tampering with him, like wax between his finger and thumb, and which he was ready shortly to seal with, smiling at the same time to himself when he beheld the Council of State giving rewards to Bletson as their faithful adherent, while he himself was secure of his allegiance, how soon soever the expected change of government should take place.

But Bletson was still more attached to his metaphysical than his political creed, and carried his doctrines of the perfectibility of mankind as far as he did those respecting the conceivable perfection of a model of government; and as in the one case he declared against all power which did not emanate from the people themselves, so, in his moral speculations, he was unwilling to refer any of the phenomena of nature to a final cause. When pushed, indeed, very hard, Bletson was compelled to mutter some inarticulate and unintelligible doctrines concerning an *Animus Mundi*, or Creative Power in the works of Nature, by which she originally called into existence, and still continues to preserve, her works. To this power, he said some of the purest metaphysicians rendered a certain degree of homage ; nor was he himself inclined absolutely to censure those, who, by the institution of holidays, choral dances, songs, and harmless feasts and libations, might be disposed to celebrate the great goddess Nature ; at least dancing, singing, feasting, and sporting, being comfortable things to both young and old, they might as well sport, dance, and feast, in honour of such appointed holidays, as under any other pretext. But then this moderate show of religion was to be practised under such exceptions as are admitted by the Highgate oath ; and no one was to be compelled to dance, drink, sing, or feast, whose taste did not happen to incline them to such divertisements ; nor was any one to be obliged to worship the creative power, whether under the name of the *Animus Mundi,* or any other whatsoever. The interference of the Deity in the affairs of mankind he entirely disowned, having proved to his own satisfaction that the idea originated entirely in priestcraft. In short, with the shadowy metaphysical exception aforesaid, Mr Joshua Bletson of Darlington, member for Littlecreed, came as near the predicament of an atheist, as it is perhaps possible for a man to do. But we say this with the necessary salvo ; for we have known many like Bletson, whose curtains have been shrewdly shaken by superstition, though their fears were unsanctioned by any religious faith. The devils, we are assured, believe and tremble ; but on earth there are many, who, in worse plight

1

than even the natural children of perdition, tremble without believing, and fear even while they blaspheme.

It follows, of course, that nothing could be treated with more scorn by Mr Bletson, than the debates about Prelacy and Presbytery, about Presbytery and Independency, about Quakers and Anabaptists, Muggletonians and Brownists, and all the various sects with which the Civil War had commenced, and by which its dissensions were still continued. " It was," he said, " as if beasts of burden should quarrel amongst themselves about the fashion of their halters and packsaddles, instead of embracing a favourable opportunity of throwing them aside." Other witty and pithy remarks he used to make when time and place suited ; for instance, at the club called the Rota, frequented by St John, and established by Harrington, for the free discussion of political and religious subjects.

But when Bletson was out of this academy, or stronghold of philosophy, he was very cautious how he carried his contempt of the general prejudice in favour of religion and Christianity further than an implied objection or a sneer. If he had an opportunity of talking in private with an ingenuous and intelligent youth, he sometimes attempted to make a proselyte, and showed much address in bribing the vanity of inexperience, by suggesting that a mind like his ought to spurn the prejudices impressed upon it in childhood ; and when assuming the *latus clavus* of reason, assuring him that such as he, laying aside the *bulla* of juvenile incapacity, as Bletson called it, should proceed to examine and decide for himself. It frequently happened, that the youth was induced to adopt the doctrines in whole, or in part, of the sage who had seen his natural genius, and who had urged him to exert it in examining, detecting, and declaring for himself; and thus flattery gave proselytes to infidelity, which could not have been gained by all the powerful eloquence, or artful sophistry, of the infidel.

These attempts to extend the influence of what was called free-thinking and philosophy, were carried on, as we have hinted, with a caution dictated by the timidity of the philosopher's disposition. He was conscious his doctrines were suspected, and his proceedings watched, by the two principal sects of Prelatists and Presbyterians, who, however inimical to each other, were still more hostile to one who was an opponent, not only to a church establishment of any kind, but to every denomination of Christianity. He found it more easy to shroud himself among the Independents, whose demands were for a general liberty of conscience, or an unlimited toleration, and whose faith, differing in all respects and particulars, was by some pushed into such wild errors, as to get totally beyond the bounds of every species of Christianity, and approach very near to infidelity itself, as extremes of each kind are said to approach each other. Bletson mixed a good deal among those sectaries; and such was his confidence in his own logic and address, that he is supposed to have entertained hopes of bringing to his opinions in time the enthusiastic Vane, as well as the no less enthusiastic Harrison, provided he could but get them to resign their visions of a Fifth Monarchy, and induce them to be contented with a reign of Philosophers in England for the natural period of their lives, instead of the reign of the Saints during the Millennium.

Such was the singular group into which Everard was now introduced; showing, in their various opinions, upon how many devious coasts human nature may make shipwreck, when she has once let go her hold on the anchor which religion has given her to lean upon; the acute self-conceit and worldly learning of Bletson—the rash and ignorant conclusions of the fierce and under-bred Harrison, leading them into the opposite extremes of enthusiasm and infidelity, while Desborough, constitutionally stupid, thought nothing about religion at all; and while the others were active in making sail on different but equally erroneous courses, he might be said to perish like a vessel, which springs a leak and founders in the roadstead. It was wonderful to behold what a strange variety of mistakes and errors, on the part of the King and his Ministers, on the part of the Parliament and their leaders, on the part of the allied kingdoms of Scotland and England towards each other, had combined to rear up men of such dangerous opinions and interested characters among the arbiters of the destiny of Britain.

Those who argue for party's sake, will see all the faults on the one side, without deigning to look at those on the other; those who study history for instruction, will perceive that nothing but the want of concession on either side, and the deadly height to which the animosity of the King's and Parliament's parties had arisen, could have so totally overthrown the well-poised balance of the English constitution. But we hasten to quit political reflections, the rather that ours, we believe, will please neither Whig nor Tory.

CHAPTER XII.

Three form a College—an you give us four,
Let him bring his share with him.
                    BEAUMONT *and* FLETCHER.

MR BLETSON arose, and paid his respects to
Colonel Everard, with the ease and courtesy of a
gentleman of the time ; though on every account
grieved at his intrusion, as a religious man who
held his free-thinking principles in detestation, and
would effectually prevent his conversion of Harrison, and even of Desborough, if any thing could be
moulded out of such a clod, to the worship of the
Animus Mundi. Moreover, Bletson knew Everard
to be a man of steady probity, and by no means disposed to close with a scheme on which he had successfully sounded the other two, and which was calculated to assure the Commissioners of some little
private indemnification for the trouble they were
to give themselves in the public business. The philosopher was yet less pleased, when he saw the
magistrate and the pastor who had met him in his
flight of the preceding evening, when he had been
seen, *parma non bene relicta,* with cloak and doublet left behind him.

The presence of Colonel Everard was as unpleasing to Desborough as to Bletson ; but the former

having no philosophy in him, nor an idea that it was possible for any man to resist helping himself out of untold money, was chiefly embarrassed by the thought, that the plunder which they might be able to achieve out of their trust, might, by this unwelcome addition to their number, be divided into four parts instead of three; and this reflection added to the natural awkwardness with which he grumbled forth a sort of welcome, addressed to Everard.

As for Harrison, he remained like one on higher thoughts intent; his posture unmoved, his eyes fixed on the ceiling as before, and in no way indicating the least consciousness that the company had been more than doubled around him.

Meantime, Everard took his place at the table, as a man who assumed his own right, and pointed to his companions to sit down nearer the foot of the board. Wildrake so far misunderstood his signals, as to sit down above the Mayor; but rallying his recollection at a look from his patron, he rose and took his place lower, whistling, however, as he went, a sound at which the company stared, as at a freedom highly unbecoming. To complete his indecorum, he seized upon a pipe, and filling it from a large tobacco-box, was soon immersed in a cloud of his own raising, from which a hand shortly after emerged, seized on the black-jack of ale, withdrew it within the vapoury sanctuary, and, after a potential draught, replaced it upon the table, its owner beginning to renew the cloud which his intermitted exercise of the tube had almost allowed to subside.

Nobody made any observation on his conduct, out of respect, probably, to Colonel Everard, who bit his lip, but continued silent; aware that censure might extract some escapade more unequivocally characteristic of a cavalier, from his refractory companion. As silence seemed awkward, and the others made no advances to break it, beyond the ordinary salutation, Colonel Everard at length said, " I presume, gentlemen, that you are somewhat surprised at my arrival here, and thus intruding myself into your meeting ?"

" Why the dickens should we be surprised, Colonel ?" said Desborough ; " we know his Excellency, my brother-in-law Noll's—I mean my Lord Cromwell's way, of over-quartering his men in the towns he marches through. Thou hast obtained a share in our commission ?"

" And in that," said Bletson, smiling and bowing, " the Lord-General has given us the most acceptable colleague that could have been added to our number. No doubt your authority for joining with us must be under warrant of the Council of State ?"

" Of that, gentlemen," said the Colonel, " I will presently advise you."—He took out his warrant accordingly, and was about to communicate the contents ; but observing that there were three or four half-empty flasks upon the table, that Desborough looked more stupid than usual, and that the philosopher's eyes were reeling in his head,

notwithstanding the temperance of Bletson's usual
habits, he concluded that they had been fortifying
themselves against the horrors of the haunted mansion, by laying in a store of what is called Dutch
courage, and therefore prudently resolved to postpone his more important business with them till
the cooler hour of morning. He, therefore, instead
of presenting the General's warrant superseding
their commission, contented himself with replying,
—" My business has, of course, some reference to
your proceedings here. But here is—excuse my
curiosity — a reverend gentleman," pointing to
Holdenough, " who has told me that you are so
strangely embarrassed here, as to require both the
civil and spiritual authority to enable you to keep
possession of Woodstock."

" Before we go into that matter," said Bletson,
blushing up to the eyes at the recollection of his
own fears, so manifestly displayed, yet so inconsistent with his principles, " I should like to know
who this other stranger is, who has come with the
worthy magistrate, and the no less worthy Presbyterian ?"

" Meaning me ?" said Wildrake, laying his pipe
aside ; " Gadzooks, the time hath been that I could
have answered the question with a better title ;
but at present I am only his honour's poor clerk, or
secretary, whichever is the current phrase."

" 'Fore George, my lively blade, thou art a frank
fellow of thy tattle," said Desborough. " There is
my secretary Tomkins, whom men sillily enough
call Fibbet, and the honourable Lieutenant-General

Harrison's secretary, Bibbet, who are now at supper below stairs, that durst not for their ears speak a phrase above their breath in the presence of their betters, unless to answer a question."

"Yes, Colonel Everard," said the philosopher, with his quiet smile, glad, apparently, to divert the conversation from the topic of last night's alarm, and recollections which humbled his self-love and self-satisfaction,—"yes; and when Master Fibbet and Master Bibbet *do* speak, their affirmations are as much in a common mould of mutual attestation, as their names would accord in the verses of a poet. If Master Fibbet happens to tell a fiction, Master Bibbet swears it as truth. If Master Bibbet chances to have gotten drunk in the fear of the Lord, Master Fibbet swears he is sober. I have called my own secretary Gibbet, though his name chances to be only Gibeon, a worthy Israelite at your service, but as pure a youth as ever picked a lamb-bone at Paschal. But I call him Gibbet, merely to make up the holy trefoil with another rhyme. This squire of thine, Colonel Everard, looks as if he might be worthy to be coupled with the rest of the fraternity."

"Not I, truly," said the cavalier; "I'll be coupled with no Jew that was ever whelped, and no Jewess neither."

"Scorn not for that, young man," said the philosopher; "the Jews are, in point of religion, the elder brethren, you know."

"The Jews older than the Christians?" said Desborough; "'fore George, they will have thee before the General Assembly, Bletson, if thou venturest to say so."

Wildrake laughed without ceremony at the gross ignorance of Desborough, and was joined by a sniggling response from behind the cupboard, which, when enquired into, proved to be produced by the serving-men. These worthies, timorous as their betters, when they were supposed to have left the room, had only withdrawn to their present place of concealment.

" How now, ye rogues," said Bletson, angrily ; " do you not know your duty better ?"

" We beg your worthy honour's pardon," said one of the men, " but we dared not go down stairs without a light."

" A light, ye cowardly poltroons ?" said the philosopher; "what—to show which of you looks palest when a rat squeaks ?—but take a candlestick and begone, you cowardly villains ! the devils you are so much afraid of must be but paltry kites, if they hawk at such bats as you are."

The servants, without replying, took up one of the candlesticks, and prepared to retreat, Trusty Tomkins at the head of the troop, when suddenly, as they arrived at the door of the parlour, which had been left half open, it was shut violently. The three terrified domestics tumbled back into the middle of the room, as if a shot had been discharged in their face, and all who were at the table started to their feet.

Colonel Everard was incapable of a moment's fear, even if any thing frightful had been seen;

but he remained stationary, to see what his companions would do, and to get at the bottom, if possible, of the cause of their alarm upon an occasion so trifling. The philosopher seemed to think that *he* was the person chiefly concerned to show manhood on the occasion.

He walked to the door accordingly, murmuring at the cowardice of the servants; but at such a snail's pace, that it seemed he would most willingly have been anticipated by any one whom his reproaches had roused to exertion. "Cowardly blockheads!" he said at last, seizing hold of the handle of the door, but without turning it effectually round—"dare you not open a door?"—(still fumbling with the lock)—"dare you not go down a staircase without a light? Here, bring me the candle, you cowardly villains!—By Heaven, something sighs on the outside!"

As he spoke, he let go the handle of the parlour door, and stepped back a pace or two into the apartment, with cheeks as pale as the band he wore.

"*Deus adjutor meus!*" said the Presbyterian clergyman, rising from his seat. "Give place, sir," addressing Bletson; "it would seem I know more of this matter than thou, and I bless Heaven I am armed for the conflict."

Bold as a grenadier about to mount a breach, yet with the same belief in the existence of a great danger to be encountered, as well as the same reliance in the goodness of his cause, the worthy man stepped before the philosophical Bletson, and taking a light from a sconce in one hand, quietly

opened the door with the other, and standing in
the threshold, said, " Here is nothing !"

" And who expected to see any thing," said
Bletson, " excepting those terrified oafs, who take
fright at every puff of wind that whistles through
the passages of this old dungeon ?"

" Mark you, Master Tomkins," said one of the
waiting-men in a whisper to the steward, — " See
how boldly the minister pressed forward before all
of them ! Ah ! Master Tomkins, our parson is the
real commissioned officer of the church—your lay-
preachers are no better than a parcel of club-men
and volunteers."

" Follow me those who list," said Master Holdenough, " or go before me those who choose, I will
walk through the habitable places of this house
before I leave it, and satisfy myself whether Satan
hath really mingled himself among these dreary
dens of ancient wickedness, or whether, like the
wicked of whom holy David speaketh, we are afraid,
and flee when no one pursueth."

Harrison, who had heard these words, sprung
from his seat, and drawing his sword, exclaimed,
" Were there as many fiends in the house, as there
are hairs on my head, upon this cause I will charge
them up to their very trenches !"

So saying, he brandished his weapon, and pressed to the head of the column, where he moved side
by side with the minister. The Mayor of Woodstock next joined the body, thinking himself safer
perhaps in the company of his pastor ; and the
whole train moved forward in close order, accom-

panied by the servants bearing lights, to search the Lodge for some cause of that panic with which they seemed to be suddenly seized.

" Nay, take me with you, my friends," said Colonel Everard, who had looked on in surprise, and was now about to follow the party, when Bletson laid hold on his cloak, and begged him to remain.

" You see, my good Colonel," he said, affecting a courage which his shaking voice belied, " here are only you and I, and honest Desborough, left behind in garrison, while all the others are absent on a sally. We must not hazard the whole troops on one sortie—that were unmilitary—Ha, ha, ha!"

" In the name of Heaven, what means all this?" said Everard. " I heard a foolish tale about apparitions as I came this way, and now I find you all half mad with fear, and cannot get a word of sense among so many of you. Fie, Colonel Desborough —fie, Master Bletson—try to compose yourselves, and let me know, in Heaven's name, the cause of all this disturbance. One would be apt to think your brains were turned."

" And so mine well may," said Desborough, " ay, and overturned too, since my bed last night was turned upside down, and I was placed for ten minutes heels uppermost, and head downmost, like a bullock going to be shot."

" What means this nonsense, Master Bletson? —Desborough must have had the nightmare."

" No, faith, Colonel, the goblins, or whatever else they were, had been favourable to honest Desborough, for they reposed the whole of his person on that part of his body which—Hark, did you not hear something ?—is the central point of gravity, namely, his head."

" Did you see any thing to alarm you ?" said the Colonel.

" Nothing," said Bletson ; " but we heard hellish noises, as all our people did ; and I, believing little of ghosts and apparitions, concluded the cavaliers were taking us at advantage ; so, remembering Rainsborough's fate, I e'en jumped the window, and ran to Woodstock, to call the soldiers to the rescue of Harrison and Desborough."

" And did you not first go to see what the danger was ?"

" Ah, my good friend, you forgot that I laid down my commission at the time of the self-denying ordinance. It would have been quite inconsistent with my duty as a Parliament-man, to be brawling amidst a set of ruffians, without any military authority. No—when the Parliament commanded me to sheathe my sword, Colonel, I have too much veneration for their authority, to be found again with it drawn in my hand."

" But the Parliament," said Desborough, hastily, " did not command you to use your heels when your hands could have saved a man from choking. Ods dickens ! you might have stopped when you saw my bed canted heels uppermost, and me half stifled in the bedclothes—you might, I say, have stopped and lent a hand to put it to rights, instead of jumping out of the window, like a new-shorn sheep, so soon as you had run across my room."

" Nay, worshipful Master Desborough," said Bletson, winking on Everard, to show that he was playing on his thickskulled colleague, "how could I tell your particular mode of reposing?—there are many tastes—I have known men who slept by choice on a slope or angle of forty-five."

" Yes, but did ever a man sleep standing on his head, except by miracle?" said Desborough.

" Now, as to miracles"—said the philosopher, confident in the presence of Everard, besides that an opportunity of scoffing at religion really in some degree diverted his fear—" I leave these out of the question, seeing that the evidence on such subjects seems as little qualified to carry conviction, as a horsehair to land a leviathan."

A loud clap of thunder, or a noise as formidable, rang through the Lodge as the scoffer had ended, which struck him pale and motionless, and made Desborough throw himself on his knees, and repeat exclamations and prayers in much admired confusion.

" There must be contrivance here," exclaimed Everard; and snatching one of the candles from a sconce, he rushed out of the apartment, little heeding the entreaties of the philosopher, who, in the extremity of his distress, conjured him by the *Animus Mundi* to remain to the assistance of a distressed philosopher endangered by witches, and a Parliament-man assaulted by ruffians. As for Desborough, he only gaped like a clown in a pantomime; and, doubtful whether to follow or stop, his natural indolence prevailed, and he sat still.

When on the landing-place of the stairs, Everard paused a moment to consider which was the best course to take. He heard the voices of men talking fast and loud, like people who wish to drown their fears, in the lower story ; and aware that nothing could be discovered by those whose enquiries were conducted in a manner so noisy, he resolved to proceed in a different direction, and examine the second floor, which he had now gained.

He had known every corner, both of the inhabited and uninhabited part of the mansion, and availed himself of the candle to traverse two or three intricate passages, which he was afraid he might not remember with sufficient accuracy. This movement conveyed him to a sort of *œil-de-bœuf*, an octagon vestibule, or small hall, from which various rooms opened. Amongst these doors, Everard selected that which led to a very long, narrow, and dilapidated gallery, built in the time of Henry VIII., and which, running along the whole south-west side of the building, communicated at different points with the rest of the mansion. This he thought was likely to be the post occupied by those who proposed to act the sprites upon the occasion ; especially as its length and shape gave him some idea that it was a spot where the bold thunder might in many ways be imitated.

Determined to ascertain the truth if possible, he placed his light on a table in the vestibule, and applied himself to open the door into the gallery. At this point he found himself strongly opposed, either by a bolt drawn, or, as he rather conceived, by somebody from within resisting his attempt. He was induced to believe the latter, because the resistance slackened and was renewed, like that of human strength, instead of presenting the permanent opposition of an inanimate obstacle. Though Everard was a strong and active young man, he exhausted his strength in the vain attempt to open the door; and having paused to take breath, was about to renew his efforts with foot and shoulder, and to call at the same time for assistance, when to his surprise, on again attempting the door more gently, in order to ascertain if possible where the strength of the opposing obstacle was situated, he found it give way to a very slight impulse, some impediment fell broken to the ground, and the door flew wide open. The gust of wind, occasioned by the sudden opening of the door, blew out the candle, and Everard was left in darkness, save where the moonshine, which the long side-row of latticed windows dimmed, could imperfectly force its way into the gallery, which lay in ghostly length before him.

The melancholy and doubtful twilight was increased by a quantity of creeping plants on the outside, which, since all had been neglected in these ancient halls, now completely overgrown, had in some instances greatly diminished, and in others almost quite choked up, the space of the lattices, extending between the heavy stone shaft-work which divided the windows, both lengthways and across. On the other side there were no windows at all, and the gallery had been once hung round with paintings, chiefly portraits, by which that side of the apartment had been adorned.   Most of the pictures had been removed, yet the empty frames of some, and the tattered remnants of others, were still visible along the extent of the waste gallery ; the look of which was so desolate, and it appeared so well adapted for mischief, supposing there were enemies near him, that Everard could not help pausing at the entrance, and recommending himself to God, ere, drawing his sword, he advanced into the apartment, treading as lightly as possible, and keeping in the shadow as much as he could.

Markham Everard was by no means superstitious, but he had the usual credulity of the times; and though he did not yield easily to tales of supernatural visitations, yet he could not help thinking he was in the very situation, where, if such things were ever permitted, they might be expected to take place, while his own stealthy and ill-assured pace, his drawn weapon, and extended arms, being the very attitude and action of doubt and suspicion, tended to increase in his mind the gloomy feelings of which they are the usual indications, and with which they are constantly associated.   Under such unpleasant impressions, and conscious of the neighbourhood of something unfriendly, Colonel Everard had already advanced about half along the gallery, when he heard some one sigh very near him, and a low soft voice pronounce his name.

" Here I am," he replied, while his heart beat thick and short.   " Who calls on Markham Everard ?"

Another sigh was the only answer.

" Speak," said the Colonel, " whoever or whatsoever you are, and tell with what intent and purpose you are lurking in these apartments ?"

" With a better intent than yours," returned the
soft voice.

" Than mine!" answered Everard in great surprise. " Who are you that dare judge of my in-
tents ?"

" What, or who are you, Markham Everard, who
wander by moonlight through these deserted halls
of royalty, where none should be but those who
mourn their downfall, or are sworn to avenge it ?"

" It is—and yet it cannot be," said Everard ;
" yet it is, and must be.—Alice Lee, the devil or
you speaks. Answer me, I conjure you ! speak
openly—on what dangerous scheme are you engaged ? where is your father ? why are you here ?
—wherefore do you run so deadly a venture ?—
Speak, I conjure you, Alice Lee !"

" She whom you call on is at the distance of
miles from this spot. What if her Genius speaks
when she is absent ?—what if the soul of an ances-
tress of hers and yours were now addressing you ?
—what if"——

" Nay," answered Everard, " but what if the
dearest of human beings has caught a touch of her
father's enthusiasm ?—what if she is exposing her
person to danger, her reputation to scandal, by tra-
versing in disguise and darkness a house filled with
armed men ? Speak to me, my fair cousin, in your
own person. I am furnished with powers to protect
my uncle, Sir Henry—to protect you too, dearest

Alice, even against the consequences of this vision-ary and wild attempt. Speak—I see where you are, and, with all my respect, I cannot submit to be thus practised upon. Trust me—trust your cousin Markham with your hand, and believe that he will die or place you in honourable safety."

As he spoke, he exercised his eyes as keenly as possible to detect where the speaker stood; and it seemed to him, that about three yards from him there was a shadowy form, of which he could not discern even the outline, placed as it was within the deep and prolonged shadow thrown by a space of wall intervening betwixt two windows, upon that side of the room from which the light was admitted. He endeavoured to calculate, as well as he could, the distance betwixt himself and the object which he watched, under the impression, that if, by even using a slight degree of compulsion, he could detach his beloved Alice from the confederacy into which he supposed her father's zeal for the cause of royalty had engaged her, he would be rendering them both the most essential favour. He could not indeed but conclude, that however successfully the plot which he conceived to be in agitation had proceeded against the timid Bletson, the stupid Desborough, and the crazy Harrison, there was little doubt that at length their artifices must necessarily bring shame and danger on those engaged in it.

It must also be remembered, that Everard's affection to his cousin, although of the most respect-ful and devoted character, partook less of the dis-tant veneration which a lover of those days entertained for the lady whom he worshipped with humble diffidence, than of the fond and familiar feelings which a brother entertains towards a younger sister, whom he thinks himself entitled to guide, advise, and even in some degree to control. So kindly and intimate had been their intercourse, that he had little more hesitation in endeavouring to arrest her progress in the dangerous course in which she seemed to be engaged, even at the risk of giving her momentary offence, than he would have had in snatching her from a torrent or conflagration, at the chance of hurting her by the violence of his grasp. All this passed through his mind in the course of a single minute ; and he resolved at all events to detain her on the spot, and compel, if possible, an explanation from her.

With this purpose, Everard again conjured his cousin, in the name of Heaven, to give up this idle and dangerous mummery; and lending an accurate ear to her answer, endeavoured from the sound to calculate as nearly as possible the distance between them.

" I am not she for whom you take me," said the voice ; " and dearer regards than aught connected with her life or death, bid me warn you to keep aloof, and leave this place."

" Not till I have convinced you of your childish folly," said the Colonel, springing forward, and endeavouring to catch hold of her who spoke to him. But no female form was within his grasp. On the contrary, he was met by a shock which could come from no woman's arm, and which was rude enough to stretch him on his back on the floor. At the same time he felt the point of a sword at his throat, and his hands so completely mastered, that not the slightest defence remained to him.

"A cry for assistance," said a voice near him, but not that which he had hitherto heard, "will be stifled in your blood!—No harm is meant you—be wise, and be silent."

The fear of death, which Everard had often braved in the field of battle, became more intense as he felt himself in the hands of unknown assassins, and totally devoid of all means of defence. The sharp point of the sword pricked his bare throat, and the foot of him who held it was upon his breast. He felt as if a single thrust would put an end to life, and all the feverish joys and sorrows which agitate us so strangely, and from which we are yet so reluctant to part. Large drops of perspiration stood upon his forehead—his heart throbbed, as if it would burst from its confinement in the bosom—he experienced the agony which fear imposes on the brave man, acute in proportion to that which pain inflicts when it subdues the robust and healthy.

"Cousin Alice,"—he attempted to speak, and the sword's point pressed his throat yet more closely, —"Cousin, let me not be murdered in a manner so fearful!"

"I tell you," replied the voice, "that you speak to one who is not here; but your life is not aimed at, provided you swear on your faith as a Christian, and your honour as a gentleman, that you will conceal what has happened, whether from the people below, or from any other person. On this condition you may rise ; and if you seek her, you will find Alice Lee at Joceline's cottage in the forest."

" Since I may not help myself otherwise," said Everard, " I swear, as I have a sense of religion and honour, I will say nothing of this violence, nor make any search after those who are concerned in it."

" For that we care nothing," said the voice. " Thou hast an example how well thou mayst catch mischief on thy own part; but we are in case to defy thee. Rise and begone !"

The foot, the sword's-point, were withdrawn, and Everard was about to start up hastily, when the voice, in the same softness of tone which distinguished it at first, said, " No haste—cold and bare steel is yet around thee. Now—now—now —[the words dying away as at a distance]—thou art free. Be secret and be safe."

Markham Everard arose, and, in rising, embarrassed his feet with his own sword, which he had dropped when springing forward, as he supposed, to lay hold of his fair cousin. He snatched it up in haste, and as his hand clasped the hilt, his courage, which had given way under the apprehension of instant death, began to return ; he considered, with almost his usual composure, what was to be done next. Deeply affronted at the disgrace which he had sustained, he questioned for an instant whether he ought to keep his extorted promise, or should not rather summon assistance, and make

haste to discover and seize those who had been
recently engaged in such violence on his person.
But these persons, be they who they would, had
had his life in their power—he had pledged his word
in ransom of it—and what was more, he could not
divest himself of the idea that his beloved Alice
was a confidant, at least, if not an actor, in the confederacy which had thus baffled him. This prepos-
session determined his conduct; for, though angry
at supposing she must have been accessory to his
personal ill-treatment, he could not in any event
think of an instant search through the mansion,
which might have compromised her safety, or that
of his uncle. " But I will to the hut," he said—
" I will instantly to the hut, ascertain her share in
this wild and dangerous confederacy, and snatch
her from ruin, if it be possible."

As, under the influence of the resolution which
he had formed, Everard groped his way through
the gallery, and regained the vestibule, he heard
his name called by the well-known voice of Wildrake. " What—ho !—holla !—Colonel Everard—
Mark Everard—it is dark as the devil's mouth—
speak—where are you ?—The witches are keeping
their hellish sabbath here, as I think.—Where are
you ?"

" Here, here !" answered Everard. " Cease your
bawling.   Turn to the left, and you will meet me."

Guided by his voice, Wildrake soon appeared,
with a light in one hand, and his drawn sword in
the other. " Where have you been ?" he said—
" what has detained you ?—Here are Bletson and

the brute Desborough terrified out of their lives, and Harrison raving mad, because the devil will not be civil enough to rise to fight him in single *duello*."

" Saw or heard you nothing as you came along?" said Everard.

" Nothing," said his friend, " excepting that when I first entered this cursed ruinous labyrinth, the light was struck out of my hand, as if by a switch, which obliged me to return for another."

" I must come by a horse instantly, Wildrake, and another for thyself, if it be possible."

" We can take two of those belonging to the troopers," answered Wildrake. " But for what purpose should we run away, like rats, at this time in the evening?—Is the house falling?"

" I cannot answer you," said the Colonel, pushing forward into a room where there were some remains of furniture.

Here the cavalier took a more strict view of his person, and exclaimed in wonder, " What the devil have you been fighting with, Markham, that has bedizened you after this sorry fashion?"

" Fighting !" exclaimed Everard.

" Yes," replied his trusty attendant, " I say fighting. Look at yourself in the mirror."

He did, and saw he was covered with dust and blood. The latter proceeded from a scratch which he had received in the throat, as he struggled to extricate himself. With unaffected alarm, Wildrake seized his friend's collar, and with eager haste proceeded to examine the wound, his hands trembling, and his eyes glistening with apprehension for his benefactor's life. When, in spite of Everard's opposition, he had examined the hurt, and found it trifling, he resumed the natural wildness of his character, perhaps the more readily that he had felt shame in departing from it, into one which expressed more of feeling than he would be thought to possess.

"If that be the devil's work, Mark," said he, " the foul fiend's claws are not nigh so formidable as they are represented; but no one shall say that your blood has been shed unrevenged, while Roger Wildrake was by your side. Where left you this same imp? I will back to the field of fight, confront him with my rapier, and were his nails tenpenny nails, and his teeth as long as those of a harrow, he shall render me reason for the injury he has done you."

"Madness—madness!" exclaimed Everard; " I had this trifling hurt by a fall—a basin and towel will wipe it away. Meanwhile, if you will ever do me kindness, get the troop-horses—command them for the service of the public, in the name of his Excellency the General. I will but wash, and join you in an instant before the gate."

"Well, I will serve you, Everard, as a mute serves the Grand Signior, without knowing why or wherefore. But will you go without seeing these people below?"

"Without seeing any one," said Everard; " lose no time, for God's sake."

He found out the non-commissioned officer, and

demanded the horses in a tone of authority, to which the corporal yielded undisputed obedience, as one well aware of Colonel Everard's military rank and consequence. So all was in a minute or two ready for the expedition.

CHAPTER XIII.

——She kneel'd, and saintlike
Cast her eyes to heaven, and pray'd devoutly.
                              King Henry VIII.

COLONEL EVERARD's departure at the late hour,
for so it was then thought, of seven in the evening,
excited much speculation.   There was a gathering
of menials and dependents in the outer chamber, or
hall, for no one doubted that his sudden departure
was owing to his having, as they expressed it, "seen
something," and all desired to know how a man of
such acknowledged courage as Everard, looked under the awe of a recent apparition. But he gave them
no time to make comments ; for, striding through
the hall wrapt in his riding suit, he threw himself
on horseback, and rode furiously through the Chase,
towards the hut of the keeper Joliffe.

It was the disposition of Markham Everard to
be hot, keen, earnest, impatient, and decisive to a
degree of precipitation. The acquired habits which
education had taught, and which the strong moral
and religious discipline of his sect had greatly
strengthened, were such as to enable him to conceal, as well as to check, this constitutional violence,
and to place him upon his guard against indulging
it. But when in the high tide of violent excitation,

the natural impetuosity of the young soldier's temper was sometimes apt to overcome these artificial obstacles, and then, like a torrent foaming over a wear, it became more furious, as if in revenge for the constrained calm which it had been for some time obliged to assume. In these instances he was accustomed to see only that point to which his thoughts were bent, and to move straight towards it, whether a moral object, or the storming of a breach, without either calculating, or even appearing to see, the difficulties which were before him.

At present, his ruling and impelling motive was to detach his beloved cousin, if possible, from the dangerous and discreditable machinations in which he suspected her to have engaged, or, on the other hand, to discover that she really had no concern with these stratagems. He should know how to judge of that in some measure, he thought, by finding her present or absent at the hut, towards which he was now galloping. He had read, indeed, in some ballad or minstrel's tale, of a singular deception practised on a jealous old man, by means of a subterranean communication between his house and that of a neighbour, which the lady in question made use of to present herself in the two places alternately, with such speed, and so much address, that, after repeated experiments, the dotard was deceived into the opinion, that his wife, and the lady who was so very like her, and to whom his neighbour paid so much attention, were two different persons. But in the present case there was no room for such a deception; the distance was too

great, and as he took by much the nearest way from
the castle, and rode full speed, it would be impossible, he knew, for his cousin, who was a timorous
horsewoman even by daylight, to have got home
before him.

Her father might indeed be displeased at his interference ; but what title had he to be so ?—Was
not Alice Lee the near relation of his blood, the
dearest object of his heart, and would he now abstain from an effort to save her from the consequences of a silly and wild conspiracy, because the
old knight's spleen might be awakened by Everard's making his appearance at their present dwelling contrary to his commands ?   No.   He would
endure the old man's harsh language, as he endured
the blast of the autumn wind, which was howling
around him, and swinging the crashing branches
of the trees under which he passed, but could not
oppose, or even retard, his journey.

If he found not Alice, as he had reason to believe
she would be absent, to Sir Henry Lee himself he
would explain what he had witnessed.   However
she might have become accessory to the juggling
tricks performed at Woodstock, he could not but
think it was without her father's knowledge, so
severe a judge was the old knight of female propriety, and so strict an assertor of female decorum.
He would take the same opportunity, he thought,
of stating to him the well-grounded hopes he entertained, that his dwelling at the Lodge might be
prolonged, and the sequestrators removed from the
royal mansion and domains, by other means than

those of the absurd species of intimidation which seemed to be resorted to, to scare them from thence.

All this seemed to be so much within the line of his duty as a relative, that it was not until he halted at the door of the ranger's hut, and threw his bridle into Wildrake's hand, that Everard recollected the fiery, high, and unbending character of Sir Henry Lee, and felt, even when his fingers were on the latch, a reluctance to intrude himself upon the presence of the irritable old knight.

But there was no time for hesitation. Bevis, who had already bayed more than once from within the Lodge, was growing impatient, and Everard had but just time to bid Wildrake hold the horses until he should send Joceline to his assistance, when old Joan unpinned the door, to demand who was without at that time of the night. To have attempted any thing like an explanation with poor dame Joan, would have been quite hopeless; the Colonel, therefore, put her gently aside, and shaking himself loose from the hold she had laid on his cloak, entered the kitchen of Joceline's dwelling. Bevis, who had advanced to support Joan in her opposition, humbled his lion-port, with that wonderful instinct which makes his race remember so long those with whom they have been familiar, and acknowledged his master's relative, by doing homage in his fashion, with his head and tail.

Colonel Everard, more uncertain in his purpose every moment as the necessity of its execution drew near, stole over the floor like one who treads in a sick chamber, and opening the door of the interior apartment with a slow and trembling hand, as he would have withdrawn the curtains of a dying friend, he saw, within, the scene which we are about to describe.

Sir Henry Lee sat in a wicker arm-chair by the fire. He was wrapped in a cloak, and his limbs extended on a stool, as if he were suffering from gout or indisposition. His long white beard flowing over the dark-coloured garment, gave him more the appearance of a hermit than of an aged soldier or man of quality ; and that character was increased by the deep and devout attention with which he listened to a respectable old man, whose dilapidated dress showed still something of the clerical habit, and who, with a low, but full and deep voice, was reading the Evening Service according to the Church of England. Alice Lee kneeled at the feet of her father, and made the responses with a voice that might have suited the choir of angels, and a modest and serious devotion, which suited the melody of her tone. The face of the officiating clergyman would have been good-looking, had it not been disfigured with a black patch which covered the left eye and a part of his face, and had not the features which were visible been marked with the traces of care and suffering.

When Colonel Everard entered, the clergyman raised his finger, as cautioning him to forbear disturbing the divine service of the evening, and pointed to a seat ; to which, struck deeply with the scene he had witnessed, the intruder stole with as light a step as possible, and knelt devoutly down as one of the little congregation.

Everard had been bred by his father what was called a Puritan; a member of a sect who, in the primitive sense of the word, were persons that did not except against the doctrines of the Church of England, or even in all respects against its hierarchy, but chiefly dissented from it on the subject of certain ceremonies, habits, and forms of ritual, which were insisted upon by the celebrated and unfortunate Laud, with ill-timed tenacity. But even if, from the habits of his father's house, Everard's opinions had been diametrically opposed to the doctrines of the English Church, he must have been reconciled to them by the regularity with which the service was performed in his uncle's family at Woodstock, who, during the blossom of his fortunes, generally had a chaplain residing in the Lodge for that special purpose.

Yet deep as was the habitual veneration with which he heard the impressive service of the Church, Everard's eyes could not help straying towards Alice, and his thoughts wandering to the purpose of his presence there. She seemed to have recognised him at once, for there was a deeper glow than usual upon her cheek, her fingers trembled as they turned the leaves of her prayerbook, and her voice, lately as firm as it was melodious, faltered when she repeated the responses. It appeared to Everard, as far as he could collect by the stolen glances which he directed towards her, that the character of her beauty, as well as of her outward appearance, had changed with her fortunes.

The beautiful and high-born young lady had now approached as nearly as possible to the brown stuff dress of an ordinary village maiden ; but what she had lost in gaiety of appearance, she had gained as it seemed in dignity. Her beautiful light-brown tresses, now folded around her head, and only curled where nature had so arranged them, gave her an air of simplicity, which did not exist when her headdress showed the skill of a curious tire-woman. A light joyous air, with something of a humorous expression, which seemed to be looking for amusement, had vanished before the touch of affliction, and a calm melancholy supplied its place, which seemed on the watch to administer comfort to others. Perhaps the former arch, though innocent expression of countenance, was uppermost in her lover's recollection, when he concluded that Alice had acted a part in the disturbances which had taken place at the Lodge. It is certain, that when he now looked upon her, it was with shame for having nourished such a suspicion, and the resolution to believe rather that the devil had imitated her voice, than that a creature, who seemed so much above the feelings of this world, and so nearly allied to the purity of the next, should have had the indelicacy to mingle in such manœuvres as he himself and others had been subjected to.

These thoughts shot through his mind, in spite of the impropriety of indulging them at such a moment. The service now approached the close ;

and a good deal to Colonel Everard's surprise as well as confusion, the officiating priest, in firm and audible tone, and with every attribute of dignity, prayed to the Almighty to bless and preserve " Our Sovereign Lord, King Charles, the lawful and undoubted King of these realms." The petition (in those days most dangerous) was pronounced with a full, raised, and distinct articulation, as if the priest challenged all who heard him to dissent if they dared. If the republican officer did not assent to the petition, he thought at least it was no time to protest against it.

The service was concluded in the usual manner, and the little congregation arose. It now included Wildrake, who had entered during the latter prayer, and was the first of the party to speak, running up to the priest, and shaking him by the hand most heartily, swearing at the same time, that he truly rejoiced to see him. The good clergyman returned the pressure with a smile, observing he should have believed his asseveration without an oath. In the meanwhile, Colonel Everard, approaching his uncle's seat, made a deep inclination of respect, first to Sir Henry Lee, and then to Alice, whose colour now spread from her cheek to her brow and bosom.

" I have to crave your excuse," said the Colonel with hesitation, " for having chosen for my visit, which I dare not hope would be very agreeable at any time, a season most peculiarly unsuitable."

" So far from it, nephew," answered Sir Henry, with much more mildness of manner than Everard had dared to expect, "that your visits at other times would be much more welcome, had we the fortune to see you often at our hours of worship."

" I hope the time will soon come, sir, when Englishmen of all sects and denominations," replied Everard, "will be free in conscience to worship in common the great Father, whom they all after their manner call by that affectionate name."

" I hope so too, nephew," said the old man in the same unaltered tone ; " and we will not at present dispute, whether you would have the Church of England coalesce with the Conventicle, or the Conventicle conform to the Church. It was, I ween, not to settle jarring creeds, that you have honoured our poor dwelling, where, to say the truth, we dared scarce have expected to see you again, so coarse was our last welcome."

" I should be happy to believe," said Colonel Everard, hesitating, " that—that—in short my presence was not now so unwelcome here as on that occasion."

" Nephew," said Sir Henry, " I will be frank with you. When you were last here, I thought you had stolen from me a precious pearl, which at one time it would have been my pride and happiness to have bestowed on you ; but which, being such as you have been of late, I would bury in the depths of the earth rather than give to your keeping. This somewhat chafed, as honest Will says, ' the rash humour which my mother gave me.' I thought I was robbed, and I thought I saw the robber before me. I am mistaken—I am not robbed; and the attempt without the deed I can pardon."

" I would not willingly seek offence in your words, sir," said Colonel Everard, " when their general purport sounds kind; but I can protest before Heaven, that my views and wishes towards you and your family are as void of selfish hopes and selfish ends, as they are fraught with love to you and to yours."

" Let us hear them, man; we are not much accustomed to good wishes now-a-days; and their very rarity will make them welcome."

" I would willingly, Sir Henry, since you might not choose me to give you a more affectionate name, convert those wishes into something effectual for your comfort. Your fate, as the world now stands, is bad, and, I fear, like to be worse."

" Worse than I expect it cannot be. Nephew, I do not shrink before my changes of fortune. I shall wear coarser clothes,—I shall feed on more ordinary food,—men will not doff their cap to me as they were wont, when I was the great and the wealthy. What of that? Old Harry Lee loved his honour better than his title, his faith better than his land and lordship. Have I not seen the 30th of January? I am neither philomath nor astrologer; but old Will teaches me, that when green leaves fall winter is at hand, and that darkness will come when the sun sets."

" Bethink you, sir," said Colonel Everard, " if, without any submission asked, any oath taken, any engagement imposed, express or tacit, excepting that you are not to excite disturbances in the public peace, you can be restored to your residence in the Lodge, and your usual fortunes and perquisites there—I have great reason to hope this may be permitted, if not expressly, at least on sufferance."

" Yes, I understand you. I am to be treated like the royal coin, marked with the ensign of the Rump to make it pass current, although I am too old to have the royal insignia grinded off from me. Kinsman, I will have none of this. I have lived at the Lodge too long ; and let me tell you, I had left it in scorn long since, but for the orders of one whom I may yet live to do service to. I will take nothing from the usurpers, be their name Rump or Cromwell—be they one devil or legion—I will not take from them an old cap to cover my grey hairs—a cast cloak to protect my frail limbs from the cold. They shall not say they have, by their unwilling bounty, made Abraham rich—I will live, as I will die, the Loyal Lee."

" May I hope you will think of it, sir ; and that you will, perhaps, considering what slight submission is asked, give me a better answer ?"

" Sir, if I retract my opinion, which is not my wont, you shall hear of it.—And now, cousin, have you more to say ? We keep that worthy clergyman in the outer room."

" Something I had to say—something touching my cousin Alice," said Everard, with embarrassment ; " but I fear that the prejudices of both are so strong against me"——

" Sir, I dare turn my daughter loose to you—I

will go join the good doctor in dame Joan's apartment. I am not unwilling that you should know that the girl hath, in all reasonable sort, the exercise of her free-will."

He withdrew, and left the cousins together.

Colonel Everard advanced to Alice, and was about to take her hand. She drew back, took the seat which her father had occupied, and pointed out to him one at some distance.

" Are we then so much estranged, my dearest Alice ?" he said.

" We will speak of that presently," she replied. " In the first place, let me ask the cause of your visit here at so late an hour."

" You heard," said Everard, " what I stated to your father ?"

" I did ; but that seems to have been only part of your errand—something there seemed to be which applied particularly to me."

" It was a fancy—a strange mistake," answered Everard. " May I ask if you have been abroad this evening ?"

" Certainly not," she replied. " I have small temptation to wander from my present home, poor as it is ; and whilst here, I have important duties to discharge. But why does Colonel Everard ask so strange a question ?"

" Tell me in turn, why your cousin Markham has lost the name of friendship and kindred, and even of some nearer feeling, and then I will answer you, Alice."

" It is soon answered," she said. " When you

drew your sword against my father's cause—almost against his person—I studied, more than I should have done, to find excuse for you. I knew, that is, I thought I knew, your high feelings of public duty—I knew the opinions in which you had been bred up ; and I said, I will not, even for this, cast him off—he opposes his King because he is loyal to his country. You endeavoured to avert the great and concluding tragedy of the 30th of January; and it confirmed me in my opinion, that Markham Everard might be misled, but could not be base or selfish."

" And what has changed your opinion, Alice ? or who dare," said Everard, reddening, " attach such epithets to the name of Markham Everard ?"

" I am no subject," she said, " for exercising your valour, Colonel Everard, nor do I mean to offend. But you will find enough of others who will avow, that Colonel Everard is truckling to the usurper Cromwell, and that all his fair pretexts of forwarding his country's liberties, are but a screen for driving a bargain with the successful encroacher, and obtaining the best terms he can for himself and his family."

" For myself—Never !"

" But for your family you have—Yes, I am well assured that you have pointed out to the military tyrant, the way in which he and his satraps may master the government. Do you think my father or I would accept an asylum purchased at the price of England's liberty, and your honour ?"

" Gracious Heaven, Alice, what is this ? You

accuse me of pursuing the very course which so lately had your approbation !"

" When you spoke with authority of your father, and recommended our submission to the existing government, such as it was, I own I thought —that my father's grey head might, without dishonour, have remained under the roof where it had so long been sheltered. But did your father sanction your becoming the adviser of yonder ambitious soldier to a new course of innovation, and his abettor in the establishment of a new species of tyranny ?—It is one thing to submit to oppression, another to be the agent of tyrants—And O, Markham—their bloodhound !"

" How! bloodhound ?—what mean you?—I own it is true I could see with content the wounds of this bleeding country stanched, even at the expense of beholding Cromwell, after his matchless rise, take a yet further step to power—but to be his bloodhound ! What is your meaning ?"

" It is false, then ?—Ah, I thought I could swear it had been false !"

" What, in the name of God, is it you ask?"

" It is false that you are engaged to betray the young King of Scotland ?"

" Betray him ! *I* betray him, or any fugitive ? Never ! I would he were well out of England—I would lend him my aid to escape, were he in the house at this instant ; and think in acting so I did his enemies good service, by preventing their soiling themselves with his blood—but betray him, never !"

"I knew it—I was sure it was impossible. Oh, be yet more honest; disengage yourself from yonder gloomy and ambitious soldier! Shun him and his schemes, which are formed in injustice, and can only be realized in yet more blood!"

"Believe me," replied Everard, "that I choose the line of policy best befitting the times."

"Choose that," she said, "which best befits duty, Markham—which best befits truth and honour. Do your duty, and let Providence decide the rest.—Farewell! we tempt my father's patience too far—you know his temper—farewell, Markham."

She extended her hand, which he pressed to his lips, and left the apartment. A silent bow to his uncle, and a sign to Wildrake, whom he found in the kitchen of the cabin, were the only tokens of recognition exhibited, and leaving the hut, he was soon mounted, and, with his companion, advanced on his return to the Lodge.

CHAPTER XIV.

——— Deeds are done on earth,
Which have their punishment ere the earth closes
Upon the perpetrators.   Be it the working
Of the remorse-stirr'd fancy, or the vision,
Distinct and real, of unearthly being,
All ages witness, that beside the couch
Of the fell homicide oft stalks the ghost
Of him he slew, and shows the shadowy wound.

Old Play.

EVERARD had come to Joceline's hut as fast as
horse could bear him, and with the same impetuosity of purpose as of speed.   He saw no choice in
the course to be pursued, and felt in his own imagination the strongest right to direct, and even re-
prove, his cousin, beloved as she was, on account of
the dangerous machinations with which she appeared to have connected herself.   He returned slowly,
and in a very different mood.

Not only had Alice, prudent as beautiful, appeared completely free from the weakness of conduct
which seemed to give him some authority over her,
but her views of policy, if less practicable, were so
much more direct and noble than his own, as led
him to question whether he had not compromised
himself too rashly with Cromwell, even although
the state of the country was so greatly divided and
torn by faction, that the promotion of the General

to the possession of the executive government seemed the only chance of escaping a renewal of the Civil War. The more exalted and purer sentiments of Alice lowered him in his own eyes ; and though unshaken in his opinion, that it were better the vessel should be steered by a pilot having no good title to the office, than that she should run upon the breakers, he felt that he was not espousing the most direct, manly, and disinterested side of the question.

As he rode on, immersed in these unpleasant contemplations, and considerably lessened in his own esteem by what had happened, Wildrake, who rode by his side, and was no friend to long silence, began to enter into conversation. " I have been thinking, Mark," said he, " that if you and I had been called to the bar—as, by the by, has been in danger of happening to me in more senses than one —I say, had we become barristers, I would have had the better oiled tongue of the two—the fairer art of persuasion."

" Perhaps so," replied Everard, "though I never heard thee use any, save to induce an usurer to lend thee money, or a taverner to abate a reckoning."

" And yet this day, or rather night, I could have, as I think, made a conquest which baffled you."

" Indeed ?" said the Colonel, becoming attentive.

" Why, look you," said Wildrake, " it was a main object with you to induce Mistress Alice Lee —by Heaven, she is an exquisite creature—I approve of your taste, Mark—I say you desire to persuade her, and the stout old Trojan her father, to consent to return to the Lodge, and live there quietly, and under connivance, like gentlefolk, instead of lodging in a hut hardly fit to harbour a Tom of Bedlam."

"Thou art right; such, indeed, was a great part of my object in this visit," answered Everard.

"But, perhaps, you also expected to visit there yourself, and so keep watch over pretty Mistress Lee—eh?"

"I never entertained so selfish a thought," said Everard; "and if this nocturnal disturbance at the mansion were explained and ended, I would instantly take my departure."

"Your friend Noll would expect something more from you," said Wildrake—"he would expect, in case the knight's reputation for loyalty should draw any of our poor exiles and wanderers about the Lodge, that you should be on the watch, and ready to snap them. In a word—as far as I can understand his long-winded speeches—he would have Woodstock a trap, your uncle and his pretty daughter the bait of toasted cheese—craving your Chloe's pardon for the comparison—you the spring-fall which should bar their escape—his Lordship himself being the great grimalkin to whom they are to be given over to be devoured."

"Dared Cromwell mention this to thee in express terms?" said Everard, pulling up his horse, and stopping in the midst of the road.

"Nay, not in express terms, which I do not believe he ever used in his life—you might as well expect a drunken man to go straight forward; but he insinuated as much to me, and indicated that you might deserve well of him—Gadzo—the damnable proposal sticks in my throat—by betraying our noble and rightful King, [here he pulled off his hat,] whom God grant in health and wealth long to reign, as the worthy clergyman says, though I fear just now his Majesty is both sick and sorry, and never a penny in his pouch to boot."

"This tallies with what Alice hinted," said Everard; "but how could she know it? didst thou give her any hint of such a thing?"

"I?" replied the cavalier, "I, who never saw Mistress Alice in my life till to-night, and then only for an instant—zooks, man, how is that possible?"

"True," replied Everard, and seemed lost in thought. At length he spoke—"I should call Cromwell to account for his bad opinion of me; for, even though not seriously expressed, but, as I am convinced it was, with the sole view of proving you, and perhaps myself, it was, nevertheless, a misconstruction to be resented."

"I'll carry a cartel for you, with all my heart and soul," said Wildrake; "and turn out with his godliness's second, with as good will as I ever drank a glass of sack."

"Pshaw," replied Everard, "those in his high place fight no single combats.—But tell me, Roger Wildrake, didst thou thyself think me capable of the falsehood and treachery implied in such a message?"

"I!" exclaimed Wildrake.—"Markham Everard, you have been my early friend, my constant benefactor. When Colchester was reduced, you saved me from the gallows, and since that thou hast twenty times saved me from starving. But, by Heaven, if I thought you capable of such villainy as your General recommended,—by yonder blue sky, and all the works of creation which it bends over, I would stab you with my own hand!"

"Death," replied Everard, "I should indeed deserve, but not from you, perhaps ;—but fortunately, I cannot, if I would, be guilty of the treachery you would punish. Know that I had this day secret notice, and from Cromwell himself, that the young man has escaped by sea from Bristol."

"Now, God Almighty be blessed, who protected him through so many dangers!" exclaimed Wildrake.—" Huzza !—Up hearts, cavaliers !—Hey for cavaliers !—God bless King Charles !—Moon and stars, catch my hat !"—and he threw it up as high as he could into the air. The celestial bodies which he invoked did not receive the present dispatched to them ; but, as in the case of Sir Henry Lee's scabbard, an old gnarled oak became a second time the receptacle of a waif and stray of loyal enthusiasm. Wildrake looked rather foolish at the circumstance, and his friend took the opportunity of admonishing him.

" Art thou not ashamed to bear thee so like a schoolboy ?"

" Why," said Wildrake, " I have but sent a Puritan's hat upon a loyal errand. I laugh to think how many of the schoolboys thou talk'st of will be cheated into climbing the pollard next year, expecting to find the nest of some unknown bird in yonder unmeasured margin of felt."

"Hush now, for God's sake, and let us speak calmly," said Everard. "Charles has escaped, and I am glad of it. I would willingly have seen him on his father's throne by composition, but not by the force of the Scottish army, and the incensed and vengeful royalists"——

"Master Markham Everard," began the cavalier, interrupting him——

"Nay, hush, dear Wildrake," said Everard; "let us not dispute a point on which we cannot agree, and give me leave to go on.—I say, since the young man has escaped, Cromwell's offensive and injurious stipulation falls to the ground; and I see not why my uncle and his family should not again enter their own house, under the same terms of connivance as many other royalists. What may be incumbent on me is different, nor can I determine my course until I have an interview with the General, which, as I think, will end in his confessing that he threw in this offensive proposal to sound us both. It is much in his manner; for he is blunt, and never sees or feels the punctilious honour which the gallants of the day stretch to such delicacy."

"I'll acquit him of having any punctilio about him," said Wildrake, "either touching honour or honesty.—Now, to come back to where we started. —Supposing you were not to reside in person at the Lodge, and to forbear even visiting there, unless on invitation, when such a thing can be brought about, I tell you frankly, I think your uncle and his daughter might be induced to come back to the Lodge, and reside there as usual. At least the clergyman, that worthy old cock, gave me to hope as much."

"He had been hasty in bestowing his confidence," said Everard.

" True," replied Wildrake ; " he confided in me at once ; for he instantly saw my regard for the church. I thank Heaven I never passed a clergyman in his canonicals without pulling my hat off— (and thou knowest, the most desperate duel I ever fought was with young Grayless of the Inner Temple, for taking the wall of the Reverend Dr Bunce) —Ah, I can gain a chaplain's ear instantly. Gadzooks, they know whom they have to trust to in such a one as I."

" Dost thou think, then," said Colonel Everard, " or rather does this clergyman think, that if they were secure of intrusion from me, the family would return to the Lodge, supposing the intruding Commissioners gone, and this nocturnal disturbance explained and ended ?"

" The old Knight," answered Wildrake, " may be wrought upon by the Doctor to return, if he is secure against intrusion. As for disturbances, the stout old boy, so far as I can learn in two minutes' conversation, laughs at all this turmoil as the work of mere imagination, the consequence of the remorse of their own evil consciences ; and says that goblin or devil was never heard of at Woodstock, until it became the residence of such men as they, who have now usurped the possession."

" There is more than imagination in it," said Everard. " I have personal reason to know there is some conspiracy carrying on, to render the house untenable by the Commissioners. I acquit my uncle of accession to such a silly trick ; but I must see it ended ere I can agree to his and my cousin's residing where such a confederacy exists ; for they are likely to be considered as the contrivers of such pranks, be the actual agent who he may."

" With reverence to your better acquaintance with the gentleman, Everard, I should rather suspect the old father of Puritans (I beg your pardon again) has something to do with the business ; and if so, Lucifer will never look near the true old Knight's beard, nor abide a glance of yonder maiden's innocent blue eyes.   I will uphold them as safe as pure gold in a miser's chest."

" Sawest thou aught thyself, which makes thee think thus ?"

" Not a quill of the devil's pinion saw I," replied Wildrake. " He supposes himself too secure of an old cavalier, who must steal, hang, or drown, in the long run, so he gives himself no trouble to look after the assured booty.   But I heard the serving-fellows prate of what they had seen and heard ; and though their tales were confused enough, yet if there was any truth among them at all, I should say the devil must have been in the dance.—But, holla! here comes some one upon us.—Stand, friend —who art thou ?"

" A poor daylabourer in the great work of England—Joseph Tomkins by name—Secretary to a godly and well-endowed leader in this poor Christian army of England, called General Harrison."

" What news, Master Tomkins?" said Everard; " and why are you on the road at this late hour?"

" I speak to the worthy Colonel Everard, as I judge?" said Tomkins; " and truly I am glad of meeting your honour. Heaven knows, I need such assistance as yours.—Oh, worthy Master Everard! —Here has been a sounding of trumpets, and a breaking of vials, and a pouring forth, and"——

" Prithee, tell me, in brief, what is the matter —where is thy master—and, in a word, what has happened?"

" My master is close by, parading it in the little meadow, beside the hugeous oak, which is called by the name of the late Man; ride but two steps forward, and you may see him walking swiftly to and fro, advancing all the while the naked weapon."

Upon proceeding as directed, but with as little noise as possible, they descried a man, whom of course they concluded must be Harrison, walking to and fro beneath the King's oak, as a sentinel under arms, but with more wildness of demeanour. The tramp of the horses did not escape his ear; and they heard him call out, as if at the head of the brigade—"Lower pikes against cavalry!—Here comes Prince Rupert—Stand fast, and you shall turn them aside, as a bull would toss a cur-dog.— Lower your pikes still, my hearts, the end secured against your foot—down on your right knee, front rank—spare not for the spoiling of your blue aprons.—Ha—Zerobabel—ay, that is the word!"

"In the name of Heaven, about whom or what is he talking?" said Everard; "wherefore does he go about with his weapon drawn?"

"Truly, sir, when aught disturbs my master General Harrison, he is something rapt in the spirit, and conceives that he is commanding a reserve of pikes at the great battle of Armageddon—and for his weapon, alack, worthy sir, wherefore should he keep Sheffield steel in calves' leather, when there are fiends to be combated—incarnate fiends on earth, and raging infernal fiends under the earth?"

"This is intolerable," said Everard. "Listen to me, Tomkins. Thou art not now in the pulpit, and I desire none of thy preaching language. I know thou canst speak intelligibly when thou art so minded. Remember, I may serve or harm thee; and as you hope or fear any thing on my part, answer straight-forward—What has happened to drive out thy master to the wild wood at this time of night?"

"Forsooth, worthy and honoured sir, I will speak with the precision I may. True it is, and of verity, that the breath of man, which is in his nostrils, goeth forth and returneth"——

"Hark you, sir," said Colonel Everard, "take care where you ramble in your correspondence with me. You have heard how at the great battle of Dunbar in Scotland, the General himself held a pistol to the head of Lieutenant Hewcreed, threatening to shoot him through the brain if he did not give up holding forth, and put his squadron in line to the front.   Take care, sir."

" Verily, the lieutenant then charged with an even and unbroken order," said Tomkins, " and bore a thousand plaids and bonnets over the beach before him into the sea. Neither shall I pretermit or postpone your honour's commands, but speedily obey them, and that without delay."

" Go to, fellow ; thou knowest what I would have," said Everard ; " speak at once—I know thou canst if thou wilt. Trusty Tomkins is better known than he thinks for."

" Worthy sir," said Tomkins, in a much less periphrastic style, " I will obey your worship as far as the spirit will permit.   Truly, it was not an hour since, when my worshipful master being at table with Master Bibbet and myself, not to mention the worshipful Master Bletson and Colonel Desborough, and behold there was a violent knocking at the gate, as of one in haste. Now, of a certainty, so much had our household been harassed with witches and spirits, and other objects of sound and sight, that the sentinels could not be brought to abide upon their posts without doors, and it was only by provision of beef and strong liquors that we were able to maintain a guard of three men in the hall, who nevertheless ventured not to open the door, lest they should be surprised with some of the goblins wherewith their imaginations were overwhelmed. And they heard the knocking, which increased until it seemed that the door was well-nigh about to be beaten down. Worthy Master

Bibbet was a little overcome with liquor, (as is his
fashion, good man, about this time of the evening,)
not that he is in the least given to ebriety, but
simply, that since the Scottish campaign he hath
had a perpetual ague, which obliges him so to nourish his frame against the damps of the night;
wherefore, as it is well known to your honour that
I discharge the office of a faithful servant, as well
to Major-General Harrison, and the other Commissioners, as to my just and lawful master, Colonel Desborough"——

" I know all that.—And now that thou art trusted by both, I pray to Heaven thou mayst merit
the trust," said Colonel Everard.

" And devoutly do I pray," said Tomkins, " that
your worshipful prayers may be answered with favour; for certainly to be, and to be called and entitled, Honest Joe, and trusty Tomkins, is to me
more than ever would be an Earl's title, were such
things to be granted anew in this regenerated government."

" Well, go on—go on—or if thou dalliest much
longer, I will make bold to dispute the article of
your honesty. I like short tales, sir, and doubt what
is told with a long unnecessary train of words."

" Well, good sir, be not hasty. As I said before,
the doors rattled till you would have thought the
knocking was reiterated in every room of the Palace. The bell rung out for company, though we
could not find that any one tolled the clapper, and
the guards let off their firelocks, merely because
they knew not what better to do. So, Master Bib-

bet being, as I said, unsusceptible of his duty, I went down with my poor rapier to the door, and demanded who was there; and I was answered in a voice which, I must say, was much like another voice, that it was one wanting Major-General Harrison. So, as it was then late, I answered mildly, that General Harrison was betaking himself to his rest, and that any who wished to speak to him must return on the morrow morning, for that after nightfall the door of the Palace, being in the room of a garrison, would be opened to no one. So the voice replied, and bid me open directly, without which he would blow the folding leaves of the door into the middle of the hall. And therewithal the noise recommenced, that we thought the house would have fallen; and I was in some measure constrained to open the door, even like a besieged garrison which can hold out no longer."

" By my honour, and it was stoutly done of you, I must say," said Wildrake, who had been listening with much interest. " I am a bold dare-devil enough, yet when I had two inches of oak plank between the actual fiend and me, hang him that would demolish the barrier between us say I—I would as soon, when aboard, bore a hole in the ship, and let in the waves; for you know we always compare the devil to the deep sea."

" Prithee, peace, Wildrake," said Everard, " and let him go on with his history.—Well, and what saw'st thou when the door was opened?—the great Devil with his horns and claws thou wilt say, no doubt."

" No, sir, I will say nothing but what is true. When I undid the door, one man stood there, and he, to seeming, a man of no extraordinary appearance. He was wrapped in a taffeta cloak, of a scarlet colour, and with a red lining. He seemed as if he might have been in his time a very handsome man, but there was something of paleness and sorrow in his face—a long love-lock and long hair he wore, even after the abomination of the cavaliers, and the unloveliness, as learned Master Prynne well termed it, of love-locks—a jewel in his ear—a blue scarf over his shoulder, like a military commander for the King, and a hat with a white plume, bearing a peculiar hatband."

" Some unhappy officer of cavaliers, of whom so many are in hiding, and seeking shelter through the country," briefly replied Everard.

" True, worthy sir—right as a judicious exposition. But there was something about this man (if he was a man) whom I, for one, could not look upon without trembling; nor the musketeers who were in the hall, without betraying much alarm, and swallowing, as they themselves will aver, the very bullets which they had in their mouths for loading their carabines and muskets. Nay, the wolf and deer-dogs, that are the fiercest of their kind, fled from this visitor, and crept into holes and corners, moaning and wailing in a low and broken tone. He came into the middle of the hall, and still he seemed no more than an ordinary man, only somewhat fantastically dressed, in a doublet of black velvet pinked upon scarlet satin under his cloak, a jewel in his ear, with large roses in his shoes, and a kerchief in his hand, which he sometimes pressed against his left side."

" Gracious Heaven!" said Wildrake, coming close up to Everard, and whispering in his ear, with accents which terror rendered tremulous, (a mood of mind most unusual to the daring man, who seemed now overcome by it)—" it must have been poor Dick Robison the player, in the very dress in which I have seen him play Philaster— ay, and drunk a jolly bottle with him after it at the Mermaid! I remember how many frolics we had together, and all his little fantastic fashions. He served for his old master, Charles, in Mohun's troop, and was murdered by this butcher's dog, as I have heard, after surrender, at the battle of Naseby-field."

" Hush! I have heard of the deed," said Eve-rard; " for God's sake hear the man to an end.— Did this visitor speak to thee, my friend?"

" Yes, sir, in a pleasing tone of voice, but somewhat fanciful in the articulation, and like one who is speaking to an audience as from a bar or a pulpit, more than in the voice of ordinary men on ordinary matters. He desired to see Major-General Harrison."

" He did!—and you," said Everard, infected by the spirit of the time, which, as is well known, leaned to credulity upon all matters of supernatural agency,—" what did you do?"

" I went up to the parlour, and related that such a person enquired for him. He started when I told him, and eagerly desired to know the man's dress; but no sooner did I mention his dress, and the jewel in his ear, than he said, ' Begone ! tell him I will not admit him to speech of me. Say that I defy him, and will make my defiance good at the great battle in the valley of Armageddon, when the voice of the angel shall call all fowls which fly under the face of heaven to feed on the flesh of the captain and the soldier, the war-horse and his rider. Say to the Evil One, I have power to appeal our conflict even till that day, and that in the front of that fearful day he will again meet with Harrison.' I went back with this answer to the stranger, and his face was writhed into such a deadly frown as a mere human brow hath seldom worn. ' Return to him,' he said, ' and say it is MY HOUR; and that if he come not instantly down to speak with me, I will mount the stairs to him. Say that I COMMAND him to descend, by the token, that, on the field of Naseby, *he did not the work negligently.*' "

" I have heard," whispered Wildrake,—who felt more and more strongly the contagion of superstition,—" that these words were blasphemously used by Harrison when he shot my poor friend Dick."

" What happened next ?" said Everard. " See that thou speakest the truth !"

" As gospel unexpounded by a steeple-man," said the Independent; " yet truly it is but little I have to say. I saw my master come down, with a blank, yet resolved air; and when he entered

the hall and saw the stranger, he made a pause.
The other waved on him as if to follow, and walked
out at the portal. My worthy patron seemed as if
he were about to follow, yet again paused, when
this visitant, be he man or fiend, re-entered, and
said, 'Obey thy doom.

> 'By pathless march, by greenwood tree,
> It is thy weird to follow me—
> To follow me through the ghastly moonlight—
> To follow me through the shadows of night—
> To follow me, comrade, still art thou bound:
> I conjure thee by the unstanched wound—
> I conjure thee by the last words I spoke,
> When the body slept and the spirit awoke,
> In the very last pangs of the deadly stroke!'

So saying, he stalked out, and my master followed
him into the wood.—I followed also at a distance.
But when I came up, my master was alone, and
bearing himself as you now behold him."

"Thou hast had a wonderful memory, friend,"
said the Colonel, coldly, "to remember these
rhymes in a single recitation—there seems something of practice in all this."

"A single recitation, my honoured sir?" exclaimed the Independent,—"alack, the rhyme is
seldom out of my poor master's mouth, when, as
sometimes haps, he is less triumphant in his wrestles
with Satan. But it was the first time I ever heard
it uttered by another; and, to say truth, he ever
seems to repeat it unwillingly, as a child after his
pedagogue, and as it was not indited by his own
head, as the Psalmist saith."

"It is singular," said Everard;—"I have heard

and read that the spirits of the slaughtered have strange power over the slayer; but I am astonished to have it insisted upon that there may be truth in such tales.—Roger Wildrake—what art thou afraid of, man?—why dost thou shift thy place thus?"

"Fear? it is not fear—it is hate, deadly hate. —I see the murderer of poor Dick before me, and —see, he throws himself into a posture of fence— Sa—sa—say'st thou, brood of a butcher's mastiff? thou shalt not want an antagonist."

Ere any one could stop him, Wildrake threw aside his cloak, drew his sword, and almost with a single bound cleared the distance betwixt him and Harrison, and crossed swords with the latter, as he stood brandishing his weapon, as if in immediate expectation of an assailant. Accordingly, the Republican General was not for an instant taken at unawares, but the moment the swords clashed, he shouted, "Ha! I feel thee now, thou hast come in body at last.—Welcome! welcome!—the sword of the Lord and of Gideon!"

"Part them, part them," cried Everard, as he and Tomkins, at first astonished at the suddenness of the affray, hastened to interfere. Everard, seizing on the cavalier, drew him forcibly backwards, and Tomkins contrived, with risk and difficulty, to master Harrison's sword, while the General exclaimed, "Ha! two to one—two to one!—thus fight demons." Wildrake, on his side, swore a dreadful oath, and added, "Markham, you have cancelled every obligation I owed you—they are all out of sight—gone, d—n me!"

" You have indeed acquitted these obligations rarely," said Everard. " Who knows how this affair shall be explained and answered ?"

" I will answer it with my life," said Wildrake.

" Good now, be silent," said Tomkins, " and let me manage.   It shall be so ordered that the good General shall never know that he hath encountered with a mortal man ; only let that man of Moab put his sword into the scabbard's rest, and be still."

" Wildrake, let me entreat thee to sheathe thy sword," said Everard, " else, on my life, thou must turn it against me."

" No, 'fore George, not so mad as that neither, but I'll have another day with him."

" Thou, another day !" exclaimed Harrison, whose eye had still remained fixed on the spot where he found such palpable resistance. " Yes, I know thee well ; day by day, week by week, thou makest the same idle request, for thou knowest that my heart quivers at thy voice.—But my hand trembles not when opposed to thine—the spirit is willing to the combat, if the flesh be weak when opposed to that which is not of the flesh."

" Now, peace all, for Heaven's sake,"—said the steward Tomkins ; then added, addressing his master, " there is no one here, if it please your Excellence, but Tomkins and the worthy Colonel Everard."

General Harrison, as sometimes happens in cases of partial insanity, (that is, supposing his to have been a case of mental delusion,) though firmly and entirely persuaded of the truth of his own visions, yet was not willing to speak on the subject to those who, he knew, would regard them as imaginary. Upon this occasion, he assumed the appearance of perfect ease and composure, after the violent agitation he had just manifested, in a manner which showed how anxious he was to disguise his real feelings from Everard, whom he considered as unlikely to participate them.

He saluted the Colonel with profound ceremony, and talked of the fineness of the evening, which had summoned him forth of the Lodge, to take a turn in the Park, and enjoy the favourable weather. He then took Everard by the arm, and walked back with him towards the Lodge, Wildrake and Tomkins following close behind and leading the horses. Everard, desirous to gain some light on these mysterious incidents, endeavoured to come on the subject more than once, by a mode of interrogation, which Harrison (for madmen are very often unwilling to enter on the subject of their mental delusion) parried with some skill, or addressed himself for aid to his steward Tomkins, who was in the habit of being voucher for his master upon all occasions, which led to Desborough's ingenious nickname of Fibbet.

" And wherefore had you your sword drawn, my worthy General," said Everard, " when you were only on an evening walk of pleasure ?"

" Truly, excellent Colonel, these are times when men must watch with their loins girded, and their lights burning, and their weapons drawn. The day draweth nigh, believe me or not as you will, that men must watch lest they be found naked and un-armed, when the seven trumpets shall sound, Boot and saddle ; and the pipes of Jezer shall strike up, Horse and away."

" True, good General ; but methought I saw you making passes even now as if you were fighting ?" said Everard.

" I am of a strange fantasy, friend Everard," answered Harrison; " and when I walk alone, and happen, as but now, to have my weapon drawn, I sometimes, for exercise' sake, will practise a thrust against such a tree as that. It is a silly pride men have in the use of weapons. I have been accounted a master of fence, and have fought prizes when I was unregenerated, and before I was called to do my part in the great work, entering as a trooper into our victorious General's first regiment of horse."

" But methought," said Everard, " I heard a weapon clash with yours ?"

" How ? a weapon clash with my sword ?—How could that be, Tomkins ?"

" Truly, sir," said Tomkins, " it must have been a bough of the tree ; they have them of all kinds here, and your honour may have pushed against one of them, which the Brazilians call iron-wood, a block of which, being struck with a hammer, saith Purchas in his Pilgrimage, ringeth like an anvil."

" Truly, it may be so," said Harrison ; " for those rulers who are gone, assembled in this their abode of pleasure many strange trees and plants, though they gathered not of the fruit of that tree which beareth twelve manner of fruits, or of those leaves which are for the healing of the nations."

Everard pursued his investigation ; for he was struck with the manner in which Harrison evaded his questions, and the dexterity with which he threw his transcendental and fanatical notions, like a sort of veil, over the darker visions excited by remorse and conscious guilt.

" But," said he, " if I may trust my eyes and ears, I cannot but still think that you had a real antagonist—Nay, I am sure I saw a fellow, in a dark-coloured jerkin, retreat through the wood."

" Did you ?" said Harrison, with a tone of surprise, while his voice faltered in spite of him— " Who could he be ?—Tomkins, did you see the fellow Colonel Everard talks of with the napkin in his hand—the bloody napkin which he always pressed to his side ?"

This last expression, in which Harrison gave a mark different from that which Everard had assigned, but corresponding to Tomkins's original description of the supposed spectre, had more effect on Everard in confirming the steward's story, than any thing he had witnessed or heard. The voucher answered the draft upon him as promptly as usual, that he had seen such a fellow glide past them into the thicket—that he dared to say he was some deer-stealer, for he had heard they were become very audacious.

" Look ye there now, Master Everard," said Harrison, hurrying from the subject—" Is it not time now that we should lay aside our controversies,

1

and join hand in hand to repairing the breaches of our Zion? Happy and contented were I, my excellent friend, to be a treader of mortar, or a bearer of a hod, upon this occasion, under our great leader, with whom Providence has gone forth in this great national controversy; and truly, so devoutly do I hold by our excellent and victorious General Oliver, whom Heaven long preserve—that were he to command me, I should not scruple to pluck forth of his high place the man whom they call Speaker, even as I lent a poor hand to pluck down the man whom they called King.—Wherefore, as I know your judgment holdeth with mine on this matter, let me urge unto you lovingly, that we may act as brethren, and build up the breaches, and re-establish the bulwarks of our English Zion, whereby we shall be doubtless chosen as pillars and buttresses, under our excellent Lord General, for supporting and sustaining the same, and endowed with proper revenues and incomes, both spiritual and temporal, to serve as a pedestal, on which we may stand, seeing that otherwise our foundation will be on the loose sand.—Nevertheless," continued he, his mind again diverging from his views of temporal ambition into his visions of the Fifth Monarchy, " these things are but vanity in respect of the opening of the book which is sealed; for all things approach speedily towards lightning and thundering, and unloosing of the great dragon from the bottomless pit, wherein he is chained."

With this mingled strain of earthly politics, and fanatical prediction, Harrison so overpowered

Colonel Everard, as to leave him no time to urge him farther on the particular circumstances of his nocturnal skirmish, concerning which it is plain he had no desire to be interrogated.   They now reached the Lodge of Woodstock.

CHAPTER XV.

Now the wasted brands do glow,
  While the screech-owl, sounding loud,
Puts the wretch that lies in woe,
  In remembrance of a shroud.
Now it is the time of night
  That the graves, all gaping wide,
Every one lets out its sprite,
  In the church-way paths to glide.
                    Midsummer Night's Dream.

BEFORE the gate of the palace the guards were now doubled. Everard demanded the reason of this from the corporal, whom he found in the hall with his soldiers, sitting or sleeping around a great fire, maintained at the expense of the carved chairs and benches, with fragments of which it was furnished.

" Why, verily," answered the man, " the *corps-de-garde*, as your worship says, will be harassed to pieces by such duty ; nevertheless, fear hath gone abroad among us, and no man will mount guard alone. We have drawn in, however, one or two of our outposts from Banbury and elsewhere, and we are to have a relief from Oxford to-morrow."

Everard continued minute enquiries concerning the sentinels that were posted within as well as without the Lodge ; and found that, as they had been stationed under the eye of Harrison himself, the rules of prudent discipline had been exactly observed in the distribution of the posts. There remained nothing therefore for Colonel Everard to do, but, remembering his own adventure of the evening, to recommend that an additional sentinel should be placed, with a companion, if judged indispensable, in that vestibule, or anteroom, from which the long gallery where he had met with the rencontre, and other suites of apartments, diverged. The corporal respectfully promised all obedience to his orders. The serving-men being called, appeared also in double force. Everard demanded to know whether the Commissioners had gone to bed, or whether he could get speech with them?

" They are in their bedroom, forsooth," replied one of the fellows; " but I think they be not yet undressed."

" What!" said Everard, " are Colonel Desborough and Master Bletson both in the same sleeping apartment?"

" Their honours have so chosen it," said the man; " and their honours' secretaries remain upon guard all night."

" It is the fashion to double guards all over the house," said Wildrake. " Had I a glimpse of a tolerably good-looking housemaid now, I should know how to fall into the fashion."

" Peace, fool!" said Everard—" and where are the Mayor and Master Holdenough?"

" The Mayor is returned to the borough on horseback, behind the trooper who goes to Oxford for the reinforcement; and the man of the steeple-house hath quartered himself in the chamber which Colonel Desborough had last night, being that in which he is most likely to meet the —— your honour understands. The Lord pity us, we are a harassed family!"

"And where be General Harrison's knaves," said Tomkins, "that they do not marshal him to his apartment?"

"Here—here—here, Master Tomkins," said three fellows, pressing forward, with the same consternation on their faces which seemed to pervade the whole inhabitants of Woodstock.

"Away with you, then," said Tomkins;—"speak not to his worship—you see he is not in the humour."

"Indeed," observed Colonel Everard, "he looks singularly wan—his features seem writhen as by a palsy stroke; and though he was talking so fast while we came along, he hath not opened his mouth since we came to the light."

"It is his manner after such visitations," said Tomkins.—"Give his honour your arms, Zedekiah and Jonathan, to lead him off—I will, follow instantly.—You, Nicodemus, tarry to wait upon me —it is not well walking alone in this mansion."

"Master Tomkins," said Everard, "I have heard of you often as a sharp, intelligent man—tell me fairly, are you in earnest afraid of any thing supernatural haunting this house?"

"I would be loath to run the chance, sir," said Tomkins very gravely; "by looking on my worshipful master, you may form a guess how the living look after they have spoken with the dead." He bowed low, and took his leave. Everard proceeded to the chamber which the two remaining Commissioners had, for comfort's sake, chosen to inhabit in company. They were preparing for bed as he went into their apartment. Both started as the door opened, both rejoiced when they saw it was only Everard who entered.

" Hark ye hither," said Bletson, pulling him aside, " sawest thou ever ass equal to Desborough? —the fellow is as big as an ox, and as timorous as a sheep. He has insisted on my sleeping here, to protect him. Shall we have a merry night on't, ha? We will, if thou wilt take the third bed, which was prepared for Harrison; but he is gone out, like a mooncalf, to look for the valley of Armageddon in the Park of Woodstock."

" General Harrison has returned with me but now," said Everard.

" Nay but, as I shall live, he comes not into our apartment," said Desborough, overhearing his answer. " No man that has been supping, for aught I know, with the Devil, has a right to sleep among Christian folk."

" He does not propose so," said Everard; " he sleeps, as I understand, apart—and alone."

" Not quite alone, I dare say," said Desborough; " for Harrison hath a sort of attraction for goblins —they fly round him like moths about a candle: But, I prithee, good Everard, do thou stay with us. I know not how it is, but although thou hast not thy religion always in thy mouth, nor speakest many hard words about it, like Harrison—nor makest long preachments, like a certain most honourable relation of mine who shall be nameless, yet somehow I feel myself safer in thy company than with any of them. As for this Bletson, he is such a mere blasphemer, that I fear the Devil will carry him away ere morning."

" Did you ever hear such a paltry coward?" said Bletson, apart to Everard. " Do tarry, however, mine honoured Colonel—I know your zeal to assist the distressed, and you see Desborough is in that predicament, that he will require near him more than one good example to prevent him thinking of ghosts and fiends."

" I am sorry I cannot oblige you, gentlemen," said Everard ; " but I have settled my mind to sleep in Victor Lee's apartment, so I wish you good-night ; and, if you would repose without disturbance, I would advise that you commend yourselves, during the watches of the night, to Him unto whom night is even as mid-day. I had intended to have spoke with you this evening on the subject of my being here ; but I will defer the conference till to-morrow, when, I think, I will be able to show you excellent reasons for leaving Woodstock."

" We have seen plenty such already," said Desborough ; " for one, I came here to serve the estate, with some moderate advantage doubtless to myself for my trouble ; but if I am set upon my head again to-night, as I was the night before, I would not stay longer to gain a king's crown; for I am sure my neck would be unfitted to bear the weight of it."

" Good-night," exclaimed Everard; and was about to go, when Bletson again pressed close, and whispered to him, " Hark thee, Colonel—you know my friendship for thee—I do implore thee to leave the door of thy apartment open, that if thou meetest with any disturbance, I may hear thee call, and be with thee upon the very instant. Do this, dear Everard, my fears for thee will keep me awake else; for I know that, notwithstanding your excellent sense, you entertain some of those superstitious ideas which we suck in with our mother's milk, and which constitute the ground of our fears in situations like the present; therefore leave thy door open, if you love me, that you may have ready assistance from me in case of need."

" My master," said Wildrake, " trusts, first, in his Bible, sir, and then in his good sword. He has no idea that the Devil can be baffled by the charm of two men lying in one room, still less that the foul fiend can be argued out of existence by the Nullifidians of the Rota."

Everard seized his imprudent friend by the collar, and dragged him off as he was speaking, keeping fast hold of him till they were both in the chamber of Victor Lee, where they had slept on a former occasion. Even then he continued to hold Wildrake, until the servant had arranged the lights, and was dismissed from the room; then letting him go, addressed him with the upbraiding question,

" Art thou not a prudent and sagacious person, who in times like these seek'st every opportunity to argue yourself into a broil, or embroil yourself in an argument ? Out on you !"

" Ay, out on me, indeed," said the cavalier; " out on me for a poor tame-spirited creature, that submits to be bandied about in this manner, by a man who is neither better born nor better bred than myself. I tell thee, Mark, you make an unfair use of your advantages over me. Why will you not let me go from you, and live and die after my own fashion ?"

" Because, before we had been a week separate, I should hear of your dying after the fashion of a dog. Come, my good friend, what madness was it in thee to fall foul on Harrison, and then to enter into useless argument with Bletson ?"

" Why, we are in the Devil's house, I think, and I would willingly give the landlord his due wherever I travel. To have sent him Harrison, or Bletson now, just as a lunch to stop his appetite, till Crom"——

" Hush ! stone walls have ears," said Everard, looking around him. " Here stands thy night-drink. Look to thy arms, for we must be as careful as if the Avenger of Blood were behind us. Yonder is thy bed—and I, as thou seest, have one prepared in the parlour. The door only divides us."

" Which I will leave open, in case thou shouldst holla for assistance, as yonder Nullifidian hath it. —But how hast thou got all this so well put in order, good patron ?"

" I gave the steward Tomkins notice of my purpose to sleep here."

" A strange fellow that," said Wildrake, " and, as I judge, has taken measure of every one's foot—all seems to pass through his hands."

" He is, I have understood," replied Everard, " one of the men formed by the times—has a ready gift of preaching and expounding, which keeps him in high terms with the Independents ; and recommends himself to the more moderate people by his intelligence and activity."

" Has his sincerity ever been doubted?" said Wildrake.

" Never, that I heard of," said the Colonel ; " on the contrary, he has been familiarly called Honest Joe, and Trusty Tomkins. For my part, I believe his sincerity has always kept pace with his interest. —But come, finish thy cup, and to bed.—What, all emptied at one draught !"

" Adzookers, yes—my vow forbids me to make two on't ; but, never fear—the nightcap will only warm my brain, not clog it. So, man or devil, give me notice if you are disturbed, and rely on me in a twinkling." So saying, the cavalier retreated into his separate apartment, and Colonel Everard, taking off the most cumbrous part of his dress, lay down in his hose and doublet, and composed himself to rest.

He was awakened from sleep by a slow and solemn strain of music, which died away as at a distance. He started up, and felt for his arms, which he found close beside him. His temporary bed being without curtains, he could look around him without difficulty; but as there remained in the chimney only a few red embers of the fire, which he had arranged before he went to sleep, it was impossible he could discern any thing. He felt, therefore, in spite of his natural courage, that undefined and thrilling species of tremor which attends a sense that danger is near, and an uncertainty concerning its cause and character. Reluctant as he was to yield belief to supernatural occurrences, we have already said he was not absolutely incredulous; as perhaps, even in this more sceptical age, there are many fewer complete and absolute infidels on this particular than give themselves out for such. Uncertain whether he had not dreamed of these sounds which seemed yet in his ears, he was unwilling to risk the raillery of his friend by summoning him to his assistance. He sat up, therefore, in his bed, not without experiencing that nervous agitation to which brave men as well as cowards are subject; with this difference, that the one sinks under it, like the vine under the hail-storm, and the other collects his energies to shake it off, as the cedar of Lebanon is said to elevate its boughs to disperse the snow which accumulates upon them.

The story of Harrison, in his own absolute despite, and notwithstanding a secret suspicion which he had of trick or connivance, returned on his mind at this dead and solitary hour. Harrison, he remembered, had described the vision by a circumstance of its appearance different from that which his own remark had been calculated to suggest to the mind of the visionary;—that bloody napkin, always pressed to the side, was then a circumstance present either to his bodily eye, or to that of his agitated imagination. Did, then, the murdered revisit the living haunts of those who had forced them from the stage with all their sins unaccounted for? And if they did, might not the same permission authorize other visitations of a similar nature, to warn—to instruct—to punish? Rash are they, was his conclusion, and credulous, who receive as truth every tale of the kind; but no less rash may it be, to limit the power of the Creator over the works which he has made, and to suppose that, by the permission of the Author of Nature, the laws of Nature may not, in peculiar cases, and for high purposes, be temporarily suspended.

While these thoughts passed through Everard's mind, feelings unknown to him, even when he stood first on the rough and perilous edge of battle, gained ground upon him. He feared he knew not what; and where an open and discernible peril would have drawn out his courage, the absolute uncertainty of his situation increased his sense of the danger. He felt an almost irresistible desire to spring from his bed and heap fuel on the dying embers, expecting by the blaze to see some strange sight in his chamber. He was also strongly tempted to awaken Wildrake; but shame, stronger than fear itself, checked these impulses. What! should it be thought that Markham Everard, held one of the best soldiers who had drawn a sword in this sad war—Markham Everard, who had obtained such distinguished rank in the army of the Parliament, though so young in years, was afraid of remaining by himself in a twilight-room at midnight ?—It never should be said.

This was, however, no charm for his unpleasant current of thought. There rushed on his mind the various traditions of Victor Lee's chamber, which, though he had often despised them as vague, unauthenticated, and inconsistent rumours, engendered by ancient superstition, and transmitted from generation to generation by loquacious credulity, had yet something in them, which did not tend to allay the present unpleasant state of his nerves. Then, when he recollected the events of that very afternoon, the weapon pressed against his throat, and the strong arm which threw him backward on the floor—if the remembrance served to contradict the idea of flitting phantoms, and unreal daggers, it certainly induced him to believe, that there was in some part of this extensive mansion a party of cavaliers, or malignants, harboured, who might arise in the night, overpower the guards, and execute upon them all, but on Harrison in particular, as one of the regicide judges, that vengeance, which was so eagerly thirsted for by the attached followers of the slaughtered monarch.

He endeavoured to console himself on this subject, by the number and position of the guards, yet still was dissatisfied with himself for not having taken yet more exact precautions, and for keeping an extorted promise of silence, which might consign so many of his party to the danger of assassination. These thoughts, connected with his military duties, awakened another train of reflections. He bethought himself, that all he could now do, was to visit the sentries, and ascertain that they were awake, alert, on the watch, and so situated, that in time of need they might be ready to support each other.—"This better befits me," he thought, "than to be here like a child, frightening myself with the old woman's legend, which I have laughed at when a boy. What although old Victor Lee was a sacrilegious man, as common report goes, and brewed ale in the font which he brought from the ancient palace of Holyrood, while church and building were in flames? And what although his eldest son was when a child scalded to death in the same vessel? How many churches have been demolished since his time? How many fonts desecrated? So many indeed, that were the vengeance of Heaven to visit such aggressions in a supernatural manner, no corner in England, no, not the most petty parish church, but would have its apparition.—Tush, these are idle fancies, unworthy, especially, to be entertained by those educated to believe that sanctity resides in the intention and the act, not in the buildings or fonts, or the form of worship."

As thus he called together the articles of his Calvinistic creed, the bell of the great clock (a token seldom silent in such narratives) tolled three, and was immediately followed by the hoarse call of the sentinels through vault and gallery, up stairs and beneath, challenging and answering each other with the usual watchword, All's well. Their voices mingled with the deep boom of the bell, yet ceased before that was silent, and when they had died away, the tingling echo of the prolonged knell was scarcely audible. Ere yet that last distant tingling had finally subsided into silence, it seemed as if it again was awakened; and Everard could hardly judge at first whether a new echo had taken up the falling cadence, or whether some other and separate sound was disturbing anew the silence to which the deep knell had, as its voice ceased, consigned the ancient mansion and the woods around it.

But the doubt was soon cleared up. The musical tones, which had mingled with the dying echoes of the knell, seemed at first to prolong, and afterwards to survive them. A wild strain of melody, beginning at a distance, and growing louder as it advanced, seemed to pass from room to room, from cabinet to gallery, from hall to bower, through the deserted and dishonoured ruins of the ancient residence of so many sovereigns; and, as it approached, no soldier gave alarm, nor did any of the numerous guests of various degrees, who spent an unpleasant and terrified night in that ancient mansion, seem to dare to announce to each other the inexplicable cause of apprehension.

Everard's excited state of mind did not permit him to be so passive. The sounds approached so nigh, that it seemed they were performing, in the very next apartment, a solemn service for the dead, when he gave the alarm, by calling loudly to his trusty attendant and friend Wildrake, who slumbered in the next chamber with only a door betwixt them, and even that ajar.

" Wildrake—Wildrake!—Up—up! Dost thou not hear the alarm ?"

There was no answer from Wildrake, though the musical sounds, which now rung through the apartment, as if the performers had actually been within its precincts, would have been sufficient to awaken a sleeping person, even without the shout of his comrade and patron.

" Alarm !—Roger Wildrake—alarm !" again called Everard, getting out of bed and grasping his weapons—" Get a light, and cry alarm !"

There was no answer. His voice died away as the sound of the music seemed also to die ; and the same soft sweet voice, which still to his thinking resembled that of Alice Lee, was heard in his apartment, and, as he thought, at no distance from him.

" Your comrade will not answer," said the low soft voice. " Those only hear the alarm whose consciences feel the call."

" Again this mummery !" said Everard. " I am better armed than I was of late ; and but for the sound of that voice, the speaker had bought his trifling dear."

It was singular, we may observe in passing, that the instant the distinct sounds of the human voice were heard by Everard, all idea of supernatural interference was at an end, and the charm by which he had been formerly fettered appeared to be broken ; so much is the influence of imaginary or su-

WOODSTOCK.

perstitious terror dependent (so far as respects strong judgments at least) upon what is vague or ambiguous; and so readily do distinct tones, and express ideas, bring such judgments back to the current of ordinary life. The voice returned answer, as addressing his thoughts as well as his words.

" We laugh at the weapons thou thinkest should terrify us—Over the guardians of Woodstock they have no power. Fire, if thou wilt, and try the effect of thy weapons. But know, it is not our purpose to harm thee—thou art of a falcon breed, and noble in thy disposition, though, unreclaimed and ill nurtured, thou hauntest with kites and carrion crows. Wing thy flight from hence on the morrow, for if thou tarriest with the bats, owls, vultures, and ravens, which have thought to nestle here, thou wilt inevitably share their fate. Away then, that these halls may be swept and garnished for the reception of those who have a better right to inhabit them."

Everard answered in a raised voice.—" Once more I warn you, think not to defy me in vain. I am no child to be frightened by goblins' tales; and no coward, armed as I am, to be alarmed at the threats of banditti. If I give you a moment's indulgence, it is for the sake of dear and misguided friends, who may be concerned with this dangerous gambol. Know, I can bring a troop of soldiers round the castle, who will search its most inward recesses for the author of this audacious frolic; and if that search should fail, it will cost but a few barrels of gunpowder to make the mansion a heap of ruins, and bury under them the authors of such an ill-judged pastime."

" You speak proudly, Sir Colonel," said another voice, similar to that harsher and stronger tone by which he had been addressed in the gallery ; " try your courage in this direction."

" You should not dare me twice," said Colonel Everard, " had I a glimpse of light to take aim by."

As he spoke, a sudden gleam of light was thrown with a brilliancy which almost dazzled the speaker, showing distinctly a form somewhat resembling that of Victor Lee, as represented in his picture, holding in one hand a lady completely veiled, and in the other his leading-staff, or truncheon. Both figures were animated, and, as it appeared, standing within six feet of him.

" Were it not for the woman," said Everard, " I would not be thus mortally dared."

" Spare not for the female form, but do your worst," replied the same voice. " I defy you."

" Repeat your defiance when I have counted thrice," said Everard, " and take the punishment of your insolence. Once—I have cocked my pistol—Twice—I never missed my aim—By all that is sacred, I fire if you do not withdraw. When I pronounce the next number, I will shoot you dead where you stand. I am yet unwilling to shed blood—I give you another chance of flight—once—twice—THRICE !"

Everard aimed at the bosom, and discharged his pistol. The figure waved its arm in an attitude of scorn; and a loud laugh arose, during which the light, as gradually growing weaker, danced and glimmered upon the apparition of the aged knight, and then disappeared. Everard's life-blood ran cold to his heart—" Had he been of human mould," he thought, " the bullet must have pierced him—but I have neither will nor power to fight with supernatural beings."

The feeling of oppression was now so strong as to be actually sickening. He groped his way, however, to the fireside, and flung on the embers which were yet gleaming, a handful of dry fuel. It presently blazed, and afforded him light to see the room in every direction. He looked cautiously, almost timidly, around, and half expected some horrible phantom to become visible. But he saw nothing save the old furniture, the reading-desk, and other articles, which had been left in the same state as when Sir Henry Lee departed. He felt an uncontrollable desire, mingled with much repugnance, to look at the portrait of the ancient knight, which the form he had seen so strongly resembled. He hesitated betwixt the opposing feelings, but at length snatched, with desperate resolution, the taper which he had extinguished, and relighted it, ere the blaze of the fuel had again died away. He held it up to the ancient portrait of Victor Lee, and gazed on it with eager curiosity, not unmingled with fear. Almost the childish terrors of his earlier days returned, and he thought the severe pale eye of the ancient warrior followed his, and menaced him with its displeasure. And although he quickly argued himself out of such an absurd belief, yet the mixed feelings of his mind were expressed in words that seemed half addressed to the ancient portrait.

" Soul of my mother's ancestor," he said, " be it for weal or for woe, by designing men, or by supernatural beings, that these ancient halls are disturbed, I am resolved to leave them on the morrow."

" I rejoice to hear it, with all my soul," said a voice behind him.

He turned, saw a tall figure in white, with a sort of turban upon its head, and dropping the candle in the exertion, instantly grappled with it.

" *Thou* at least are palpable," he said.

" Palpable?" answered he whom he grasped so strongly—" 'Sdeath, methinks you might know that without the risk of choking me; and if you loose me not, I'll show you that two can play at the game of wrestling."

" Roger Wildrake!" said Everard, letting the cavalier loose, and stepping back.

" Roger Wildrake? ay, truly. Did you take me for Roger Bacon, come to help you to raise the devil?—for the place smells of sulphur consumedly."

" It is the pistol I fired—Did you not hear it?"

" Why, yes, it was the first thing waked me—for that nightcap which I pulled on, made me sleep like a dormouse—Pshaw, I feel my brains giddy with it yet."

" And wherefore came you not on the instant? —I never needed help more."

" I came as fast as I could," answered Wildrake;

"but it was some time ere I got my senses collected, for I was dreaming of that cursed field at Naseby—and then the door of my room was shut, and hard to open, till I played the locksmith with my foot."

"How! it was open when I went to bed," said Everard.

"It was locked when I came out of bed, though," said Wildrake, "and I marvel you heard me not when I forced it open."

"My mind was occupied otherwise," said Everard.

"Well," said Wildrake, "but what has happened?—Here am I bolt upright, and ready to fight, if this yawning fit will give me leave—Mother Redcap's mightiest is weaker than I drank last night, by a bushel to a barleycorn—I have quaffed the very elixir of malt—Ha—yaw."

"And some opiate besides, I should think," said Everard.

"Very like—very like—less than the pistol-shot would not waken me; even me, who with but an ordinary grace-cup sleep as lightly as a maiden on the first of May, when she watches for the earliest beam to go to gather dew. But what are you about to do next?"

"Nothing," answered Everard.

"Nothing?" said Wildrake, in surprise.

"I speak it," said Colonel Everard, "less for your information, than for that of others who may hear me, that I will leave the Lodge this morning, and, if it is possible, remove the Commissioners."

" Hark," said Wildrake, " do you not hear some noise, like the distant sound of the applause of a theatre? The goblins of the place rejoice in your departure."

" I shall leave Woodstock," said Everard, " to the occupation of my uncle Sir Henry Lee, and his family, if they choose to resume it; not that I am frightened into this as a concession to the series of artifices which have been played off on this occasion, but solely because such was my intention from the beginning. But let me warn," (he added, raising his voice,)—" let me warn the parties concerned in this combination, that though it may pass off successfully on a fool like Desborough, a visionary like Harrison, a coward like Bletson"——

Here a voice distinctly spoke, as standing near them—" Or a wise, moderate, and resolute person, like Colonel Everard."

" By Heaven, the voice came from the picture," said Wildrake, drawing his sword; " I will pink his plated armour for him."

" Offer no violence," said Everard, startled at the interruption, but resuming with firmness what he was saying,—" Let those engaged be aware, that however this string of artifices may be immediately successful, it must, when closely looked into, be attended with the punishment of all concerned—the total demolition of Woodstock, and the irremediable downfall of the family of Lee. Let all concerned think of this, and desist in time."

He paused, and almost expected a reply, but none such came.

" It is a very odd thing," said Wildrake ; " but
—yaw-ha—my brain cannot compass it just now ;
it whirls round like a toast in a bowl of muscadine ;
I must sit down—ha-yaw—and discuss it at leisure—Gramercy, good elbowchair."

So saying, he threw himself, or rather sank gradually down, on a large easy-chair, which had been
often pressed by the weight of stout Sir Henry
Lee, and in an instant was sound asleep. Everard
was far from feeling the same inclination for slumber, yet his mind was relieved of the apprehension
of any farther visitation that night ; for he considered his treaty to evacuate Woodstock, as made
known to, and accepted in all probability by, those
whom the intrusion of the Commissioners had induced to take such singular measures for expelling
them. His opinion, which had for a time bent towards a belief in something supernatural in the disturbances, had now returned to the more rational
mode of accounting for them, by dexterous combination, for which such a mansion as Woodstock
afforded so many facilities.

He heaped the hearth with fuel, lighted the
candle, and, examining poor Wildrake's situation,
adjusted him as easily in the chair as he could, the
cavalier stirring his limbs no more than an infant.
His situation went far, in his patron's opinion, to
infer trick and confederacy, for ghosts have no
occasion to drug men's possets. He threw himself
on the bed, and while he thought these strange
circumstances over, a sweet and low strain of music
stole through the chamber, the words " Good-night

—good-night—good-night," thrice repeated, each
time in a softer and more distant tone, seeming to
assure him that the goblins and he were at truce,
if not at peace, and that he had no more disturbance to expect that night. He had scarcely the
courage to call out a " good-night ;" for, after all
his conviction of the existence of a trick, it was so
well performed as to bring with it a feeling of fear,
just like what an audience experience during the
performance of a tragic scene, which they know to
be unreal, and which yet affects their passions by
its near approach to nature. Sleep overtook him
at last, and left him not till broad daylight on the
ensuing morning.

CHAPTER XVI.

And yonder shines Aurora's harbinger,
At whose approach ghosts, wandering here and there,
Troop home to churchyard————
Midsummer Night's Dream.

WITH the fresh air, and the rising of morning, every feeling of the preceding night had passed away from Colonel Everard's mind, excepting wonder how the effects which he had witnessed could be produced. He examined the whole room, sounding bolt, floor, and wainscot, with his knuckles and cane, but was unable to discern any secret passages; while the door, secured by a strong cross bolt, and the lock besides, remained as firm as when he had fastened it on the preceding evening. The apparition resembling Victor Lee next called his attention. Ridiculous stories had been often circulated, of this figure, or one exactly resembling it, having been met with by night among the waste apartments and corridors of the old palace; and Markham Everard had often heard such in his childhood. He was angry to recollect his own deficiency of courage, and the thrill which he felt on the preceding night, when, by confederacy doubtless, such an object was placed before his eyes.

"Surely," he said, "this fit of childish folly could

not make me miss my aim—more likely that the bullet had been withdrawn clandestinely from my pistol."

He examined that which was undischarged—he found the bullet in it. He investigated the apartment opposite to the point at which he had fired, and, at five feet from the floor, in a direct line between the bedside and the place where the appearances had been seen, a pistol-ball had recently buried itself in the wainscot. He had little doubt, therefore, that he had fired in a just direction; and indeed to have arrived at the place where it was lodged, the bullet must have passed through the appearance at which he aimed, and proceeded point blank to the wall beyond. This was mysterious, and induced him to doubt whether the art of witchcraft or conjuration had not been called in to assist the machinations of those daring conspirators, who, being themselves mortal, might, nevertheless, according to the universal creed of the times, have invoked and obtained assistance from the inhabitants of another world.

His next investigation respected the picture of Victor Lee itself. He examined it minutely as he stood on the floor before it, and compared its pale, shadowy, faintly-traced outlines, its faded colours, the stern repose of the eye, and deathlike pallidness of the countenance, with its different aspect on the preceding night, when illuminated by the artificial light which fell full upon it, while it left every other part of the room in comparative darkness. The features seemed then to have an unnatural glow, while the rising and falling of the flame in the chimney gave the head and limbs something which resembled the appearance of actual motion. Now, seen by day, it was a mere picture of the hard and ancient school of Holbein; last night, it seemed for the moment something more. Determined to get to the bottom of this contrivance if possible, Everard, by the assistance of a table and chair, examined the portrait still more closely, and endeavoured to ascertain the existence of any private spring, by which it might be slipt aside,—a contrivance not unfrequent in ancient buildings, which usually abounded with means of access and escape, communicated to none but the lords of the castle, or their immediate confidants. But the panel on which Victor Lee was painted was firmly fixed in the wainscoting of the apartment, of which it made a part, and the Colonel satisfied himself that it could not have been used for the purpose which he had suspected.

He next aroused his faithful squire Wildrake, who, notwithstanding his deep share of the " blessedness of sleep," had scarce even yet got rid of the effects of the grace-cup of the preceding evening. " It was the reward," according to his own view of the matter, " of his temperance; one single draught having made him sleep more late and more sound than a matter of half-a-dozen, or from thence to a dozen pulls, would have done, when he was guilty of the enormity of rere-suppers,* and of drinking deep after them."

* Rere-suppers (*quasi arrière*) belonged to a species of luxury introduced in the jolly days of King James's extravagance,

" Had your temperate draught," said Everard, " been but a thought more strongly seasoned, Wildrake, thou hadst slept so sound that the last trump only could have waked thee."

" And then," answered Wildrake, " I should have waked with a headach, Mark ; for I see my modest sip has not exempted me from that epilogue. —But let us go forth, and see how the night, which we have passed so strangely, has been spent by the rest of them. I suspect they are all right willing to evacuate Woodstock, unless they have either rested better than we, or at least been more lucky in lodgings."

" In that case, I will dispatch thee down to Joceline's hut, to negotiate the re-entrance of Sir Henry Lee and his family into their old apartments, where, my interest with the General being joined with the indifferent repute of the place itself, I think they have little chance of being disturbed either by the present, or by any new Commissioners."

" But how are they to defend themselves against the fiends, my gallant Colonel ?" said Wildrake. "Methinks, had I an interest in yonder pretty girl, such as thou dost boast, I should be loath to expose her to the terrors of a residence at Woodstock, where these devils—I beg their pardon, for I sup-

and continued through the subsequent reign. The supper took place at an early hour, six or seven o'clock at latest—the reresupper was a postliminary banquet, a *hors d'œuvre*, which made its appearance at ten or eleven, and served as an apology for prolonging the entertainment till midnight.

pose they hear every word we say—these merry goblins—make such gay work from twilight till morning."

"My dear Wildrake," said the Colonel, "I, as well as you, believe it possible that our speech may be overheard; but I care not, and will speak my mind plainly. I trust Sir Henry and Alice are not engaged in this silly plot; I cannot reconcile it with the pride of the one, the modesty of the other, or the good sense of both, that any motive could engage them in so strange a conjunction. But the fiends are all of your own political persuasion, Wildrake, all true-blue cavaliers; and I am convinced, that Sir Henry and Alice Lee, though they be unconnected with them, have not the slightest cause to be apprehensive of their goblin machinations. Besides, Sir Henry and Joceline must know every corner about the place: it will be far more difficult to play off any ghostly machinery upon him than upon strangers. But let us to our toilet, and when water and brush have done their work, we will enquire what is next to be done."

"Nay, that wretched puritan's garb of mine is hardly worth brushing," said Wildrake; "and but for this hundred-weight of rusty iron, with which thou hast bedizened me, I look more like a bankrupt Quaker than any thing else. But I'll make *you* as spruce as ever was a canting rogue of your party."

So saying, and humming at the same time the cavalier tune,—

" ' Though for a time we see Whitehall
With cobwebs hung around the wall,
Yet Heaven shall make amends for all,
    When the King shall enjoy his own again' "——

" Thou forgettest who are without," said Colonel Everard.

" No—I remember who are within," replied his friend. " I only sing to my merry goblins, who will like me all the better for it. Tush, man, the devils are my *bonos socios*, and when I see them, I will warrant they prove such roaring boys as I knew when I served under Lumford and Goring, fellows with long nails that nothing escaped, bottomless stomachs that nothing filled,—mad for pillaging, ranting, drinking, and fighting,—sleeping rough on the trenches, and dying stubbornly in their boots. Ah! those merry days are gone! Well, it is the fashion to make a grave face on't among cavaliers, and specially the parsons that have lost their tithe-pigs ; but I was fitted for the element of the time, and never did or can desire merrier days than I had during that same barbarous, bloody, and unnatural rebellion."

" Thou wert ever a wild sea-bird, Roger, even according to your name ; liking the gale better than the calm, the boisterous ocean better than the smooth lake, and your rough, wild struggle against the wind, than daily food, ease, and quiet."

" Pshaw ! a fig for your smooth lake, and your old woman to feed me with brewer's grains, and the poor drake obliged to come swattering whenever she whistles ! Everard, I like to feel the wind rustle

against my pinions,—now diving, now on the crest
of the wave, now in ocean, now in sky—that is the
wild-drake's joy, my grave one ! And in the Civil
War so it went with us—down in one county, up
in another, beaten to-day, victorious to-morrow—
now starving in some barren leaguer—now revel-
ling in a Presbyterian's pantry—his cellars, his
plate-chest, his old judicial thumb-ring, his pretty
serving-wench, all at command !"

" Hush, friend," said Everard ; " remember I
hold that persuasion."

" More the pity, Mark, more the pity," said
Wildrake ; " but, as you say, it is needless talking
of it. Let us e'en go and see how your Presbyterian
pastor, Mr Holdenough, has fared, and whether he
has proved more able to foil the foul Fiend than
have you his disciple and auditor."

They left the apartment accordingly, and were
overwhelmed with the various incoherent accounts
of sentinels and others, all of whom had seen or
heard something extraordinary in the course of the
night. It is needless to describe particularly the
various rumours which each contributed to the common stock, with the greater alacrity that in such
cases there seems always to be a sort of disgrace
in not having seen or suffered as much as others.

The most moderate of the narrators only talked
of sounds like the mewing of a cat, or the growling
of a dog, especially the squeaking of a pig. They
heard also as if it had been nails driven and saws
used, and the clashing of fetters, and the rustling
of silk gowns, and the notes of music, and in short

all sorts of sounds which have nothing to do with each other. Others swore they had smelt savours of various kinds, chiefly bituminous, indicating a Satanic derivation; others did not indeed swear, but protested, to visions of men in armour, horses without heads, asses with horns, and cows with six legs, not to mention black figures, whose cloven hoofs gave plain information what realm they belonged to.

But these strongly-attested cases of nocturnal disturbances among the sentinels had been so general, as to prevent alarm and succour on any particular point, so that those who were on duty called in vain on the *corps-de-garde*, who were trembling on their own post; and an alert enemy might have done complete execution on the whole garrison. But amid this general *alerte*, no violence appeared to be meant, and annoyance, not injury, seemed to have been the goblin's object, excepting in the case of one poor fellow, a trooper, who had followed Harrison in half his battles, and now was sentinel in that very vestibule upon which Everard had recommended them to mount a guard. He had presented his carabine at something which came suddenly upon him, when it was wrested out of his hands, and he himself knocked down with the but-end of it. His broken head, and the drenched bedding of Desborough, upon whom a tub of ditch water had been emptied during his sleep, were the only pieces of real evidence to attest the disturbances of the night.

The reports from Harrison's apartment were, as

2

delivered by the grave Master Tomkins, that truly the General had passed the night undisturbed, though there was still upon him a deep sleep, and a folding of the hands to slumber; from which Everard argued that the machinators had esteemed Harrison's part of the reckoning sufficiently paid off on the preceding evening.

He then proceeded to the apartment doubly garrisoned by the worshipful Desborough, and the philosophical Bletson. They were both up and dressing themselves, the former open-mouthed in his feeling of fear and suffering. Indeed, no sooner had Everard entered, than the ducked and dismayed Colonel made a dismal complaint of the way he had spent the night, and murmured not a little against his worshipful kinsman, for imposing a task upon him which inferred so much annoyance.

"Could not his Excellency, my kinsman Noll," he said, "have given his poor relative and brother-in-law a sop somewhere else, than out of this Woodstock, which seems to be the devil's own porridge-pot? I cannot sup broth with the devil; I have no long spoon—not I. Could he not have quartered me in some quiet corner, and given this haunted place to some of his preachers and prayers, who know the Bible as well as the muster-roll? whereas I know the four hoofs of a clean-going nag, or the points of a team of oxen, better than all the books of Moses. But I will give it over, at once and for ever; hopes of earthly gain shall never make me run the risk of being carried away bodily by the devil, besides being set upon my head one

whole night, and soused with ditch water the next
—No, no—I am too wise for that."

Master Bletson had a different part to act.   He
complained of no personal annoyances ; on the contrary, he declared he should have slept as well as
ever he did in his life, but for the abominable disturbances around him, of men calling to arms every
half hour, when so much as a cat trotted by one of
their posts—He would rather, he said, " have slept
among a whole sabaoth of witches, if such creatures
could be found."

" Then you think there are no such things as
apparitions, Master Bletson ?" said Everard.   " I
used to be sceptical on the subject ; but, on my life,
to-night has been a strange one."

" Dreams, dreams, dreams, my simple Colonel,"
said Bletson, though his pale face, and shaking
limbs, belied the assumed courage with which he
spoke.   " Old Chaucer, sir, hath told us the real
moral on't—He was an old frequenter of the forest
of Woodstock, here"——

" Chaser ?" said Desborough ; " some huntsman
belike, by his name—Does he walk, like Hearne
at Windsor?"

" Chaucer," said Bletson, "my dear Desborough,
is one of those wonderful fellows, as Colonel Everard knows, who live many a hundred years after
they are buried, and whose words haunt our ears
after their bones are long mouldered in the dust."

" Ay, ay ! well," answered Desborough, to whom
this description of the old poet was unintelligible
—" I for one desire his room rather than his com-

pany—one of your conjurers, I warrant him. But what says he to the matter?"

" Only a slight spell, which I will take the freedom to repeat to Colonel Everard," said Bletson; " but which would be as bad as Greek to thee, Desborough.—Old Geoffrey lays the whole blame of our nocturnal disturbance on superfluity of humours,

> ' Which causen folke to dred in their dreams
> Of arrowes, and of fire with red gleams,
> Right as the humour of Melancholy
> Causeth many a man in sleep to cry
> For fear of great bulls and bears black,
> And others that black devils will them take.' "

While he was thus declaiming, Everard observed a book sticking out from beneath the pillow of the bed lately occupied by the honourable member.

" Is that Chaucer?" he said, making to the volume—" I would like to look at the passage"——

" Chaucer?"—said Bletson, hastening to interfere; "no—that is Lucretius, my darling Lucretius. I cannot let you see it—I have some private marks."

But by this time Everard had the book in his hand. " Lucretius?" he said; "no, Master Bletson—this is not Lucretius, but a fitter comforter in dread or in danger—Why should you be ashamed of it?—Only, Bletson, instead of resting your head, if you can but anchor your heart upon this volume, it may serve you in better stead than Lucretius or Chaucer either."

" Why, what book is it?" said Bletson, his pale

cheek colouring with the shame of detection.—
"Oh, the Bible?" throwing it down contemptuous-
ly—" some book of my fellow Gibeon's—these
Jews have been always superstitious—ever since
Juvenal's time, thou knowest—

      ' Qualiacunque voles Judæi somnia vendunt.'

He left me the old book for a spell, I warrant you,
for 'tis a well-meaning fool."

"He would scarce have left the New Testament,
as well as the Old," said Everard. "Come, my
dear Bletson, do not be ashamed of the wisest
thing you ever did in your life, supposing you took
your Bible in an hour of apprehension, with a view
to profit by the contents."

Bletson's vanity was so much galled, that it over-
came his constitutional cowardice. His little thin
fingers quivered for eagerness, his neck and cheeks
were as red as scarlet, and his articulation was as
thick and vehement as—in short, as if he had been
no philosopher.

"Master Everard," he said, "you are a man of
the sword, sir,—and, sir, you seem to suppose yourself entitled to say whatever comes into your mind
with respect to civilians, sir—But I would have
you remember, sir, that there are bounds beyond
which human patience may be urged, sir,—and
jests which no man of honour will endure, sir,—
and therefore, I expect an apology for your present
language, Colonel Everard, and this unmannerly
jesting, sir,—or you may chance to hear from me
in a way that will not please you."

Everard could not help smiling at this explosion of valour, engendered by irritated self-love.

" Look you, Master Bletson," he said, " I have been a soldier, that is true, but I was never a bloody-minded one ; and as a Christian, I am unwilling to enlarge the kingdom of darkness by sending a new vassal thither before his time. If Heaven gives you time to repent, I see no reason why my hand should deprive you of it, which, were we to have a rencontre, would be your fate in the thrust of a sword, or the pulling of a trigger—I therefore prefer to apologize ; and I call Desborough, if he has recovered his wits, to bear evidence that I *do* apologize for having suspected you, who are completely the slave of your own vanity, of any tendency, however slight, towards grace or good sense. And I farther apologize for the time that I have wasted in endeavouring to wash an Ethiopian white, or in recommending rational enquiry to a self-willed atheist."

Bletson, overjoyed at the turn the matter had taken—for the defiance was scarce out of his mouth ere he began to tremble for the consequences— answered with great eagerness and servility of manner,—" Nay, dearest Colonel, say no more of it—an apology is all that is necessary among men of honour—it neither leaves dishonour with him who asks it, nor infers degradation on him who makes it."

" Not such an apology as I have made, I trust," said the Colonel.

" No, no—not in the least," answered Bletson,—

"one apology serves me just as well as another, and Desborough will bear witness you have made one, and that is all there can be said on the subject."

. "Master Desborough and you," rejoined the Colonel, "will take care how the matter is reported, I dare say, and I only recommend to both, that, if mentioned at all, it may be told correctly."

"Nay, nay, we will not mention it at all," said Bletson, "we will forget it from this moment. Only, never suppose me capable of superstitious weakness. Had I been afraid of an apparent and real danger—why such fear is natural to man—and I will not deny that the mood of mind may have happened to me as well as to others. But to be thought capable of resorting to spells, and sleeping with books under my pillow to secure myself against ghosts,—on my word, it was enough to provoke one to quarrel, for the moment, with his very best friend.—And now, Colonel, what is to be done, and how is our duty to be executed at this accursed place? If I should get such a wetting as Desborough's, why I should die of catarrh, though you see it hurts him no more than a bucket of water thrown over a posthorse. You are, I presume, a brother in our commission; how are you of opinion we should proceed?"

"Why, in good time here comes Harrison," said Everard, "and I will lay my commission from the Lord General before you all; which, as you see, Colonel Desborough, commands you to desist from acting on your present authority, and intimates his pleasure accordingly, that you withdraw from this place."

Desborough took the paper and examined the signature.—" It is Noll's signature sure enough," said he, dropping his under jaw; "only, every time of late he has made the *Oliver* as large as a giant, while the *Cromwell* creeps after like a dwarf, as if the surname were like to disappear one of these days altogether. But is his Excellency, our kinsman, Noll Cromwell, (since he has the surname yet,) so unreasonable as to think his relations and friends are to be set upon their heads till they have the crick in their neck—drenched as if they had been plunged in a horsepond—frightened, day and night, by all sort of devils, witches, and fairies, and get not a penny of smart-money? Adzooks, (forgive me for swearing,) if that's the case, I had better home to my farm, and mind team and herd, than dangle after such a thankless person, though I *have* wived his sister. She was poor enough when I took her, for as high as Noll holds his head now."

" It is not my purpose," said Bletson, " to stir debate in this honourable meeting; and no one will doubt the veneration and attachment which I bear to our noble General, whom the current of events, and his own matchless qualities of courage and constancy, have raised so high in these deplorable days. —If I were to term him a direct and immediate emanation of the *Animus Mundi* itself—something which Nature had produced in her proudest hour, while exerting herself, as is her law, for the preservation of the creatures to whom she has given existence—I should scarce exhaust the ideas which I entertain of him. Always protesting, that I am by no means to be held as admitting, but merely as granting for the sake of argument, the possible existence of that species of emanation, or exhalation, from the *Animus Mundi*, of which I have made mention. I appeal to you, Colonel Desborough, who are his Excellency's relation—to you, Colonel Everard, who hold the dearer title of his friend, whether I have overrated my zeal in his behalf?"

Everard bowed at this pause, but Desborough gave a more complete authentication. "Nay, I can bear witness to that! I have seen when you were willing to tie his points or brush his cloak, or the like—and to be treated thus ungratefully—and gudgeoned of the opportunities which had been given you"——

"It is not for that," said Bletson, waving his hand gracefully. "You do me wrong, Master Desborough—you do indeed, kind sir—although I know you meant it not—No, sir—no partial consideration of private interest prevailed on me to undertake this charge. It was conferred on me by the Parliament of England, in whose name this war commenced, and by the Council of State, who are the conservators of England's liberty. And the chance and serene hope of serving the country, the confidence that I—and you, Master Desborough—and you, worthy General Harrison—superior, as I am, to all selfish considerations—to which I am sure you also, good Colonel Everard, would be superior,

had you been named in this commission, as I would
to Heaven you had—I say, the hope of serving the
country, with the aid of such respectable associates,
one and all of them—as well as you, Colonel Everard, supposing you to have been of the number,
induced me to accept of this opportunity, whereby
I might, gratuitously, with your assistance, render
so much advantage to our dear mother the Commonwealth of England.—Such was my hope—my
trust—my confidence. And now comes my Lord
General's warrant to dissolve the authority by which
we are entitled to act. Gentlemen, I ask this honourable meeting, (with all respect to his Excellency,) whether his commission be paramount to
that from which he himself directly holds *his* commission ? No one will say so. I ask whether he
has climbed into the seat from which the late Man
descended, or hath a great seal, or means to proceed by prerogative in such a case ? I cannot see
reason to believe it, and therefore I must resist such
doctrine. I am in your judgment, my brave and
honourable colleagues ; but, touching my own poor
opinion, I feel myself under the unhappy necessity
of proceeding in our commission, as if the interruption had not taken place ; with this addition,
that the Board of Sequestrators should sit, by day,
at this same Lodge of Woodstock, but that, to
reconcile the minds of weak brethren, who may be
afflicted by superstitious rumours, as well as to
avoid any practice on our persons by the malignants,
who, I am convinced, are busy in this neighbour-

hood, we should remove our sittings after sunset to the George Inn, in the neighbouring borough."

" Good Master Bletson," replied Colonel Everard, " it is not for me to reply to you; but you may know in what characters this army of England and their General write their authority. I fear me the annotation on this precept of the General, will be expressed by the march of a troop of horse from Oxford to see it executed. I believe there are orders out for that effect; and you know by late experience, that the soldier will obey his General equally against King and Parliament."

" That obedience is conditional," said Harrison, starting fiercely up. " Know'st thou not, Markham Everard, that I have followed the man Cromwell as close as the bull-dog follows his master?—and so I will yet;—but I am no spaniel, either to be beaten, or to have the food I have earned snatched from me, as if I were a vile cur, whose wages are a whipping, and free leave to wear my own skin. I looked, amongst the three of us, that we might honestly and piously, and with advantage to the Commonwealth, have gained out of this commission three, or it may be five thousand pounds. And does Cromwell imagine I will part with it for a rough word? No man goeth a warfare on his own charges. He that serves the altar must live by the altar—and the saints must have means to provide them with good harness and fresh horses against the unsealing and the pouring forth. Does Cromwell think I am so much of a tame tiger as to permit him to rend from me at pleasure the miserable dole he hath thrown

me? Of a surety I will resist; and the men who
are here, being chiefly of my own regiment—men
who wait, and who expect, with lamps burning and
loins girded, and each one his weapon bound
upon his thigh, will aid me to make this house
good against every assault—ay, even against Cromwell himself, until the latter coming—Selah!
Selah!"——

"And I," said Desborough, "will levy troops
and protect your out-quarters, not choosing at present to close myself up in garrison"——

"And I," said Bletson, "will do my part, and
hie me to town and lay the matter before Parliament, arising in my place for that effect."

Everard was little moved by all these threats.
The only formidable one, indeed, was that of Harrison, whose enthusiasm, joined with his courage,
and obstinacy, and character among the fanatics of
his own principles, made him a dangerous enemy.
Before trying any arguments with the refractory
Major-General, Everard endeavoured to moderate
his feelings, and threw something in about the late
disturbances.

"Talk not to me of supernatural disturbances,
young man—talk not to me of enemies in the body
or out of the body. Am I not the champion chosen
and commissioned to encounter and to conquer the
great Dragon, and the Beast which cometh out of
the sea? Am I not to command the left wing and
two regiments of the centre, when the Saints shall
encounter with the countless legions of Gog and
Magog? I tell thee that my name is written on

the sea of glass mingled with fire, and that I will keep this place of Woodstock against all mortal men, and against all devils, whether in field or chamber, in the forest or in the meadow, even till the Saints reign in the fulness of their glory !"

Everard saw it was then time to produce two or three lines under Cromwell's hand, which he had received from the General, subsequently to the communication through Wildrake. The information they contained was calculated to allay the disappointment of the commissioners. This document assigned as the reason of superseding the Woodstock Commission, that he should probably propose to the Parliament to require the assistance of General Harrison, Colonel Desborough, and Master Bletson, the honourable member for Littlefaith, in a much greater matter, namely, the disposing of the royal property, and disparking of the King's forest at Windsor. So soon as this idea was started, all parties pricked up their ears ; and their drooping, and gloomy and vindictive looks began to give place to courteous smiles, and to a cheerfulness, which laughed in their eyes, and turned their mustaches upwards.

Colonel Desborough acquitted his right honourable and excellent cousin and kinsman of all species of unkindness ; Master Bletson discovered, that the interest of the state was trebly concerned in the good administration of Windsor more than in that of Woodstock. As for Harrison, he exclaimed, without disguise or hesitation, that the gleaning of the grapes of Windsor was better than the vintage of Woodstock. Thus speaking, the glance of his dark eye expressed as much triumph in the proposed earthly advantage, as if it had not been, according to his vain persuasion, to be shortly exchanged for his share in the general reign of the Millennium. His delight, in short, resembled the joy of an eagle, who preys upon a lamb in the evening with not the less relish, because she descries in the distant landscape an hundred thousand men about to join battle with daybreak, and to give her an endless feast on the hearts and lifeblood of the valiant.

Yet though all agreed that they would be obedient to the General's pleasure in this matter, Bletson proposed, as a precautionary measure, in which all agreed, that they should take up their abode for some time in the town of Woodstock, to wait for their new commissions respecting Windsor; and this upon the prudential consideration, that it was best not to slip one knot until another was first tied.

Each commissioner, therefore, wrote to Oliver individually, stating, in his own way, the depth and height, length and breadth, of his attachment to him. Each expressed himself resolved to obey the General's injunctions to the uttermost; but with the same scrupulous devotion to the Parliament, each found himself at a loss how to lay down the commission intrusted to them by that body, and therefore felt bound in conscience to take up his residence at the borough of Woodstock, that he might not seem to abandon the charge committed to them, until they should be called to administrate the weightier matter of Windsor, to which they expressed their willingness instantly to devote themselves, according to his Excellency's pleasure.

This was the general style of their letters, varied by the characteristic flourishes of the writers. Desborough, for example, said something about the religious duty of providing for one's own household, only he blundered the text. Bletson wrote long and big words about the political obligation incumbent on every member of the community, on every person, to sacrifice his time and talents to the service of his country; while Harrison talked of the littleness of present affairs, in comparison of the approaching tremendous change of all things beneath the sun. But although the garnishing of the various epistles was different, the result came to the same, that they were determined at least to keep sight of Woodstock, until they were well assured of some better and more profitable commission.

Everard also wrote a letter in the most grateful terms to Cromwell, which would probably have been less warm had he known more distinctly than his follower chose to tell him, the expectation under which the wily General had granted his request. He acquainted his Excellency with his purpose of continuing at Woodstock, partly to assure himself of the motions of the three Commissioners, and to watch whether they did not again enter upon the execution of the trust, which they had for the present renounced,—and partly to see that some extraordinary circumstances, which had taken place in the Lodge, and which would doubtless transpire, were not followed by any explosion to the disturbance of the public peace. He knew (as he expressed himself) that his Excellency was so much the friend of order, that he would rather disturbances or insurrections were prevented than punished; and he conjured the General to repose confidence in his exertions for the public service by every mode within his power; not aware, it will be observed, in what peculiar sense his general pledge might be interpreted.

These letters being made up into a packet, were forwarded to Windsor by a trooper, detached on that errand.

CHAPTER XVII.

We do that in our zeal,
Our calmer moments are afraid to answer.
Anonymous.

WHILE the Commissioners were preparing to
remove themselves from the Lodge to the inn at
the borough of Woodstock, with all that state and
bustle which attend the movements of great persons, and especially of such to whom greatness is
not entirely familiar, Everard held some colloquy
with the Presbyterian clergyman, Master Holdenough, who had issued from the apartment which
he had occupied, as it were in defiance of the spirits
by whom the mansion was supposed to be disturbed, and whose pale cheek and pensive brow gave
token that he had not passed the night more com-
fortably than the other inmates of the Lodge of
Woodstock.　Colonel Everard having offered to
procure the reverend gentleman some refreshment,
received this reply :—" This day shall I not taste
food, saving that which we are assured of as sufficient for our sustenance, where it is promised that
our bread shall be given us, and our water shall be
sure.　Not that I fast, in the papistical opinion that
it adds to those merits, which are but an accumu-
lation of filthy rags ; but because I hold it needful

that no grosser sustenance should this day cloud my understanding, or render less pure and vivid the thanks I owe to Heaven for a most wonderful preservation."

" Master Holdenough," said Everard, " you are, I know, both a good man and a bold one, and I saw you last night courageously go upon your sacred duty, when soldiers, and tried ones, seemed considerably alarmed."

" Too courageous—too venturous," was Master Holdenough's reply, the boldness of whose aspect seemed completely to have died away. " We are frail creatures, Master Everard, and frailest when we think ourselves strongest. Oh, Colonel Everard," he added, after a pause, and as if the confidence was partly involuntary, " I have seen that which I shall never survive !"

" You surprise me, reverend sir," said Everard; —" may I request you will speak more plainly? I have heard some stories of this wild night, nay, have witnessed strange things myself; but, methinks, I would be much interested in knowing the nature of your disturbance."

" Sir," said the clergyman, " you are a discreet gentleman; and though I would not willingly that these heretics, schismatics, Brownists, Muggletonians, Anabaptists, and so forth, had such an opportunity of triumph, as my defeat in this matter would have afforded them, yet with you, who have been ever a faithful follower of our church, and are pledged to the good cause by the great National League and Covenant, surely I would be more open.

Sit we down, therefore, and let me call for a glass of pure water, for as yet I feel some bodily faltering; though, I thank Heaven, I am in mind resolute and composed as a merely mortal man may after such a vision.—They say, worthy Colonel, that looking on such things foretells, or causes, speedy death—I know not if it be true; but if so, I only depart like the tried sentinel when his officer releases him from his post; and glad shall I be to close these wearied eyes against the sight, and shut these harassed ears against the croaking, as of frogs, of Antinomians, and Pelagians, and Socinians, and Arminians, and Arians, and Nullifidians, which have come up into our England, like those filthy reptiles into the house of Pharaoh."

Here one of the servants who had been summoned, entered with a cup of water, gazing at the same time in the face of the clergyman, as if his stupid grey eyes were endeavouring to read what tragic tale was written on his brow; and shaking his empty scull as he left the room, with the air of one who was proud of having discovered that all was not exactly right, though he could not so well guess what was wrong.

Colonel Everard invited the good man to take some refreshment more genial than the pure element, but he declined: " I am in some sort a champion," he said; " and though I have been foiled in the late controversy with the Enemy, still I have my trumpet to give the alarm, and my sharp sword to smite withal; therefore, like the Nazarites of old, I will eat nothing that cometh of the vine, neither drink wine nor strong drink, until these my days of combat shall have passed away."

Kindly and respectfully the Colonel anew pressed Master Holdenough to communicate the events that had befallen him on the preceding night ; and the good clergyman proceeded as follows, with that little characteristical touch of vanity in his narrative, which naturally arose out of the part he had played in the world, and the influence which he had exercised over the minds of others. " I was a young man at the University of Cambridge," he said, " when I was particularly bound in friendship to a fellow-student, perhaps because we were esteemed (though it is vain to mention it) the most hopeful scholars at our college ; and so equally advanced, that it was difficult, perhaps, to say which was the greater proficient in his studies. Only our tutor, Master Purefoy, used to say, that if my comrade had the advantage of me in gifts, I had the better of him in grace ; for he was attached to the profane learning of the classics, always unprofitable, often impious and impure ; and I had light enough to turn my studies into the sacred tongues. Also we differed in our opinions touching the Church of England, for he held Arminian opinions, with Laud, and those who would connect our ecclesiastical establishment with the civil, and make the Church dependent on the breath of an earthly man. In fine, he favoured Prelacy both in essentials and ceremonial ; and although we parted with tears and embraces, it was to follow very different courses. He obtained a living, and became a great controversial writer in behalf of the Bishops and of the Court. I also, as is well known to you, to the best of my poor abilities, sharpened my pen in the cause of the poor oppressed people, whose tender consciences rejected the rites and ceremonies more befitting a papistical than a reformed Church, and which, according to the blinded policy of the Court, were enforced by pains and penalties. Then came the Civil War, and I—called thereunto by my conscience, and nothing fearing or suspecting what miserable consequences have chanced, through the rise of these Independents—consented to lend my countenance and labour to the great work, by becoming chaplain to Colonel Harrison's regiment. Not that I mingled with carnal weapons in the field —which Heaven forbid that a minister of the altar should—but I preached, exhorted, and, in time of need, was a surgeon, as well to the wounds of the body as of the soul. Now, it fell, towards the end of the war, that a party of malignants had seized on a strong house in the shire of Shrewsbury, situated on a small island, advanced into a lake, and accessible only by a small and narrow causeway. From thence they made excursions, and vexed the country; and high time it was to suppress them, so that a part of our regiment went to reduce them; and I was requested to go, for they were few in number to take in so strong a place, and the Colonel judged that my exhortations would make them do valiantly. And so, contrary to my wont, I went forth with them, even to the field, where there was valiant fighting on both sides. Nevertheless, the

malignants shooting their wall-pieces at us, had so
much the advantage, that after bursting their gates
with a salvo of our cannon, Colonel Harrison ordered his men to advance on the causeway, and try
to carry the place by storm.   Natheless, although
our men did valiantly, advancing in good order,
yet being galled on every side by the fire, they at
length fell into disorder, and were retreating with
much loss, Harrison himself valiantly bringing up
the rear, and defending them as he could against
the enemy, who sallied forth in pursuit of them,
to smite them hip and thigh.   Now, Colonel Everard, I am a man of a quick and vehement temper
by nature, though better teaching than the old law
hath made me mild and patient as you now see me.
I could not bear to see our Israelites flying before
the Philistines, so I rushed upon the causeway,
with the Bible in one hand, and a halberd, which
I had caught up, in the other, and turned back the
foremost fugitives, by threatening to strike them
down, pointing out to them at the same time a
priest in his cassock, as they call it, who was among
the malignants, and asking them whether they
would not do as much for a true servant of Heaven, as the uncircumcised would for a priest of
Baal. My words and strokes prevailed ; they turned at once, and shouting out, Down with Baal and
his worshippers ! they charged the malignants so
unexpectedly home, that they not only drove them
back into their house of garrison, but entered it
with them, as the phrase is, pellmell.   I also was
there, partly hurried on by the crowd, partly to

prevail on our enraged soldiers to give quarter; for it grieved my heart to see Christians and Englishmen hashed down with swords and gunstocks, like curs in the street when there is an alarm of mad dogs. In this way, the soldiers fighting and slaughtering, and I calling to them to stay their hand, we gained the very roof of the building, which was in part leaded, and to which, as a last tower of refuge, those of the cavaliers, who yet escaped, had retired. I was myself, I may say, forced up the narrow winding staircase by our soldiers, who rushed on like dogs of chase upon their prey; and when extricated from the passage, I found myself in the midst of a horrid scene. The scattered defenders were, some resisting with the fury of despair; some on their knees, imploring for compassion in words and tones to break a man's heart when he thinks on them; some were calling on God for mercy; and it was time, for man had none. They were stricken down, thrust through, flung from the battlements into the lake; and the wild cries of the victors, mingled with the groans, shrieks, and clamours, of the vanquished, made a sound so horrible, that only death can erase it from my memory. And the men who butchered their fellow-creatures thus, were neither Pagans from distant savage lands, nor ruffians, the refuse and offscourings of our own people. They were in calm blood reasonable, nay, religious men, maintaining a fair repute both heavenward and earthward. Oh, Master Everard, your trade of war should be feared and avoided, since it

converts such men into wolves towards their fellow-creatures!"

"It is a stern necessity," said Everard, looking
down, "and as such alone is justifiable—But proceed, reverend sir; I see not how this storm, an
incident but e'en too frequent on both sides during
the late war, connects with the affair of last night."

"You shall hear anon," said Mr Holdenough;
then paused as one who makes an effort to compose himself before continuing a relation, the tenor
of which agitated him with much violence.—"In
this infernal tumult," he resumed—"for surely
nothing on earth could so much resemble hell, as
when men go thus loose in mortal malice on their
fellow-creatures,—I saw the same priest whom I
had distinguished on the causeway, with one or
two other malignants, pressed into a corner by the
assailants, and defending themselves to the last,
as those who had no hope.—I saw him—I knew
him—Oh, Colonel Everard!"

He grasped Everard's hand with his own left
hand, and pressed the palm of his right to his face
and forehead, sobbing aloud.

"It was your college companion?" said Everard,
anticipating the catastrophe.

"Mine ancient—mine only friend—with whom
I had spent the happy days of youth!—I rushed
forward—I struggled—I entreated.—But my eagerness left me neither voice nor language—all was
drowned in the wretched cry which I had myself
raised—Down with the priest of Baal—Slay Mat-
tan—slay him were he between the altars!—Forced

over the battlements, but struggling for life, I could see him cling to one of those projections which were formed to carry the water from the leads—but they hacked at his arms and hands.—I heard the heavy fall into the bottomless abyss below.—Excuse me —I cannot go on !"

" He may have escaped ?"

" Oh ! no, no, no—the tower was four stories in height. Even those who threw themselves into the lake from the lower windows, to escape by swimming, had no safety ; for mounted troopers on the shore caught the same blood-thirsty humour which had seized the storming party, galloped around the margin of the lake, and shot those who were struggling for life in the water, or cut them down as they strove to get to land. They were all cut off and destroyed.—Oh ! may the blood shed on that day remain silent !—Oh ! that the earth may receive it in her recesses ! Oh ! that it may be mingled for ever with the dark waters of that lake, so that it may never cry for vengeance against those whose anger was fierce, and who slaughtered in their wrath !—And, oh ! may the erring man be forgiven who came into their assembly, and lent his voice to encourage their cruelty !—Oh ! Albany, my brother, my brother—I have lamented for thee even as David for Jonathan !" *

The good man sobbed aloud, and so much did Colonel Everard sympathize with his emotions, that he forbore to press him upon the subject of his own

* Note, p. 346. Dr Michael Hudson.

curiosity until the full tide of remorseful passion had for the time abated. It was, however, fierce and agitating, the more so, perhaps, that indulgence in strong mental feeling of any kind was foreign to the severe and ascetic character of the man, and was therefore the more overpowering when it had at once surmounted all restraints. Large tears flowed down the trembling features of his thin, and usually stern, or at least austere countenance; he eagerly returned the compression of Everard's hand, as if thankful for the sympathy which the caress implied.

Presently after, Master Holdenough wiped his eyes, withdrew his hand gently from that of Everard, shaking it kindly as they parted, and proceeded with more composure: " Forgive me this burst of passionate feeling, worthy Colonel. I am conscious it little becomes a man of my cloth, who should be the bearer of consolation to others, to give way in mine own person to an extremity of grief, weak at least, if indeed it is not sinful; for what are we, that we should weep and murmur touching that which is permitted? But Albany was to me as a brother. The happiest days of my life, ere my call to mingle myself in the strife of the land had awakened me to my duties, were spent in his company.—I—but I will make the rest of my story short."—Here he drew his chair close to that of Everard, and spoke in a solemn and mysterious tone of voice, almost lowered to a whisper —" I saw him last night."

"Saw *him*—saw whom?" said Everard. "Can you mean the person whom"——

"Whom I saw so ruthlessly slaughtered," said the clergyman—"My ancient college-friend—Joseph Albany."

"Master Holdenough, your cloth and your character alike must prevent your jesting on such a subject as this."

"Jesting!" answered Holdenough; "I would as soon jest on my death-bed—as soon jest upon the Bible."

"But you must have been deceived," answered Everard, hastily; "this tragical story necessarily often returns to your mind, and in moments when the imagination overcomes the evidence of the outward senses, your fancy must have presented to you an unreal appearance. Nothing more likely, when the mind is on the stretch after something supernatural, than that the imagination should supply the place with a chimera, while the over-excited feelings render it difficult to dispel the delusion."

"Colonel Everard," replied Holdenough, with austerity, "in discharge of my duty I must not fear the face of man; and, therefore, I tell you plainly, as I have done before with more observance, that when you bring your carnal learning and judgment, as it is but too much your nature to do, to investigate the hidden things of another world, you might as well measure with the palm of your hand the waters of the Isis. Indeed, good sir, you err in this, and give men too much pretence to confound your honourable name with witch-advocates, free-thinkers, and Atheists, even with such as this man Bletson, who, if the discipline of the church had its hands strengthened, as it was in the beginning of the great conflict, would have been long ere now cast out of the pale, and delivered over to the punishment of the flesh, that his spirit might, if possible, be yet saved."

" You mistake, Master Holdenough," said Colonel Everard; " I do not deny the existence of such preternatural visitations, because I cannot, and dare not, raise the voice of my own opinion against the testimony of ages, supported by such learned men as yourself. Nevertheless, though I grant the possibility of such things, I have scarce yet heard of an instance in my days so well fortified by evidence, that I could at once and distinctly say, This must have happened by supernatural agency, and not otherwise."

" Hear, then, what I have to tell," said the divine, " on the faith of a man, a Christian, and, what is more, a servant of our Holy Church; and therefore, though unworthy, an elder and a teacher among Christians.—I had taken my post yester evening in the half-furnished apartment, wherein hangs a huge mirror, which might have served Goliath of Gath to have admired himself in, when clothed from head to foot in his brazen armour. I the rather chose this place, because they informed me it was the nearest habitable room to the gallery in which they say you had been yourself assailed that evening by the Evil One.—Was it so, I pray you?"

" By some one with no good intentions I was assailed in that apartment. So far," said Colonel Everard, " you were correctly informed."

" Well, I chose my post as well as I might, even as a resolved general approaches his camp, and casts up his mound as nearly as he can to the besieged city. And, of a truth. Colonel Everard, if I felt some sensation of bodily fear,—for even Elias, and the prophets, who commanded the elements, had a portion in our frail nature, much more such a poor sinful being as myself—yet was my hope and my courage high ; and I thought of the texts which I might use, not in the wicked sense of periapts, or spells, as the blinded Papists employ them, together with the sign of the cross, and other fruitless forms, but as nourishing and supporting that true trust and confidence in the blessed promises, being the true shield of faith wherewith the fiery darts of Satan may be withstood and quenched. And thus armed and prepared, I sat me down to read, at the same time to write, that I might compel my mind to attend tó those subjects which became the situation in which I was placed, as preventing any unlicensed excursions of the fancy, and leaving no room for my imagination to brood over idle fears. So I methodized, and wrote down what I thought meet for the time, and peradventure some hungry souls may yet profit by the food which I then prepared."

" It was wisely and worthily done, good and

reverend sir," replied Colonel Everard; " I pray you to proceed."

" While I was thus employed, sir, and had been upon the matter for about three hours, not yielding to weariness, a strange thrilling came over my senses,—and the large and old-fashioned apartment seemed to wax larger, more gloomy, and more cavernous, while the air of the night grew more cold and chill; I know not if it was that the fire began to decay, or whether there cometh before such things as were then about to happen, a breath and atmosphere, as it were, of terror, as Job saith in a well-known passage, ' Fear came upon me, and trembling, which made my bones to shake;' and there was a tingling noise in my ears, and a dizziness in my brain, so that I felt like those who call for aid when there is no danger, and was even prompted to flee, when I saw no one to pursue. It was then that something seemed to pass behind me, casting a reflection on the great mirror before which I had placed my writing-table, and which I saw by assistance of the large standing light which was then in front of the glass. And I looked up, and I saw in the glass distinctly the appearance of a man—as sure as these words issue from my mouth, it was no other than the same Joseph Albany— the companion of my youth—he whom I had seen precipitated down the battlements of Clidesthrough Castle into the deep lake below !"

" What did you do ?"

" It suddenly rushed on my mind," said the divine, " that the stoical philosopher Athenodorus had eluded the horrors of such a vision by patiently pursuing his studies ; and it shot at the same time across my mind, that I, a Christian divine, and a Steward of the Mysteries, had less reason to fear evil, and better matter on which to employ my thoughts, than was possessed by a Heathen, who was blinded even by his own wisdom. So, instead of betraying any alarm, or even turning my head around, I pursued my writing, but with a beating heart, I admit, and with a throbbing hand."

" If you could write at all," said the Colonel, " with such an impression on your mind, you may take the head of the English army for dauntless resolution."

" Our courage is not our own, Colonel," said the divine, " and not as ours should it be vaunted of. And again, when you speak of this strange vision as an impression on my fancy, and not a reality obvious to my senses, let me tell you once more, your worldly wisdom is but foolishness touching the things that are not worldly."

" Did you not look again upon the mirror ?" said the Colonel.

" I did, when I had copied out the comfortable text, ' Thou shalt tread down Satan under thy feet.' "

" And what did you then see ?"

" The reflection of the same Joseph Albany," said Holdenough, " passing slowly as from behind my chair, the same in member and lineament that I had known him in his youth, excepting that his cheek had the marks of the more advanced age at which he died, and was very pale."

" What did you then ?"

" I turned from the glass, and plainly saw the figure which had made the reflection in the mirror retreating towards the door, not fast, nor slow, but with a gliding, steady pace. It turned again when near the door, and again showed me its pale, ghastly countenance, before it disappeared. But how it left the room, whether by the door, or otherwise, my spirits were too much hurried to remark exactly; nor have I been able, by any effort of recollection, distinctly to remember."

" This is a strange, and, as coming from you, a most excellently well-attested apparition," answered Everard. " And yet, Master Holdenough, if the other world has been actually displayed, as you apprehend, and I will not dispute the possibility, assure yourself there are also wicked men concerned in these machinations. I myself have undergone some rencontres with visitants who possessed bodily strength, and wore, I am sure, earthly weapons."

" Oh ! doubtless, doubtless," replied Master Holdenough ; " Beelzebub loves to charge with horse and foot mingled, as was the fashion of the old Scottish general, Davie Leslie. He has his devils in the body as well as his devils disembodied, and uses the one to support and back the other."

" It may be as you say, reverend sir," answered the Colonel.—" But what do you advise in this case ?"

"For that I must consult with my brethren," said the divine; "and if there be but left in our borders five ministers of the true kirk, we will charge Satan in full body, and you shall see whether we have not power over him to resist till he shall flee from us. But failing that ghostly armament against these strange and unearthly enemies, truly I would recommend, that as a house of witchcraft and abomination, this polluted den of ancient tyranny and prostitution should be totally consumed by fire, lest Satan, establishing his headquarters so much to his mind, should find a garrison and a fastness from which he might sally forth to infest the whole neighbourhood. Certain it is, that I would recommend to no Christian soul to inhabit the mansion; and, if deserted, it would become a place for wizards to play their pranks, and witches to establish their Sabbath, and those, who, like Demas, go about after the wealth of this world, seeking for gold and silver to practise spells and charms to the prejudice of the souls of the covetous. Trust me, therefore, it were better that it were spoiled and broken down, not leaving one stone upon another."

"I say nay to that, my good friend," said the Colonel; "for the Lord General hath permitted, by his license, my mother's brother, Sir Henry Lee, and his family, to return into the house of his fathers, being indeed the only roof under which he hath any chance of obtaining shelter for his grey hairs."

"And was this done by your advice, Markham Everard?" said the divine, austerely.

" Certainly it was," returned the Colonel.— " And wherefore should I not exert mine influence to obtain a place of refuge for the brother of my mother ?"

" Now, as sure as thy soul liveth," answered the presbyter, " I had believed this from no tongue but thine own.   Tell me, was it not this very Sir Henry Lee, who, by the force of his buff-coats and his green-jerkins, enforced the Papist Laic's order to remove the altar to the eastern end of the church at Woodstock ?—and did not he swear by his beard, that he would hang in the very street of Woodstock whoever should deny to drink the King's health ? —and is not his hand red with the blood of the saints ?—and hath there been a ruffler in the field for prelacy and high prerogative more unmitigable or fiercer ?"

" All this may have been as you say, good Master Holdenough," answered the Colonel ; " but my uncle is now old and feeble, and hath scarce a single follower remaining, and his daughter is a being whom to look upon would make the sternest weep for pity ; a being who"——

" Who is dearer to Everard," said Holdenough, " than his good name, his faith to his friends, his duty to his religion ;—this is no time to speak with sugared lips.   The paths in which you tread are dangerous. You are striving to raise the papistical candlestick which Heaven in its justice removed out of its place—to bring back to this hall of sorceries those very sinners who are bewitched with them.

I will not permit the land to be abused by their witchcrafts.—They shall not come hither."

He spoke this with vehemence, and striking his stick against the ground; and the Colonel, very much dissatisfied, began to express himself haughtily in return. "You had better consider your power to accomplish your threats, Master Holdenough," he said, "before you urge them so peremptorily."

"And have I not the power to bind and to loose?" said the clergyman.

"It is a power little available, save over those of your own church," said Everard, with a tone something contemptuous.

"Take heed—take heed," said the divine, who, though an excellent, was, as we have elsewhere seen, an irritable man.—"Do not insult me; but think honourably of the messenger, for the sake of Him whose commission he carries.—Do not, I say, defy me—I am bound to discharge my duty, were it to the displeasing of my twin brother."

"I can see nought your office has to do in the matter," said Colonel Everard; "and I, on my side, give you warning not to attempt to meddle beyond your commission."

"Right—you hold me already to be as submissive as one of your grenadiers," replied the clergyman, his acute features trembling with a sense of indignity, so as even to agitate his grey hair; "but beware, sir, I am not so powerless as you suppose. I will invoke every true Christian in Woodstock to gird up his loins, and resist the restoration of prelacy, oppression, and malignancy within our bor-

ders. I will stir up the wrath of the righteous
against the oppressor—the Ishmaelite—the Edomite—and against his race, and against those who
support him and encourage him to rear up his horn.
I will call aloud, and spare not, and arouse the many
whose love hath waxed cold, and the multitude who
care for none of these things. There shall be a
remnant to listen to me ; and I will take the stick
of Joseph, which was in the hand of Ephraim, and
go down to cleanse this place of witches and sorce-
rers, and of enchantments, and will cry and exhort,
saying—Will you plead for Baal?—will you serve
him ? Nay, take the prophets of Baal—let not a
man escape !"

"Master Holdenough, Master Holdenough,"
said Colonel Everard, with much impatience, "by
the tale yourself told me, you have exhorted upon
that text once too often already."

The old man struck his palm forcibly against his
forehead, and fell back into a chair as these words
were uttered, as suddenly, and as much without
power of resistance, as if the Colonel had·fired a
pistol through his head. Instantly regretting the
reproach which he had suffered to escape him in
his impatience, Everard hastened to apologize, and
to offer every conciliatory excuse, however inconsistent, which occurred to him on the moment. But
the old man was too deeply affected—he rejected
his hand, lent no ear to what he said, and finally
started up, saying sternly, " You have abused my
confidence, sir—abused it vilely, to turn it into my
own reproach ; had I been a man of the sword, you

dared not—But enjoy your triumph, sir, over an old man, and your father's friend—strike at the wound his imprudent confidence showed you."

"Nay, my worthy and excellent friend," said the Colonel——

"Friend!" answered the old man, vehemently —"We are foes, sir—foes now, and for ever!"

So saying, and starting from the seat into which he had rather fallen than thrown himself, he ran out of the room with a precipitation of step which he was apt to use upon occasions of irritable feeling, and which was certainly more eager than dignified, especially as he muttered while he ran, and seemed as if he were keeping up his own passion, by recounting over and over the offence which he had received.

"Soh!" said Colonel Everard, "and there was not strife enough between mine uncle and the people of Woodstock already, but I must needs increase it, by chafing this irritable and quick-tempered old man, eager as I knew him to be in his ideas of church-government, and stiff in his prejudices respecting all who dissent from him! The mob of Woodstock will rise; for though he would not get a score of them to stand by him in any honest or intelligible purpose, yet let him cry havoc and destruction, and I will warrant he has followers enow. And my uncle is equally wild and unpersuadable. For the value of all the estate he ever had, he would not allow a score of troopers to be quartered in the house for defence; and if he be alone, or has but Joceline to stand by him, he will be as sure to fire upon those who come to attack the Lodge, as if he had a hundred men in garrison; and then what can chance but danger and bloodshed?"

This progress of melancholy anticipation was interrupted by the return of Master Holdenough, who, hurrying into the room, with the same precipitate pace at which he had left it, ran straight up to the Colonel, and said, " Take my hand, Markham—take my hand hastily; for the old Adam is whispering at my heart, that it is a disgrace to hold it extended so long."

" Most heartily do I receive your hand, my venerable friend," said Everard, " and I trust in sign of renewed amity."

" Surely, surely"—said the divine, shaking his hand kindly; " thou hast, it is true, spoken bitterly, but thou hast spoken truth in good time; and I think—though your words were severe—with a good and kindly purpose. Verily, and of a truth, it were sinful in me again to be hasty in provoking violence, remembering that which you have upbraided me with"——

" Forgive me, good Master Holdenough," said Colonel Everard, " it was a hasty word; I meant not in serious earnest to *upbraid*."

" Peace, I pray you, peace," said the divine; " I say, the allusion to that which you have *most justly* upbraided me with—though the charge aroused the gall of the Old Man within me, the inward tempter being ever on the watch to bring us to his lure— ought, instead of being resented, to have been ac-

knowledged by me as a favour, for so are the wounds
of a friend termed faithful. And surely I, who
have by one unhappy exhortation to battle and
strife sent the living to the dead—and I fear brought
back even the dead among the living—should now
study peace and good-will, and reconciliation of
difference, leaving punishment to the Great Being
whose laws are broken, and vengeance to Him who
hath said, I will repay it."

The old man's mortified features lighted up with
a humble confidence as he made this acknowledg-
ment; and Colonel Everard, who knew the constitutional infirmities, and the early prejudices of
professional consequence and exclusive party opinion, which he must have subdued ere arriving at
such a tone of candour, hastened to express his
admiration of his Christian charity, mingled with
reproaches on himself for having so deeply injured
his feelings.

" Think not of it—think not of it, excellent
young man," said Holdenough; " we have both
erred—I in suffering my zeal to outrun my charity,
you, perhaps, in pressing hard on an old and peevish
man, who had so lately poured out his sufferings
into your friendly bosom. Be it all forgotten. Let
your friends—if they are not deterred by what has
happened at this manor of Woodstock—resume
their habitation as soon as they will. If they can
protect themselves against the powers of the air,
believe me, that if I can prevent it by aught in
my power, they shall have no annoyance from
earthly neighbours; and assure yourself, good sir,

that my voice is still worth something with the worthy Mayor, and the good Aldermen, and the better sort of housekeepers up yonder in the town, although thé lower classes are blown about with every wind of doctrine. And yet farther, be assured, Colonel, that should your mother's brother, or any of his family, learn that they have taken up a rash bargain in returning to this unhappy and unhallowed house, or should they find any qualms in their own hearts and consciences which require a ghostly comforter, Nehemiah Holdenough will be as much at their command by night or day, as if they had been bred up within the holy pale of the church in which he is an unworthy minister; and neither the awe of what is fearful to be* seen within these walls, nor his knowledge of their blinded and carnal state, as bred up under a prelatic dispensation, shall prevent him doing what lies in his poor abilities for their protection and edification."

" I feel all the force of your kindness, reverend sir," said Colonel Everard, " but I do not think it likely that my uncle will give you trouble on either score. He is a man much accustomed to be his own protector in temporal danger, and in spiritual doubts to trust to his own prayers and those of his Church."

" I trust I have not been superfluous in offering mine assistance," said the old man, something jealous that his proffered spiritual aid had been held rather intrusive. " I ask pardon if that is the case

—I humbly ask pardon—I would not willingly be superfluous."

The Colonel hastened to appease this new alarm of the watchful jealousy of his consequence, which, joined with a natural heat of temper which he could not always subdue, were the good man's only faults.

They had regained their former friendly footing, when Roger Wildrake returned from the hut of Joceline, and whispered his master that his embassy had been successful. The Colonel then addressed the divine, and informed him, that as the Commissioners had already given up Woodstock, and as his uncle, Sir Henry Lee, proposed to return to the Lodge about noon, he would, if his reverence pleased, attend him up to the borough.

" Will you not tarry," said the reverend man, with something like inquisitive apprehension in his voice, "to welcome your relatives upon their return to this their house ?"

" No, my good friend," said Colonel Everard ; " the part which I have taken in these unhappy broils—perhaps also the mode of worship in which I have been educated—have so prejudiced me in mine uncle's opinion, that I must be for some time a stranger to his house and family."

" Indeed ! I rejoice to hear it, with all my heart and soul," said the divine. " Excuse my frankness —I do indeed rejoice,—I had thought—no matter what I had thought,—I would not again give offence. But truly though the maiden hath a pleasant feature, and he, as all men say, is in human things unexceptionable,—yet—but I give you pain —in sooth, I will say no more unless you ask my sincere and unprejudiced advice, which you shall command, but which I will not press on you superfluously. Wend we to the borough together—the pleasant solitude of the forest may dispose us to open our hearts to each other."

They did walk up to the little town in company, and, somewhat to Master Holdenough's surprise, the Colonel, though they talked on various subjects, did not request of him any ghostly advice on the subject of his love to his fair cousin, while, greatly beyond the expectation of the soldier, the clergyman kept his word, and, in his own phrase, was not so superfluous as to offer upon so delicate a point his unasked counsel.

NOTE TO CHAPTER XVII.

Note, p. 328.—Dr MICHAEL HUDSON.

Michael Hudson, the *plain-dealing* chaplain of King Charles I., resembled, in his loyalty to that unfortunate monarch, the fictitious character of Doctor Rochecliffe ; and the circumstances of his death were copied in the narrative of the Presbyterian's account of the slaughter of his school-fellow ;—he was chosen by Charles I., along with John Ashburnham, as his guide and attendant, when he adopted the ill-advised resolution of surrendering his person to the Scots army.

He was taken prisoner by the Parliament, remained long in their custody, and was treated with great severity. He made his escape for about a year in 1647 ; was retaken, and again escaped in 1648, and, heading an insurrection of cavaliers, seized on a strong moated house in Lincolnshire, called Woodford House. He gained the place without resistance ; and there are among Peck's Desiderata Curiosa several accounts of his death, among which we shall transcribe that of Bishop Kenneth, as the most correct and concise :—

" I have been on the spot," saith his Lordship, " and made all possible enquiries, and find that the relation given by Mr Wood may be a little rectified and supplied.

" Mr Hudson and his party did not fly to Woodford, but had quietly taken possession of it, and held it for a garrison, with a good party of horse, who made a stout defence, and frequent sallies, against a party of the Parliament at Stamford, till the colonel commanding them sent a stronger detachment, under a captain, his own kinsman, who was shot from the house, upon which the colonel himself came up to renew the attack, and to demand surrendry, and brought them to capitulate upon terms of safe quarter. But the colonel, in base revenge, commanded that they should not spare that rogue Hudson. Upon which Hudson fought his way up to the leads; and when he saw they were pushing in upon him, threw himself over the battlements (another account says, he caught hold of a spout or outstone), and hung by the hands as intending to fall into the moat beneath, till they cut off his wrists and let him drop, and then ran down to hunt him in the water, where they found him paddling with his stumps, and barbarously knocked him on the head."—PECK's *Desiderata Curiosa*, Book ix.

Other accounts mention he was refused the poor charity of coming to die on land, by one Egborough, servant to Mr Spinks, the intruder into the parsonage. A man called Walker, a chandler or grocer, cut out the tongue of the unfortunate divine, and showed it as a trophy through the country. But it was remarked, with vindictive satisfaction, that Egborough was killed by the bursting of his own gun; and that Walker, obliged to abandon his trade through poverty, became a scorned mendicant.

For some time a grave was not vouchsafed to the remains of this brave and loyal divine, till one of the other party said, "Since he is dead, let him be buried."

CHAPTER XVIII.

Then are the harpies gone—Yet ere we perch
Where such foul birds have roosted, let us cleanse
The foul obscenity they've left behind them.

Agamemnon.

THE embassy of Wildrake had been successful, chiefly through the mediation of the Episcopal divine, whom we formerly found acting in the character of a chaplain to the family, and whose voice had great influence on many accounts with its master.

A little before high noon, Sir Henry Lee, with his small household, were again in unchallenged possession of their old apartments at the Lodge of Woodstock ; and the combined exertions of Joceline Joliffe, of Phœbe, and of old Joan, were employed in putting to rights what the late intruders had left in great disorder.

Sir Henry Lee had, like all persons of quality of that period, a love of order amounting to precision, and felt, like a fine lady whose dress has been disordered in a crowd, insulted and humiliated by the rude confusion into which his household goods had been thrown, and impatient till his mansion was purified from all marks of intrusion. In his anger he uttered more orders than the limited

number of his domestics were likely to find time
or hands to execute. " The villains have left such
sulphureous steams behind them, too," said the old
knight, " as if old Davie Leslie and the whole
Scottish army had quartered among them."

" It may be near as bad," said Joceline, " for
men say, for certain, it was the Devil came down
bodily among them, and made them troop off."

" Then," said the knight, " is the Prince of
Darkness a gentleman, as old Will Shakspeare
says. He never interferes with those of his own
coat; for the Lees have been here, father and son,
these five hundred years, without disquiet; and no
sooner came these misbegotten churls, than he plays
his own part among them."

" Well, one thing he and they have left us,"
said Joliffe, " which we may thank them for; and
that is, such a well-filled larder and buttery as has
been seldom seen in Woodstock Lodge this many
a day;—carcasses of mutton, large rounds of beef,
barrels of confectioners' ware, pipes and runlets of
sack, muscadine, ale, and what not. We shall have
a royal time on't through half the winter; and Joan
must get to salting and pickling presently."

" Out, villain!" said the knight; " are we to
feed on the fragments of such scum of the earth as
these ?—Cast them forth instantly !—Nay," check-
ing himself, " that were a sin; but give them to
the poor, or see them sent to the owners.—And,
hark ye, I will none of their strong liquors—I
would rather drink like a hermit all my life, than
seem to pledge such scoundrels as these in their

leavings, like a miserable drawer, who drains off the ends of the bottles after the guests have paid their reckoning, and gone off.—And, hark ye, I will taste no water from the cistern out of which these slaves have been serving themselves—fetch me down a pitcher from Rosamond's spring."

Alice heard this injunction, and well guessing there was enough for the other members of the family to do, she quietly took a small pitcher, and flinging a cloak around her, walked out in person to procure Sir Henry the water which he desired. Meantime, Joceline said, with some hesitation, " that a man still remained, belonging to the party of these strangers, who was directing about the removal of some trunks and mails which belonged to the Commissioners, and who could receive his honour's commands about the provisions."

" Let him come hither."—(The dialogue was held in the hall.)—" Why do you hesitate and drumble in that manner?"

" Only, sir," said Joceline, " only perhaps your honour might not wish to see him, being the same who, not long since"——

He paused.

" Sent my rapier a-hawking through the firmament, thou wouldst say?—Why, when did I take spleen at a man for standing his ground against me?—Roundhead as he is, man, I like him the better of that, not the worse. I hunger and thirst to have another turn with him. I have thought on his passado ever since, and I believe, were it to try again, I know a feat would control it.—Fetch him directly."

Trusty Tomkins was presently ushered in, bearing himself with an iron gravity, which neither the terrors of the preceding night, nor the dignified demeanour of the high-born personage before whom he stood, were able for an instant to overcome.

" How now, good fellow ?" said Sir Henry; " I would fain see something more of thy fence, which baffled me the other evening—but truly, I think the light was somewhat too faint for my old eyes —Take a foil, man—I walk here in the hall, as Hamlet says; and 'tis the breathing-time of day with me—Take a foil, then, in thy hand."

" Since it is your worship's desire," said the steward, letting fall his long cloak, and taking the foil in his hand.

" Now," said the knight, " if your fitness speaks, mine is ready. Methinks the very stepping on this same old pavement hath charmed away the gout which threatened me—Sa—sa—I tread as firm as a game cock !"

They began the play with great spirit; and whether the old knight really fought more coolly with the blunt than with the sharp weapon, or whether the steward gave him some grains of advantage in this merely sportive encounter, it is certain Sir Henry had the better in the assault. His success put him into excellent humour.

" There," said he, " I found your trick,—nay, you cheat me not twice the same way—There was a very palpable hit. Why, had I had but light

enough the other night—But it skills not speaking
of it—Here we leave off.   I must not fight, as we
unwise cavaliers did with you roundhead rascals,
beating you so often that we taught you to beat us
at last.—And good now, tell me why you are leaving your larder so full here?—Do you think I or
my family can use broken victuals?—What, have
you no better employment for your rounds of sequestrated beef than to leave them behind you
when you shift your quarters?"

"So please your honour," said Tomkins, "it
may be that you desire not the flesh of beeves, of
rams, or of goats.   Nevertheless, when you know
that the provisions were provided and paid for out
of your own rents and stock at Ditchley, sequestrated to the use of the state more than a year since,
it may be you will have less scruple to use them
for your own behoof."

"Rest assured that I shall," said Sir Henry;
"and glad you have helped me to a share of mine
own. Certainly I was an ass to suspect your masters of subsisting, save at honest men's expense."

"And as for the rumps of beeves," continued
Tomkins, with the same solemnity, "there is a
rump at Westminster, which will stand us of the
army much hacking and hewing yet, ere it is dis-
cussed to our mind."

Sir Henry paused, as if to consider what was the
meaning of this innuendo; for he was not a person
of very quick apprehension. But having at length
caught the meaning of it, he burst into an explo-

sion of louder laughter than Joceline had seen him indulge in for a good while.

"Right, knave," he said, "I taste thy jest—It is the very moral of the puppetshow. Faustus raised the devil, as the Parliament raised the army—and then, as the devil flies away with Faustus, so will the army fly away with the Parliament—or the rump, as thou call'st it, or sitting part of the so-called Parliament.—And then, look you, friend, the very devil of all hath my willing consent to fly away with the army in its turn, from the highest general down to the lowest drum-boy.—Nay, never look fierce for the matter; remember there is daylight enough now for a game at sharps."

Trusty Tomkins appeared to think it best to suppress his displeasure; and observing that the wains were ready to transport the Commissioners' property to the borough, took a grave leave of Sir Henry Lee.

Meantime the old man continued to pace his recovered hall, rubbing his hands, and evincing greater signs of glee than he had shown since the fatal 30th of January.

"Here we are again in the old frank, Joliffe—well victualled too.—How the knave solved my point of conscience!—the dullest of them is a special casuist where the question concerns profit. Look out if there are not some of our own ragged regiment lurking about, to whom a bellyful would be a godsend, Joceline—Then his fence, Joceline—though the fellow foins well—very sufficient well

VOL. XXXIX.   z

—But thou saw'st how I dealt with him when I had fitting light, Joceline?"

" Ay, and so your honour did," said Joceline. " You taught him to know the Duke of Norfolk from Saunders Gardner. I'll warrant him he will not wish to come under your honour's thumb again."

" Why, I am waxing old," said Sir Henry ; " but skill will not rust through age, though sinews must stiffen. But my age is like a lusty winter, as old Will says—frosty but kindly—And what if, old as we are, we live to see better days yet! I promise thee, Joceline, I love this jarring betwixt the rogues of the board and the rogues of the sword. When thieves quarrel, true men have a chance of coming by their own."

Thus triumphed the old cavalier, in the treble glory of having recovered his dwelling—regained, as he thought, his character as a man of fence, and finally, discovered some prospect of a change of times, in which he was not without hopes that something might turn up for the royal interest.

Meanwhile, Alice, with a prouder and a lighter heart than had danced in her bosom for several days, went forth with a gaiety to which she of late had been a stranger, to contribute her assistance to the regulation and supply of the household, by bringing the fresh water wanted from fair Rosamond's well.

Perhaps she remembered, that when she was but a girl, her cousin Markham used, among others, to make her perform that duty, as presenting the character of some captive Trojan princess, condemned by her situation to draw the waters from some Grecian spring, for the use of the proud victor. At any rate, she certainly joyed to see her father reinstated in his ancient habitation ; and the joy was not the less sincere, that she knew their return to Woodstock had been procured by means of her cousin, and that even in her father's prejudiced eyes, Everard had been in some degree exculpated of the accusations the old knight had brought against him ; and that, if a reconciliation had not yet taken place, the preliminaries had been established on which such a desirable conclusion might easily be founded. It was like the commencement of a bridge ; when the foundation is securely laid, and the piers raised above the influence of the torrent, the throwing of the arches may be accomplished in a subsequent season.

The doubtful fate of her only brother might have clouded even this momentary gleam of sunshine ; but Alice had been bred up during the close and frequent contests of civil war, and had acquired the habit of hoping in behalf of those dear to her, until hope was lost. In the present case, all reports seemed to assure her of her brother's safety.

Besides these causes for gaiety, Alice Lee had the pleasing feeling that she was restored to the habitation and the haunts of her childhood, from which she had not departed without much pain, the more felt, perhaps, because suppressed, in order to avoid irritating her father's sense of his misfortune. Finally, she enjoyed for the instant the gleam of self-satisfaction by which we see the young and well-disposed so often animated, when they can be, in common phrase, helpful to those whom they love, and perform at the moment of need some of those little domestic tasks, which age receives with so much pleasure from the dutiful hands of youth. So that, altogether, as she hasted through the remains and vestiges of a wilderness already mentioned, and from thence about a bow-shot into the Park, to bring a pitcher of water from Rosamond's spring, Alice Lee, her features enlivened and her complexion a little raised by the exercise, had, for the moment, regained the gay and brilliant vivacity of expression which had been the characteristic of her beauty in her earlier and happier days.

This fountain of old memory had been once adorned with architectural ornaments in the style of the sixteenth century, chiefly relating to ancient mythology. All these were now wasted and overthrown, and existed only as moss-covered ruins, while the living spring continued to furnish its daily treasures, unrivalled in purity, though the quantity was small, gushing out amid disjointed stones, and bubbling through fragments of ancient sculpture.

With a light step and laughing brow the young Lady of Lee was approaching the fountain usually so solitary, when she paused on beholding some one seated beside it. She proceeded, however, with confidence, though with a step something less gay, when she observed that the person was a female; —some menial perhaps from the town, whom a fanciful mistress occasionally dispatched for the water of a spring, supposed to be peculiarly pure, or some aged woman, who made a little trade by carrying it to the better sort of families, and selling it for a trifle. There was no cause, therefore, for apprehension.

Yet the terrors of the times were so great, that Alice did not see a stranger even of her own sex without some apprehension. Denaturalized women had as usual followed the camps of both armies during the Civil War; who, on the one side with open profligacy and profanity, on the other with the fraudful tone of fanaticism or hypocrisy, exercised nearly in like degree their talents for murder or plunder. But it was broad daylight, the distance from the Lodge was but trifling, and though a little alarmed at seeing a stranger where she expected deep solitude, the daughter of the haughty old Knight had too much of the lion about her, to fear without some determined and decided cause.

Alice walked, therefore, gravely on towards the fount, and composed her looks as she took a hasty glance of the female who was seated there, and addressed herself to her task of filling her pitcher.

The woman, whose presence had surprised and somewhat startled Alice Lee, was a person of the lower rank, whose red cloak, russet kirtle, handkerchief trimmed with Coventry blue, and a coarse steeple hat, could not indicate at best any thing higher than the wife of a small farmer, or, perhaps, the helpmate of a bailiff or hind. It was well if she proved nothing worse. Her clothes, indeed, were of good materials; but, what the female eye discerns with half a glance, they were indifferently adjusted and put on. This looked as if they did not belong to the person by whom they were worn, but were articles of which she had become the mistress by some accident, if not by some successful robbery. Her size, too, as did not escape Alice, even in the short perusal she afforded the stranger, was unusual; her features swarthy and singularly harsh, and her manner altogether unpropitious. The young lady almost wished, as she stooped to fill her pitcher, that she had rather turned back, and sent Joceline on the errand; but repentance was too late now, and she had only to disguise as well as she could her unpleasant feelings.

" The blessings of this bright day to one as bright as it is!" said the stranger, with no unfriendly, though a harsh voice.

" I thank you," said Alice in reply; and continued to fill her pitcher busily, by assistance of an iron bowl which remained still chained to one of the stones beside the fountain.

" Perhaps, my pretty maiden, if you would accept my help, your work would be sooner done," said the stranger.

" I thank you," said Alice; " but had I needed assistance, I could have brought those with me who had rendered it."

" I do not doubt of that, my pretty maiden," answered the female; " there are too many lads in Woodstock with eyes in their heads—No doubt you could have brought with you any one of them who looked on you, if you had listed?"

Alice replied not a syllable, for she did not like the freedom used by the speaker, and was desirous to break off the conversation.

" Are you offended, my pretty mistress?" said the stranger; " that was far from my purpose.— I will put my question otherwise—Are the good dames of Woodstock so careless of their pretty daughters as to let the flower of them all wander about the wild chase without a mother, or a somebody to prevent the fox from running away with the lamb?—that carelessness, methinks, shows small kindness."

" Content yourself, good woman, I am not far from protection and assistance," said Alice, who liked less and less the effrontery of her new acquaintance.

" Alas! my pretty maiden," said the stranger, patting with her large and hard hand the head which Alice had kept bended down towards the water which she was laving, " it would be difficult to hear such a pipe as yours at the town of Woodstock, scream as loud as you would."

Alice shook the woman's hand angrily off, took up her pitcher, though not above half full, and as she saw the stranger rise at the same time, said, not without fear doubtless, but with a natural feeling of resentment and dignity, " I have no reason to make my cries heard as far as Woodstock; were there occasion for my crying for help at all, it is nearer at hand."

She spoke not without a warrant; for, at the moment, broke through the bushes, and stood by

her side, the noble hound Bevis; fixing on the
stranger his eyes that glanced fire, raising every
hair on his gallant mane as upright as the bristles
of a wild boar when hard pressed, grinning till a
case of teeth, which would have matched those of
any wolf in Russia, were displayed in full array,
and, without either barking or springing, seeming,
by his low determined growl, to await but the signal for dashing at the female, whom he plainly considered as a suspicious person.

But the stranger was undaunted. " My pretty
maiden," she said, " you have indeed a formidable
guardian there, where cockneys or bumpkins are
concerned; but we who have been at the wars know
spells for taming such furious dragons; and therefore let not your four-footed protector go loose on
me, for he is a noble animal, and nothing but self-
defence would induce me to do him injury." So
saying, she drew a pistol from her bosom, and cocked it—pointing it towards the dog, as if apprehensive that he would spring upon her.

" Hold, woman, hold!" said Alice Lee; " the
dog will not do you harm.—Down, Bevis, couch
down—And ere you attempt to hurt him, know he
is the favourite hound of Sir Henry Lee of Ditchley, the keeper of Woodstock Park, who would
severely revenge any injury offered to him."

" And you, pretty one, are the old knight's
housekeeper, doubtless? I have often heard the
Lees have good taste."

" I am his daughter, good woman."

" His daughter!—I was blind—but yet it is

true, nothing less perfect could answer the description which all the world has given of Mistress Alice Lee. I trust that my folly has given my young mistress no offence, and that she will allow me, in token of reconciliation, to fill her pitcher, and carry it as far as she will permit."

" As you will, good mother ; but I am about to return instantly to the Lodge, to which, in these times, I cannot admit strangers. You can follow me no farther than the verge of the wilderness, and I am already too long from home : I will send some one to meet and relieve you of the pitcher." So saying, she turned her back, with a feeling of terror which she could hardly account for, and began to walk quickly towards the Lodge, thinking thus to get rid of her troublesome acquaintance.

But she reckoned without her host; for in a moment her new companion was by her side, not running, indeed, but walking with prodigious long unwomanly strides, which soon brought her up with the hurried and timid steps of the frightened maiden. But her manner was more respectful than formerly, though her voice sounded remarkably harsh and disagreeable, and her whole appearance suggested an undefined, yet irresistible feeling of apprehension.

" Pardon a stranger, lovely Mistress Alice," said her persecutor, " that was not capable of distinguishing between a lady of your high quality and a peasant wench, and who spoke to you with a degree of freedom, ill-befitting your rank, certainly, and condition, and which, I fear, has given you offence."

" No offence whatever," replied Alice ; " but, good woman, I am near home, and can excuse your farther company.—You are unknown to me."

" But it follows not," said the stranger, " that *your* fortunes may not be known to *me*, fair Mistress Alice. Look on my swarthy brow—England breeds none such—and in the lands from which I come, the sun which blackens our complexion, pours, to make amends, rays of knowledge into our brains, which are denied to those of your lukewarm climate. Let me look upon your pretty hand,— [attempting to possess herself of it,]—and I promise you, you shall hear what will please you."

" I hear what does *not* please me," said Alice, with dignity ; " you must carry your tricks of fortune-telling and palmistry to the women of the village—We of the gentry hold them to be either imposture or unlawful knowledge."

" Yet you would fain hear of a certain Colonel, I warrant you, whom certain unhappy circumstances have separated from his family ; you would give better than silver if I could assure you that you would see him in a day or two—ay, perhaps sooner."

" I know nothing of what you speak, good woman ; if you want alms, there is a piece of silver —it is all I have in my purse."

" It were pity that I should take it," said the female ; " and yet give it me—for the princess in the fairy tale must ever deserve, by her generosity, the bounty of the benevolent fairy, before she is rewarded by her protection."

" Take it—take it—give me my pitcher," said Alice, "and begone,—yonder comes one of my father's servants.—What, ho !—Joceline—Joceline !"

The old fortune-teller hastily dropped something into the pitcher as she restored it to Alice Lee, and, plying her long limbs, disappeared speedily under cover of the wood.

Bevis turned, and backed, and showed some inclination to harass the retreat of this suspicious person, yet, as if uncertain, ran towards Joliffe, and fawned on him, as to demand his advice and encouragement. Joceline pacified the animal, and coming up to his young lady, asked her, with surprise, what was the matter, and whether she had been frightened ? Alice made light of her alarm, for which, indeed, she could not have assigned any very competent reason, for the manners of the woman, though bold and intrusive, were not menacing. She only said she had met a fortune-teller by Rosamond's Well, and had had some difficulty in shaking her off.

" Ah, the gipsy thief," said Joceline, " how well she scented there was food in the pantry !—they have noses like ravens these strollers. Look you, Mistress Alice, you shall not see a raven, or a carrion-crow, in all the blue sky for a mile round you; but let a sheep drop suddenly down on the greensward, and before the poor creature's dead you shall see a dozen of such guests croaking, as if

inviting each other to the banquet.—Just so it is
with these sturdy beggars. You will see few
enough of them when there's nothing to give, but
when hough's in the pot, they will have share on't."

" You are so proud of your fresh supply of pro-
vender," said Alice, " that you suspect all of a
design on't. I do not think this woman will venture
near your kitchen, Joceline."

" It will be best for her health," said Joceline,
" lest I give her a ducking for digestion.—But
give me the pitcher, Mistress Alice—meeter I bear
it than you.—How now? what jingles at the bottom? have you lifted the pebbles as well as the
water?"

" I think the woman dropped something into
the pitcher," said Alice.

" Nay, we must look to that, for it is like to be
a charm, and we have enough of the devil's ware
about Woodstock already—we will not spare for
the water—I can run back and fill the pitcher."
He poured out the water upon the grass, and at
the bottom of the pitcher was found a gold ring,
in which was set a ruby, apparently of some value.

" Nay, if this be not enchantment, I know not
what is," said Joceline. " Truly, Mistress Alice,
I think you had better throw away this gimcrack.
Such gifts from such hands are a kind of press-
money which the devil uses for enlisting his regiment of witches ; and if they take but so much as
a bean from him, they become his bond slaves for
life—Ay, you look at the gewgaw, but to-morrow

you will find a lead ring and a common pebble in its stead."

" Nay, Joceline, I think it will be better to find out that dark-complexioned woman, and return to her what seems of some value. So, cause enquiry to be made, and be sure you return her ring. It seems too valuable to be destroyed."

" Umph! that is always the way with women," murmured Joceline. " You will never get the best of them, but she is willing to save a bit of finery. —Well, Mistress Alice, I trust that you are too young and too pretty to be enlisted in a regiment of witches."

" I shall not be afraid of it till you turn conjurer," said Alice; " so hasten to the well, where you are like still to find the woman, and let her know that Alice Lee desires none of her gifts, any more than she did of her society."

So saying, the young lady pursued her way to the Lodge, while Joceline went down to Rosamond's Well to execute her commission. But the fortune-teller, or whoever she might be, was nowhere to be found; neither, finding that to be the case, did Joceline give himself much trouble in tracking her farther.

" If this ring, which I dare say the jade stole somewhere," said the under-keeper to himself, " be worth a few nobles, it is better in honest hands than in those of vagabonds. My master has a right to all waifs and strays, and certainly such a ring, in possession of a gipsy, must be a waif. So I shall confiscate it without scruple, and apply the produce to the support of Sir Henry's household, which is like to be poor enough. Thank Heaven, my military experience has taught me how to carry hooks at my finger-ends—that is trooper's law. Yet, hang it, after all, I had best take it to Mark Everard and ask his advice—I hold him now to be your learned counsellor in law where Mistress Alice's affairs are concerned, and my learned Doctor, who shall be nameless, for such as concern Church and State and Sir Henry Lee—And I'll give them leave to give mine umbles to the kites and ravens if they find me conferring my confidence where it is not safe."

END OF VOLUME THIRTY-NINTH.

EDINBURGH:
PRINTED BY BALLANTYNE AND COMPANY,
PAUL'S WORK, CANONGATE.

The Codes Of Hammurabi And Moses
W. W. Davies

QTY

The discovery of the Hammurabi Code is one of the greatest achievements of archaeology, and is of paramount interest, not only to the student of the Bible, but also to all those interested in ancient history...

Religion   **ISBN:** *1-59462-338-4*   **Pages:132**
MSRP $12.95

The Theory of Moral Sentiments
Adam Smith

QTY

This work from 1749. contains original theories of conscience amd moral judgment and it is the foundation for systemof morals.

Philosophy **ISBN:** *1-59462-777-0*   **Pages:536**
MSRP $19.95

Jessica's First Prayer
Hesba Stretton

QTY

In a screened and secluded corner of one of the many railway-bridges which span the streets of London there could be seen a few years ago, from five o'clock every morning until half past eight, a tidily set-out coffee-stall, consisting of a trestle and board, upon which stood two large tin cans, with a small fire of charcoal burning under each so as to keep the coffee boiling during the early hours of the morning when the work-people were thronging into the city on their way to their daily toil...

Pages:84

Childrens   **ISBN:** *1-59462-373-2*   **MSRP $9.95**

My Life and Work
Henry Ford

QTY

Henry Ford revolutionized the world with his implementation of mass production for the Model T automobile. Gain valuable business insight into his life and work with his own auto-biography... "We have only started on our development of our country we have not as yet, with all our talk of wonderful progress, done more than scratch the surface. The progress has been wonderful enough but..."

Pages:300

Biographies/   **ISBN:** *1-59462-198-5*   **MSRP $21.95**

www.bookjungle.com *email: sales@bookjungle.com fax: 630-214-0564 mail: Book Jungle PO Box 2226 Champaign, IL 61825*

The Art of Cross-Examination
Francis Wellman

QTY

I presume it is the experience of every author, after his first book is published upon an important subject, to be almost overwhelmed with a wealth of ideas and illustrations which could readily have been included in his book, and which to his own mind, at least, seem to make a second edition inevitable. Such certainly was the case with me; and when the first edition had reached its sixth impression in five months, I rejoiced to learn that it seemed to my publishers that the book had met with a sufficiently favorable reception to justify a second and considerably enlarged edition. ..

Pages:412

Reference   ISBN: *1-59462-647-2*   *MSRP $19.95*

On the Duty of Civil Disobedience
Henry David Thoreau

QTY

Thoreau wrote his famous essay, On the Duty of Civil Disobedience, as a protest against an unjust but popular war and the immoral but popular institution of slave-owning. He did more than write—he declined to pay his taxes, and was hauled off to gaol in consequence. Who can say how much this refusal of his hastened the end of the war and of slavery ?

Law   ISBN: *1-59462-747-9*

Pages:48

MSRP $7.45

Dream Psychology Psychoanalysis for Beginners
Sigmund Freud

QTY

Sigmund Freud, born Sigismund Schlomo Freud (May 6, 1856 - September 23, 1939), was a Jewish-Austrian neurologist and psychiatrist who co-founded the psychoanalytic school of psychology. Freud is best known for his theories of the unconscious mind, especially involving the mechanism of repression; his redefinition of sexual desire as mobile and directed towards a wide variety of objects; and his therapeutic techniques, especially his understanding of transference in the therapeutic relationship and the presumed value of dreams as sources of insight into unconscious desires.

Pages:196

Psychology   ISBN: *1-59462-905-6*   *MSRP $15.45*

The Miracle of Right Thought
Orison Swett Marden

QTY

Believe with all of your heart that you will do what you were made to do. When the mind has once formed the habit of holding cheerful, happy, prosperous pictures, it will not be easy to form the opposite habit. It does not matter how improbable or how far away this realization may see, or how dark the prospects may be, if we visualize them as best we can, as vividly as possible, hold tenaciously to them and vigorously struggle to attain them, they will gradually become actualized, realized in the life. But a desire, a longing without endeavor, a yearning abandoned or held indifferently will vanish without realization.

Pages:360

Self Help   ISBN: *1-59462-644-8*   *MSRP $25.45*

www.**bookjungle**.com *email: sales@bookjungle.com fax: 630-214-0564 mail: Book Jungle PO Box 2226 Champaign, IL 61825*

QTY

The Rosicrucian Cosmo-Conception Mystic Christianity *by Max Heindel* ISBN: *1-59462-188-8* **$38.95**
The Rosicrucian Cosmo-conception is not dogmatic, neither does it appeal to any other authority than the reason of the student. It is: not controversial, but is: sent forth in the, hope that it may help to clear... New Age/Religion Pages 646

Abandonment To Divine Providence *by Jean-Pierre de Caussade* ISBN: *1-59462-228-0* **$25.95**
"The Rev. Jean Pierre de Caussade was one of the most remarkable spiritual writers of the Society of Jesus in France in the 18th Century. His death took place at Toulouse in 1751. His works have gone through many editions and have been republished... Inspirational/Religion Pages 400

Mental Chemistry *by Charles Haanel* ISBN: *1-59462-192-6* **$23.95**
Mental Chemistry allows the change of material conditions by combining and appropriately utilizing the power of the mind. Much like applied chemistry creates something new and unique out of careful combinations of chemicals the mastery of mental chemistry... New Age Pages 354

The Letters of Robert Browning and Elizabeth Barret Barrett 1845-1846 vol II ISBN: *1-59462-193-4* **$35.95**
*by **Robert Browning** and **Elizabeth Barrett*** Biographies Pages 596

Gleanings In Genesis (volume I) *by Arthur W. Pink* ISBN: *1-59462-130-6* **$27.45**
Appropriately has Genesis been termed "the seed plot of the Bible" for in it we have, in germ form, almost all of the great doctrines which are afterwards fully developed in the books of Scripture which follow... Religion/Inspirational Pages 420

The Master Key *by L. W. de Laurence* ISBN: *1-59462-001-6* **$30.95**
In no branch of human knowledge has there been a more lively increase of the spirit of research during the past few years than in the study of Psychology, Concentration and Mental Discipline. The requests for authentic lessons in Thought Control, Mental Discipline and... New Age/Business Pages 422

The Lesser Key Of Solomon Goetia *by L. W. de Laurence* ISBN: *1-59462-092-X* **$9.95**
This translation of the first book of the "Lemegton" which is now for the first time made accessible to students of Talismanic Magic was done, after careful collation and edition, from numerous Ancient Manuscripts in Hebrew, Latin, and French... New Age/Occult Pages 92

Rubaiyat Of Omar Khayyam *by Edward Fitzgerald* ISBN: *1-59462-332-5* **$13.95**
Edward Fitzgerald, whom the world has already learned, in spite of his own efforts to remain within the shadow of anonymity, to look upon as one of the rarest poets of the century, was born at Bredfield, in Suffolk, on the 31st of March, 1809. He was the third son of John Purcell... Music Pages 172

Ancient Law *by Henry Maine* ISBN: *1-59462-128-4* **$29.95**
The chief object of the following pages is to indicate some of the earliest ideas of mankind, as they are reflected in Ancient Law, and to point out the relation of those ideas to modern thought. Religiom/History Pages 452

Far-Away Stories *by William J. Locke* ISBN: *1-59462-129-2* **$19.45**
"Good wine needs no bush, but a collection of mixed vintages does. And this book is just such a collection. Some of the stories I do not want to remain buried for ever in the museum files of dead magazine-numbers an author's not unpardonable vanity..." Fiction Pages 272

Life of David Crockett *by David Crockett* ISBN: *1-59462-250-7* **$27.45**
"Colonel David Crockett was one of the most remarkable men of the times in which he lived. Born in humble life, but gifted with a strong will, an indomitable courage, and unremitting perseverance... Biographies/New Age Pages 424

Lip-Reading *by Edward Nitchie* ISBN: *1-59462-206-X* **$25.95**
Edward B. Nitchie, founder of the New York School for the Hard of Hearing, now the Nitchie School of Lip-Reading, Inc, wrote "LIP-READING Principles and Practice". The development and perfecting of this meritorious work on lip-reading was an undertaking... How-to Pages 400

A Handbook of Suggestive Therapeutics, Applied Hypnotism, Psychic Science ISBN: *1-59462-214-0* **$24.95**
*by **Henry Munro*** Health/New Age/Health/Self-help Pages 376

A Doll's House: and Two Other Plays *by Henrik Ibsen* ISBN: *1-59462-112-8* **$19.95**
Henrik Ibsen created this classic when in revolutionary 1848 Rome. Introducing some striking concepts in playwriting for the realist genre, this play has been studied the world over. Fiction/Classics/Plays 308

The Light of Asia *by sir Edwin Arnold* ISBN: *1-59462-204-3* **$13.95**
In this poetic masterpiece, Edwin Arnold describes the life and teachings of Buddha. The man who was to become known as Buddha to the world was born as Prince Gautama of India but he rejected the worldly riches and abandoned the reigns of power when... Religion/History/Biographies Pages 170

The Complete Works of Guy de Maupassant *by Guy de Maupassant* ISBN: *1-59462-157-8* **$16.95**
"For days and days, nights and nights, I had dreamed of that first kiss which was to consecrate our engagement, and I knew not on what spot I should put my lips..." Fiction/Classics Pages 240

The Art of Cross-Examination *by Francis L. Wellman* ISBN: *1-59462-309-0* **$26.95**
Written by a renowned trial lawyer, Wellman imparts his experience and uses case studies to explain how to use psychology to extract desired information through questioning. How-to/Science/Reference Pages 408

Answered or Unanswered? *by Louisa Vaughan* ISBN: *1-59462-248-5* **$10.95**
Miracles of Faith in China Religion Pages 112

The Edinburgh Lectures on Mental Science (1909) *by Thomas* ISBN: *1-59462-008-3* **$11.95**
This book contains the substance of a course of lectures recently given by the writer in the Queen Street Hall, Edinburgh. Its purpose is to indicate the Natural Principles governing the relation between Mental Action and Material Conditions... New Age/Psychology Pages 148

Ayesha *by H. Rider Haggard* ISBN: *1-59462-301-5* **$24.95**
Verily and indeed it is the unexpected that happens! Probably if there was one person upon the earth from whom the Editor of this, and of a certain previous history, did not expect to hear again... Classics Pages 380

Ayala's Angel *by Anthony Trollope* ISBN: *1-59462-352-X* **$29.95**
The two girls were both pretty, but Lucy who was twenty-one who supposed to be simple and comparatively unattractive, whereas Ayala was credited, as her Bombwhat romantic name might show, with poetic charm and a taste for romance. Ayala when her father died was nineteen... Fiction Pages 484

The American Commonwealth *by James Bryce* ISBN: *1-59462-286-8* **$34.45**
An interpretation of American democratic political theory. It examines political mechanics and society from the perspective of Scotsman James Bryce Politics Pages 572

Stories of the Pilgrims *by Margaret P. Pumphrey* ISBN: *1-59462-116-0* **$17.95**
This book explores pilgrims religious oppression in England as well as their escape to Holland and eventual crossing to America on the Mayflower, and their early days in New England... History Pages 268

QTY

The Fasting Cure *by Sinclair Upton*   **ISBN: 1-59462-222-1** **$13.95**

In the Cosmopolitan Magazine for May, 1910, and in the Contemporary Review (London) for April, 1910, I published an article dealing with my experiences in fasting. I have written a great many magazine articles, but never one which attracted so much attention... New Age/Self Help/Health Pages 164

Hebrew Astrology *by Sepharial*   **ISBN: 1-59462-308-2** **$13.45**

In these days of advanced thinking it is a matter of common observation that we have left many of the old landmarks behind and that we are now pressing forward to greater heights and to a wider horizon than that which represented the mind-content of our progenitors... Astrology Pages 144

Thought Vibration or The Law of Attraction in the Thought World   **ISBN: 1-59462-127-6** **$12.95**

by William Walker Atkinson   *Psychology/Religion Pages 144*

Optimism *by Helen Keller*   **ISBN: 1-59462-108-X** **$15.95**

Helen Keller was blind, deaf, and mute since 19 months old, yet famously learned how to overcome these handicaps, communicate with the world, and spread her lectures promoting optimism. An inspiring read for everyone... Biographies/Inspirational Pages 84

Sara Crewe *by Frances Burnett*   **ISBN: 1-59462-360-0** **$9.45**

In the first place, Miss Minchin lived in London. Her home was a large, dull, tall one, in a large, dull square, where all the houses were alike, and all the sparrows were alike, and where all the door-knockers made the same heavy sound... Childrens/Classic Pages 88

The Autobiography of Benjamin Franklin *by Benjamin Franklin*   **ISBN: 1-59462-135-7** **$24.95**

The Autobiography of Benjamin Franklin has probably been more extensively read than any other American historical work, and no other book of its kind has had such ups and downs of fortune. Franklin lived for many years in England, where he was agent... Biographies/History Pages 332

Name	
Email	
Telephone	
Address	
City, State ZIP	

☐ **Credit Card**   ☐ **Check / Money Order**

Credit Card Number	
Expiration Date	
Signature	

Please Mail to: *Book Jungle*
PO Box 2226
Champaign, IL 61825
or Fax to: *630-214-0564*

ORDERING INFORMATION

web*: www.bookjungle.com*
email*: sales@bookjungle.com*
fax*: 630-214-0564*
mail*: Book Jungle PO Box 2226 Champaign, IL 61825*
or PayPal *to sales@bookjungle.com*

Please contact us for bulk discounts

DIRECT-ORDER TERMS

**20% Discount if You Order
Two or More Books**
Free Domestic Shipping!
Accepted: Master Card, Visa,
Discover, American Express